Praise for the Writing of Nadine Gonzalez

"A spirited, sexy tale from a promising new author of contemporary romance."

—*Kirkus Reviews* on *Exclusively Yours*

"I loved this story! The setting is well described, the opulence and sunny tropical locale of Miami's Ocean Drive . . . I'm looking forward to reading more from this author!"

—*Harlequin Junkie* on *Scandal in the VIP Suite*

"Nadine Gonzalez weaves the perfect Hollywood fairy tale that has the heroine obtaining not just the hero, but the dream and the power of her voice. I adored this book!"

—Naima Simone, *USA TODAY* bestselling author, on *Scandal in the VIP Suite*

"Sharp, witty banter with laugh-out-loud puns—Nadine Gonzalez's *Scandal in the VIP Suite* is one of the most entertaining 'only one bed' stories I've ever had the pleasure of reading."

—LaQuette, award-winning author of *Vanessa Jared's Got a Man*

ALSO BY NADINE GONZALEZ

Harlequin Desire

Miami Famous
Miami Marriage Pact
What Happens in Miami . . .
Scandal in the VIP Suite

Texas Cattleman's Club
Oh So Wrong with Mr. Right
Rivalry at Play
The Rebel's Return

Harlequin Kimani

Unconditionally Mine
Exclusively Yours

ONLY LOVERS IN THE BUILDING

NADINE GONZALEZ

CANARY STREET PRESS

CANARY STREET PRESS™

ISBN-13: 978-1-335-90334-1

Only Lovers in the Building

For questions and comments about the quality of this book, please contact us at CustomerService@Harlequin.com.

TM is a trademark of Harlequin Enterprises ULC.

Canary Street Press
22 Adelaide St. West, 41st Floor
Toronto, Ontario M5H 4E3, Canada
CanaryStPress.com

Printed in U.S.A.

For Ariel and Nathaniel, always and forever.

Thursday, June 1, 12:30 a.m.
From: Lily.Lyon@AceStaffingSolutions.com
To: Kendal.Hill@AceStaffingSolutions.com

Dear Mr. Hill:

I hereby resign from the position of associate general counsel.

Respectfully,
Liliane Lyon
Associate General Counsel, Ace Staffing Solutions
New York, New York

Prologue

There was nothing to rush home to except her prized Monstera plant.

Lily pondered this at the airport gate, boarding pass in hand. She'd quit her job, walked out mid–corporate retreat in Miami. Now what? Her life revolved around work. Without it, she was stuck, wheels spinning. While her fellow passengers rushed to board flight 826 to JFK International Airport, she stumbled into the past.

How did I get here?

Like all bad choices, her late-night decision to quit was spurred by social media. Would she have walked out of the banquet if her Instagram feed weren't flooded with photos of her ex's wedding? Then again, would she have been held up in the ladies' room, scrolling Instagram, if the idea of a drawn-out dinner with colleagues hadn't left her numb? Finally, without the images of her ex—now someone's new husband—dancing in her head, would she have snapped when the CEO gave a new colleague full credit for her work? Well, probably. But she would never know for sure. Such was the vicious circle of doomscrolling.

Yesterday evening, Lily slipped on a little black dress, swiped on red lipstick, and left her hotel room for the final event of the week. She shared an elevator with a woman in a bikini who spent the entire ride rummaging through her tote for a vape pen. In the lobby, Bikini Lady joined her friends, and they trotted off toward the pool. Lily followed the signs leading to Ballroom 2, her heels catching on the carpet. Had that been the fork in the road? It was summer in Miami, one of the most colorful cities in the world, and Lily could only peek out at it from behind sheer curtains. A pool party raged outside. She would spend the night making small talk with her boss, her boss's boss, and a battalion of VPs. The thought alone drained her. The night hadn't yet started, and already she needed a break.

She dipped into the ladies' room and took a seat in the adjoining lounge for a social media scroll. On Facebook she liked a photo of her mother's orchids. She posted a status update on her favorite new app, BookTap.

@LilyLyon: Busy week. Did not get much reading done. Currently halfway through The Sweetest Lie by Teresa Star. Will finish up on the flight home tomorrow.

Eventually she got around to Instagram and lurked a bit until she came across a college friend's post. It was a photo from a wedding they'd attended, bride and groom in standard attire, kissing on a beach. She might have scrolled past if the proud groom hadn't caught her attention. With a fit of nausea, she recognized Darren Gordy.

From then on, it was impossible to put the phone down. Even at the dinner, she kept it open on her lap, scrolling between bites of chicken parmesan. By dessert, she'd gathered enough images to recreate, with some imagination, the entire wedding in her mind: vows, cocktail reception, dinner and dancing, the cutting of the coconut cream cake (his favorite), and fireworks to cap off the night.

"Is that your brother?"

The question came from Gus, a new attorney on the team.

"My brother? Where?" Lily looked up, half expecting to see her brother stroll into the ballroom in his hospital scrubs.

Gus pointed to the phone on her lap. "There."

Darren's face lit up the screen. His dark brown skin glowed, and his brown eyes sparkled with unfiltered joy. She had never seen him so happy.

"He's *not* my brother," Lily replied. "He's a friend. We went to college together."

She silenced her blabbing with a sip of wine. *My first boy-friend, my one true love. Haven't thought about him in ages. Split at graduation, went our separate ways. Mr. What-If.*

"Did you skip the wedding to be here?" Gus asked. "A shame. If you want my advice, don't ever let work take over your life. That's a mistake you'll regret."

Gus was a good decade older than Lily and positioned him-self in a fatherly role, the hip office dad, of sorts. Like her own dad, he was a fountain of so-called advice, sharing his opinion on anything from taxes to real estate to car maintenance—not that anyone in their Manhattan office owned a car. As it turned out, she didn't want his advice. If Darren had invited her to his wedding, she would have RSVPed *no*. Gus Porter was new to the ACE ecosystem. Poached from a top law firm, he'd been given princess treatment since he'd started the job late January. He clearly wasn't aware that skipping the annual retreat was unthinkable. This year in Miami, last year in Aspen—it was always a show, a three-ring circus under a fancy big top. Their role as good little employees was to clap and squeal and eat the cotton candy. Gus was a smart man: he'd figure it out soon enough.

Kendall Hill, their CEO, rose from the head of the table and launched into his speech. As always, he assured them the state of the union was strong. Lily zoned out to replay the wedding from start to finish in her mind. That could have been us, she thought. Had she gambled and lost?

Kendall called out her name, and Lily straightened up. It was that time in the speech when he acknowledged the year's strong contributors. This year she'd done well, closing a major deal. But Kendall didn't mention it. Instead, he thanked her for creating a welcoming environment for Gus. He thanked Gus for simply existing and for taking the reins of the Brooks merger. Great, except the Brooks merger had been *her* deal.

Gus bowed humbly. "I couldn't have done it without Lily."

So thoughtful of him to acknowledge her in this way, but what had he done, exactly? Aside from breezing in and out of the office, regaling the support staff with dad jokes, taking a few calls, and sitting in on a few meetings, she couldn't think of one significant contribution to the merger deal in particular or the company as a whole.

"Your friend's a handsome guy," Gus whispered, picking up their conversation as if nothing had happened, as if they were office besties mid–gossip session. "The bride is mid, don't you think?"

Lily clocked it: the straw that broke her back. The last two years had been consumed by this one big fucking deal. If it had dragged on so long, it wasn't because of some failing on her part. It was a complicated deal with many moving parts. Gus's timely arrival hadn't made those parts move any faster. Was that why they'd brought him in, to take the reins? God . . . if this was a circus, she was the clown.

Lily threw down her napkin and pushed back her chair. She caught her wineglass before it toppled over and took it with her, leaving everything else behind. She was vaguely aware of Gus asking if she was feeling okay. She ignored Gus and the others and did the unthinkable: she quit the circus.

By the time final boarding was announced, her mind was made up. She could not get on that plane. She could not fly home. Like a child who'd misbehaved, she needed a time-out. Lily returned to the business travelers' lounge to plan. She set up her laptop, ordered a late lunch, and posted a status update to her 710 BookTap followers, not that any of them would care.

@LilyLyon: Change of plans: nothing but sunshine, beach reads, and cocktails for the summer. Follow for more. #MiamiBeach #Beachbumming

One follower replied straight away.

@Angieslittlelibrary: Sounds good! Keep us posted on the books you read.

Lily needed no further encouragement. She was on the right track. Down and out, where better to wash up than the hot sands of Miami Beach?

She booked an Airbnb.

Chapter One

The Icon, a classic Art Deco building on Washington Avenue, was home for the summer. Old but new: Lily imagined the bones were stripped bare at some point, polished, lacquered, and covered in gold leaf. She walked through archway after archway, in the golden light of so many chandeliers, rolling her carry-on case over the ivory tile with onyx inlay, thinking *My God . . . this is perfect.* If she was going to do this—escape reality, bake in the sun, drink unreservedly, waste her days, ruin her nights, and generally behave irresponsibly—the setting mattered. She'd do it in style.

However, retreating to paradise wasn't without its complications. It was a logistical nightmare. Her Airbnb wouldn't be ready for a while, and the property manager's laissez-faire attitude grated her nerves. "Immediate occupation allows for twenty-four hours' notice," he explained. "It's in the fine print."

When you wanted a thing badly enough, even corporate lawyers quickly scrolled to the bottom of the contract, tapped the big fat red button marked *Accept*, and assumed all conditions and consequences.

To make up for the inconvenience, he offered her a voucher for a complimentary glass of rosé. That was how Lily found herself alone at the rooftop bar overlooking Miami Beach, e-reader open to *The Sweetest Lie*, a spicy romance set in Malibu, waiting to be served. She didn't even *like* rosé, but she needed something to take the edge off. The people around her exuded coolness, while she sat with her luggage piled at her side, huffing and puffing, ready to blow her top.

She'd been on the run since two in the afternoon. Fueled by adrenaline, there'd been no stopping her. No time to pause, reflect or second-guess the string of rash decisions that had landed her here. To sit still, even at a bar, was to run the risk of succumbing to doubt. You couldn't just run away from your life, could you? Who would water her Monstera? She arrived at one conclusion: this was a big fat costly mistake.

What was she even doing here? Lily felt completely out of place at the trendy bar. She couldn't even catch the bartender's attention. He had his back to her the whole time, busy with worthier patrons. She watched as he rattled a shaker, poured the mix into a chilled glass, garnished it with a lemon twist, and offered the cocktail to a lucky woman, who rewarded him with a smile.

He answered to Ben, Benny, Bro, or Benito:

"Yo, Ben!"

"Yeah?"

"Bro!"

"What's up?"

"Hey, Benny!"

"Hey, man! Where've you been?"

"Benito. Two vodka tonics for the high top."

"You got it."

He was good at his job. He doted on the few who managed to get his attention. He laughed at jokes, got the indecisive to make up their minds, and handed napkins to the ladies who spilled their drinks. He opened tabs, swiped credit cards, and collected tips. Lily was forever in awe of happy workers. A job was a job, as far as she was concerned. You showed up, toiled away for eight hours or more, and went home exhausted and spent. There was no joy in it. No pleasure. All it caused was stress, which quitting, she'd learned today, didn't do much to alleviate. That was the fate of all those born into late-stage capitalism.

A guy slid onto the stool next to hers. Eyeing her e-reader, he spoke over the music. "What am I interrupting here? Sad-girl solo date?"

French, she could tell, from the accent and attitude. He could take that somewhere else. Today was *not* the day.

"Excuse me?" she snapped.

"You've got your book," he observed. "All you're missing is a glass of chardonnay."

A fuse ignited in Lily's gut. But when she met his water-blue eyes, it instantly died out. He meant no harm. Besides, he wasn't too far from the truth. She felt no shame. Solo dates were a pillar of the self-care doctrine.

"Tonight's sad drink of choice is a complimentary glass of rosé," she said. "But I can't get the bartender's attention."

He let out a tortured sound. "You're too pretty to be so tragic."

"Thanks. Sort of."

He was pretty, too, with slick blond hair and a deep tan that made his blue eyes pop.

"Cheer up," he said. "If the guy I'm here to meet doesn't show, I'll join you. This is our third attempt at a first date."

Lily gasped, any residual resentment gone. There ought to be a three-strike rule in the contact sport known as dating.

"He's a lawyer," her barmate explained. "Justice for all requires human sacrifice."

"I'm a lawyer," she said. "I can attest that's true."

He looked her over. She returned the favor, only she had to crane her neck to do so properly. In a pair of linen pants and a button-down shirt with most buttons left undone, he had obviously put a lot of effort into looking effortless, and it paid off handsomely. He was too good-looking to be ghosted, but it was a spooky world.

Next to him, Lily felt drab. She'd fled a corporate retreat, but she was still in corporate uniform. In a cashmere knit, pleated trousers, and sling-back pumps, she was as prim and proper as Miami allowed. Her reflection in the smoky mirror behind the bar confirmed this. She'd turned thirty last month, and every birthday card assured her that she was fun and fabulous. Well, not tonight. Her wide eyes stared back at her with a war-weary expression. The weight she'd lost to better fit in her bathing suit at the retreat had hollowed her cheeks and collarbones. Her copper-brown complexion was as dull as an old penny. Her hair, ever so curly in Miami's record-breaking humidity, was gathered on top of her head, giving her the air of a deranged pineapple. Coppery, wiry, and overdressed, it was a wonder they hadn't escorted her thirty-year-old self off the premises.

"I'm Noah," he said, finally.

"Lily."

"What's with the luggage, Lily? Are you on the run?"

"In a way. I'll be hiding out here a bit."

"Moving in?"

"For the summer," she replied. No one in their right mind would stay in Miami past Labor Day. "I quit my job."

He nodded approvingly. "Good for you."

It *was* good for her. She shouldn't doubt it, even if it was reckless and foolish and prohibitively expensive. None of that mattered. She'd earned this.

Noah's phone lit up in his hand. He glanced at the screen. "Bet he's calling to cancel." He let the call die out.

"Give him the benefit of the doubt," she said. "I'm sure he'd rather be with you than working on a brief. It's early. Still time to turn things around."

"Is that how it works out in books?" Noah asked, skeptical.

"In real life, too."

A lie, but Noah couldn't handle the truth. Lily was willing to bet anything that his supposedly overworked lawyer had swiped a picture-perfect profile from LinkedIn and was using it as bait. Classic catfish. The dating game was brutal. People had twisted and selfish motives, Lily chief among them. She broke Darren's heart all those years ago when she was too young or too foolish to value their relationship. "We're so good together," he'd pleaded. "This is true love. We want all the same things." That couldn't be further from the truth. She'd only wanted to be free. At thirty, she no longer believed in true love—but a romance novel delivered every time.

"I should call him back," Noah said with a little frown.

"I think so."

"Well, welcome to the building, Lily. I'm on the tenth floor, but I live at the pool." Noah sealed their new friendship with a double air kiss. Before slipping away, he whispered, "The hot bartender will get to you eventually. By the way, he's straight . . . and single. That's a rare combination here."

Stung, she replied, "Why should I care?"

Hot or not, she'd ruled out bartenders, bouncers, DJs, and dancers a long time ago. There came a time for every girl to grow up, sober up, shake the glitter out of her hair, and kiss the party boys goodbye. They called it growing pains for a reason. Now that she was old enough to appreciate the Darrens of the world—loyal, steadfast, a little boring, but so what?—she would limit her search to the men who fell neatly onto that pile.

Noah looked at her pointedly, a look so sharp it cut through her bullshit like butter. "Good luck," he mouthed and walked away, phone pinned to his ear. Lily knew instinctively that if she didn't panic and bolt, aborting her impromptu fun-filled summer, if she stuck it through, she and Noah from the tenth floor would be the best of friends.

But first, that drink.

The sun was setting over Miami Beach, and the rooftop deck had filled up. What was she doing, brandishing a coupon as if she were at the checkout line of a big box store? No wonder she wasn't getting any service. Free wasn't *free*. She had to entice the hot bartender with a tip.

Lily rummaged in her quilted leather bag for her silver money clip. As she rifled through the wad of twenties in search of a ten, she had the odd feeling of being watched. She glanced up, and there he was. She'd spent so long trying to get the man's attention, and now that she had it, it burned. His eyes were midnight black, but his gaze flashed blue then red then gold, catching the colors of the neon lights strung over the bar. For a fraction of a second, her world went silent—no music, no chatter, no distant sounds of traffic. Even the noise in her head quieted down, which was unheard of. He leaned close to speak to her, setting her pulse at an erratic pace.

"Ma'am," he said.

Was that necessary? They had to be about the same age.

He pointed over his shoulder. "The gentleman over there would like to buy you a drink."

Gentleman! *National Geographic* had declared that species extinct. Besides, the bar was too crowded to spot anyone who might fit the bill. "Who? Where?" Lily asked. She scanned for a top hat and coattails.

Hot Bartender Benny dropped his elbows onto the glass counter, exposing the black ink tattoos of knotted vines, curling around his wrists and up his golden-brown arms. "The guy in the suit."

There was only one guy in a tailored blue suit, and that was the most remarkable thing about him. Naturally he was drawn to her. Like attracts like, she concluded grimly.

"No, thanks," Lily said. "He's not my type, and I have a voucher."

He plucked it from her and held it up as he addressed the suit. "Sorry, man. Your money is no good here. The lady has a voucher."

The man's friends—he had quite a few—let out a collective *Awww!* Lily could have crumbled on the spot. The suit handled it better. He brandished a black credit card and cried, "Shots for everyone!" His words were met with cheers. The DJ bellowed, "Shot time!"

It seemed she'd left one circus for another. Lily washed her hands of the whole thing.

"He's celebrating his divorce," Hot Bartender Benny explained.

Lily chanced one last look the man's way. Pink-faced and bleary-eyed, he was in a hell of his own making. "I wish him well."

"How do you like your rosé, ma'am?" he asked, already retreating, while she wanted him to stay close and whisper all the secrets of every person pressed around the bar. "On the sweet side or—"

"I don't like it," Lily stammered. "I don't like rosé." She'd only liked that it was free, which in retrospect was stupid. "After the day I've had, just splash some vodka in a cold glass. I don't even care what kind. Any celebrity brand will do."

He narrowed his eyes at her. In the kaleidoscope of neon colors, she caught a glimmer of amusement. He crumpled the voucher. "How about I make you something?"

"Please." She peeled two twenties from the clip and set the bills onto the bar. "Anything you'd like."

He glanced at the money. "Put that away. It's on the house."

This time, Lily had the distinct pleasure of watching him at work for her. He poured and dashed the ingredients of a classic vodka martini into a shaker. Blessedly, he bypassed the celebrity brands and reached for the top shelf. Thrilled, she called out a final request. "Make it filthy!" Her words sailed across the bar at the exact moment the DJ cut the music. *Make. It. Filthy.* Oh God . . . She had to get out more often. How had she become this stiff, awkward, cashmere-clad woman? Be cool, she told herself. Her attempt at playing it cool failed as soon as she caught Benny's smirk. Her cheeks caught fire. Nothing could douse it, not even the chilled, dirty martini he placed before her like an offering at an altar.

"For you."

"Thank you."

"My pleasure."

She slid a tip across the bar. He dropped it in a jar.

"This looks amazing," she said. "You have skills."

"Enough to keep me afloat through grad school."

She refrained from asking where he went to school and what he studied. This wasn't a networking event. She would not produce a business card and ask him to circle back or touch base.

"Taste your martini before you praise my work," he said. "It might be too dry."

The perfect martini was a cut diamond in a chilled glass. Dirty or not, you checked for clarity and color. So far, so good. The choice of garnish was an art. She went with stuffed olives, always—blue cheese, garlic, jalapeño. Those choices weren't on offer here. The skewered olive in her glass was standard, plain. She was willing to let that slide. Lily raised the glass to her lips, took a sip. The chilled vodka slid down her throat. She instinctively closed her eyes and wished the day's stress would drain away. When she opened her eyes again, he was gone, off pouring shots for the suit and his friends. She took a couple more sips. Just when she was ready to resume her sad, solo date, he returned. "Filthy enough?"

Lily nearly did a spit take. With a half smile, he handed her a cocktail napkin. "Tell me about your day."

"What do you mean?"

The question was clear enough. Lily was buying time.

"You said 'after the day I've had.' That's a setup for a story."

"I don't want to bore you."

"Lucky for you, I love stories. It's part of the job. I serve drinks and advice."

Where Noah was a Mediterranean golden boy, Hot Bartender Benny was rough sea salt extracted from the Caribbean, geotag as yet unknown. Dark hair, dark eyes, dark honey skin made brown by the sun. His face was all hard, sharp lines. And beneath that black T-shirt, there was an equally hard and angled body—she just knew it.

"Come on," he said. "You can trust me."

Lily gave the martini glass a little swirl and thought it over. A minute ago, she'd told Noah the truth without flinching. The big difference was she wasn't trying to impress Noah. If a decade of happy hours had taught her anything, it was this: emotionally unloading on a bartender would not get you laid. Not that it was her objective in this case, but why cancel it altogether? She offered him a version of the truth. "I'm on sabbatical."

"Are you in academia?"

"No. I'm taking a break from corporate America."

"Congratulations," he said. "Are you sure he's not your type? He's corporate, too."

Across the bar, the suit was downing shots and miming tossing money. Lily shuddered. "Thanks, I'll pass. He's *not* my type."

He folded his arms on the bar again, keeping a respectful distance, but just close enough. "So who is?"

If her life were a novel, the dominant trope would be Good Girl Gone Bad. She'd never met a dark-haired, tattooed guy in a tight T-shirt she didn't like. The one exception had been Darren, the all-around nice guy. Since she left him, it had been a parade of losers, one disastrous affair after another. One broke her heart, but that was to be expected. One had dated her for her apartment. Another stole her identity and ruined her credit. She got ghosted, gaslit, lectured on her spending habits, and ridiculed for her taste in books. She'd sworn off men after that and lived a chaste and pure life, the kind the nuns of her former Catholic school would approve of. For the most part, it had served her well. She'd applied herself to her career, soaring to new heights, only to crash into the glass ceiling.

The bartender was waiting for an answer. Now that it counted most, Lily couldn't bring herself to spin the wheel of truth. She couldn't even hold eye contact. Therefore, she punted. Lily lowered her eyes and finished her martini.

"Another round?" he offered.

"No," she said, far too quickly.

His face remained impassive, but deep in his eyes, amid the swirling neon colors and the glimmer of amusement, was sparkling certainty. He knows, she thought. He knows he can get it.

Her phone chimed with the message she'd been waiting for. **The studio is ready. Meet you in the lobby.**

"That's it for me," she said, grateful for the excuse. "I have to go."

"All right, ma'am. Do you need a ride?"

"No, thanks. I'm sorted." She grabbed her large tote and the handle of her small suitcase and stepped away from the bar.

"Need help with that?" he asked.

"I can manage! Thanks again! Good night!"

"Are you sure?"

"Oh, I'm sure."

She dashed across the terrace, head low, clutching the handle of her suitcase as if it held the nuclear codes. She made her way to the elevators and punched the Down button, furious with herself. If every hot bartender in Miami made her fluster, how was she going to survive the summer?

Lily stepped into the elevator just as she heard him call out to her. At least she thought she'd heard him. The martini had kicked in, and the world had gone soft at the edges. She should not have downed the cocktail on an empty stomach. Her last meal had been half a club sandwich at the airport.

"Ma'am! Wait!"

It *was* him. He chased her into the elevator. The doors sealed shut behind him, the car started its rocky descent. It was an awkward situation to be sure, but Lily was consumed by other thoughts. "Do you have to call me *ma'am*?"

This was the fourth time, and she was having none of it.

He drew a shaky breath. When he spoke, his voice was even. "At the bar, I can't keep names straight, and you strike me as a woman who wants respect."

What gave him that impression? Was it the cashmere?

He held up her money clip. "You forgot this."

"Oh." She cleared her throat, somewhat embarrassed, yet determined to see this issue to its painful end. "My name is on it."

The silver clip was a law school graduation gift from her father. Her full name was engraved in cursive letters.

He squinted to read it. "Marie-Louise Liliane Lyon."

A faint Spanish accent added a lilt to the many *L*s.

"Now you know my name," she said. "Please use it."

He ran his thumb over the engraved letters. "Bet no one calls you that."

He had a point there. "It's Lily."

He handed her the clip. A current passed between them when their fingertips touched.

"Nice to meet you, Lily," he said.

"Likewise."

"Who carries a money clip anymore?" he asked.

"Me. It was a gift."

"Ah."

He leaned against a far wall, head tossed back. A moment ago, in the sultry light of the bar, he was dark and mysterious.

In the unforgiving light of the elevator, he was just as dark, just as mysterious, only now she could appreciate the wave in his hair, the angle of his brows, the cut of his jaw. But those eyes . . . black, glossy, and bottomless.

"May I ask, do you have gray eyes?"

"Hazel." Her eyes were a mix of brown and swamp green with streaks of silver, depending on the light.

"Beautiful."

The word came out in a breath, the softest of whispers. Had he meant for her to hear? Only she *had* heard it, and it worked like a skeleton key, unlocking her innermost thoughts. "You're my type," she blurted.

That half smirk returned, and it was glorious, irresistible. Guess she hadn't sworn off the party boys, after all.

Given that the word of the day was *implosion*, Lily would not stop until she acted on every impulse, no matter how self-destructive, stupid, or rash. When the urge to kiss him struck her, and struck *hard*, she did not hesitate. She stepped toward him, grabbed his strong shoulders, and kissed him full on the mouth.

It was one-sided.

When she released him and stepped back, he said nothing. Silence quickly filled the elevator like poison gas. Thank the patron saint of bad decisions, whoever it might be, the ride came to a crashing stop on the ground floor. The elevators exposed the building's age. The heavy doors squeaked open with excruciating slowness. Lily grabbed her suitcase and her tote and charged out. To make a painful situation worse, she rolled the suitcase over his foot.

"Good night, Lily!" he called out. "Hope to see you around."

The words landed like darts on her back. She glanced over her shoulder and stole one last look at his rugged, handsome face. After this, she hoped never to see him again.

Chapter Two

@**LegalLyon** Four ways to blow up your life in twenty-four hours. A thread.

1. Quit your job. Walk out and don't look back.
2. Pay a premium for a flight home, then miss it.
3. Book an Airbnb. Hit a bar and thirst over the bartender. Kiss him without consent and wait to be slapped with a lawsuit.

Delete.

Lily chucked her phone clear across the bed. Best to stay off The App Formerly Known as Twitter. What good was it to telegraph to the world how badly she'd screwed up? As a sage woman once said, she could do bad all by herself.

Alone and awake at six in the morning in her strange new home, Lily was shaking with anxiety. The events of the past few days rattled her. What had possessed her to quit her job on the flimsiest of excuses? Regret, hurt feelings, and bruised pride were no reason to give up a six-figure salary and top-notch benefits. The way she'd gone about it, too . . . She hadn't just burned a bridge, she'd polluted the stream beneath it. Then to turn around and book a summer rental in the heart of Miami Beach like it was nothing!

It had seemed like such a good idea at the time. Now she felt lost and disoriented in this sterile white box of a studio apartment. When startled awake in the dead of night, she'd fumbled about for the light switch for an eternity. Okay, it was just a minute or so, but that's a long time when a) you desperately need to pee and b) have no muscle memory of the way to the bathroom.

And then there was the mishap with Hot Bartender. She would have done better by kissing the guy in the suit. He was straight and single, too! More likely than not, she had far more in common with that guy than him. Sad women on solo dates were most definitely *not* his type. Why had she gone and made a fool of herself when she wasn't even all that drunk? Now she could never show her face at the rooftop bar again. It was going to be one cruel-ass summer.

Lily scrambled out of bed. She was in the throes of a meltdown and needed caffeine. The kitchenette was stark white and spotless. A Mr. Coffee machine was tucked in a cabinet, but with no ground coffee or filters. No matter that the sun had barely peaked. Time for a coffee run.

She rummaged through the open suitcase at the foot of the bed for something to wear. Everything she'd packed was work appropriate, tasteful, and neutral. Even her bathing suit and other beachy things fit the bill. No cutoff denim shorts, no cute halter tops, no bright-colored sarongs or faded T-shirts. She'd have to add a whole new wardrobe to her online cart if she wanted to fit in. But there was no need to fit in at six in the morning. Her pajamas were fine. The classic navy two-piece with contrasting piping had a touch of old-Hollywood glam befitting an Art Deco building. She secured her wild hair with a clip and was ready to go. No. Wait. She wasn't ready at all. No money, no keys, no phone, and . . . no shoes.

She slid on the pointy-toed kitten heels abandoned by the door and found the set of keys the property manager had given her the night before. The official title of Property Manager was a bit of a stretch. Dr. Jake Goldman, a clinical psychologist in his thirties, had inherited the condo from his grandmother who'd retired to Miami Beach. He lived with his family in Sunny Isles and rented out this property, but only for extended stays. "Fewer hassles," he'd explained during their friendly walk-through. Lily had struggled to pay attention to Dr. Jake. She was still stinging with embarrassment from the elevator-ride fiasco.

Her money clip was on the kitchen counter next to the keys. As she headed out, she caught her reflection in a large round mirror and scurried back to the bedroom for a pair of dark sunglasses to hide her puffy, bloodshot eyes. Then she was off, on a mission to buy a gallon of coffee. She locked her door just as the door directly across the narrow hall swung open. That's how at six thirty she found herself face-to-face with the hot bartender.

She closed her eyes and wished him away. For a moment, her world went still, and she was fool enough to believe it had worked. Unfortunately, his image was seared into her retinas. Dressed in a hoodie and sweatpants. Chiseled face soft with morning scruff. This was Miami, she reasoned. There were loads of men who looked like that. It could be anyone, not just the one she'd attacked the night before.

"Lily?"

Nothing to do now but smile. "Hey there, Ben! Or is it Benny?"

"It's Benedicto."

"Ha! Bet no one calls you that!"

Her smile was so tight, her neck muscles ached.

"Not even my mother. Call me Ben."

"Okay, Ben! Good seeing you . . . at this early hour!"

She took a few sidelong steps toward the stairwell, preferring to walk down seven flights of stairs in heels than get on an elevator with him.

"Did you move in last night?" he asked.

She stopped and fidgeted. "Yes. This is home for the summer."

"Ah," he said. "We have a landlord in common."

Curiosity got the best of her. She moved toward him. "Dr. Jake owns your unit, too?"

"And an apartment on the tenth floor."

"Are you kidding? He said his grandmother—"

"His grandmother was a real estate mogul. She left him several properties."

"Jesus . . ."

"I know," he said. "We should all be so lucky. All I got from my grandmother is a statue of *la Virgen de la Caridad*."

They laughed rather mechanically. Internally, Lily was freaking out. How could he be so bright and shiny so freaking early in the morning after working all evening? She was thankful for the sunglasses that ate up half her face. Quickly, she thought of something clever to say. "All I got from my grandmother is my stupid name."

"Don't say that. Your name is beautiful."

That word again! "Are you off to the gym?"

"Going for a run."

"Me, too." His gaze slid from her face, taking in her outfit. She prayed he thought it eclectic and cool. "A *coffee* run."

"This early?" He checked the time on the watch he likely only used to count steps. "Liliana, nothing is open. The nearest coffee shop is blocks away. Trust me, I know."

She wondered if he realized he'd changed her name. Normally, she objected when people did that. Not this time.

"Let me make you coffee," he offered.

"No way!"

"Why not?"

Lily gesticulated wildly at his sporty attire. "You're headed out for a run."

"I'm not up for it this morning," he said. "That was wishful thinking on my part. Let me make you coffee."

Lily considered him. She should not have lumped him in with all the losers she'd loved before. Badass bartender aura and all, he had a certain elegance in his manners and speech. Last night, he'd said something about grad school. She hadn't asked about it then but was curious now.

"If you insist," she said.

"It's the neighborly thing to do. Come inside."

And that's how, at six forty-five in the morning, Lily found herself in her hot *neighbor's* apartment.

Ben's place was the mirror opposite of hers, with more natural light and a nicer view from the kitchen window. Only his apartment looked like a Before picture, and hers the After. The parquet floor had a yellowish-orange tint. The walls were textured, not smooth like hers, and painted a shade of alabaster, whereas hers were a stark white. The kitchen countertop was butcher block, the backsplash vintage tile, and the black cabinet doors were uneven on brass hinges. It was perfection, every detail.

"You have patina, and texture, and warmth, and brass, and . . . a gooseneck faucet!"

"Don't get excited. It leaks."

"My point is you've got character."

"Jake isn't done remodeling. He'll get to my side of the street eventually."

"Could we stop him?"

"Join forces?" he suggested.

"Yes!"

"Not likely," he said. "Sit down."

Lily sidled up to the breakfast bar and watched him work, stricken by déjà vu. It was like last night except with caffeine.

"How do you take your coffee?" he asked.

"Bitter and strong," she said. "I'm a New Yorker to the core."

If he had a standard-issued coffee machine, he wasn't using it. Instead, he rinsed out a moka pot and filled the reservoir with hot water. "I'm Cuban," he said. "I take it creamy and sweet."

When he started grinding coffee beans and the aroma filled the kitchen, she thanked the coffee gods above. "Do you always go all out like this, or are you trying to impress me?"

He tossed her a grin and went on working. "It's just coffee, Lily."

"No," she said. "Mr. Coffee is just coffee."

He cut her a glance. "Come here. You've got a lot to learn."

Now, why was that so hot?

Ben walked her through the steps of filling the reservoir with water and the little metal basket with the freshly ground coffee. He placed a hand over hers and showed her how to tamp it down and apply the right pressure, even though a child could do it. "Remember," he said, "we want to pack the grounds tight."

Lily looked up and studied his focused expression. This was who he was at the core: focused, attentive to detail. Last night, she'd treated him like man candy. That wasn't right. She was stressed, not in her right mind, but that was no excuse. All the man had done was smirk at her, and she'd somehow taken that as an invitation.

He twisted the moka pot shut and set it on the stovetop. "Let's give it a minute."

Lily returned to the barstool and pressed her hands between

her knees. There was something intimate about a man making you coffee first thing in the morning.

"This is awkward," she whispered.

"Why?" he asked.

"I . . . don't know." Women likely jumped him all the time. Why bring it up? She switched topics. "Last night you mentioned grad school. What do you study?"

"I said a lot of things last night and forgot them all after you kissed me."

Lily screeched.

"Sorry!" He grinned. "Had to poke the elephant in the room."

"Not true! We could've kept ignoring it!"

"Don't you feel less awkward?"

"No!" she cried. "I can hardly look at you!"

"Lily," he said softly. "It's okay."

Was he saying that to make her feel better? "It's not. And I'm sorry."

He shrugged. "I'm not."

Now *that* was a lie. "Oh, come on! You didn't kiss back!"

"I had my reasons."

"Such as?"

What if he wasn't straight or single, despite what Noah from the tenth floor had attested? She hadn't asked. Instead, she'd taken the word of a virtual stranger . . . to make a move on another stranger.

"It felt to me like you dared yourself to do it," he replied. "And that's just not how I like to be kissed."

"Oh really?"

Funny, she thought. You go your whole life wanting to be seen and understood. When it happens, you don't care for it. You feel fragile and exposed. In fact, you hate it.

The coffeepot percolated, and her phone rang at the same

time. He turned his back to her, and she glanced at the screen. The name on her caller ID had her in a cold sweat. *The Saint.*

Lily slid off the barstool. "Sorry, I have to take this."

"I'm almost done," he said. "Sugar?"

"Uh-huh . . ." She was already at the door, phone still ringing in her hand. "I'll be back, but honestly, I'm not sure when. I'm really sorry!" Lily was across the hall and back in her apartment in no time. With her back to the locked door, she answered the call. "Hello?"

"Liliane!"

Not everyone called her Lily. To her parents, she would always be Marie-Louise Liliane Lyon.

"Good morning, Dad."

It was early, even for him. Her parents had expected to hear from her last night, a quick text to reassure them she'd landed safely. If she didn't answer this call, they'd alert the National Guard.

"What's this I'm reading on BookTap?" her father said. "You're a beach bum now? Aren't you coming home? What about work?"

She needn't have worried. They were up to speed.

"Dad, since when are you on BookTap?"

BookTap was the book community's answer to social media upheaval. It provided a safe space to share hot takes on books, publishing news, and author drama—all genres included. Founded by a former Instagram exec, members included the likes of Obama, Oprah, and Deepak Chopra.

Her father sighed. "Liliane, the whole world is on that app now."

Lily focused her thoughts, took a breath, and presented oral arguments to Judge Yves Lyon of New York's Second District Court. These were the lies she told: after working for months to close a deal, she was granted a sabbatical. No way was she tapping into her savings: her bonus would cover the expense. And she would put her free time to good use by signing up for pro bono work and finally learning Spanish. Fifteen long minutes later, after promising she would no longer post about frivolous things and instead use her account to establish herself in the legal community, she said goodbye to her father, sent her love to her mother, and promptly blocked him on BookTap.

Lily slid onto the floor, weighed down by her deception. It made no sense, lying to everyone and anyone. She'd quit her job! So what? She had savings, resources, a law license, and years of experience under her belt. She was going to see her way through. Why couldn't she stand her ground, own her truth, or whatever?

She spiraled back in time to the moment her career had gone up in smoke. Not smoke, exactly. Eucalyptus-scented steam pumped out in thick tufts at a five-star Miami Beach spa, of all places. She'd stormed out of the banquet hall and sought refuge in the spa. There, she exchanged her cocktail dress for a towel and settled in the steam room for a good cry. She mourned her career as much as the life with Darren that she hadn't wanted but now seemed so full, so rich. When at twenty she'd envisioned her future with the aid of magazine cutouts of her life and legal career in the city, she could not have imagined it would shape out like this. "I need to know what else is out there for me," she'd told him. Well, now she knew, and it wasn't great.

She blinked the image away. Now was not the time for a meltdown. Her neighbor was making her coffee. Although, by now, the coffee had surely gone cold and Ben had given up on her.

Head throbbing, she set out for a caffeine fix, once again. If Ben did not come to the door, she was hopeful a coffee shop would be open by now.

A small package on the welcome mat outside her door

stopped her in her tracks. Wrapped in a tea towel was a stainless-steel travel mug along with a Ziploc bag filled with sugar packets of the type collected at random drive-through windows. There was even a handwritten note.

Love thy neighbor.
—Ben

Chapter Three

Ben's coffee revitalized her, propelled her into the day. Determined to start her pseudosabbatical right, Lily slipped on a swimsuit and found her way to the pool. She spotted Noah sprawled on a lounge chair, wet hair slicked back. He called out to her. *"La belle Lily!"*

"Well, hello!" she replied. "You weren't kidding when you said you lived by the pool."

"Is there a better way to start the day?" he asked.

"None that I know of."

She tossed her tote onto a vacant chaise and stretched out next to him. It was Friday, the start of the weekend. And yet, while she slathered sunscreen on her legs, hordes of people commuted to work. Back home, the early birds were flocking to the office. The news of her departure would have already made the rounds. They'd laugh and call her a flake. Gus would update his comedic material to better cover his involvement. They'd fight for her office and the minifridge with her snacks. In a few weeks, they'd forget all about her. What did it matter? The morning air was fresh, the sun gentle. A blue pool stretched out before her. Her former colleagues could congregate in cold conference rooms with coffee and doughnuts. She was drinking in sunshine. They could go screw themselves.

Her phone rang.

Lily and Noah groaned in unison.

Lily scrambled to silence the offending thing. She'd made the mistake of taking her father's call and had no intention of repeating that mistake. Without reading the screen, she shut it off and shoved it into the tote. Out of sight, out of mind.

"Désolée!" she apologized in his native French in the hopes of getting back in his good graces.

Noah shielded his eyes from the sun. "You speak a little French?"

"A little," she admitted.

"Where'd you pick it up?" he asked.

She laughed. "I'll never tell you about my slutty semester abroad."

"Okay." Noah turned away. "I won't tell you about last night."

Oh no! Anything but that! Other people's love lives were her raison d'être, so to speak. Had Noah been stood up, after all? If so, how did he take it? Did he need a hug? Her inquiring mind had to know.

"I'm bilingual," she admitted. "My parents are from Haiti. Dad insisted we speak French in the house. He's fussy like that."

"Ah . . ." he said. "We have that in common."

Lily had no idea what he was getting at. "Fussy dads?"

"No," he said. "My dad is a mechanic. Not fussy at all."

"Lucky you."

"We haven't spoken in years."

"Oh. Sorry to hear that."

"It's nothing," he said, although his tone hinted otherwise. "We're both Caribbean."

She eyed him skeptically. "Are we?"

"My parents are from Martinique. I grew up there."

"Really? Here I thought you were raised in a Parisian sidewalk café."

Noah smirked. "Because of my je ne sais quoi?"

"Exactly."

"I work in fashion," he explained. "Although, I did move to Paris when I was fifteen."

"How did you end up here?" she asked.

"When you're lost, all paths lead to Miami."

He had a point there. "We've so much in common. Are we soulmates, you think?"

"I wouldn't go that far," Noah said. "How about kindred spirits?"

"I'll take that." Lily sat back on her chair's bright yellow cushions and fired up her e-reader. "When I need a soulmate, I read a book."

"And how's that going?" Noah asked. "Have they kissed yet?"

"They've done more than that."

The Sweetest Lie was an instant *New York Times* bestseller and, by all accounts, the romance of the summer. Exes Max and Emma reunite at a mutual friend's wedding in Malibu. For reasons Lily had yet to discover, Emma resents Max for the way things ended.

"Details, please," Noah said.

Lily tossed the e-reader aside. "I'm more interested in *your* love story. Come on. How did the date go?"

"He was an hour late."

"He showed up?" So much for her catfish theory.

"Yes, but something is off with him."

"Bad vibe?"

"Not exactly."

"Go on! Tell me more."

"Not without a drink," he said. "Meet you on the rooftop later?"

She thought it over. If she agreed to meet with Noah for

drinks, she'd encounter Ben. He'd fix her a martini, and she'd want to kiss him. Again. Although, she could run into him outside her door in the morning. He'd make her coffee, and she'd want to kiss him. So really, she risked nothing by meeting Noah later this evening.

"Okay, cool," she said. "What time?"

Noah rolled up to his feet and slipped on a rumpled cotton shirt. "Oh, you know, happy hour."

Lily watched him stroll off and enter the building. Her gaze then skimmed the lines of the narrow building up to its tiered crown, a birthday cake with white icing and lemon-yellow piping. So cheery and quirky, nothing like her stern brick building in New York. She let out a breath and relaxed. She could be happy here.

Lily finished the novel by noon. Afterwards, she waded into the pool to keep from drowning in a sea of conflicting emotions. Max and Emma got their happy ending, but was it earned? She wasn't convinced. Bobbing about on a pink raft, she applied analytic skills honed at law school to deconstruct the deceptively simple narrative.

Max and Emma are exes. They dated for a few months straight out of college.

Max breaks Emma's heart when, on a business trip, he wakes up married in Vegas.

The pair reunites in Malibu, at the wedding.

Max is divorced. A changed man, he's determined to win Emma back.

Spoiler: he does.

It was more nuanced than that, obviously, but Lily was stuck on one point. All Max had to do to regain Emma's trust was admit to his mistake—in an emotionally fraught scene that brought Lily to tears, but still.

She climbed out of the pool and toweled off. Before heading

out for lunch, she hopped on BookTap and crafted a quick book review.

@LegalLyon: 1/3 Chemistry eclipses common sense in The Sweetest Lie by Teresa Star. The only lie detected in this fiery romance is that people change. They don't.

@LegalLyon: 2/3 Max is two margaritas away from waking up married in Cancun.

@LegalLyon: 3/3 In the end, this book still gave me all the feels. The chemistry between Max and Emma was off the charts. 4 stars.

She added a couple of hashtags, #bookreview #romance, and posted the thread.

After lunch, a quick trip to the grocery store, and a nap that stretched out far too long, Lily woke up with a kink in her neck and hair stuck to her cheek. Had she missed happy hour? She reached for her phone to check the time and . . . *wow!* BookTap alerts crowded the home screen. Apparently, her short review of *The Sweetest Lie* had taken off. Thrilled, she took the phone into the bathroom and scrolled through the comments as she went about the tedious work of detangling her hair.

@RoséAllDayyyy: LMAO!!! Love your take on this! Please review Blurred Lines next! Highly overrated IMO

@TheTrilogyGoddess: Exactly! Our girl is 2 tequila shots away from heartbreak!

@BookBae89: Ha! 4 stars?!!! You can't be serious. It was MID at best. 2.5 stars.

Two and a half stars? Rude! Lily was insulted on the author's behalf. What of the whip-smart dialogue and sexy banter that had made her blush? What of those lush descriptions of the California sunrise?

@Ben_Romero: You're wrong. "Changing," or evolving, is inherently human. Only those with limited insight into the complexities of the human psyche would fail to acknowledge this.

That caught her attention. Very limited . . . what? She read it again and again. Each time, her annoyance spiked. Who was this pretentious person? Were they calling her dumb? She noted the user's blue check mark. This was a verified account, a BookTap VIP. Curious, she tapped on the handle.

Benedicto Romero
Literary Translation
Current Read: Miami, by Joan Didion
All opinions are my own.

Lily stared at her phone. The thumbnail photo was blurry, yet there were those keen eyes staring back at her. Unless her neighbor had a doppelgänger with the exact same first name, she could only reasonably conclude that Benedicto, the literary translator, and Ben, the bartender, were one and the same. Could it be?

She was about to find out.

Lily marched across the hall and knocked on Ben's door. He was home, likely on the phone. She could hear him laughing. Irritated, she knocked again. He yanked the door open and, surprised to see her, smiled. She didn't reciprocate.

"What's wrong?" he asked.

"I have enough *insight* to know when I've been insulted."

He went silent, which infuriated her. She could kiss him or accuse him of libel—it didn't matter. He would keep his cool. Lily had no doubt that this quiet, focused man was a literary scholar in disguise. She felt suddenly self-conscious, aware of what she must look like in the plushy robe stolen from the resort she'd fled the day before, clutching a hairbrush in one hand and a phone in the other. What must he think of her!

"Is it the coffee?" he asked. "You didn't like it?"

"No!" she cried, appalled. "Why would you say that? Didn't you get my note?"

She'd rinsed the mug and returned it with a note scribbled on a page ripped from her daily planner. It read *Thanks for the love.*

"I got it." He was leaning against the doorway now, arms folded across his chest. "It was sweet."

"If that's the case, why are you trolling me?"

"Trolling you?" He considered her carefully. "I don't understand. I would never insult or troll you. What are you talking about?"

Trolling was a little strong, but she would not back down. "I'll read the record to refresh your memory."

"All right, then." He mimicked her tone. "Go on."

Lily tapped on the phone screen and read the comment aloud. Ben's face registered his surprise. "I posted that a minute ago."

"More like five minutes."

"What does it have to do with you?" he asked. "I was disputing a point made in a book review."

"That was *my* point you were disputing, *my* book review, *my* lack of insight into the complexities of the human psyche."

"Was it?"

She held up her phone. He narrowed his eyes as he read the screen. "@LegalLyon . . . That's you?" he asked.

"As if you didn't know."

"I didn't," he insisted. "I comment on book reviews all the time. It's my thing."

She scoffed. "You comment on random reviews? Even of books you haven't read?"

Who was she to question him? Up until minutes ago, she'd thought he was a grad student, wrapping up an MFA or similar.

"No, never," he said. "What would be the point of that?"

"You read *The Sweetest Lie*?" Lily asked, incredulous. Back in New York, it wasn't uncommon to spot a hot guy on the subway with his nose buried in a book. Yet it was generally accepted among her friends that those men were posers or figments of their collective imagination. Once they stepped off the train, these men disappeared, dissolved into the city, never to be seen again.

"It's not my preferred genre," he admitted. "But I'll read anything that isn't nailed down. I found it lying around my place, read it, and kind of liked it. Your review was harsh. You're essentially saying people can't change."

"They can, but they rarely do," Lily retorted. "And what do you mean you found the book lying around your place?" She found it hard to picture the hot bartender curled up with a romance novel.

"Someone left it behind."

"Who?"

He stepped back and opened the door wider, giving her a glimpse into his apartment and of the woman, a raven-haired beauty with coal eyes like his, lounging on his sectional sofa, feet propped up on the coffee table. She waved hello to Lily, smiling, friendly.

Lily went up in flames.

"Believe me now?" Ben asked.

She nodded and, without another word, stepped away from his door. Moving slowly, oh so carefully, so as to not set the entire building on fire, she retreated to her apartment to die, alone, in shame.

Chapter Four

Ben knocked and called to her from the hall. "May I come in?"

"No!" Lily cried.

She lacked sufficient insight into her own psyche to interact with her neighbor in any way. What had gotten into her? She was *spiraling*. This was not a good look for a fun and fabulous thirty-year-old.

"Come on, Lily."

"No!"

There was no need to drag this out. She knew full well where this was headed. In the last twenty-four hours, she'd become his Crazy Next-door Neighbor. Everybody had one; she'd lived in the city long enough to know. Gradually, he'd start avoiding her, timing his comings and goings to keep from running into her in the hall or joining her in an elevator.

Ben knocked again. This time the door, which wasn't locked or even shut properly, swung open. There he stood, filling her doorway just as he had his own a moment earlier. His demeanor did not match the moment. His face was strained to control his laughter.

"Why are you here when your date is waiting?" she snapped.

"Date?" He ran a hand through his hair. When left to its own devices, it was thick, curly, and a little wild. "She's my cousin, Roxanna. Honestly, she's more like a sister."

"Your . . . cousin?"

"Yes."

If leaping to conclusions were an Olympic sport, she'd win gold.

"Go back," she insisted. "It's rude to leave her alone."

"I wouldn't worry about her," he said. "She's raiding my refrigerator for day-old pasta. She likes to hang out at my place before her shift at the bar."

"She's a bartender, too?"

"No." A pause. "She's *the* bartender. I covered for her last night because her baby—God, there are so many things to clear up."

Lily stood in the middle of her living room, feeling help-less, her phone and hairbrush still clutched in her hands like weapons. She set them down on the nearest surface and ca-pitulated. "Come in."

Ben stepped inside and gingerly shut the door. He looked at her for a long while, saying nothing, until the silence became unbearable.

"Who are you?" she asked.

"I'm Ben," he said. "Professor, literary translator, occasional part-time bartender."

"You could've said any of those things last night or this morning," she said. "You had me thinking you were working your way through grad school."

"You liked the bartender," he said. "Besides, that's who you met last night. Did you really want to hear my PhD thesis?"

Lily shrugged. "Why not?"

"Most people's eyes glaze over when I tell them what I do," he said. "Maybe you're the exception. Forgive me?"

Who was she to judge? Miami was truly the multiverse: no one was who they claimed they were, not even herself.

She sighed. "Of course . . . And I'm sorry I jumped all over you. All I want for this summer is to chill by the pool and read, not pick fights with my neighbor. This is not who I am, not really. My life has been stagnant for so long. I hoped a change in scene might work, but it's painfully clear I can't function outside of my daily routines. I've never felt so scattered, so insecure."

"Who are you, really?" he asked.

Her answer mirrored his. "I'm Lily, a failed corporate lawyer from New York who quit her job on a whim and booked an Airbnb in Miami for the summer to avoid going home and dealing with the fallout."

He seemed to take that in without judgment. "Nice to meet you, Lily."

"Nice to meet you, too, Ben. I wish we could start over," she said.

"We are," he said. "This is what we're doing."

It wasn't enough. She would give anything for a second chance at a first impression.

"May I hold you?" he asked. "You look like you could use a hug."

"Yes, of course. But do you see what you did there?" she said. "Asking to hold me instead of just grabbing me? I should have been that considerate of your feelings in the elevator."

He pulled her in his arms and held her close. "Let's forget the elevator."

"I can't." Lily rested her head against his chest, felt the steady beat of his heart. "It's just one in a string of bad decisions I've made in an alarmingly short time."

"Think of it this way. If you hadn't decided to stay in Miami, you wouldn't have booked this apartment and ended up at the bar. We wouldn't have met at all. I had no plans for the summer, and now I have you."

"Sweet of you to say. I'm one gaff away from being the neighbor you'll have to hide from."

"Never."

He released her, and the air between them stirred. Longing for his warmth, she struggled to find something meaningful to say. "So . . . you translate books?"

"Poetry, mainly."

"Any particular language?"

"Spanish."

"Are you any good?"

His gaze sharpened with pride. "Yes."

There was a knock on the door, and a woman called out. "Hey! It's me!"

"Roxanna," Ben said.

"Right."

Lily tightened the knot of her robe and went to the door. Ben's cousin stood in the hall with her arms akimbo. From this close, it was obvious that Roxanna and Ben were related. The resemblance was striking. They had the same thick black hair, dark eyes, and golden honey complexion. They even had similar tattoos. Roxanna's ink was more colorful and floral, but the craftsmanship was the same. Her smile was benign, but her words were direct.

"If you're running a secret book club, I want in," she said. "I read *The Sweetest Lie*, too, and I have thoughts."

Lily was curious to get her take on Max and Emma, but Ben was quicker to reply. From inside her apartment, he said, "You're going to have to troll her on BookTap like everyone else."

"Would you like to come in?" Lily offered.

"I'm heading to work," Roxanna replied. "Come up to the bar when you're free. The first drink is on the house."

Technically, she'd already had her complimentary first drink. Roxanna didn't have to know that. "Thanks. How about later? I'm meeting . . ." *Crap!* Lily brought her hands to her tangled hair. "I'm supposed to meet Noah for happy hour."

"Relax," Roxanna said. "Noah won't show up until sunset. He never does. If he gets there early, I'll keep him entertained."

"Thanks!"

This was the sort of sisterhood and allyship the world needed right now!

Roxanna left Lily standing in a cloud of rose-scented perfume. Ben approached and touched her arm. "I should get out of your way," he said. "Also, don't go inviting random people to join our book club. It's just for us."

"Roxanna is your cousin," she reminded him. "Actually, she's more like a sister."

"I know, and I love her," he said. "It doesn't change that three's a crowd. When do we meet by the pool?"

"Tomorrow, around ten?"

He made a face. "Can you do early? The pool is deserted at eight or nine."

"I can do early. How about eight?"

"Perfect. What are we reading?"

"*Blurred Lines* by Kayla Clark."

"Come by for coffee first."

"If you insist."

"I insist."

Lily waited until she heard the door across the hall click shut before plugging his name into a search engine.

Benedicto Romero is a Cuban American academic who specializes in literary translations . . . on the faculty of the University of Miami . . . works include *War and Reason,*

Light before Dawn, The Lamb . . . recipient of a PEN award for translation and a MacArthur Fellowship . . .

Lily blinked and read that last bit again. The man she'd accused of trolling, just for poking holes into her hot take on a romance novel, was a MacArthur Fellow—or stated more plainly, a certified genius.

Chapter Five

The next morning, Ben presented her with a coffee and a copy of *Blurred Lines*, picked up the night before at a local bookstore. Affection bubbled up inside her. Quickly, she used her iron will to pop those bubbles, putting an end to that.

"Thanks, neighbor."

"You're welcome." He grabbed his keys off a hook. "Elevator or stairs?"

"You'd get in an elevator with me?" she asked.

"I'll take my chances," he said. "How was happy hour?"

"Postponed until later today," she replied. "Noah couldn't make it. He left a message with your cousin. Are you bartending tonight?"

"No," he answered. "I'm grading papers."

Lily stomped on the sprouting weed of disappointment. "Ah . . . sounds like fun!"

"I'm teaching a seminar this summer. It's short but intense."

"Well, we can't all be on sabbatical," she said.

"I envy you," he said. "If you only knew how much."

They rode to the pool deck without incident. Ben pulled close two lounge chairs and adjusted the yellow sun umbrella for maximum shade. Then he peeled off his T-shirt, balled it up, and stuffed it into a duffel bag. Lily stole a glance, then another . . . and another. He might be a scholar, but his body told the story of another kind of life. His back was broad, chiseled, and seared by the sun. He did not have the regular assortment of tattoos: daggers on forearms, barbed wire around wrists, requisite angel, wings outstretched over biceps. Instead, vines crawled up his forearms, flowers bloomed on his chest, and a flock of tiny black birds soaring up his spine. Was that all? Were there more concealed somewhere? The little birds held her attention. She wanted to follow their flight with her fingertips.

He caught her staring. She blushed but didn't look away. Lily no longer felt awkward and jittery around him, which was a minor miracle that deserved its own holiday.

She stripped off her cotton button-up shirt. Underneath, she wore the most provocative of her swimsuit collection, a navy tankini that she was going to get rid of the minute her online orders arrived. Ben didn't steal glances at her newly unveiled body, he stared with keen, observant eyes. He could see right down to her last cell of insecurity, and yet there was no judgment, only warmth and admiration.

She stretched out next to him in her chair. "We should set some ground rules."

"I'm listening," he said.

"This is a romance book club, so let's be clear on what a romance is and is not."

"I don't need a primer, but go on."

"A romance is not a tragic love story. We won't read *Wuthering Heights* or *Madame Bovary*."

"Now I'm disappointed," he deadpanned.

"Rule number two," she continued. "There's no such thing as highbrow or lowbrow. We'll read trad, indie, and everything in between. No judgment."

"I wouldn't worry about that. People will judge regardless," he said. "I promise if you pick up Tolstoy, someone will tell you to read Chekhov, instead."

"I won't be picking up either," Lily said. "Not this summer. I'm fried."

"How did you lose your job?" he asked.

She hadn't lost her job. It wasn't a puppy or a cat. She could find her way back to it if she wanted to. She knew exactly who to call, whose ass to kiss. Only, she didn't want to. That was the crux of the problem, wasn't it? She didn't want to go back and hadn't begun to explore how to move forward.

He brushed the back of her hand with his. "We don't have to talk about it now."

Lily didn't want to talk about it ever. There was something to leaving the past, even the very recent past, firmly behind you.

"It's just so boring." She raised herself onto an elbow. "Let's talk about you," she said. "You're a board-certified genius. I'm impressed."

"That's not a thing," he said, laughing.

"You won a MacArthur!"

"I'm the flavor of the month. It doesn't mean anything, Lily."

"In case the meaning is lost on you, let's review the criteria." She whipped out her phone and read from the source material. *"The fellows are selected for the exceptional work they've already done, their ability to do more, and—"*

"It's just words," he said.

"Words have meaning," she reminded him. "Tell me about your exceptional work, past, present, and future."

"It's just so boring."

He used her own line against her, a genius move.

Then he did something that outraged her. He folded back the cover of the paperback, creasing the edge. It was a striking cover, too. The story was set in Chicago. The city's skyline extended from the front to the back.

"Why would you do that?" Lily cried.

"Do what?" he asked, genuinely confused.

"Fold the cover like that! It'll never lie flat again."

"Lie flat? It won't be in one piece by the time I'm done. I might even rip it off and use it as a bookmark."

This, as far as she was concerned, was the first red flag. She should've known Ben was too good to be true.

He pulled a pen from his bag. "I mark them up, too."

"No!" she gasped.

"Oh yes."

Lily pinched the bridge of her nose. She could feel a migraine coming on.

"Tell me your book kinks," he said. "Don't you have any?"

"I stamp them," she replied.

"Spank them? You're into that?"

"Keep this up and I'll spank *you*!"

In the back of her mind, Lily wondered, Is this banter? Good banter was the product of novels, plays, movies. In real life, men didn't engage in repartee. They said things like *Hey* or *What's up?* and the oh-so-popular *So can I call you sometime?* Other times, they sent random texts in the dead of night with an urgent question: *U up??*

Lily had started reading romance at the tender age of twelve over her parents' objections. Her father was dismayed by her taste in books. Her mother worried the steamy novels might *give her ideas*. They did. Word play was just as good as foreplay. Now that it was happening, now that she'd found a sparring partner, Lily's mind went blank. Or was she reading too much into this? It was a sunny day. They were by the pool, poking fun. Either way, she ought to know for sure.

In the real world, in New York, she wouldn't have gone so long without asking a man some pertinent questions. Though Miami had revealed itself to be an alternate universe, this was no reason to go rogue.

"Are you single?" she asked.

Ben had already started with the prologue. He looked up from his book, startled by the question. If he hoped she'd take it back, she wouldn't. She might have jumped to conclusions where Roxanna was concerned, but that didn't mean Ben wasn't hiding a girlfriend somewhere. Men these days were crafty.

"Technically, I am."

Lily turned away abruptly and flipped open her book. However, there was no *unseeing* it, the huge red flag unfurling, flapping noisily in the morning breeze.

"You either are or you aren't," she said.

"Yes, but you forget the undefinable gray area," he said.

She wanted to forget this conversation. "We should start reading."

Lily had no interest in hearing what he had to say. It was always the same. His girlfriend was either away on an extended trip, or they were on an official break, or they were one of those on again–off again couples, running hot and cold.

He sat up and turned to her. "You've judged and sentenced me without a preliminary hearing. Is that how the judicial system works?"

"You're not on trial! Being *technically single* is not a crime, last I checked."

"I'd like to say a few words in my defense."

"Fine." She sat up to face him. "Go ahead. Just don't perjure yourself."

"I *am* single," he said. "That's the truth. A relationship ended, and it was painful. It's only been a week."

"I'm sorry to hear that. Are you okay?"

"Yeah. It's been a wild week."

In the back of her mind, Lily did the math. One week was nothing when it came to a breakup. You needed a month to see clearly again and six months to a year to feel like your old self.

Her phone rang. This time, she checked the caller ID before silencing it. It was her brother, Patrick. He'd called yesterday when she was at the pool with Noah. She couldn't go too long without calling him back. Their parents were likely driving him crazy. Even so, she tucked the phone away.

He took in her furtive movements and asked, "What about you? Is someone waiting back home?"

"No."

"Are you sure?"

Had she raised a red flag of her own? Dodging phone calls was shady behavior, for sure. In her defense, she wasn't hiding a man, but her melodramatic family. "I've been single a while. I'll stay single until I find what I want."

"What do you want?" he asked.

"I have no clue."

She knew what she didn't want, which was to not repeat the same old mistakes. No way was she getting involved with a man fresh out of a relationship. Two weeks in and he'd ask for *space*, claiming that he couldn't get too involved because he had *inner work* to do.

Even as far back as when she was dating Darren, Lily had trouble imagining their future. He was a Midwesterner, born and raised in Cleveland. He'd come to the East Coast for college but had no intention of staying. He studied podiatry and would take over his father's practice someday. Lily, pre-law and political science, born and raised in Long Island, did not see where she fit in his plan. Now, thanks to Instagram, she didn't have to rely on imagination. The images were there for her to peruse at will. They would have a lakeside wedding with a hundred or so guests. Darren, heavier than she remembered, hairline receding, would nonetheless look handsome in his tuxedo. He would tear up when she showed up in her wedding gown for a First Look moment captured by their photographer. He would vow to be forever by her side. They'd honeymoon in South Carolina. Who wouldn't want that? It was all so wholesome. Why had she thrown it away?

"What do you want in general?" he asked. "No need to get specific."

"I want something stable," Lily replied. She'd never yearned for stability before. When drowning in a pool, you don't dream of the sea. Her life was a testament to what a stable upbringing could produce. Her parents, both highly educated and firmly planted in the middle class, had given her brother and her everything required to succeed. What she'd always wanted, more than anything, was to shake things up.

Click!

Lily and Ben both caught the sound of the camera shutter. The photographer was a young woman in a lime-green bikini. Brown skin, loose curly hair. Camera dangling from her neck. She was stunning.

"Hey there! I'd kill to know what you two are chatting about."

Lily held up *Blurred Lines*. "This!"

"It must be a banger," she said. "Are you two buddy-reading? That's so cute!"

"It's an exclusive book club," Ben informed her. "And we haven't read a word."

"So far we've only set some ground rules."

"Exclusive! How sexy! I'm Sierra, by the way."

Ben took over the introductions from there. "Lily, this is Sierra Jay, the resident vlogger. Sierra, this is Lily. She's new."

"Hey, Lily! Nice to meet you."

"Same. Are you going to shoot video?"

"Just some photos. I've got to catch this gorgeous light." She pointed to the far side of the pool. "I'll be over there. You won't even know I'm here."

Sierra left them and got busy, setting up her tripods.

"She's a swimwear influencer with a million followers on YouTube," Ben said. "Bikinis are big business."

"I could never," Lily said. "I'm far too self-conscious."

She went on a crash diet just to go on a corporate retreat and never once wore her bathing suit. There hadn't been any time.

"That's a shame," he said. "If there was a *Lily* channel, I'd subscribe."

"Be careful. You could get hooked."

"Hey!" Sierra called out from the deep end of the pool. "Is that book any good?"

"Don't know yet," Lily replied. "It's gotten a lot of hype. We'll see."

"What's it about?" she asked.

The nuanced answer came from Ben. "The exploration of the generational divide, with an older female protagonist and a younger male love interest, through the lens of a contemporary romance embedded with a friends-to-lovers trope."

"What the hell was that?" Lily asked.

"What? . . . You disagree?"

How would she know? She hadn't read past the tagline: *In matters of the heart, where do you draw the line?*

"Is this how it's going to be?" she asked. "You showing off your genius at every turn?"

Ben smirked. "I'll try not to."

Lily took in his smirk, attitude, and even his body posture. He was adorable.

Sierra waded over to their end of the pool. "Hey! While you two sort that out, hand over the book. I could use a prop."

Lily wouldn't let her precious copy, a gift no less, go anywhere near the water. She tossed over Ben's copy instead. "Here you go!"

"Thanks, doll!"

They watched, heads close as Sierra stretched out on the pool's edge, twisting, turning, posing, the book open on her lap or propped under her head.

"That's going to be a good shot," Lily whispered.

"She's a pro," Ben whispered back.

"I didn't know *Blurred Lines* was about a May–December relationship."

"I prefer age-gap romance," he said. "How old are you, by the way?"

"Old enough to practice law in New York, New Jersey, and Connecticut."

It was easier to make a joke than simply say her age. Lily was patient with herself. It took effort to shut the doors on a defining decade, even though it was for the best.

"Who's showing off now?" Ben said.

"I'm thirty," she said.

"Thirty-two." Ben took her hand and curled his fingers tightly around hers. He might as well have taken her heart in his hands. "Are we going to read this book or not?"

Lily sighed. "Likely not. It's so hot already."

The sun was creeping higher. The light Sierra had wanted to catch had turned harsh. She wrapped up her photo shoot. All the while, Lily's hand was still in Ben's. Hadn't he noticed?

Before leaving, Sierra returned the book. The warped cover broke Lily's heart. "I'll tag you on Instagram," she said. "What's your handle?"

"I'm @LegalLyon everywhere. Lyon with a *Y*."

"Got it. How about you, Ben?"

"I'm on BookTap," he said. "Tag me there."

"BookTap?" Sierra scoffed. "Is that a real thing?"

"Wow," Lily said, watching her go. "I don't think I've ever felt so irrelevant."

"At least you're on Instagram," Ben said. He stood and stretched. "I'd tell her I'm on X, but I don't like how it sounds."

"Sounds like a misdemeanor with a heavy fine."

He laughed. "Come. Let's swim."

"We can't!" Lily protested. "First rule of book club is that we have to read, even a single page."

"And then we swim?" he asked.

"Of course."

"Fine."

They finished the first chapter. They swam. They rode the elevator back to their floor, the fourth, wrapped in beach towels. Ben told her he had a full day ahead, teaching a Saturday poetry seminar. He said most of the students had signed up to meet graduation credit requirements. Some, however, were eager and showed promise.

"I'm sure you're a great professor," she said.

Again, that hint of pride in his eyes. "I do all right," he said. "How's your day shaping up?"

Lily had nothing to do except wash her hair and meet Noah later, for happy hour. "A whole lot of nothing."

He laughed. "You're my hero. Same time tomorrow, or a little later? I'd like to run first."

"Sure," she said, sunshine in her heart. "How about nine? We'll meet by the pool."

"That's a plan." He left her with a wink goodbye.

Lily let herself into her place. Her summer was off to an excellent start.

Chapter Six

True to her word, that evening Roxanna kept Noah entertained at the bar. When Lily arrived for happy hour fifteen minutes late, still glowing from her morning with Ben, Roxanna had him engrossed in what seemed like a spicy story. Brows raised to his golden hairline, Noah was hanging on the bartender's every word. Lily caught the tail end of the story when she slid onto the stool beside him. "And now they've started a private book club!"

The hot story was about her and Ben. So much for allyship!

"Roxanna!" Lily protested.

Roxanna poured her a glass of white wine. "Sorry," she said without a drip of remorse.

Noah clinked his glass to hers. "When I told you to go for the bartender, I didn't think you had it in you."

"And this is the book that started it all." Roxanna pulled out a water-stained paperback copy of *The Sweetest Lie* from under the counter and handed it to Noah.

He thumbed the frayed pages. "Should I read it?"

Roxanna shrugged. "Up to you. I loved it."

Lily watched this exchange in shock. Wasn't this the man who'd ridiculed her for reading at the bar? She tapped Noah's shoulder. "You gave me so much shit the other night. Yet here you are, a book in one hand, a glass of wine in the other."

Noah dropped the paperback as if it were contaminated.

Lily wouldn't let him get away with it. "Too late for that! You're reading this book, and you owe me an apology."

"All I owe you is a recount of my date. Ready?"

Lily sipped her wine and gestured for him to spill the tea.

"It's a short story. We met for dinner, went back to my place."

"Sounds promising. Go on."

"We watched a movie, something with Timothée Chalamet."

She nodded approvingly. "And then what?"

"He left."

"Hmm . . . Maybe he had an early morning. Will you see him again?"

"What's the point? He's wasting my time. There's more chemistry between you and that glass of wine."

"Maybe it's a good thing." Lily set the wineglass down and pointed to the book lying on the bar between them. "I won't spoil it for you, but the couple was so hot for each other it clouded their judgment."

She had no business sounding so sure of herself. Her lack of chemistry with Darren hadn't sharpened her judgment. He was a good catch, as her mother had said repeatedly. Yet she'd released him to marry a girl named Mandy, who was not *mid* as Gus had so gutlessly declared. She was lovely and smart enough to see the value in the Darrens of the world.

"I don't want to see clearly," Noah said. "I want to see stars."

A while later, Noah left to say hello to a friend, and Roxanna circled back. She filled a highball with ice and stuffed it with lemon wedges. "That's good advice," she said.

Lily startled. She hadn't realized Roxanna had been listening to them the whole time.

"He won't take it, of course," Roxanna continued. "But you had a point about the book. I didn't think of it that way."

"He has a point, too," Lily said. "If there's no smoke, there's no fire."

"If there's no fire, you can't torch your life."

"So true."

"Are *you* open to advice?" Roxanna asked.

Lily nodded. "Always."

This wasn't true, naturally.

"God knows my life is a mess. Add a kid and it just gets messier. Believe me. I've got no business telling you what to do, but ask me if I care." Roxanna reached for a bottle of gin. "Ben is not the one."

"The one . . . what?" Lily asked, confused. Had she missed something? Happy hour was in full swing, and the rooftop bar was getting loud.

"Your one true love," Roxanna replied.

Lily stiffened. "What makes you say that?"

"I caught the vibes between you two."

"We're neighbors! It's a neighborly vibe!"

Roxanna laughed. "We've all got neighbors. There's no such thing."

"Anyway, he told me he just ended something, and for me, that's a red flag," Lily said. "I'm no idiot!"

Roxanna went on as if Lily had said nothing. "I get it. He's irresistible, particularly when you compare him to those losers." She pointed with her chin at a group of guys at the far end of the bar who could only be described as *bros*. "But my cousin has issues—and that's all I'll say."

"He's a genius. Is that the problem?"

Roxanna stared at her blankly. "My God," she muttered under her breath. "That stupid grant has everyone tripping."

"It's a big deal," Lily said.

"Ben has been translating poems in his bedroom since he

was fourteen. If the world is catching on now, that's on them. And it shouldn't be a shock to anyone! He *is* his father's son."

Lily was about to ask if his father worked in publishing when Roxanna added a new spin to the story. "*That's* the problem. He's got some trauma to unpack."

So his father was the problem. Had he been overbearing, negligent, an abuser, narcissist, deadbeat dad, gambler, workaholic, alcoholic, serial cheater, polygamist, politician, or felon? What could be so bad that, at thirty-two, Ben was still messed up about it?

"You're a smart woman," Roxanna said. "But at the end of the day, you're just a girl standing in front of a boy asking him to read romance books by the pool, and we know how that story ends."

She could ignore good advice; however, when the truth slapped you in the face there was no denying it. Lily didn't have to feign a headache, she really had one. Blame it on the early morning sun, the wine, or Roxanna's words of caution. She said goodnight to Noah and went straight to bed. Tucked in tight, she resumed her search, this time typing *Benedicto Romero father* into the search bar. She found these illuminating gems:

OBITUARY
SABATO ROMERO, CUBAN POET, DIES AT 78
Born in a coastal town in Cuba, educated in Havana . . .
emigrated to the US as a young man . . . published several
acclaimed collections, notably *Aurore*, which won a
Pulitzer Prize in 2000 . . . delivered the inaugural poem at
President . . .

LITERARY TRANSLATOR BENEDICTO ROMERO RECEIVES
MACARTHUR FELLOWSHIP
The *World Tribune's* Lesly Kennedy speaks with Benedicto
Romero about the MacArthur Fellowship and his father's
influence on his work.

This year's roster of MacArthur Foundation fellowship winners includes thirty-two-year-old Benedicto "Ben" Romero. Born and raised in South Florida, the respected literary translator is the son of the late poet Sabato Romero. Ben distinguished himself by, as he put it, "eliminating the imaginary barrier of language and bridging cultures." Each so-called Genius Grant comes with an award for $800,000. I started by asking what led him to this line of work.

Romero: It came naturally. Like many children growing up in South Florida, I grew up in a Spanish-speaking household. My grandmother struggled with English. I routinely translated her correspondence, her shows, magazine clippings, coupons . . . At some point, there was no veil between English and Spanish, her world and mine.

Kennedy: Tell us how you came to translate the collection of poems that catapulted Cuban author Juaquin Tomas to literary fame.

Romero: The collection tells a quiet coming-of-age story of two brothers in 1950s Havana. They were first published in the original Spanish by a small press out in Indiana. A year later, they decided to translate the poems into English to widen the audience. That's when I got the call.

Kennedy: The plan worked because the critics praised Tomas's literary achievement. He went on to win the Pulitzer Prize, and you, a PEN/Faulkner award, now the MacArthur Fellowship grant. Let's talk about early influences. Your father, the poet Sabato Romero, passed away last year. What influence has he had on your work?

Romero: None that I can think of. He's an artist. I'm a wordsmith, if anything.

Kennedy: Still, you captured the musicality of Tomas's words beautifully. Your work is extremely precise.

Romero: The author had a point of view. I did not want to dilute it in a torrent of words.

Kennedy: You're being modest.

Romero: I promise I'm not.

Kennedy: What's your take on your father's most famous work, his inaugural poem, "Promise of Dawn"?

Romero: I'd have chosen a better title. [Laughs]. Otherwise, I've nothing to add. It stands on its own.

Lily set her phone aside and got out of bed for a glass of water. She played with the words of the interview in her mind, moving them around. What journalist Lesly Kennedy took for modesty she took for caginess. Ben had danced around the questions about his father and his impressive body of work. This morning, by the pool, he'd danced around her questions about his own impressive body of work. No harm, no foul: she'd danced around his questions, too. At this rate, they could join the Alvin Ailey dance company.

He is *his father's son*, Roxanna had said. That's *the problem*.

Lily was her mother's daughter, a woman who never left a single stone unturned—not in her garden or anywhere else. A licensed social worker, it was literally her job. She would discover the secrets buried in Ben's beautiful mind.

Chapter Seven

Ben's Journal

April 19, Death in Late Spring

April is the cruelest month. —T.S. Eliot

Outside the hospital, spring shows its colors. The parking lot is slick from a sun-shower. The air smells of grass. Birds sing, and one craps on your windshield. A tree dumps pink flowers everywhere. All this life, and he is dead.

Dying alone is a joke, an empty threat, until you watch it play out. If you hadn't dragged your feet, delayed this visit, you might've saved him from this fate, but every story has the ending it deserves.

The first time you visited, you got lost in the hospice ward's long, dim, ghostly halls. By the time you found his room, he was either asleep or unconscious. The bed was a boat tethered to land by tubes pumping fluids or oxygen. You hated seeing him like that, but you couldn't look away.

Head propped up to ease his breathing; thin and waxy skin, once golden, now a dull brown; sunken eyes, coal-black hair turned ash gray. There was nothing left of the titan who loomed so large over your life, the myth who held so much space in your mind. It was a shock seeing him like this, reduced to nothing, like any abuelito on his last days. How different from that man who, one frigid January morning in Washington, DC, stepped up to the inaugural podium and made history.

That poem is not his best work. The message is generic, expected. A new administration ushers in change, an opportunity for a nation to make whole those shattered by the hammer of injustice. But who are these nameless victims, exactly? And what injustice had they suffered? It was anyone's guess.

Here, you could show some mercy. It was likely the best he could do. Riddled with disease, as he was at the time, his once-sharp mind was dulled by radiation and chemotherapy and whatever else. No one would know it. With some makeup, a tailored suit, a fake tan, and a hairpiece, he'd fooled them all, including you.

That first visit didn't last long. You hadn't made the pilgrimage to pray and weep at his bedside. You left disappointed, itching for a fight.

This time, he isn't asleep: he's dead.

The nurse hands you a worn leather box. "For you," she says.

"What's in it?" you ask.

"You'll have to open it to find out," she says. "He set it aside for you last week."

A current of judgment runs through her words.

You could've laughed in her face. His father had waited a week for his visit? You'd waited a lifetime for visits, phone calls, birthday cards, a letter of explanation. You owed the dead man nothing.

Most fathers were a mystery to their sons; yours was a total stranger. What you knew of him were facts and opinions found in books and articles. Everyone agreed—critics, scholars, former wives, jilted lovers, everyone the poet had ever encountered—that he was great. A great man of letters!

Early on, at ten or twelve, you'd been fool enough to believe that life had spared you. No father to look up to meant no legacy to uphold. You could be whatever, do whatever, and what did you do? You wrote a poem and won a prize.

Life father, like son! they cheered.

You hadn't been spared a thing. His legacy was a weight that would drag you to the bottom of the sea if you let it.

The box is heavier than expected. It holds a collection of journals, letters, a few photos, and a watch. It slides from the seat to the floor as you drive off the lot. Bougainvillea trees line the road.

Death in late spring.

Full blooms for a funeral.

Birds sing a eulogy.

Daisies push through the grave.

Chapter Eight

The App Formerly Known as Twitter: "At the end of the day, we all just miss our plants."

Post.

Delete Post.

Lily had to quit this pity party on social media and start her days journaling, like the wellness gurus recommended. Besides, it wasn't smart; someday, her dark thoughts could be held against her in the court of public opinion. She missed her Monstera and the rituals of watering, pruning, and repotting it when necessary. Tending to it in the morning calmed her before heading into the office. The plant had been a housewarming gift from her mother when she moved into the apartment in Murray Hill. But why long for an emotional support plant when new rituals were taking shape? She was meeting Ben by the pool, around nine.

New bikini, flip-flops, floppy hat, sunglasses, sunblock, sarong, a swipe of red lipstick (because why not?), iced coffee (which she'd gotten herself like a grown-up), a tote with corporate branding . . . and Lily was out the door, Roxanna's warnings trailing behind her. The plan was to get to the pool early, settle down, and maintain a steady heartbeat. He'd arrive after his run to find her, as she'd found Noah the other day, looking like a sun goddess, immersed in the book.

Nothing went according to plan. Ben was already there. His stuff was piled on a chair along with his copy of *Blurred Lines*, its pages flipping in the breeze while he swam long, lazy laps. Lily marched to the pool's edge and dropped the tote at her feet. He swam over and emerged like Triton. There was no controlling her heart rate now.

"Good morning, beautiful!"

"Don't call me that. You know it makes me crazy."

He wiped water out of his eyes. "I'll stop."

"Don't! Obviously, I love it!"

"It's not that obvious," he said, grinning. "What's the matter?"

"You're early!" she said reproachfully.

"I decided to come down for an early swim instead of a run," he explained. "Why is that a problem?"

"Never mind."

She felt foolish for making such a fuss. Life wasn't a staged event. She would never have pulled off sun goddess, anyway. Lily was about to suggest reading sprints when he nodded toward her drink.

"I see you have coffee," he said stiffly. "I was about to head up to make you some."

She raised her stainless-steel cup. "This isn't real coffee. It has so much caramel syrup it's more like dessert."

Drops of water had gathered at his lashes, making his eyes sparkle as he gazed up at her. "What happened? Mr. Coffee didn't deliver?"

"Don't get carried away," Lily said. "I stocked up on cold brew and creamer at the bodega down the street and ordered this cup online."

"That corner store is no bodega, Lily. I wish it was, but it isn't. Words have meaning, remember?"

She wanted to argue, but what could she say? The NYC bodega supplied all you needed to start the day, the tastiest egg sandwiches, the richest coffee, the best bagels, along with the daily paper, flowers, a lotto ticket, and a cheap bottle of wine for later. There was truly nothing like it here.

"Next time, come over for coffee," he said. "Bring your shiny new cup."

"I can't keep knocking on your door for daily essentials."

"Would you like a key?" he asked.

"No, Ben!" she cried. "You can't offer your key to just anyone! What are you thinking?"

"You're not just anyone," he said. "As long as you're my neighbor, I'll make you coffee."

"With ice?"

"With whatever you'd like."

With that promise, Ben smoothly climbed out of the pool while she tried hard not to look. Still, her imagination offered her everything she did not see. The way his muscles pulled tight against the weight of the water. The way the water poured down his back. When he came close, a blue towel draped around his neck, her fingertips tingled she wanted so badly to reach out and trace the outline of his tattoos.

"Can we talk?" he asked. "I scrolled your social media."

The day had come for her to answer for her random social media posts, but she was not without her defenses. "I've done some research on you, too."

"Research? All I did was scroll your social media. That doesn't count as research."

"It's not my fault you're not prepared, Counselor."

He scooped up her tote and dropped it onto a chair. "Should we spend some time reading or get down to it?"

Her insides were corroding with curiosity. She couldn't possibly wait any longer to ask the questions that had kept her up half the night. "Let's get straight to it."

"I like your style."

They sat shoulder to shoulder at the pool's edge on the towel he'd rolled out for them to share, feet in the water. The sun was peaking up over the building's crowned roof. Lily slipped on her sunglasses. "I'm ready."

"What've you got in terms of research?" he asked.

"Interview transcripts."

"That's it?" he said. "Good luck with that. I've lied in every interview I've ever given."

"Don't worry. I'm working on getting your arrest record."

He smiled. "You're funny."

"Funny in a good way or what?" she said, poorly mimicking Joe Pesci.

"In a brilliant way."

"Too bad I have to bring the heat now. Are you ready?"

"Ready."

"Your father was a presidential inaugural poet. That's major. Were you at the inauguration? I got to see my dad sworn onto New York's Second District Court, and that's nowhere near as cool."

He shook his head. "I was nowhere near that event."

"Why?" she asked.

"Wasn't invited," he said coolly. "This leads me to my question. Is your dad @TheSaint on social media? He comments on most of your posts."

"Not anymore. I blocked him."

"That's going to make for an awkward Father's Day."

"I had no choice," Lily said. "He read my posts on BookTap the other day and demanded to know what I was up to for the summer. I had to defend my life choices, cite case law and everything."

Ben picked up his phone, opened the app, and found her dad's profile. "I see he's read every book by Barack and Michelle."

"Don't forget every memoir written by a supreme court justice," Lily added.

Ben kept scrolling. *"Rich Dad, Poor Dad? How to Win Friends and Influence People, Retire Rich . . ."*

"I know! It's embarrassing!"

"He won't be joining our discussion of *Blurred Lines*, I'm guessing."

"He would sooner die."

"I'm going to follow him," Ben said. "To keep an eye on his reading list."

"Please don't troll him! His ego can't stand it."

Ben set the phone down. "How did he react to the news about your job?"

"He had none."

"In other words, you didn't tell him."

"Correct." Lily kicked her feet in the water. If anything, this conversation was drawing out her daddy issues, not Ben's. It was embarrassing, at her age, to admit she still yearned for her father's approval. Yves Lyon was dubbed The Saint, after the patron saint of lawyers, by his peers and the voters of his district alike. Compared to his star-spangled legal career, hers was a flop. At her age, he'd won his first election. She loved the law, was good at it, yet she'd never found her niche. She'd stumbled into corporate by default. Not a day went by when she didn't think of this.

"Let's drop this," he said. "Judge Lyon has no jurisdiction on us. But if you ever want to talk, knock on my door, anytime, night or day."

He was ready to wrap up their Q and A, but she still had more questions than answers. "Hold on. Back to your dad," she said. "What's going on there?"

"Well, he's dead, for one thing. I don't have to worry what he thinks."

"I'm sorry, Ben."

He waved away her condolences. "Don't be. You can't lose what you never had."

Lily studied him closely, taking in the damp dark hair, the angled nose, the sharp jaw. In the photos she'd seen of the great Sabato Romero, the poet was well into middle age. However, there was no denying the resemblance between father and son.

"I have something to tell you," Ben said solemnly. His gaze was lost in the water.

"Yes?"

"I've finished *Blurred Lines*."

"What?!"

"Read it last night. I was done with work earlier than expected and got bored."

"I'll finish it today," Lily promised.

"Easy!" he teased, as if she were a spirited horse. "Go at your own pace. This isn't a competition."

"Of course it is."

"That's not what I wanted to tell you, though."

"What, then?"

"I had a chat with Roxy last night. She told me what she told you."

"You had a very eventful night, Mr. Romero."

"She was worried. She said you left the bar looking upset."

"I had a headache," Lily said, jaw tight.

"Is that all?"

"She warned me not to fall in love with you," she said. "The shock gave me a headache."

He brought his fingertips to her left temple and massaged gently. "Roxanna can be so blunt. She was out of line. It won't happen again."

"Just so you know," Lily said bluntly, "I have no plans to fall in love with you or anyone else. Summer love is for suckers. I'm looking for something with longevity."

Ben studied her in his quiet way.

"Even if that weren't the case," she continued, "I'd never catch feelings for a man on the rebound. That way lies madness."

"I'm not hung up on my ex, if that's what you're saying."

"That's exactly what I'm saying."

"It's over," he said quietly. "Still, not catching feelings—your term, not mine—is probably a good idea. I'm a mess. The breakup was rocky, plus there's other stuff I'm dealing with."

Suddenly he looked every bit the tortured poet, the fourteen-year-old boy who honed his craft in his bedroom.

"Roxanna said your father is the issue. She says you have some trauma to unpack."

"I wouldn't go *that* far."

"How far would you go?"

They were doing it again, that delicate dance.

"His death brought back a bunch of stuff."

"That's normal. I think."

After a bit of silence, he said, "The morning we met out in the hall, I'd decided to dedicate the summer to figuring this out. No fun, no games, no distractions, just unflinching self-inspection."

"We can't have that on my watch," Lily quipped. "We've got books to read."

"And reviews to write," he added.

"Seriously, though, have you considered therapy?" she asked.

"There's little I haven't considered."

"If you ever want to talk, free of charge, I'm across the hall. Just knock."

"You're sweet, Lily."

"Don't go falling in love with me," she cautioned. "Braver men have tried and failed."

"Lucky bastards." He smiled wanly.

"I wouldn't be so sure. They're dead to me, and look at us, hanging out, drinking in sunshine."

"Guess I'm lucky we're friends . . . We *are* friends, right?"

He seemed so earnest, as if his well-being hinged on the answer to that question.

"We'll see," Lily said and slipped into the pool.

She'd have to get back to him on that. How could they be friends if he couldn't keep pace with a buddy read?

Chapter Nine

Blurred Lines by Kayla Clark is an age-gap romance with a significant plot hole. #mindthegap

Back at her place, Lily threw herself onto the couch, finished the novel, and posted an update. Then she reached out to her brother. Her call went straight to voice mail, which was only right, considering she'd ignored three of his calls. However, Patrick was decent enough to follow up with a text.

Pat: Can't talk now. At a conference. What are you up to? Dad says you're on sabbatical.

Lily imagined her serious brother concealing his phone like back in high school, texting from under a conference table, while someone droned on about mortality rates or MRSA.

Lily: I quit my job.

Pat: No shit. Who goes on sabbatical? That's not a real thing.

Lily: Are you shocked? Surprised? Disappointed?

Pat: I'm none of those things. You hated that stupid job.

Lily: How do you know?

Pat: That's what you called it. My stupid job.

Lily: I had enough.

Pat: I get it.

Lily: Dad doesn't.

Pat: He won't. Mom won't talk to you until you come to your senses. She didn't raise a beach bum.

Lily: 😳 Can you work your magic on her?

Pat: Not this time.

Lily: Could you ask her to check in on Monster?

Pat: What?

Lily: Just do it!

Lily chucked her phone. She went to the kitchen to eat crunchy peanut butter out of the jar, then to the bathroom to file her nails. When there was nothing left to do but sit in silence and replay her earlier conversation with Ben, a knock on the door saved her. She opened to a stone-faced brunette with raging green eyes.

"You're Lily, right?" she asked. "I'm Kylie from the third floor. Noah sent me your way."

Any friend of Noah's was a potential friend of hers, so Lily studied the woman's unsmiling face. Kylie was pretty with short brown hair and pale freckles scattered over the bridge of her nose. She was taller and curvier than Lily and more direct.

"Noah and I had dinner plans," she said. "He bailed last minute. The reservation was tough to get, and I don't want to cancel. He said you might be free. Are you? Dinner is on me."

Under any other circumstances than her current one, Lily might have resented this lazy, last-minute invitation. Kylie from the third floor didn't care who joined her for dinner: she was looking for a seat-filler. Honestly, she did not seem like a pleasant dinner partner. That aside, Lily had no plans for the night, except sitting in silence and all that. Plus, she'd meant to check out Miami's restaurant scene. Now was as good a time as any.

"Sure. Why not?"

"You should know I'm a food blogger," Kylie warned her. "I'll take pics of everything. Some people find it cringe, and I get it, but that's what's happening."

"I don't mind."

Who better to discover a new restaurant with if not a bona fide foodie? Might be fun.

They agreed to meet in the lobby in an hour. Kylie had booked an Uber, and it was waiting when Lily got there. By Manhattan standards, the Italian restaurant was within walking distance. In Miami, this was unthinkable. "Not in this heat," Kylie said, holding open the car door. They rode to the newly opened restaurant, which turned out to be an old New York spot. Everything made its way south, eventually.

As soon as the bread basket hit their corner table, Kylie whipped out her phone and started snapping pictures. This earned her sidelong glances from a couple at the next table. She ignored them and went about her business, switching angles, moving the bottles of olive oil and balsamic vinegar until she was satisfied. This was work, not fun.

"I can't count on him," she said. "One text from a guy and poof! He's gone!"

"Who? Noah?" Lily asked.

Kylie's silence said everything.

In the books she'd picked up lately, friendships were uncomplicated. The main character's pal was an unwavering ally who never let them down. In real life, friends could be flaky. They followed boyfriends across country, took jobs in Europe, or quit social media to focus on inner peace. Work friends weren't friends at all: the competition was too fierce. There were only so many promotions, perks, and corner offices to go around. Often, what you were left with, particularly as you entered your thirties, was a former roommate with whom you have little in common aside from shared memories of a beloved apartment, a girl at your gym who's up for coffee after Pilates, the friend who travels too often to make plans, and a guy you'd love to hang out with if he didn't live way out in Long Island.

Their waiter set their cocktails before them. "Take all the photos you want," he said. "Just no flash, please."

Kylie turned red in the ears.

Lily sipped her perfectly crafted martini. She preferred the one Ben had made her, for some unknown reason, but this one was strong enough to get her through dinner—that's what counted.

Kylie set down her phone and picked up her glass of white wine. "So . . . when did you move in?"

"Over the weekend. I'm glad you stopped by. I've made a few friends, but they're busy working."

That was the wrong thing to say. Kylie's reaction was swift. "I work!" she exclaimed.

"I didn't mean to suggest—"

"Blogging isn't all I do. I'm a private chef. Before that, I owned a food truck. It went bust in 2020. Before that, I was a cook at a popular restaurant. Before that, I waitressed."

"Didn't mean to offend."

Kylie deflated. "No . . . It's fine. You've been wonderful. I'm a bitch tonight."

"I understand," Lily said. "My career is a sore spot, too."

"Noah says you're a lawyer."

"Did he brief the whole building?" Lily asked.

"He keeps us informed," Kylie answered. "It's a public service."

Every building needed an informant, Lily reasoned. Back home, she had Mrs. Appleton on the ground floor, who kept track of everyone's comings and goings.

"If you really are a lawyer—" Kylie started.

"I really am," Lily interrupted.

"I know someone, this guy, Jeremy, who could use one."

"I'm not licensed to practice in Florida. Is he in jail?"

"God, no! He's an artist on your floor."

"I never see anyone on my floor," Lily said.

The fourth floor was hers and Ben's private retreat, as far as she could tell.

"That's because you're at that weird dead end near the elevator," Kylie said. "Anyway, back to Jeremy. He could use some help with a contract. I think they're taking him for a ride."

"I'll help if I can."

"Thanks."

The conversation was fizzling. Lily grappled for something to say. "Is it tough being a private chef? Long hours?"

"Not this summer," Kylie replied. "My client is spending eight weeks in Italy."

"Nice."

"He's on a family vacation in Lake Como. I'm so jealous."

Lily raised her glass to the lucky bastards currently sipping Aperol spritz at posh beach clubs across Europe. Screw them!

"I recommend reading a book set in Italy," she suggested. "God knows there are so many to choose from. It's not like traveling to Europe, but you'll get the vibes."

Kylie tapped the menu. "I recommend the lemon spaghetti."

"Perfetto."

"If I make tiramisu, could I join your book club?" Kylie asked. "I'm bored out of my mind."

Lily was low-key impressed. Noah's briefing had been thorough. However, she thought of Ben, of their cozy club for two, and how much she would've loved to keep it that way. But Roxanna *was* right. She was courting trouble.

"I make an amazing tiramisu," Kylie added. She'd likely picked up on Lily's hesitation.

Oh, what the hell. "You're in!"

"Awesome."

"My loves!"

The familiar voice had them twisting around, searching for a familiar face. They spotted Noah making his way toward them. He wore a slim-fitting dark suit, as was required at the jewelry store where he worked as a sales assistant. He sailed to their table, pulled up a seat, and poured himself a glass of sparkling water from the bottle on the table.

"You made it!" Kylie cried.

"I told you I would!"

"No, you said you had a date."

"An *appointment*," he said, correcting her. "A client called last minute. Nothing I could do. Before you give me a hard time, he bought a fifty-thousand-dollar watch. It was his first time. He was nervous, and I had to hold his hand. For that commission, I'll hold whatever he needs me to hold for as long as he needs me to hold it."

"I bet," Kylie said.

"I thought I'd find you here alone, crying at the bar."

"I've been crying on Lily's shoulder instead."

"Hi there," Lily said, feeling like a prop in their two-person play.

Noah leaned over and planted a kiss on her cheek. "Thanks for doing this," he whispered. "Also, you smell amazing."

Lily blushed. "Thank you."

"One last thing." Noah reached for the bread basket. "I wouldn't dump you for a date. My dates are dull lately."

Kylie expertly mixed olive oil and balsamic vinegar in a dipping dish. "What about that guy?"

"What about him?" Noah asked.

"I thought it was promising."

"I called it after the second date. It's over."

"Second date?" Kylie and Lily cried in unison. Finally, something they could bond over! If there'd been a second date with the reclusive state attorney, or anyone, they wanted to hear about it. The story was coming, they could feel it, but they'd have to wait. Noah took his time, dipping a bit of artisanal bread in the olive oil and vinegar mix, savoring it, before he was ready to share.

"We met for drinks this time," Noah said. "No movies. No Timothée Chalamet. Nothing to distract us."

Lily and Kylie exchanged knowing looks. It *was* the attorney.

"He wanted to talk, get to know me, know where I've lived, where my family's from, whether or not I liked my job, if I had ambitions for the future, secret passions, hobbies, pets, an OnlyFans account, my thoughts on voting, my thoughts on immigration, my favorite song, favorite book, favorite actor, favorite movie of all time, and my dream vacation destination."

"OnlyFans!" Kylie screeched. This earned her another sidelong look from the exasperated couple at the next table.

"I threw that in there."

Kylie made a face. "Too bad. That would've spiced things up."

Lily felt compelled to cut through the nonsense. "Sounds like he was trying to get to know you."

"Exactly," Kylie chimed in. "Did you answer any of his questions? Or did you just sit there, brooding, smoking, drinking wine?"

"Vaping, but yeah. Pretty much."

Lily was starting to think the lawyer's only fault was being a normal person and a decent human being.

Kylie scoffed. "You're hopeless."

Noah returned fire. "You're in love with your boss. That's a hopeless situation!"

"Which boss?" Lily asked. The current one in Lake Como, or any one of the previous ones?

"There's only one," Kylie admitted quietly. "Presently, he's sipping limoncello at a plaza by a fountain. There's an IG post to prove it."

"Oh no . . ." Lily whispered. Falling for your boss was the world's oldest mistake. No good could come of it.

"It's tragic," Noah said.

"You'd be in love with him, too, if you met him."

She handed over her phone open to the Instagram account of one blindingly handsome Frederico Costa, Miami-based architect. Lily recoiled in horror.

"What is it?" Kylie asked, alarmed.

"A hot, single, Italian architect is the stuff of movies and books. They don't exist in real life."

"He's very real," Kylie assured her. "But I wouldn't mind reading one of those books. Could you recommend one?"

"Books are great, but this is real life," Lily said. "Quit your job. Save yourself."

Noah touched Lily's arm. "We can't all quit our jobs."

That was a fair point, but Lily saw no other option.

"Speaking of books," Noah said, in an obvious attempt to

change the subject that he'd introduced, "I'm almost done with *The Sweetest Lie*. Two chapters to go. Don't spoil it."

"Spoiler. The guy gets the girl," Kylie said bitterly. "In real life, the guy ignores the girl, barely notices when she walks into a room. All he wants from her is a protein-packed breakfast and his favorite pasta for dinner, stacked in containers in the Sub-Zero fridge."

"Oh, honey," Lily said.

"It's okay. I'll get over it."

Lily looked around the table. They were living embodiments of the tropes. Noah, as bold as he seemed, was scared shitless of intimacy. Kylie was in the throes of unrequited love. As for Lily, she was the spinster anguishing over the one who got away. If this was the Regency, she'd cry over his perfumed letters. Sadly, she'd deleted all of Darren's texts. There was little physical evidence left of their love affair. More realistically, she was the new girl in town, obsessed with her handsome neighbor. That girl would end up in tears at Terminal 4 of Miami International Airport come departure day.

If this were an e-book, these overlapping storylines would tie up neatly around the 90 percent mark, but this was real life. Everything was up in the air.

Desperate to save the night, Noah asked Kylie what she was drinking.

"A sauvignon blanc," she replied. "It's not bad."

"It's your birthday! We should drink champagne!"

"Hold on!" Lily looked from one to the other. "Is this a *birthday* dinner?"

"Yes, unfortunately," Kylie replied, miserable.

It all made sense. The attitude, the drama, the low-grade depression . . . This was a birthday dinner, and there was honestly nothing worse. "Happy birthday!" Lily managed to say. "Noah's right. We should celebrate."

"I love it when I'm right." Noah flagged the waiter and tried ordering champagne. "A good bottle, but not too good, within reason."

"It's my thirtieth," Kylie intervened. "I need the good stuff to get through it. You and your fat commission can afford it."

"Within reason," Noah repeated.

The waiter gave up. "I'll send the sommelier."

"I can't get over it," Kylie moaned. "Thirty! Jesus!"

"I just turned thirty, and it's not so bad," Lily said with a slight one-shoulder shrug.

Noah and Kylie cut her a look.

Though her track record didn't set her up as a subject matter expert on aging with grace, she would share what she'd learned these past months. They could do with it what they wished.

"You get clear about some things," Lily said. "You know what you don't want and what you won't put up with. That's the best I can explain it."

"I'm thirty-three," Noah said. "I know what I don't want."

"Let's hear it," Kylie said.

Noah itemized his list on his fingers. "I don't want to answer a million questions. I don't want to meet anyone's parents or even their siblings. I don't want to make long-term plans. I don't want to know my lover's favorite author, book, movie, or song. I just want to know what they like in bed and what they do for fun. It's really that simple. I didn't move to Miami to become some man's wife."

"Well, I don't want to be alone on my birthday," Kylie said. "I had to practically beg a stranger to come out tonight."

"Hey!" Lily protested.

"No offense. I'm grateful for you, but can you see how it's depressing for me?"

"I had dinner with my parents on my thirtieth," Lily said. "That was truly depressing."

"My parents are back Minnesota," Kylie said. "I don't have many friends in Miami."

"I'm sitting right here," Noah pointed out.

"Plus, there's that guy, Jeremy, right?" Lily said. "He's a friend of yours."

"He's a baby," Kylie said.

"What about my neighbor, Ben?" Lily asked. "He's friendly."

"He's a *flirt*," Kylie said. "There's a difference."

"He's a poet," Noah said, correcting them both. "It goes with the territory."

"Anyway, when I first moved in, Belle kept him all to herself," Kylie said. "Or was it Bella? I have no idea."

Noah shrugged. "It doesn't matter. She's not coming around anymore. Too bad. I liked her."

Lily's fingers tightened around the stem of her martini glass. Were they serious? Was it Belle, or was it Bella? These were crucial questions. Ben's ex now had a name. She'd interacted with people in the building. Noah had *liked* her.

"I should have more friends," Kylie insisted. "All I've done this past decade was hop from job to job. Each one brought a new friend group. Today, I couldn't tell you where half those people are. I don't have their numbers and can't recall most of their names. I've got to do better."

"You got me," Lily said. "We've spent a milestone birthday together. This means we're friends for life."

"Thanks, but you're only here for the summer."

"Take what you can get, Kylie," Noah said. "Not everything has to last until the end of time."

The sommelier dispatched to their table suggested a good, but not too good, bottle of champagne. They toasted to the birthday girl, to friendship, to knowing what you don't want and leaving the rest to chance, and to the fat commission that would pay for dinner.

Chapter Ten

I mind the gap very much.
Come over. Let's talk.
—Ben

One of life's joys was coming home to a note taped to your door with the potential of taking your night in a whole new direction. This note would join the first one he'd written her, in the top drawer of her nightstand. For the moment, it went into her purse. Giddy, she knocked on her neighbor's door.

Ben opened right away. With his five-o'clock shadow and unkempt hair, he looked scruffy—just as she liked. "I'm not jealous," he said, taking her in—her midnight-blue dress, the same one she'd worn to the corporate retreat's welcome reception. "I just need to know who you're stepping out on me with."

He was teasing in his flirty way, but Lily struggled to hide her very real jealousy of the infamous—in her mind only—Belle/Bella. "You *should* be jealous," she said. "I had a great night with Kylie from the third floor and Noah from the tenth."

"There are twenty-one floors," he said. "Are you going to work your way through each one? Is that your strategy?"

"What's your strategy? They say you keep to yourself."

"Not true. I have my favorites. Have you met Cecily Joy on the seventeenth floor, or Rachel Stark on the twentieth?"

"I didn't take you for a social climber. Do you only talk to the girls on the top floors?"

"Golden girls," he said. "No one under retirement age."

"Ah . . . If you're looking for a sugar mama, Ben, just say!" Lily teased. "I won't judge."

"I appreciate that."

"I've got news," Lily said. "Our book club is open to everyone, no matter which floor they're on. Kylie, Noah, and Roxanna are full members now."

"That's okay," he said, though his expression clouded. "But only if we still get to do this."

If by *this* he meant mornings by the pool and late-night meetings, just the two of them, with the stated purpose to shred a novel apart, the answer was yes. Every club had a managing board, and that's what they were.

"Of course."

"Good," he said. "Because I need to talk about that book now, so I can move on with my life. I can't wait until you convene a panel."

"I'll take you out of your misery," she said. "Give me a second to grab my copy and I'll be right back."

"The door is open. Just come in."

A quick whirl at her place and she was back, in monogrammed slippers lifted from a hotel in Paris, her copy of *Blurred Lines*, and a box of mint tea. When she let herself into his place, Lily was struck, once again, by how homey it felt. Her eyes traveled from the crammed bookcase to the desk stacked high with paperbacks, the wire bin holding a collection of laptops from different eras that he ought to recycle, and the frayed copies of *The New Yorker* magazine scattered on the dinner table. The soft light from the lamps cast a warm glow on all of this. She made a mental note to change her stark-white bulbs immediately.

Ben was in the kitchen, wiping down the counter as she had seen him do at the bar. Occupational habit, no doubt.

She handed over the box of tea. "If you heat a cup of water and a tea bag in the microwave, I'll have this."

"You've heard of a kettle, right?" he asked.

"Who has one of those?" she replied. "I mean in real life, not on Pinterest."

He pointed to a well-loved copper kettle sitting on the stovetop. Lily tossed her hands up. "I give up! You win!"

"You don't take care of yourself," he said.

Lily dropped onto the couch. "Why should I when you're so willing to pick up the slack?"

"Too willing," he muttered.

"Would you consider moving to New York with me?" Lily asked. "I'll email my landlord to check for vacancies on my floor. I need you close."

"There's a reason we met here, and not in New York," he said. "Frigid winters."

He filled the kettle and placed it on a burner. "Let's get into that age gap, Lily."

"What's your issue with it?" she asked. "You think they went too far?"

"They didn't go far enough," he said. "Justine is eight years older than Mike. That's no big deal. Men date younger women every day."

"I agree," Lily said. "The only scandal here is that the woman was older than her partner. The issue feels dated."

"Mike killed me," Ben said. "He was young, dumb, broke, and so fucking cocky. No notes there—that's any guy at twenty-three."

"Justine is only thirty-one. Why did she have to be so insecure? That scene when she checks her legs for cellulite before they have sex broke me. Like, what?"

"They fought about money all the damn time. Makes me think the wage gap was the real problem."

"She outearned him by a lot, and I don't have to tell you that men are fragile."

"Why couldn't she let him pay for the deep-dish pizza?"

"He'd paid for the cab from O'Hare!"

"It was just pizza, Lily!"

"If it makes you feel better, I'll let you buy me pizza . . . tomorrow night . . . for dinner."

"I appreciate it."

The kettle started to gurgle and whistle. Ben dropped a tea bag in a cup and filled it with the boiling water. He brought it to her with the usual assortment of sugar packets.

"Thanks," she said. "I'm adding sugar to our shopping list. You won't have to stuff your pockets anymore."

"I get them on campus, but that'll stop soon. The summer term is nearly over. I still have to meet with students, but once I turn in my grades, I'm free."

Why did she love the sound of that? His free time wasn't hers to take. He likely had plans. Perhaps he'd join Frederico Costa on the Amalfi Coast.

"Will you travel?" She kept her tone light, conversational, even though her happiness and hope for the immediate future was riding on his answer.

Ben grabbed an iPad off his desk and joined her on the couch. "I'm not going anywhere," he said. "Who would make your morning coffee?"

"And my filthy martinis?"

"Leave it all to me. I'm devoted to you until Labor Day."

"Actually, August 31. I'll be long gone before Labor Day. There's nothing like autumn in New York." Lily set the mug down on the low coffee table. "But whatever. I'm fine either way. It's your life."

"August 31. I'll mark my calendar."

His tone was flat without its ring of flirtatiousness. Lily tried not to read too much into it and returned to the book discussion. "I think we've skipped over one huge point. Justine is a highly successful Black woman from a wealthy family. Mike is . . . Mike."

"So you agree it's not about age."

"Yup."

"All right. Are we ready? Let's get to it."

BOOK REVIEW
BOOKTAP @LegalLyon in collaboration with @Ben_Romero

BLURRED LINES, by Kayla Clark
Couple: Justine and Mike
Trope: age gap, older woman/younger man

Review: The plot relies heavily on the age difference of the couple when, really, the difference in their tax brackets is the problem. In this interracial romance, Justine is the daughter of a famous Black artist and successful gallery owner. She is accustomed to the finer things, namely wine, taxis, trips, and Uber Eats. Mike is charismatic, Caucasian, and cocky. He is a basement-apartment dweller, surviving on a waiter's salary while working the Windy City's improv circuit. Mostly, they can't seem to agree on who should pick up the check. They fight. They fuck. A vicious cycle, but a fun read.

Lily's Rating: 3.5 stars

Ben's Rating: 3 stars

P.S.: We loved the setting. Chicago comes alive in this novel. Although we think this couple doesn't stand a chance in the long run, the steamy afternoons in the chilly basement apartment will live rent-free in our minds forever.

The next morning, Lily woke up to the exciting news that their joint review had gone viral. Unfortunately, the news was delivered by her father, which dampened the excitement a bit. Her phone rang at seven sharp. She could just picture her father at the breakfast table with the iPad that had replaced the morning paper.

"Hello," he said. "I'm trying to reach my ungrateful daughter."

Her father still had the Caribbean lilt to his voice that made even his admonishments sound lyrical.

"Good morning, Dad. How's Mom?"

"Her blood pressure is under control. The new medication is working. But that's not why I called."

"What is it, then?"

"Your silly romance post is everywhere!"

Lily shot upright. "What? I thought I block—"

"You thought you blocked me?" he interrupted. "Aren't you ashamed? I'm your father!"

"You are," Lily said. "I love and respect you, but BookTap is my playground. I'm setting healthy boundaries."

"Is that why you left your job? Are you setting boundaries with your employer, too?"

"I'm on sabbatical," she insisted. "How do you even know about my posts?"

"Cynthia sent it my way with a smiley-face emoji, as if there was anything to smile about. She's under the impression you've found a boyfriend. A man named Romeo."

Cynthia was her father's long-suffering assistant who'd married off her two daughters and pinned her hopes on Lily.

"His name is Ben *Romero*, and he's not my boyfriend. He's my new neighbor."

"It looks to me that he's a bright young man," her father said grudgingly. "Is everyone in Miami just wasting away in the sun?"

Lily snapped: it was far too early for this. "Dad, I get that my choices and my interests and my hobbies and my career path are deeply unserious and troubling to you. I get it! But this routine is getting old. There's nothing you can do about it. Now, if you'll excuse me, I've got to reserve my place in the sun. Say hi to Mom. Tell her I love her, and we'll talk soon."

Lily ended the call and hopped on BookTap. If Cynthia had seen their post, then it had to have made the rounds. She was right. Over two hundred and fifty thousand impressions on a silly little book post! Thousands of comments! Unheard of!

U 2 are 2 much!

The dynamic duo I didn't know I needed!

Ben Romero Romance wasn't on my bingo card. Here for it!

More!! Give us more!!!

This is the chemistry that was missing from the story.

I need visuals. Could this be a YouTube series?

Their first post had gone viral! She couldn't wait to share the news with her Romeo.

Lily leaped across the hall. Ben came to the door in his boxers, toothbrush in his mouth.

"Guess what?" she blurted.

He ignored the question. "Do you always look so adorable?"

"Always." She looked like she always looked, faintly ridiculous in a demure nightie, pineapple hair gathered with a silk scrunchie, and socks. And she hadn't so much as rinsed with mouthwash.

He stepped aside. "Come in."

She pointed to the toothbrush angling out of the corner of his mouth. "I'll be back in a sec. I need to do that."

He opened the door even wider. "I have an extra one."

"You just happen to have an extra toothbrush lying around?"

She couldn't sand the edge off that question quickly enough. Lily imagined a parade of women who, after spending the night, were offered a cup of coffee and a toothbrush before they were sent on their way. If not a parade, then maybe just one special person, Belle/Bella, not that it was any of Lily's business.

"They're sold in packs at the drugstore. You know this, right?"

She squirmed. "I'm aware."

"Usually, there's a pink one I can't bring myself to use."

"Does the pink toothbrush threaten your masculinity?"

"It did, when I was ten. Old habits die hard."

With a bit of chitchat, Ben had lured her into his apartment and silently shut the door behind her. Damn! He'd figured out that the way to get her to do anything was to distract her with inane conversation.

He led her to the bathroom and produced a bright pink toothbrush. "Here you go."

She snatched it from him. "Boys will be boys."

With a goofy, childlike grin, Ben pointed out the toothpaste and mouthwash. He reached for a fresh towel in a basket stored under the sink and froze. "You have a bruise," he said. "What happened?"

"A bruise? Where?"

He pointed to a minor scrape on her left knee.

"Oh, that," she said. "Last night I banged into the nightstand. I don't do well in new spaces."

"Lily, I don't like to see you hurt."

"Don't be silly," she said. "I'm not hurt. I'm not even that bruised. It's just a scratch."

He moved some stuff around and tapped the vanity countertop. "Hop on," he said. "I'll take care of it."

Lily did as she was told and watched as he tended to her scratch as if it were an open wound earned on a battlefield.

"Wait!" she said. "Will it hurt? Should I take a swig of whiskey?"

He glanced up. "Funny girl."

Suddenly, the little bathroom steamed up. There was such a thing as too much kindness and attention. If he was going to do all this, he should back it up with action. She wanted him to carryher to his unmade bed. Yes, she'd noticed the rumpled white sheets earlier, and it was sexy as hell.

He applied a small Band-Aid and tapped her thigh. "I don't think we have to amputate."

"Oh, thank God!"

"If you need anything, holler." He left her to brush her teeth in peace. She slid off the counter, turned on the tap, and splashed cold water on her neck.

Ben had coffee going when she came out of the bathroom.

"What did you rush over to tell me?" he asked.

"Right!" she cried. "Have you seen the reaction to our post?"

"No. I mute alerts at night."

"Well, unmute them! We're a hit, and people have lots to say."

"This I have to see."

He went for his phone, swiped, scrolled, and found the post. "Fuck. They love us."

"They love *you*," Lily said.

"There's no me without you," he said as he scrolled. "You bring out the best in me."

Lily was grateful his eyes were glued to his screen because she was melting, turning into a puddle in his kitchen.

"Is the coffee ready?" she asked in a scratchy voice.

They took their coffee to the couch and spent an hour laughing at comments and interacting with the hundreds of new followers they'd gained overnight.

Finally, Lily set her phone down. "This was so much fun."

"The most fun I'd ever had on this app," he said.

"*Spring Fever* is next. Yes?"

"Of course. We're locked in now."

She stood and stretched and drifted toward the door. "I'm meeting with Kylie in a bit. We're going food shopping. I'll stock up on coffee supplies."

He followed. "You don't have to."

"I want to."

They lingered at the doorway, each reluctant to move, until the ding of the elevator caught their attention. A moment later, a tall and lanky guy with shaggy brown hair headed down the hall, carrying a large canvas.

"Hey, Jeremy," Ben said.

"Oh, hey," he said, eyeing their appearance. With Ben in his boxers and the T-shirt he'd thrown on while she was in the bathroom, and Lily looking like she'd just rolled out of bed, there was only one conclusion, although false, to arrive at.

Jeremy rounded the corner. "Good seeing you."

Only then did it click. That was Kylie's Jeremy, the artist in need of legal advice. Knowing how this building operated, it wouldn't take long for the rumors to fly.

"He's going to tell everyone he saw us together," Lily whispered. "They already think something is going on between us."

"Something *is* going on between us," Ben said. "We haven't labeled it yet."

"We're friends," she said. "I thought we agreed."

"We didn't agree on anything. If I remember right, when I brought it up you swam away."

"Fair point," she said. "Let's settle this now. We're the best of friends."

He reached out and tucked an errant curl behind her ear, and like in the movies, she came undone.

"To be clear, we could be more than friends," he said. "We're choosing not to."

"It's the smart thing to do," she whispered.

"And we're smart people."

"One of us is too smart for their own good."

"It couldn't be me," he said softly. "I missed my chance that first night in the elevator. A part of me regrets it."

Her thoughts slid to Darren. He'd held nothing back, pledging his love on their first date. As flighty as Ben was by comparison, a part of her was sure they could be so much more than friends. This thing between them was more than neighborly love. He *liked* her. It was obvious in the way he looked at her, scheduled time to be with her, and read the books she read. It was evident in the notes he left her and the coffee he insisted on making, always to her taste. For some, that might be the bare minimum. To her, it meant the world. Too bad it wasn't enough. Nothing short of devotion would do. Ben could pocket his regrets. He had no business liking her if his heart and mind were otherwise occupied. Lily knew what she didn't want. No more half-baked, halfhearted love affairs that would ultimately fizzle out. She'd drawn a line in Miami Beach's famed white sands and would not cross it.

Chapter Eleven

Unemployment was no cure for the Sunday scaries. A week into her summer sabbatical, Lily was still overwhelmed with dread about all the things she wouldn't be doing come Monday. No waking up with purpose, no commuting, no coffee on the go. It didn't help that Ben had to spend the day grading papers and could not meet with her. By midmorning, her anxiety had reached its peak. She was grateful when Noah called to check in on her. On Sundays, he didn't indulge in mental breakdowns. He had back-to-back appointments for all his maintenance work: hair, nails, brows. "Do you have a local spot?" he asked. "If not, I can take you to mine."

"How would I have a spot?" she asked. "I just got here."

"When I show up in a new city, I ask for the best day spas, wine bars, gay bars. I'm guessing you just ask for the nearest bookstore."

"Good guess," Lily said. "Where *is* the closest bookstore?"

"On Lincoln."

"Thanks. I'll check it out."

"Since we're on the topic of books—"

"A topic you seem to like."

"I finished yours."

"I didn't write it, but go on. What did you think?"

"*The Sweetest Lie* is a deceiving title. You didn't tell me it's basically soft core—"

"It's not!" Lily interrupted. "It's explicit, but we're all adults."

"It's definitely not for kids!" he said cheerily. "About the spa, are you coming or not?"

Her skin was fried. She needed a facial. "I'm in!"

Located in a boutique hotel with a side door reserved for *non-guests*, the lovely day spa was officially Lily's local spot. She and Noah reclined in the Relaxation Suite between various treatments, sipped green tea, and snacked on fruits and nuts. Noah gave her a full update. He told her about the latest watch he'd sold, the new shoes he'd bought, and the guy he'd ghosted. "How about you, little Lily?" he asked. "How are things moving along with Ben?"

"We're friends. That's good enough," she said. "My life is too complicated as it is."

"You're the only new friend I plan on making this year," he said dryly. "Everyone else better come with some benefits."

They parted ways in the early afternoon. Noah gave her directions to the bookstore and strode off with a jaunty wave. Lily took her time, stopping at the stalls of a farmers market where she picked up an assortment of artisanal soap. Next she perused the shops on Lincoln Road, reminding herself every few blocks that, with no immediate source of income, she couldn't afford to splurge. Eventually she found the bookstore. It was a glossy tourist trap filled with travel books, city guides, and novels of various genres with *Miami* in the title. Even so, she found what she was looking for: the fancy leatherbound journals all bookstores were required to carry. No more posting her embarrassing thoughts online. Journaling was the way to go. She made her purchase and was on her way out when someone tapped her shoulder.

"I'm not surprised you found your way here."

Ben's warm voice filled her ear. Lily closed her eyes to savor it, before swiveling around to face him as if it cost her nothing. He looked like he always looked, that is, a little rumpled in an untucked button-up shirt that would have looked fantastic if ironed. The look was slightly elevated by a smart pair of rimless eyeglasses. The man was a dream.

"What are you doing here?" she asked. "Did you misplace your *Michelin Guide* or map of the Florida Keys?"

"I told you. I'm grading papers," he answered.

"Here?" She looked around. "Where?"

"Come. I'll show you."

Ben extended an ink-stained hand, which she readily accepted. He led her through the store and up a flight of stairs to what looked like a coffee bar. However, the walls were lined with shelves of clothbound classics and weathered paperbacks. Farther back were crates of vinyl records and a whole section devoted to vintage magazines.

Lily clutched his hand and brought it to her thumping heart. "What is this place?"

"A lounge, a bar, a used bookshop."

"Oh my God!" She pointed to the stack of classic romance novels. "Why isn't any of this stuff on the ground floor?"

"We like it like this."

She imagined so. The lounge had a private-club vibe where small groups gathered to talk over Latin jazz. Ceiling fans rotated overhead, and tall windows let in fractured light through hurricane shutters. It was marvelous.

Ben showed her to his table. He had a corner booth to himself. "Most Sundays, you'll find me here."

"If you were stationed up here, how did you know I was downstairs?" she asked.

"I didn't," he said. "It's just luck that I went down to grab this." He held up a highlighter. "The manager is a friend. He lets me borrow office supplies. What do you have there?" Ben pointed to the paper bags still clutched in her hand.

She opened one and pulled out a chunky yellow bar. "Handmade soap," she said. "This one has lemon, turmeric, and beeswax."

He took it from her and brought it to his nose. "Nice. You better smell like this every day."

Lily laughed. She pulled out a journal from the other bag. "I got this downstairs. Thought I'd try journaling instead of posting random thoughts online."

"You should start writing," he said.

"Write what?"

"Romance. You know the genre like the back of your hand."

Lily had considered it, way back when. Ultimately, she'd rejected the idea. "It's my escape. I don't want to monetize it."

"What about your thoughts on the genre? You could monetize that. It's called literary criticism."

"I do that for free on BookTap."

"I mean an exploration of the themes—"

"I know what you mean, Professor."

"Think about it. You have a distinctive voice, an audience, and subject matter expertise. Men have gone to war over far less."

"Well," Lily said, "when you put it like that."

"So much about writing is having a unique point of view."

Was the translator looking into writing original work? Lily wondered.

"What are you working on?" she asked.

"It's unclear for the moment, but I've got to put that grant money to use. It's all anyone asks me about."

Lily heard the hum of anxiety in his voice. Was this something he was struggling with?

"Aren't you free to do whatever? Isn't that how it works?"

From what she'd read, the grant was awarded with no strings

attached. He could pay off student debt, travel, or use it as a down payment on a house.

"Ideally, I'd put it toward something meaningful," he said. "The only problem is I'm fresh out of ideas."

"I think the best way to tackle a problem is to avoid it all together!" Lily declared.

"It's one way."

Ben slipped off his glasses and pressed his fingers to the bridge of his nose, as if her suggestion had given him a headache.

"You'll figure it out," she said softly. "You're too smart not to."

"Thank you," he said. "What can I get you from the bar?"

Lily eyed his laptop, pile of notebooks, assortment of pens, and the highlighter he'd just retrieved from downstairs. "I should go. You're working."

"I was, but now I get to spend time with you."

He tossed out words like this as if they didn't cause mini earthquakes deep inside her, leaving large cracks in the barren landscape of her soul.

"Okay. I guess," she said. "What's good here?"

"Most people like the sangria. The lemon cake is popular, too. What would you like to try?"

"C. All of the above."

"I'll be right back."

When he returned with cake and beverages, she asked, "How did you get your start in such a niche field?"

Lily was genuinely curious. Who dreamed of becoming a literary translator? What rare breed was he?

"I read a novel by a Colombian author. I was just a kid, and so fucking grateful someone had taken the time to translate it into English. I would've burned a fuse had I tried to read a five-hundred-page novel in the original Spanish."

"You once said you liked to translate things for your grandmother."

He stared at her, connecting dots. "The interview with Lesly Kennedy," he said. "I don't think I mentioned it any other time."

"Yes, for the *World Tribune*."

"I'm impressed. You did a deep dive, Lily. I hope you remembered to come up for air."

"Don't worry about me. I've made it my life's mission to find out who you really are."

"This is who I really am," he said.

By that, he meant this bookshop, his books, his collection of pens, his ink-stained hands, his rumpled shirt, rimless glasses, and beer—he hadn't gone for the sangria. If this was who he was, she liked him very much.

Ben shut his laptop and pushed it away. "I'll take a chance and ask again. What happened with your job?"

"If I tell you, I'll lose all mystery."

"That's not possible."

He touched her cheek, ostensibly to wipe away a crumb. Lily was on to him. His hands were always reaching for her, and she was forever turning to him, heart eager, full of longing.

"Want to pick up copies of *Spring Fever* on the way out?" he offered.

"Here?"

"There's a romance section downstairs, except it's practically hidden from view. You might've missed it."

"Ugh! I hate when they do that!" Lily cried in frustration.

"I know the owner. I'll talk to him."

They did not leave the bookstore until closing time. With their new book selection tucked in Ben's backpack, they walked home. The lively promenade crammed with tourists gave way to quiet residential neighborhoods, streets lined with apartment buildings that flaunted their midtwentieth-century heritage. Ben told her about growing up in Miami Beach. "It's not as glamorous as it sounds," he assured her. His family lived in a cramped duplex, his high school was run-down. He and his friends spent their time biking, skating, and prowling the beaches. Spring breaks were golden. All of Miami was flooded with college girls ready to party.

Lily poked him in the ribs. "Fuckboy! How many hearts did you break?"

"They never stuck around long enough for that," he said. "I was a story they could tell their friends back home."

Wait. Had he lumped her in with those girls? She'd announced the exact date of her departure, had even made a joke of it. *I'll be long gone before Labor Day. There's nothing like autumn in New York.* What was the rush? Having lived her entire life in the Northeast, she could use a change of scenery. Besides, if you've seen one maple tree turn colors, you've seen them all.

"How about you?" he asked. "Where did you grow up?"

"Long Island," she replied. "It was an ordinary childhood until my father became a judge and local celebrity."

Lily divided her childhood, distinguishing from the time before her father won a seat on the county court and the following years. Until then, he was an assistant public defender. They'd lived a quiet life. Winning that election boosted his ego. He set his sights higher and higher. He expected Lily and her older brother Patrick to do the same. They'd lived up to his expectations. Patrick had gone into medicine, and Lily had followed in their father's footsteps, but only so far.

"Your dad is reading *Crime and Punishment*, by the way."

"Is he?"

"No. He's reading *The Warren Buffett Way.*"

"Again?"

They'd made it back to The Icon. The building was quiet this Sunday night. Most of the apartment windows reflected the blue light of television screens.

Inside, they rode up to their floor. Ben walked her to her door and waited for her to find her key. Lily opened her bag and searched and searched and searched.

"What's the matter? Can't find your keys?" Ben asked.

"No. I hope I didn't leave them behind."

"Let's check."

He pulled out his phone and placed a call to someone named Randy. "Hey! Did I leave anything behind? Keys and a bag of soap? Thanks, man."

Lily covered her eyes with her hands. "The soap, too!"

"Sorry," Ben said. "He's left them at the register. I'll pick them up in the morning."

Lily grabbed her doorknob and rattled it. What would she do until then? "Do you think Dr. Jake would be willing to bring me a spare?"

"It's past eight on a Sunday night, and he's got two kids."

Lily let out a sigh. "Maybe we could drive over?"

Ben gave her a look, as if he were waiting for her to see reason.

"What?" she demanded.

"I have to take you in," he said. "It's the neighborly thing to do."

She moved away from him, but there was nowhere to go. "That won't be necessary."

"I can't have you sleeping out in the hall, Lily."

She rattled the doorknob again, harder this time. "It won't come to that!"

"I'll feed you and give you a warm place to sleep," he whispered as if speaking to a petrified cat. "And I'll be on my best behavior."

That only meant she'd have to be on her best behavior, too. How was that fun?

"Would you be more comfortable at Noah's or Kylie's?" he asked.

"I'd be more comfortable with you," she admitted.

"I would hope so." Ben found his keys with no problem and unlocked his door. "Welcome, neighbor. *Mi casa es su casa.*"

Lily pushed past him. "Please, no clichés! I won't last the night."

Chapter Twelve

Ben switched on the lights and moved a stack of books off the round dining table to the kitchen island. "Would you like to shower?"

She desperately needed one. It was a hot June night, and the walk from the bookstore had left her sweaty. "I don't have anything to change into."

Lily supposed she could sleep in the airy linen dress she wore to the day spa, but honestly, she didn't want to.

"Take something of mine," he said. "Believe it or not, I've had women stay the night. We've always managed."

She believed it; she just didn't want to think about it now. How Belle/Bella had made herself cozy in his apartment was not something she wanted to contemplate.

Ben opened his closet, and she was amused to see that his doors jammed on the glider just as hers did. He pulled out a short black silky robe sliding off a skinny hanger, the kind you buy to leave at a guy's apartment—just in case. "Will this work?"

She snatched it from him, begrudgingly, yet grateful to Belle/Bella even so. The kimono style robe was perfect. "It'll work," she mumbled.

Ben did not owe her any explanations regarding the robe or

anything else. If she hadn't been so absent-minded, hearts for
eyes, butterflies fluttering in her chest, she might not have left
her keys behind. Presently, she would be in her studio, where
she belonged, curled up in bed with a cup of tea and a new
book.

"I'll order dinner while you shower," he said. "What would
you like?"

Lily was starving. They'd gone straight past the busy restau-
rants along Lincoln Road with their long lines. Now the mention of food had her salivating.

"You never did order that pizza," she replied.

"Deep-dish it is."

In the tiny bathroom, Lily tried and failed to get a grip. Ben's
soap smelled fresh, and his toiletries were semi decent. But she
couldn't appreciate any of it. She didn't even snoop through the
medicine cabinet, as reason dictated. She had other things on
her mind. She and Ben were going to sleep together. There'd
been no talk of him taking the couch or her using a futon.
Their apartments were nearly identical, down to the quirks, and
unless his leather couch pulled out to a bed, they were going
to have to share his. Somehow, she would have to hold it together and not turn into a sex-craved werewolf at the stroke of
midnight.

When she finally ventured out of the bathroom, the soft
glow of Ben's many mismatched lamps instantly calmed her.
Determined to enjoy this night, Lily tightened the knot of the
robe and joined him in the kitchen.

"Couldn't get you deep-dish, darling," he said. "The place I
had in mind is closed. I hope you're okay with New York–style
from a spot down the street."

"I'm not picky," Lily said. "Except when it comes to New
York–style anything. So I'll be the judge of that."

"I'm sure you will." He presented her with two bottles of
wine. "This red or this red?" he asked.

"Any red is fine."

"Oh, that's right. You're not picky." He flashed a killer smile and opened a bottle.

The pizza arrived piping hot, and to be fair, it was decent. Although, it wouldn't rank very high in the city. Maybe it had to do with the NYC water or something, but NYC–style pizza was hard to replicate. She didn't tell any of this to Ben. He'd been so kind to her, she could leave him to his illusions.

After dinner, she helped him tidy up, then it was his turn to shower. He handed her a glass of wine and a remote control. "Watch, read, or listen to whatever you like. If you're into games . . ." He pointed out an old school gaming console on the shelf. "The games are in the boxes up there. Make yourself at home. I'll be in the shower."

Lily didn't relax until she heard running water. Even then, she was faking it. When Ben came out of the bathroom in a T-shirt and striped boxer shorts, smelling of fresh soap, she was curled up in bed, glass of wine in hand, book on her lap, seemingly engrossed in a passage that she had not even attempted to read.

"Want to stay up and read the whole book?" he asked.

"I'm game if you are," she said.

He grabbed his copy of *Spring Fever* and stretched out at the foot of the bed, his head to her feet. Their bodies formed a perfect ninety-degree angle. Why did she think that spending the night with Ben would be anything but fun?

"By the way, what's this fine novel about?" he asked.

"I . . . don't know."

She flipped over her copy and read the back cover. "Says here it's *a fast-paced, thrilling romance between a political strategist and a newspaper journalist . . . Set in DC in the spring, when the cherry blossoms are in bloom . . . Clive and Celine are tangled in the world of intrigue and half-truths . . . They find passion in each other's arms.*"

He balked. "What does that even mean?"

Lily wiggled her toes, tickling his ear. "Guess we'll find out."

"What fun tropes are in store for us?" he asked.

"Enemies to lovers, I bet. Usually with this setup, that's what you get."

"I don't get the appeal," he said dryly.

"The drama!"

"It's your sworn enemy, Lily. Think about it. You'll have to sleep with one eye open just to sleep with them."

"Benedicto Romero, you are a man of principle."

"And you're a romantic. Your eyes say so."

She blinked at him. It occurred to her that this might be the root cause of her problems. Was she waiting for a proposal in a hot-air balloon or some other grand gesture to fall in love? A miscommunication device to drum up excitement? She was a grown woman and no longer believed in fairy tales. However, she believed that a well-timed meet-cute could lead to a happily ever after. That was the green rolling hill in Scotland she was willing to die on.

"It's not a bad thing," he said. "I like that about you."

"If I tell you something embarrassing, promise not to laugh?"

Ben chucked his book across the bed and sat up to face her, giving her his full attention. "Go on."

"I've never been courted." His silence gave her pause. He was staring at her as if she'd morphed into an alien before his eyes. "Don't look at me like that! It's not like I've never been kissed."

"Not that there would be anything wrong with that," he said. "Being asexual is fine, more than fine."

"I'm not asexual, Ben."

"Oh, I know it."

"You promised not to make fun!"

"I made no such promise. Check the transcript."

"Forget I said anything."

"Forget that!" he volleyed back. "What do you mean by *never been courted*?"

The man was full of questions tonight. "What do you think I mean?"

"No one has ever sent you flowers or bought you chocolates on Valentine's Day?" he ventured.

"I got chocolates and bodega flowers from this one guy I was really into."

"That's kind of sweet."

"It's the bare minimum, Ben!"

He sat up straighter. "Obviously, I'm lost in the weeds. Walk me through this. Make me understand."

Lily shrugged, unsure where to begin. "Depending on what stage you are in life, a friend, classmate, or a coworker slides into your DMs, ask if you're free for coffee, drinks, or even a game over the weekend. One thing always leads to another with no fuss and no grand gestures." She studied his face for a reaction. What did he make of all this? Was he the type to go all out when he wanted a woman? "Maybe it's New York. The bar is in hell."

"Or maybe you're just a sweet person who deserves more."

"What's your track record?" she asked.

"Not great, I admit," he said. "All through college, and for years after, I was mainly a bartender. There were a lot of late nights, last-minute calls. Most of my relationships were fluid, undefined."

"I'm familiar with the dynamics," Lily said. She chucked her copy of *Spring Fever*. They were not going to get much reading done tonight.

"There was this one girl, though. She had raven hair, and I fell hard for her. I wrote her reams of poems. She sent them down the trash compactor."

"Rude!"

"She was ten, and I was seven. Someone had to put me in my place."

Lily folded over, laughing. "The age-gap thing doesn't always work, does it?"

"No," he said with a quirky little smile.

To be ten and worshipped by a little Ben Romero! Lily would have changed places with that girl in a second.

"We're not going to read this book tonight, are we?" Ben asked.

"Not likely," Lily replied.

"Should we watch a movie?" he suggested.

Nothing on a screen could be more entertaining than this.

"How about you tell me your war stories and I'll tell you mine," she said. "Let's talk about the breakups that broke us."

"We'd be up all night," he said.

"Nothing heavy. We'll keep it to the highlight reel," she said. "Feel free to change names to protect the innocent. I don't mind telling you that one of my exes is named Brad. Don't hold it against me."

"What does he do?"

"He's a financial consultant."

"I hate him already."

"Wait," Lily said. "It gets better."

"I love a good story." He inched closer. "Tell me everything."

"He took me on a few dates to noisy jazz bars and complained he couldn't hear my laugh over the music. I suggested slower, quieter dates. We met for ice cream at the park and visited museums after dark. He worked long hours and welcomed the slower pace. Imagine my surprise when I found out that Brad didn't have a job. He hadn't worked in *months*."

"If I were to play devil's advocate for a minute," Ben said, "I'd point out that women are not kind to broke men."

"You're *my* advocate," she reminded him.

"How did you learn the truth?" he asked. "Was his platinum card declined at the ice cream shop?"

"We made plans for my birthday, dinner at a new French restaurant I was dying to try. Thinking back, I made those plans, reserved the table, everything. All he had to do was meet me at the restaurant."

"He stood you up on your birthday?"

"No," Lily said. "He ghosted me the day before, ignoring my calls and texts. Like an idiot, I thought he might be planning a surprise. He wasn't. When I didn't hear from him on the day, I gave up and had dinner with my parents. It was hellish."

"I'm sorry he put you through that," Ben said gravely. "And I'm sorry I wasted my breath defending him."

"Aw. Thanks."

"Did you ever hear from him after that?"

"The feds got him," Lily said. "He's under indictment. No time to date, I guess."

"No fucking way."

"Yes way."

"That's better than the plot of the last book we read."

"My life is stranger than fiction." Lily joined her hands with a loud clap. "That's my sad story. Your turn!"

"Sadly, I'm the villain in my stories."

"I find that hard to believe. You're so . . . good."

"Lily, you only see the good in people," he said. "You should work on that."

Lily cackled. "I'll tell my therapist!"

"Your laugh is music," Ben said. "Brad had that right."

"Liar. It's maniacal," Lily said. Flattery would not get him off the hook. "Now, get on with the story."

"All right," he said. "There was this one woman I was dating casually."

Lily reached for her glass of wine on the bedside table. "Here we go!"

"One night, we were together, and I forgot her name at the worst time."

"Please don't say it was during sex."

"It was during sex."

"Oh, Ben!"

"Her name is Kimberly," he said. "I kept calling her Cora, a character in a novella I was translating. The project wasn't coming together. I was stressed, tired as fuck, and on deadline. I should've canceled our date, but I'd canceled twice before."

"Three strikes, you're out."

"Those are the rules."

Would the women in his life always come second to his love for literature? Lily wondered. Had that played a hand in his most recent break up? Whatever the case, she would not find out tonight. Ben would not share the story of Belle/Bella, she was sure of it. Similarly, she wouldn't bring up Darren. They were even.

"I've got ice cream," he said. "Want to move this conversation to the kitchen?"

"Happily."

If they were going to talk all night, while skirting the important issues, they might as well have ice cream.

Chapter Thirteen

They were on their best behavior all through the night. Come morning, it was a different story. Lily couldn't lay the blame squarely on Ben: it was partly her fault. Forgetting where she was, she rolled over and flung her leg over him, taking his muscular thighs for the body pillow left behind in New York. Ben, who'd been sleeping like a log until then, stirred to life. His erection knocked against her knee. Instead of pulling away, she went full body-pillow mode and tightened her hold on him. She breathed in the scent of his soap mixed with the warmth of his skin, rubbed her cheek against the scruff of his chin, and on and on until he eased off her.

Breath heavy, lids low, he studied her face in the soft darkness, questioning her intentions. Her only intention was to stay stock-still. No sudden moves.

"Sorry," she whispered. "I took you for my body pillow."

Ben's hands went to her face. "Is that your excuse?"

"I have no excuse."

Her resolve had softened since yesterday. It occurred to her that she might be going about this all wrong. Miami wasn't the city for rebirth and growth. It was the city to get messy. And why not see where this goes? her inner voice whispered. What's the harm? You wanted chemistry, and here it is. You wanted romance? You've been served.

He brushed back her unruly hair. "We agreed it was a bad idea."

"That was last week. We've grown so much since then. I'm a new woman."

His laughter caressed her skin. "You're making a new man out of me."

"Am I?"

"Incrementally."

"I think we're being overly cautious. I mean . . . we can't let a perfect one-bed trope go to waste. Let's do it for the plot."

He wasn't convinced. "Beautiful, we can't do this."

"May I approach the bench, Your Honor?"

His smile flashed in the dark. "Of course."

She reached down and grabbed his cock. "I present to you Exhibit A."

"You little—"

Ben kissed her like she'd wanted to be kissed since the dawn of her sexual awakening, with tongue and teeth and feeling, their bodies twisting to fit, his hands in her tangled hair. A knock on the door startled her. He managed to ignore it, pulling her closer, pinning her beneath his thigh, telling her not to squirm because it was undoing him. She squirmed even more until another knock forced them apart.

"Maybe you should get that," she whispered.

He took in a ragged breath. "It's for the best. We can't do this."

"Why not?" she demanded, frustrated.

"Lily, sweet—"

She pressed a finger to the lips she'd just kissed. "Don't sweet talk me! Just give it to me straight."

"I'm trying to change."

This admission left her baffled. What was he changing into? A monk?

Another knock on the door, more urgent this time. Lily threw up her hands. "Who is it this early?"

"It's probably Roxy," he said. "And I bet it's not that early." He rolled off the bed and drew back the heavy drapes to a glorious, sun-filled Miami day.

Another round of knocks caused the door to rattle in its frame. "Ben! Open the door! I know you're in there, and I've got to pee!"

"Bella?"

In one breath, the mystery was solved. Ben's ex-girlfriend *Bella* was at his door, clamoring to get in. Lily felt as though she'd been caught red-handed, deep in a bank's vault. Where could she hide? The bathroom was out of the question if Bella had to use it!

"Stay here," Ben ordered. "I'll see what she needs."

No sound escaped her throat. Ben was at the door, working the lock, yanking it open.

Before he could say anything, Bella shoved a gym bag into his chest. "Here's your shit," she said and pushed past him. "Now, if you'll excuse me, I'll use the restroom and will be out of your hair in five."

The tall brunette invaded the apartment. She might've made it past the bed, where Lily sat motionless, not even breathing for fear of making a sound. However, the day a woman failed to notice another woman in her ex-lover's bed would likely be the last day on earth.

Bella paused midstride and nearly tripped over her feet. She was one of those Jane Birkin girls. Her chestnut hair flowed past her narrow shoulders. Thick bangs hid her brows. She wore a loose, white button-up shirt, narrow slacks, and worn loafers. She studied Lily with open hostility before rushing to the bathroom to answer the call of nature. In the short time she was in there, Lily could not bring herself to look at Ben, even though she knew he sought out her eyes with a silent apology. He wasn't at fault here. This wound was self-inflicted. She'd ignored her best instincts and his expressed warnings that he was in no position to start something new, however casual.

The bathroom door flew open. Composed, Bella strode out, holding up the tub of body lotion Lily had moisturized with after her shower. "I'll take this, thanks," she announced. "You can keep the robe," she said to Lily. "It looks good on you."

Ben's gaze snapped to Lily, that silent apology amplified tenfold. Bella exited the apartment. He followed, closing the door behind them. At first, their voices were muffled. Lily could not follow the conversation until Bella's voice spiked. "I get it! It's over! Do you have to rub it in my face?"

Ben argued, rightly, that she had been the one to show up unannounced. Bella entered an unanswered text message into evidence. "I texted you like an hour ago to tell you I was swinging by."

"I was asleep an hour ago."

"Since when do you sleep in?"

"It was a long night."

"I bet!"

"Bella—"

"Your new girlfriend is pretty. Can't she afford her own lingerie?"

If Lily weren't naked under the robe, she would have ripped it off. She was breaking out in hives.

"Lily is my neighbor."

"How convenient for you!" Bella spat. "You won't have to leave your special razor at her apartment, and when it's over, it'll be like you were never there."

Lily buried her face in her hands. She knew better than to get involved with a man post breakup. Or mid breakup, more likely. They were still collecting their things from each other's apartments. The wrecking ball had swung, but the dust had not yet settled. She had to ditch this robe and put on some protective gear to keep her heart safe.

@novelnews: After influencer @Swimwithsierra posed in a bikini with a copy of Blurred Lines, her 710K followers dove right in. The contemporary romance jumped six spots on the NYT Bestseller's List to No. 2. When asked about it, the fashionista replied "My neighbors are doing a buddy read. It's the cutest thing." Her neighbors are @Ben_Romero and @LilyLyon. To read their review, click here.

Chapter Fourteen

The reason to avoid getting romantically involved with a neighbor was obvious: privacy. The universal right to privacy was the backbone of human dignity. How unnerving to open your door in your bathrobe to collect packages, only to encounter your crush out in the hall, looking handsome and smelling wonderful, on his way to work. How devastating to return home with bags full of groceries and run into him stepping out for the evening, unencumbered, ready to lend a hand. To avoid any of these scenarios, Lily pressed her ear to her door before leaving her apartment. A limited strategy—the elevators, open areas, and lobby were fair game. How long could this go on?

A few days had passed since the Bella incident. Lily had not returned to Ben's place, not for coffee, not to borrow sugar or return a book, not for anything. He'd stayed away, as well, respecting her request for space when they parted ways after retrieving her key at the bookstore. There was such a thing as too much space. The gulf between two people could widen to such a degree that they never find their way back to one another.

On Thursday evening, Lily's trained ear picked up the faint ding of the elevator down the hall, the familiar cadence of his footsteps, the jingle of his keys—then nothing. Pure silence.

Lily had made herself a cup of tea, preparing to read in bed. She held the mug tightly, burning her fingertips. She knew without knowing exactly what was going on out there: Ben was staring at her closed door, fighting the impulse to knock as she fought a similar impulse to throw open the door.

In the end, common sense won out. He entered his apartment. She climbed into bed and called it a night until . . .

BookTap Direct Messages
@BenRomero ➜ @LegalLyon
12:36 a.m.

BR: The first sentence is an insult to my intelligence.

LL: Ha!

BR: Lily? What are you doing up?

LL: You messaged me!

BR: For you to read in the morning. I didn't expect you to be up.

LL: Technically, it's morning.

BR: Did I wake you?

LL: No. I'm reading in bed.

BR: May I join you? Virtually?

LL: All right. Okay. Sure.

Although she'd consented to it, when the phone buzzed with the video call, Lily froze. One ring. Two. Heart racing, she sat up, ripped the silk tie out of her hair and straightened her pajama top. Her face was slick with layers of moisturizing serums, but it was too late to do anything about it now. She tapped on the icon of the videocam, and Ben instantly filled the tiny screen. He was at his desk and wearing his glasses. Her smaller reflection, framed in a box at the bottom left of the screen, showed that she was wearing forgotten undereye patches.

"Oh God!" Lily cried and ripped them off.

"Don't do that on my account," he said. "It's cute."

"Fat chance," she replied, the patches already curling onto themselves on her nightstand. "I'll battle my dark circles in private."

"Fair enough," he said. "Hi there, pretty."

Lily saw herself blushing in real time. "Hi."

"I've missed you."

"Me, too," she admitted.

"Let's not do that again."

"Never," she said. "I'd like very much for us to stay friends."

All week, she'd thought of the men she'd dated and discarded, some whose names she could not remember, and wondered why she'd been so eager to add another log to that bonfire. Flings were fleeting, but true friendship could last a lifetime.

"Me, too," he said.

"Good."

"I just got around to starting *Spring Fever*," he said, steering them back to familiar territory. "Work was more hectic than expected."

"What's so wrong with the first sentence that you felt the need to DM me in the middle of the night?"

"You don't remember it, do you?"

"The first line? Ben, I'm on chapter thirty-five. I'm nearly done."

"A first line should be memorable," he insisted.

"Not everyone is Charles Dickens!" Lily protested. "It can't always be the best and worst of times."

"Read it again and tell me what you think."

Lily picked up the paperback and flipped to the first chapter. *"That spring day, the frosty air did not keep my soul from catching fire,"* she read. "Perfectly fine. What's your objection?"

"It should be obvious," he said. "Souls don't catch fire."

"You'd have to have one to know for sure, wouldn't you?"

"Are you implying that I'm soulless? How did you figure that out, and so soon?"

Those dark, soulful eyes made a liar out of him. With some effort, she focused on the words on the page. "It's not exceptional, but it does the job. We know it's spring, for one thing."

"Spring has sprung," he said agreeably.

"It gets the ball rolling. Something's ignited a fire in our main character."

"Could it be last night's takeout?" he asked.

With a laugh, Lily tossed the book aside. "It's not love! It's heartburn!"

"There's that laugh I missed," he said. "It's like wind chimes."

The wind must have settled because they both fell quiet.

"We should talk," he said softly.

"No, we shouldn't."

We should talk was the most dreadful of first lines. Nothing good would stem from it.

"I want to explain what happened with Bella and apologize properly."

"Not tonight."

"Tomorrow?" he suggested.

"Not tomorrow, either."

"When?"

"We don't have to talk, and you don't have to apologize," she said. "It's summer! Let's forget it ever happened."

"It's summer yearlong here," he said, suggesting there was no point squirreling away tough talks for the winter.

"I don't live here, do I? Your logic doesn't apply," Lily said.

"I give up."

Ben ran a palm down his face, looking suddenly weary. He'd had a tough week. Good thing the weekend was ahead.

"When can we meet for book club?" she asked.

"Tomorrow morning, if you're free."

"Like a bird."

"See you tomorrow, little bird," he said. "Good night."

"Good night."

In the morning, a bold sun greeted them, and their lounge chairs sat empty by the pool. Lily and Ben eased into their roles as if nothing had happened. It was time to get back to scheduled programming. They stretched out to read for a bit. Lily finished *Spring Fever* and Ben put a dent in it. After a swim, they gathered their things and headed inside for breakfast.

In the elevator, riding to their floor, he reached for her hand, linking a finger around hers. This was the proper apology and a silent reassurance that they were okay. Lily swayed with relief. To think they could have lost this.

Ben let her into his apartment, and that marked the end of their quiet, cozy morning. Roxanna greeted them at the door, stern-faced, as if they were teens breaking curfew. She wore a floral dress, and her dark hair was gathered in a loose ponytail. Lily had only ever seen her in the T-shirt and jeans she wore to work at the bar.

"Finally!" Roxanna cried. "I've been waiting forever."

"I didn't know you were stopping by," Ben said.

"I texted an hour ago!"

"I was reading with Lily. We silenced our phones."

It was déjà vu, except with his cousin. The women in Ben's life were the bold sort.

Roxanna turned to Lily with a knowing little smirk. "What are you two reading?"

"*Spring Fever,*" Lily answered.

"Funny. This looks like *Summer Love* to me."

"Quit it," Ben warned.

"We're just friends," Lily said.

Roxanna raised her hands. "It's none of my business!"

"It isn't," Ben said. "In the future, please remember that."

"I should go," Lily said, hovering at the entryway. She didn't want to intrude.

"Go where?" Ben asked.

"Across the hall."

"Don't go." He relieved her of her soggy tote bag. "I'm making us breakfast."

"If you leave, he'll never forgive me," Roxanna added.

"I still don't know why you're here so early," Ben mumbled, heading into the kitchen.

"I've got the day off, and I've got some news."

"What's the news?" Ben rummaged through the fridge and produced eggs and butter. "Did Oscar say his first word? Is it *Benito*? I've been coaching him."

"It's not about Oscar."

"It better not be about Slick Rick."

"It is about Ricky. We're getting married."

"*No!*" Ben dropped the word in Spanish.

Roxanna raised her brows in surprise. "I'm not asking for your permission."

Lily took a seat at the breakfast bar, no longer concerned about intruding. They'd roped her in, and she was fully invested. Who was this Slick Rick person, and why would Ben react this way? Not everyone was cut out for marriage. What if he was abusive, or miserly, or lazy, or one of those undecided voters who pissed everyone off come election time?

"I'm sorry, but I'm not cosigning this," Ben said.

"No one is asking you to, asshole!" Roxanna retorted. "But you'll have to walk me down the aisle, like you promised. There's no getting out of it."

"Oh, fuck that!" Ben scoffed.

"No, fuck *you*!" Roxanna fired back. She collected her things off the couch and marched to the door. "The wedding will be sometime this summer. We haven't pinned down a date, but the sooner, the better. That means you won't have long to get your head out of your ass."

Roxanna left, slamming the door behind her.

"Ben!" Lily cried. She had never thought him rude. Regardless of how he felt about this wedding, whether he liked Ricky or not, the only thing to do was congratulate his cousin and support her choices.

"Lily," he said, weary, "there's a lot of history you know nothing about."

Now wasn't the time for a history lesson. "Go and get her! You have to apologize!"

As if on cue, the door swung open. Roxanna, who likely hadn't gone far, strode back in. "Yeah!" she shouted. "Apologize!"

"I'm sorry you think marrying that guy is a good idea," Ben said smoothly.

Lily could hit him over the head with this prized moka pot.

"What kind of bullshit apology is that?" Roxanna demanded.

Ben shrugged. "I'm being honest. You don't have to do this."

"My son deserves to grow up in a two-parent home. I shouldn't have to rely on my cousins to step in as father figures."

"We don't mind," Ben said.

"I know you don't, but Oscar deserves more."

Lily fit the puzzle pieces together. Ricky was the father of Roxanna's child. He'd likely been MIA for a while. A team of cousins had filled in as best they could. Ben picked up shifts at the bar so Roxanna could spend more nights at home. He would have gone on doing so without complaint. For Roxanna, though, it wasn't enough.

"Do you remember what he did to you?" Ben asked.

"Yes, of course. But he's changed. He's not that person anymore."

Change. They'd been back and forth with this one issue. Both Ben and Lily were trying to change. Roxanna was betting her and her child's future on the hope that a partner had changed. These were high-wire acts that should only be attempted by professionals.

"Could you be happy for us?" Roxanna implored him.

Lily looked to one then the other, wondering what Ricky could have done that was so awful that Ben, the man with such keen insight into the complexities of the human psyche, could not forgive or forget. Yet it broke her heart to see Roxanna, seemingly so confident, so self-possessed, crack open like this. It showed how much his approval mattered to her. The swelling tension in the room suddenly deflated when Ben pulled his cousin to his chest. The very strong, very proud Roxanna buried her face in his shoulder and let herself go. These cousins, as close as siblings, had navigated life together. Ben couldn't abandon her now.

"I just want you to be happy, Rox," Ben whispered. "I know you think Oscar needs his dad, but I promise you, he'll be fine either way."

Roxanna snorted. "Says the guy with his dad's ashes under his bed."

Lily gasped. Which bed? Certainly not the one they'd slept in the other night?

Ben abandoned his cousin to reassure Lily. "Don't listen to her."

Lily moved to peek under the bed. Her motto was When in Doubt, Trust Women. Ben grabbed her by the arm and stopped her. "There's nothing there," he promised. "My father's ashes are scattered off the coast of Key West like he wanted."

"Okay," Roxanna said. "But what's in that box?"

Lily followed Roxanna's pointed gaze to the bookcase. A worn leather box the color of tobacco sat between the PS5 and a collection of vintage police procedurals.

"Papers," Ben said flatly.

That small box grew large in their collective imaginations, taking up space, until Ben cleared his throat and said, "I'm making coffee."

Roxanna collapsed on the couch and invited Lily to join her. "Poor thing. You must be so confused. This is what you get for hooking up with Ben."

"Ben and I are just friends," Lily repeated, stupidly.

"If we hook up, we'll send out a press release. Okay?" Ben called out. "For now, we're friends."

"Ricky was my friend until I got pregnant."

"Tell her the whole story," Ben said from the kitchen. "Tell her how he abandoned you."

"He didn't abandon me!"

"What do you call what he did?" Ben asked.

Roxanna pleaded her case to Lily. "It's not as dramatic as all of that. Ricky and I were on-and-off for years. It was a situationship, at best. Then I got pregnant. We decided to lock it down, raise the kid, start a family. It was going to be simple, just a trip to city hall."

"Don't stop there," Ben said. "Tell her everything."

"He never showed."

"He abandoned you at the altar?!" Lily cried.

"Not on the wedding day," Roxanna said quickly. "The week before. We'd planned to meet at the courthouse to apply for the marriage license."

Lily shook her head. As if that minute point made any difference.

"Keep talking," Ben said.

"He got overwhelmed," Roxanna said in her man's defense. "Everything was happening so fast. We hadn't thought it through."

From the kitchen island, Ben caught Lily's eye and, without uttering a word, asked if she'd heard the ringing desperation in Roxanna's voice. The short answer was *yes*. Loud and clear.

"Things are different now," Roxanna continued. "You'll have to trust us."

"I trust you with my life, Rox," Ben said.

The implication was obvious. He would never trust Ricky again.

When the coffee was ready, they all gathered around the kitchen island. Roxanna stirred sugar into her dark espresso. "Do you still have that thing tomorrow night?" she asked Ben.

He nodded, though his expression was inscrutable.

Lily had no idea what that thing might be and no clue why Ben had seemingly retreated into himself. That was the thing with him, she realized. He was the great unknown, a continent on the horizon that she would never reach. Lily felt the ring of desperation in her hollow chest. She did not have Roxanna's blind faith. People simply didn't change all that much, including herself.

Chapter Fifteen

At The Icon, it all went down in the lobby. Sierra met her dates, Kylie routinely got into shouting matches over the phone with her sister, Noah had broken up with at least two men, and this evening, Lily bumped into Ben on his way out for a night on the town. She didn't immediately recognize him: he was a new man in his dark tailored suit, white shirt, and oxfords. When he called out to her, she startled.

"Lily! I've been looking for you."

"I'm sorry," she said. "Who are you, and what have you done to my neighbor?"

"A little cologne and I'm a new man," he said.

His cologne had hints of tobacco and leather. Very warm and cozy. Very Ben. Lily smelled like the dusty back room of a thrift shop on Drexel Avenue. She and Noah had gone shopping. He'd left her, midafternoon, to meet the lawyer for coffee. "A fucking coffee date!" he complained. "I hate those!"

"And yet you're going," Lily pointed out.

"If nothing comes of this, I'm blocking him."

"Harsh!" she said. "He's trying. The least you can do is meet him halfway."

Noah tousled her hair and took off, leaving her elbows deep

in a pile of vintage leather bags. Lily spent the afternoon digging for vintage treasures, and as a result, she was a sweaty mess.
She had no regrets. She'd walked away with two Pucci dresses
and a thirty-dollar pair of Manolo mules.

Ben relieved her of her shopping bags. "I've got a thing
tonight."

"Right." The *thing* that Roxanna had brought up yesterday,
yet he'd been tight-lipped about.

"How about you? What are your plans?"

"The usual."

She was on her way up to order dinner, try on her new purchases, and make a cup of tea before scrolling herself to sleep.

"Listen, I know it's last minute," he said. "If you don't mind
too much, I was wondering if maybe . . ."

"Maybe what?" she asked.

"You'd like to come out with me."

"Tonight?"

"Yes, tonight."

"To the . . . *thing*?"

"Yes."

It wasn't only last minute; it was borderline inconsiderate.
Why hadn't he asked her last night on their video call after he'd
wrapped up *Spring Fever* or last Sunday when she'd slept over?
There'd been ample opportunity to ask her out.

"Am I filling in for a date?" she asked.

It was possible that someone had canceled, and like Kylie, he
needed a seat-filler.

"I wouldn't subject a date to this," he said.

"Oh?" Lily blinked. How presumptuous of her.

"That came out wrong," he said. "It's not a fun event, okay?
If anyone would be gracious about it, it would be you."

"Oh." She blinked again. What was she to make of that?

"I've put you on the spot," he said. "Forget it."

"What is this *thing*?" she asked. "You never said."

"A dinner at a museum."

"Dinners at museums are typically galas."

"I guess," he said. "It's for charity."

"A charity gala?"

An uneasy look passed over his beautiful face. "Unfortunately, yes. I told you I wouldn't subject just anyone to this."

"Where I come from, Ben, we take charity galas quite seriously. We go all out. Hair, makeup, gowns, the works. Is that what we're looking at?"

"Maybe." He inspected her shopping bags. "What do you have in here? Would any of it work?"

"No!" she snapped. Nothing would work, not even the pair of Manolos, which were a vibrant shade of green. "Don't worry," she relented. "All I need is a black dress and red lipstick."

She had a half hour to get ready. It took Lily no time to shower, slick back her hair, swipe on red lipstick, spritz perfume, and slip on the black formal dress she'd retired for the summer. She might not have the right outfits for happy hour, but a black-tie event was no problem at all.

Ben was waiting at his place. He assured her they wouldn't be late because nothing in Miami ever started on time. With a tap on his door, she let him know that she was ready. Stunned by her transformation, he let out a low whistle. Flattering, sure, but for her, this attire was business as usual.

"This is the real me," she admitted.

He disagreed. "The real Lily wears heels and pajamas to run out for coffee."

She laughed. "That might be true."

"Let's hope so."

Ben drove a midnight-blue BMW convertible, a vintage model from the eighties. It suited him. Everything about his life suited him. His profession, hobbies, apartment, car, and clothes—it all suited him. This was the way to be. Figure out who you are and build your world accordingly. Nothing added or subtracted.

"Which museum is it?" she asked.

"Freedom Tower."

"Never heard of it."

Miami had a respectable art scene, and she'd hoped to visit a few of the modern museums over the summer. That was about it.

"It's a landmark. You'll see."

What she saw when they arrived some twenty minutes later was an old-world cathedral, cupola piercing the night sky. It was dropped in the middle of downtown Miami, neighboring modern high-rises, not unlike St. Patrick's on Fifth Avenue.

"Is it a church?" she asked.

"No. It just looks like one," he replied. "It's our Ellis Island. Back in the fifties, Cubans who'd arrived on Freedom Flights were taken here to be processed, hence the name."

They left the car with the valet and climbed the steps to the lobby. They were talking and laughing and might have missed the easel to the side of the entrance with a message from the Day Foundation welcoming the guests, championing the cause (art education), and announcing the keynote speaker, Benedicto Romero.

Lily stopped in her tracks. Pointing to the board, she cried, "Ben! Have you seen this?"

He gave her a weary look. "I've seen it."

It all made sense. This was a function, not a fun night out. If he was nervous, she could help him loosen up.

"I'm so honored to be here," she teased, "I could cry."

"That's enough, Lily."

He steered her toward the elevators, but the supply far exceeded the demand, and the line was out the door. Their choices were to wait forever or take the stairs to the event room. To her mind, there was but one choice. The keynote speaker could not arrive late, not on her watch.

"Stairs?" she suggested.

He pointed to her stilettos. "In those shoes?"

She took his hand and led him to the stairwell. There, she twisted into a pretzel to loosen the tiny buckles of the ankle straps. It would've been easier to sit on the steps, but her fitted dress had no give and wouldn't allow it.

"Let me help you."

Ben kneeled before her, as if proposing marriage or guiding her foot into a glass slipper. The dim stairwell created an intimate setting. She grabbed onto the handrail for support and watched him work. Was it her imagination, or had his fingers lingered at her ankles as he loosened the stubborn straps? The thrill that ran through her was not imagined. The glow in his eyes when he looked up at her wasn't imagined, either.

"You look beautiful tonight," he said.

Lily's grip tightened on the rail. "Thank you."

Ben straightened up and shoved her shoes into the pockets of his jacket. He glanced at the steep steps. "Are you sure you're up for this?"

"I used to live on the fifth floor of a walkup," she said. "I can handle this."

"Show me."

Lily charged the stairs with Ben, laughing close behind. When they made it to the top, panting, he returned her shoes and helped slip them on. Then he helped straighten her dress, smoothing the fabric at her hips. She dabbed at the shine at his temples and made sure he looked all right. He was the man of the hour, after all.

"Thanks," he said.

"No problem."

"I mean for coming tonight. It's going to be a circus."

She took his arm. "In that case, you're in good hands."

They entered the ballroom. The hostess checked their names off a list: *Benedicto Romero* and *Guest*. She pinned a *Keynote* label to his lapel. They were offered champagne and escorted to the main table. It was all going great, until they took their seats. From then on, after some brief introductions, Ben fielded questions from all sides. Most concerned his father. How was he coping with the loss? Had he read the exposé in *The New Yorker* about the famous poet? Did he know that PBS had greenlit a documentary about Caribbean writers which would feature his father? And what of the grant he'd won—wouldn't his father be proud? What was the plan?

"Lily and I are reading romance novels all summer," he said smoothly. "That's the only plan."

All eyes darted to her. As a thank-you, Lily kicked him under the table.

"Who did you say you are?" someone asked.

There was no distinguishing one from the other. Men and women in suits, sequin gowns, jewels, watches, cuff links, and *Guerlain's Shalimar*, her mother's preferred perfume.

"Lily Lyon, Ben's neighbor for the summer."

"Are you a critic? Or a writer?"

Unlike Ben, who was so many things—bartender, lecturer, writer, speaker—she was one thing. "An attorney."

"Oh."

"The grant money," a cranky old man repeated. "What do you plan to do with it?"

"For the love of God," a woman moaned. "Whatever you do, please don't start a podcast. The last thing the world needs is another damn podcast. I can hardly stand it."

"A podcast about romance novels!" a man exclaimed. "Ha!"

It was clearly a joke, and the table laughed.

"Oh, leave them alone!" Finally, someone spoke up in their defense. She was a woman in her fifties with silver hair and gray eyes. "They're young. If they want to read romance all summer long, let them. If they want to podcast about it, I think it's a fantastic idea. The world is a dumpster fire, and we could all use a little romance."

The table raised a toast to love and romance. The conversation turned to local politics, and Ben was left alone.

"Who is she?" Lily whispered to Ben.

"Allison Leigh. She's in media."

"I like her."

He agreed. "She's cool."

The others were decidedly not cool. Their disapproval of Ben still hung in the air. They were the reason he'd put off inviting her. Anyone would be intimidated by all this. Lily, though, could hold her own. This was her kind of circus, not much different than a room full of lawyers, judges, politicians, or corporate drones. She wasn't afraid of these clowns.

Just when Ben leaned close to whisper something in her ear, he was called away. It was time for the keynote address.

Ben took the stage and, without hesitation or nervousness, delivered a simple and effective speech. "In my work," he began hesitantly, "I consider myself something of a ferryman or gondolier." He paused and gazed out at the audience. "Every etymologist worth his salt knows the root word of *translate*, from the Latin *translatio* for *a transfer* or *a handing over*. That's my job, you see, to bring languages together, to row one across a foggy lagoon to another without losing the author's voice or intent. It's a challenge. Language is slippery as a seal. It hides as much as it reveals." Now his eyes rested on Lily. "If you surrender yourself to the rhythm of the words, however, to the emotions those words evoke, you'll make it to the other side without running aground."

Lily checked the time on her vintage Cartier watch. She fell in love with Ben Romero at exactly 8:04 p.m. Eastern time.

Chapter Sixteen

After dinner, dessert, and one last tour around the room—at Lily's insistence—to thank all the right people, she and Ben ducked out. Having beat the crowds, they easily caught an elevator.

Ben shoved his prepared remarks into his jacket pocket. "Lily, you made this night infinitely more pleasurable. I can't thank you enough."

"You're welcome." Lily stumbled back and leaned against the paneled wall. Socializing was a competitive sport. Like any athlete who'd left it all on the field, she was ready to drop.

He stepped closer. "Why so far away? I won't kiss you again, if that's what you're worried about."

"Again?" she asked. "If you mean our first elevator kiss, you don't get to claim a kiss you didn't give."

"A kiss is shared, Lily," he said. "It's not a territory. No one person gets to claim it."

Suddenly, it got very hot and steamy in the elevator. Lily's face was still hot when the valet attendant brought their car around.

Lily slipped into the low passenger seat and winced. The corset bodice of her dress dug into her ribs.

Ben took the wheel. "Are you okay?" he asked.

"It's the dress," she answered. "I think I'll sell it online. I'm done with it."

The midi-length crepe cocktail dress wasn't the vibe for the summer.

"Too bad. You look good in it."

"Oh, I know," she said with a grin. "I quit my job in this dress."

He put the car in gear with a low whistle. "I would've loved to see that. Paint me a picture. How did it go down?"

Lily considered how to answer his question without dragging Darren into it. *Corporate lawyer quits jobs after seeing ex's wedding pics on Instagram.* There was no way to admit to that without coming across as a flake, or flakier than she already did.

"We flew to Miami for our yearly retreat."

"What does a corporate retreat entail?" he asked. "Group therapy? Trust exercises?"

"A whole lot of drinking and endless rounds of golf," Lily said. "Family isn't invited, so it's the perfect excuse to get away from husbands, wives, and significant others."

"Sounds right. Then what happened?"

"It was the night of the big banquet. Kendal Hill, president and CEO, rises to give the toast. Generally, this is when he announces big shifts in trajectory, expansions, promotions, and the like. This year, we acquired a major asset. I worked hard on those negotiations and delivered more than was asked for. I got a bonus, but no recognition. Ken gave full credit to Gus Porter, praising his hard work and hinting at a future promotion."

"Who's Gus?" Ben asked.

"A new attorney, legendary negotiator," Lily replied. "They'd poached him from a rival and promised him the moon. I get that's how the game is played, but he didn't work on this deal. He showed up at a few meetings, shook a few hands, that's it!"

"Lily, I'm sorry."

"No, it's okay."

"How is that okay?"

"It happens more often than you'd think," she said. "Men steal credit for women's work all the time. It's just a thing they do."

"It pisses me off. You shouldn't have to put up with that."

"I didn't," she said. "I got up and left. Made quite a scene, too."

"Did you push back your chair, toss your napkin, knock over a glass of wine?"

"I took my wine with me," she replied. "It was damn good, and I wasn't going to waste it! But I slammed the door behind me."

"Did anyone come after you?" he asked.

"I wouldn't know," Lily said. "The banquet hall was on the same floor as the hotel spa, so I hid there. I traded this dress for a robe, locked myself in the sauna, and cried."

"Lily . . ."

"Not gonna lie, I panicked," she admitted. "While I turned into a prune in the sauna, I thought of a thousand ways to undo what I'd just done. The best I could come up with was a sudden allergy attack."

"Blame it on a bad oyster," he said. "It works every time."

"In the end, I couldn't bring myself to grovel for a job I secretly hated. I'd been unhappy for so long. I was ready for a change. So in the morning, I packed my bag, sent Ken an email, and left for the airport."

"But you're still here," Ben said. "You didn't fly home. What made you stay?"

"I didn't want to face my family," she said. "I needed time to clear my head. And I was exhausted. Believe it or not, the retreat had drained me. Rubbing elbows is work. Making yourself seen by senior management is work. Small talk is tedious and tiresome."

"I'd rather write a grant proposal than make small talk," Ben said. "But if you turn down too many invitations, you're labeled a recluse. In fact, any writer who doesn't socialize is a recluse. Guess what that gets you? More attention." He loosened the knot of his tie. "Wait. How did I make this about me?"

She rolled her eyes. "Typical man!"

"All right, I'll take that," he said. "So you're riding to the airport. It's a beautiful Miami day. What goes through your mind?"

"I'm thinking . . . what's the rush? You know? All that's waiting for me is my lovely plant baby."

"What kind?"

"A Monstera."

"Do you have a photo?"

"Do *I* have a photo? Ha!"

She had a folder full of photos of her little monster at various stages of development. When they pulled up to a traffic light, Lily showed him her favorite shot of the houseplant basking in sunlight. At the time, it was positioned under the living room window, which happened to be her kitchen window. Her apartment was that small.

"Pretty," he said. "Will it survive without you? You've been away for more than two weeks now."

"I've asked my mom to check in on her." They rode the rest of the way in comfortable silence. At the building, Ben walked her to her door, which was no big deal considering it was directly across from his.

Determined to play it cool, she took a breezy tone and said, "Thanks for a lovely—"

It was tough playing it cool with trembling hands. Her little satin clutch slipped out of her grip. Her keys, lipstick, breath mints, and money clip scattered across the floor. Ben gathered everything and dropped it all into her purse, except the keys. He first unlocked her door and then placed them in the palm of her hand.

Suddenly, there was nothing but their breath and a heady si-

lence between them. At the end of the hall, static noise crack-
led from a faulty Art Deco sconce. Lily was desperate to kiss
him, but she wouldn't. If he wanted her, he'd have to make the
move. She'd made a fool of herself once—never again! She was
so caught in these thoughts that when Ben pressed his mouth to
hers, she was completely caught off guard.

The unexpected kiss was scorching hot, lighting a fuse deep
inside her, setting her soul on fire.

Despite having opened her door, they ended up stumbling
into his apartment. Kissing madly, hands roaming each other's
bodies, they made their way to the bed. Ben pulled her onto
his lap. She took his face in her hands, looking for assurances in
his heated gaze. *Are we really going to do this?*

He kissed her again. It seemed the answer was *yes*.

As she worked off his jacket, his phone slipped out of the
pocket, landing face up on the bed. It lit up suddenly with
a text message. The words *PODCAST*, *I'M SERIOUS*, and
CALL ME leaped at her.

"Oh my God!" she cried.

"What's wrong?" Ben asked.

He'd pulled the pin out of her hair and rushed his fingers
through her curls with urgency, as if he'd been waiting to do it
all night.

"You have a text message. Read it."

Ben pounced on his phone, scanned the message, and
laughed. "It's just Allison," he said. "Thank God. For a second
I thought it was . . ."

He didn't have to finish the sentence. Lily slipped off his lap
and onto the bed beside him. The memory of his ex-girlfriend
knocking on his door had knocked sense into her. After Bella
had returned his things, had they gone no-contact? Or did they
still exchange the odd text message after midnight, as recent
exes are wont to do?

Ben scanned the message and dismissed it, tossing his phone aside.

Lily cleared her throat. "She mentioned a podcast."

"She's not serious," he said.

"It's in all caps! Of course she's serious."

"No way," Ben insisted. "Allison's a major snob when it comes to literature."

"She didn't come across that way to me. She was the only one who supported our romance-reading."

"For the intellectual upper hand," Ben said. "Everyone was against it, so she had to be for it."

"You're clearly against it."

He paused. "Is this something you'd be interested in?"

"No, of course not."

"Lily, you're a lot of things, but not a good liar."

"I'm just surprised, that's all."

"I know Allison," he said. "It's probably the champagne talking. She might regret sending the text in the morning."

Unfortunately, regretting decisions in the morning was a thing Lily knew all too well. If anything, Alison's interest proved that she and Ben made a good team. They didn't have to go pro with a podcast, but they could keep things professional. She got up and collected her bag, keys, and hairpin. "Good night," she said. "I think we've all had a little too much champagne."

Ben looked up at her. A current of understanding passed between them. They had a plan, a good one, to rest and heal over the summer, not to overheat, crash out, and burn. Now they had to stick with it.

"When will I see you again?" he asked.

"Tomorrow morning, obviously," she replied. "To wrap up our next review."

"All right," he said. "Tomorrow night I'm covering for Roxanna. Will you come up for a drink?"

"I will."

"Good. I'll make you a martini."

"Make it extra dirty."

"Anything you like."

With that, he walked her out. Lily crossed the hall while he waited at the threshold of his apartment for her to supposedly make it home safely.

"I made it!" she announced.

"One more thing," he called out before she closed her door.

"Yes?"

"When you enter this last kiss into the record, make sure I get full credit."

BOOKTAP @LegalLyon in collaboration with @Ben_Romero

Spring Fever, by Ella Green
Couple: Celine and Clive
Trope: enemies to lovers

REVIEW: Celine Campbell, 31, chief of staff of a powerful US senator, falls for Clive Brown, 39, a washed-up reporter out to make a name for himself. Clive unearths the long-buried secrets of Celine's boss. The published story reveals corruption on a scale that Celine could not have imagined and paints her as either complicit or clueless. When the senator resigns, Celine loses her job and her reputation. Regretful, Clive offers to write a puff piece on her for a leading magazine. He shadows her around for two weeks in March. Their attraction blooms with the first cherry blossoms.

Lily's Rating: 3 stars

Clive sucks as a reporter and sucks even harder as a potential life partner. After profiting off Celine's misery, he circles back—like the vulture he is—to pick on the ruins of her career. Our girl Celine is destined to be roadkill, left on the side of the road to rot, when Clive runs her over in a fevered rush to land another scoop.

Ben's Rating: 2.5 stars

Spring Fever is a thinly veiled political thriller with a wild sex scene tossed in at the halfway mark to spice things up. However, by the end of this sluggish saga, I lost my faith in America and my interest in this couple. I question Clive's integrity and Celine's intelligence. It might've been best if these two had never met.

Chapter Seventeen

The bar was nearly empty when Lily arrived, but even if that hadn't been the case, she wouldn't have had to compete for the hot bartender's attention. She took her regular seat, and within minutes, he placed a martini in front of her.

"Dirty enough?" he asked with a wink.

She brought the olive pick to her lips. "It'll do."

She now shared inside jokes with the man who'd so intimidated her only two weeks earlier. What a seismic change! Her reflection in the smoky mirror glowed, the person she was striving to be staring back at her. Gone was the tense, awkward woman who'd arrived at The Icon with a suitcase full of anxiety.

"Have you received any interesting text messages lately?" she asked.

"I didn't hear from Allison, if that's what you're asking."

Of course it was. She didn't point out that Allison had requested that *he* reach out to *her*. Ben was obviously pleased with the way it had played out, so she left it alone. She couldn't blame him. Yesterday, at this time, if anyone had suggested she host a podcast, she would've laughed in their face. Allison must be incredible at her job because, as soon as she'd introduced the idea, Lily could think of nothing else. It thrilled and terrified her in equal measure. It could be fun, but her father could die of a stroke just at the thought of it.

"Any thoughts on our next read?" Ben asked.

"I polled our followers and . . ." Lily trailed off, feeling the weight of someone's stare on her back. She glanced over her shoulder and saw a frantic Kylie charging at them from across the terrace. Kylie was often frantic, so Lily thought nothing of it. She waved. "Hey there!"

"Hey." Kylie slid onto the seat beside hers. "I've got an axe to grind."

"Grind away!"

"Or don't," Ben said, leaning forward on his elbows. "I don't know what your complaint is, but can prosecco fix it?"

"Pour me a glass, but I won't shut up," Kylie said and held up her phone. "This is your take? Seriously?"

Lily was too distracted by the curve of Ben's arms—and re-membering how those arms had tightened around her—to pay attention. This pushed Kylie over the edge.

"Lily, I'm talking to you!" she cried.

"Me? What did I do?" Lily asked.

"You did Clive so dirty!"

"Clive . . . ? Is this about *Spring Fever*?"

"The book you made me read," Kylie said.

That was a stretch. Lily hadn't made her do anything. If memory served, she'd recommended books set in Italy. How-ever, she was glad Kylie had read the novel and wanted to talk about it. Could this be the first meeting of the book club?

"So you liked it?"

"It was so good. I loved it."

"That's all that matters!" Lily said reassuringly. "It comes down to personal preference."

"You were so tough on Clive, though!" Kylie cried. "Couldn't you cut the guy some slack? He was just doing his job."

Lily wasn't having that. "Please! He killed her career."

"Her boss was on Big Pharma's payroll. She had to have known."

"I stand by my review," Lily said stubbornly.

Kylie turned on Ben. "What about you, Ben? Two and a half stars? Really?"

"I knocked off a half-star because Clive pissed Lily off," Ben replied and uncorked the prosecco.

Lily beamed at him. How could she not love this man? As a reading buddy, obviously.

Kylie watched them like a cat. "You two are not beating the boning allegations."

Ben placed a glass of sparkling wine before her. "We're not boning."

"Not yet! Who knows what the future holds?"

That was Noah, still in his navy work suit, a silk tie trailing out of his pants pocket. He took the seat next to Kylie and seamlessly joined the conversation. Arriving late and blending in was his true talent.

"What are we talking about?" he asked.

Kylie got him up to speed between long sips. Noah absorbed the information, nodding. When she was done, he said, "I haven't read the book."

"Don't let a small detail like that keep you from speaking your mind," Ben said.

"I never have," Noah said. He looked Kylie in the eye. "You love toxic men, even in books."

"I do not!" Kylie cried.

The few patrons at the bar on that slow Sunday evening startled, looking up from their martinis and mojitos. "Settle down," Ben said.

Noah doubled-down on his review of Kylie. "Admit it," he said. "Clive sounds like a nightmare, and that's the kind of man who turns you on."

Lily reached out for Kylie's hand. "Girl, you're in good company. I can't date a nice guy to save my life."

"Nice guys are the fucking worst," Noah said.

"Oh fuck no," Ben said, but not in response to Noah. He was staring at his phone.

"Is something wrong?" Lily asked.

"Well, I've heard from Allison."

Stunned, Lily asked, "What did she say?"

He showed her the message. The text was written in Allison Leigh's signature style, to the point and all caps. I'M SERIOUS. CALL ME.

"Holy shit," Lily whispered.

"What is it?" Kylie asked. "What's going on?"

"Just someone who wants to discuss hosting a podcast," Lily replied. "We didn't think they were serious, but it looks like they are."

"Pas un autre putin de podcast," Noah moaned.

"Hold on," Kylie said. "It's not a bad thing. I love a podcast. What's it about?"

"Love and romance," Lily replied.

Kylie gave her a skeptical look. "Would you be giving advice?"

"What would qualify us to give advice?" Lily asked.

"Absolutely nothing," Kylie said. "You told me to quit my job, and that was terrible advice."

"That's sound advice," Ben said. "You need a fresh start."

"Hold on!" Lily confronted Ben. "How do you know about Kylie's . . . situation?"

"Is that what we're calling it?" Ben asked, amused. "How do you think I know? She told me."

Lily confronted Kylie. "I thought you two didn't talk."

"All I meant is that he doesn't hang out," Kylie said. "Of course we talk at the bar."

"All this time, I didn't say a word because I didn't want to spread gossip!"

"You'd be the only one," Noah said, cutting in. "A glass of red," he said to Ben. "Whatever you have."

"I told you, Lily," Ben said, pouring Noah's wine. "Listening to stories and giving advice is half the job."

"Then, you might as well start that podcast," Kylie said. "You're already doing it for free. Might as well get paid."

Lily let out a nervous laugh. "I don't know about that. This building is our jurisdiction."

"I can't believe Allison is serious," Ben said. "I thought it was a joke."

"Why a joke?" Lily asked.

"Because we both have careers and reputations to uphold," he said.

Now he sounded like her father. "Who knew you were a snob, Ben?" she said. "I bet you'd be all for it if the podcast were about Proust."

"Leave Proust out of it." He left to serve two newcomers.

Lily swiveled in her seat and bumped against Noah and Kylie's hard disapproval. "What?"

"He's standoffish," Kylie said, "but he's not a snob."

"You can't blame the man if he doesn't want to be a podcast bro," Noah added. "I don't fuck them, and I don't fuck with them."

"That's smart," Kylie said. "They're the actual worst."

Who could argue with that? Although, in her heart of hearts, Lily knew she was right. Ben was a *literary* snob. Reading romance and posting reviews on social was just a bit of fun for him, something to mention at galas to ruffle a few feathers. It wasn't meant to go any further than that. On the other hand, he wasn't one hundred percent wrong. Her professional reputation was at stake. She was a lawyer, and lawyers were limited to hosting true crime podcasts.

"Hey, gang! What's up?"

Sierra, in her finest athleisure, thick hair held in place with a claw clip, popped up out of nowhere, startling them all. It was rare to spot her on the rooftop. Of everyone, excluding Noah, she had the liveliest social life. On any given night, she could be seen sailing through the lobby in the most extravagant of looks, heading out with friends or on a date.

"Ben and Lily may start a podcast. Or not. It's still up in the air," Kylie said.

"Nice." Sierra banged a straw cup on the bar to get Ben's attention. "Hey, hottie, could I get some of that free rosé? I'm binge-watching a show tonight. I've got snacks, but no wine."

"We're out of rosé," Ben said. He held up the bottle of prosecco that he'd opened for Kylie. "How about this?"

"You're really pushing that stuff," Kylie commented.

"We received a shit ton of it," Ben explained. "It's a promotional thing."

Kylie shrugged. "It's not bad."

Sierra tapped her cup for ASMR. "Fill her up, baby."

Ben obliged her, filling the cup to the brim.

"So, Lily," Sierra said. "Remember that book you let me use as a prop? The engagement I got from that post was insane. People lost their minds. Some magazines reached out for a quote. It was crazy!"

"Good for you!" Lily said.

"Celebrities pay people to curate books for them," Sierra said. "You guys could do that for me."

"I have an idea," Ben said. "Go to a library and go to a local bookstore, wander the aisles, and see what speaks to you."

"Who has time for that?"

"You do, Sierra. I'm willing to bet money on it."

"Stay out of my business, Ben," Sierra shot back.

"You made it my business," Ben said. "That was my book you used as a prop."

"Lily, I know you don't gatekeep," Sierra said. "What are you reading next?"

"Our followers recommended *Around Midnight* by Charlotte Mitchel," Lily replied. "It's set in Italy, so that works for Kylie. Ben, does that sound good to you?"

"Whatever you'd like. I'll order our copies tonight."

"Oh, really?" Sierra said. "She picks your books? What happened to going to the library and seeing what speaks to you, Ben?"

"Shut up, Sierra," Kylie said. "They've got something going on. Why are you trying to mess with that?"

"I'm not, I promise. I'm a big fan!"

To bolster her defense, Sierra showed everyone the photo she'd taken the day Lily had first met her. She and Ben were hanging poolside, side by side on their lounge chairs, his long brown legs stretched out, hers crossed. Lily was not a body language expert, but even the untrained eye could pick up on the way their bodies tilted toward each other. Ben's expression was thoughtful. The gears of his mind were always spinning, no matter how relaxed he appeared to be. She, well, was fucking gorgeous! There was no subtle way to put it. Coppery, curvy, radiant. Miami had done her well.

"Could you send me that pic?" Lily asked Sierra.

"I tagged you on Insta."

"Hmm . . . I might've missed it."

"Check your notifications."

Kylie examined the photo closely and declared, "If you're not going to sleep together, start that podcast. That's my advice. Don't waste the sexual chemistry. Put it to use."

"Definitely," Sierra said. "In or out of the bedroom, it's time to level up. Tell me more about this podcast."

"It would be about whatever the heck they're doing in that

photo," Kylie said. "Sitting around, talking about books, and falling in love."

"And giving advice," Noah added. "So far, Lily told Sierra to quit her job, and she told me to give this guy I'm talking to a second chance."

"Not a second chance," Lily said. "We don't necessarily believe in those. All I ask is that you give him a chance before you write him off."

"I agree," Sierra said. "Second chances are bullshit."

"Any boy trouble we can help you with tonight?" Kylie asked her.

"Not really," she said in her flippant way. "I don't mess with boys anymore. I date *high value* men. I won't settle for less. Boys are a waste of time."

"Could you send some my way?" Noah asked.

"Wait!" Lily grabbed her phone and opened her Notes app. "Define *high value*, please."

Sierra lifted her straw cup to her lips and thought it over. "The high value man has his act together," she declared. "He has a great job or his own business. Either way, his hustle is strong. He owns or rents—no roommates. He's well-traveled. If he doesn't have a passport with lots of stamps, he's not the man for me."

"You got all that, Lily?" Kylie teased.

"Got it!"

The high value man is worldly, wealthy, and well-rounded. He is the antithesis to the podcast bro or bro of any kind. But where does one find this most elusive species?

"I have one question. Where do you meet these men?"

"You've got to move in the right circles."

"Right. What's the equivalent of the high value woman?"

"Every woman is a high value woman," Sierra answered. "But we can all agree that some men are trash."

"When did you become so wise?" Kylie teased her. "It seems

like only yesterday you moved in with a vlogging camera and a dream."

"Maybe *you* should host the podcast," Lily said.

Sierra slammed down her cup of prosecco. "Are you telling me you have a legit offer to host a podcast, and you're turning it down?"

"Not a legit offer," Ben said. "A text. It means nothing still."

"We're flattered, obviously," Lily said.

"Forget flattered," Sierra said. "You should be interested. Get your social media manager on that text."

"I don't have one of those," Lily said. "I'm a lawyer."

"I'd hold your hand to say this, but you're grown-up," Sierra said. "No one cares. Do you know how much money successful podcast babes make? I would jump on that."

The more the idea took shape, the less Lily was inclined to accept. "It's a cool offer, but a silly idea. I love to read and to share that love on social media—and with you guys—but that's as far as it ought to go. I'm not making a career out of it. Ben is right. We're professionals. It would only distract us from everything else we've got going on and likely be a lot of work. Ben still hasn't figured out how to apply his grant, and when would I find time to study Spanish? I'd like to return home with some marketable skills."

"Wow," Sierra said.

"I'm a chef, and that was a word salad," Kylie said.

Noah rolled his eyes and sipped his wine.

Ben reached for his phone and dialed a number. "Allison, it's Ben. So you're serious? You'd have to get in touch with my agent to make it happen. On our end, we'd request total creative freedom. Okay? Okay. Let's start there. We'll wait for your call."

When he set the phone down, everyone started talking at the same time.

Lily: "Ben, why?"

Sierra: "That's a boss!"

Noah: *"Mec!"*

Kylie: "I need another drink!"

Lily: "Why?"

"Because why the fuck not?" Ben said. "I was wrong. Our careers are fine. They'll survive this summer."

"Are you sure?"

He covered Lily's hand with his. "It's just a call. If we don't like the terms, we'll walk away."

Sierra scoffed. "You people are soft! I'm twenty-two. How is it that I'm the most business-savvy person here? If I didn't make the most of every opportunity that came my way, I'd still be stuck in Tallahassee working at some outlet mall."

"She's right," Kylie said. "A friend of mine, a chef, was stagnant. His career was going nowhere until he started a podcast. Now he has a book deal and merch. You just never know. The exposure alone is worth it."

Lily glanced at the others . . . at Ben . . . at his hand over hers on the glossy bar. "All right," she said. "Why not?"

She was going to make the most of this summer if it killed her.

Everyone cheered. Ben lined up flutes and uncorked another bottle of prosecco. They toasted to the podcast and the books that made it possible.

Chapter Eighteen

The Total Package

The Italian architect, French baker, American rancher, rock star, and prince of some imaginary kingdom—what do they have in common, aside from their height and their sun-kissed skin? These are the romantic leads, the heroes, in novels written by women.

In my experience, holding out for the total package is a strategy that leaves you empty-handed. The architect's career is crumbling. The rock star has poor impulse control. The hockey player is in training and can't commit. We'll make excuses. "He's not so bad," we'll confess to our friends at the bottom of a bottomless-mimosa brunch. "He's just stressed with work."

All this to say we are not well-crafted characters but flawed human beings, and—

Lily dropped her pen and picked up her buzzing phone. There was a message from Ben: **You up?**

Ever since they'd started texting, he would send her the loveliest messages at all times of day or night. Then, as a palette cleanser, he'd send her something like this—a reminder that he was just a guy and not the romance hero she was building him up to be in her mind. Going forward, she would see potential love interests for who they were and not who she wished them to be—a mindset that would have saved her so much heartache in the past, starting with Darren. Had she not read too much into his sweet smile and Midwestern manners, she might have seen him for the flat tire that he was.

Lily: I expect better from you.

Ben: I'm done for the night. Can we talk?

Lily: That's better.

It was a Wednesday night, and Ben had once again filled in for Roxanna. Her baby was colicky and needed his mother. The way Ben selflessly gave of his time only added to the myth that he was better than any main character.

Lily: Want to meet out in the hall in 10?

The hall was neutral territory. She wasn't going to his place this late at night or inviting him over. Any friendship required boundaries. The romance genre had taught her one undeniable truth: you can meet the right person at the wrong time, and nothing you do can change the doomed outcome.

Ben: I'll be waiting.

Ben had seen her in every possible state, and his hands had been everywhere. She should feel comfortable enough to step out to meet him in the oversize T-shirt she'd worn to bed but, again, boundaries. She grabbed her robe off the hook in the bathroom. He was waiting outside his door, a backpack in hand. His black T-shirt was rumpled and water-stained. She suppressed the urge to invite him in to take a load off.

"I heard from my agent," he said. "They've agreed to our terms. She'll forward the contract in the morning for us to take a first look."

"Oh my God," she murmured. "That's fast!"

In her world, any contractual agreement took months and months of negotiating. However, this was Ben's world, and she lacked subject matter expertise. She took a back seat and let him spearhead the negotiations. So far, he'd done an excellent job fast-tracking the deal. Good thing, too. The takeaway from their initial call with the producers of *Pop Shop*, a high-ranking pop culture podcast, was that there was no time to waste. A sudden vacancy had to be filled. They were looking for someone to cover a few episodes over the summer with smart and fun content until a permanent host could be found. Allison was convinced that a limited series on romance from the perspective of smart young professionals was the perfect fit. For Lily, it was an opportunity to raise her profile in the book community and earn money over the summer.

He tilted his head to study her. "How do you feel?"

"I'm excited," Lily admitted.

The idea had enticed her from the start, though she'd been reluctant to admit it. She'd considered the negative impact on the future of her legal career and factored in her father's opinion. None of that mattered now that the opportunity was at hand.

The elevator whirred and dinged and opened at the end of the hall. Jeremy, who Lily had yet to talk to about anything substantive, let alone his legal dilemmas, stumbled out. This time, there was no awkwardness. Ben said, "Hey." Jeremy waved hello as if swatting a fly and rounded the corner to his apartment. It was enough to make Lily change her mind about the hall. This was no safe space. "Let's head inside."

Ben let her into his apartment. He switched on a soft light and dropped his backpack at the doorway. "Roxanna found a new job at a resort," he announced. "In a few weeks, she'll start a day shift at the hotel bar. The new schedule works for her family."

This meant he wouldn't have to cover shifts for her anymore. "Is this the end of your bartending career?"

"Could be," he said. "I'd miss it."

"Well . . . I'll take a glass of water, please."

"Lemon?"

"No, thanks."

"Coming right up. Have a seat."

Lily sat at the table. Her eyes were instantly drawn to the leather box on the bookshelf.

"Why were you up so late?" Ben asked.

"Hmm?" she asked, distracted by the box.

"Were you reading?" he asked.

She turned away from the box. "No, actually . . . I was working out my perspective on romantic fiction."

"Really?" he asked, rummaging through the refrigerator.

"Yes, really," she said. "You only have yourself to blame."

His laugh was low, warm, and familiar. "You give me too much credit."

"Enjoy it," Lily replied. "It won't happen again."

"What is the Lily Lyon perspective on romantic fiction?" he asked.

"It's a work in progress."

He dropped a container onto the counter. "Let's hear it."

She launched into her theory. "One of the main complaints about the genre is that it sets up unrealistic expectations. One false expectation is that men will *man up*, for lack of a better term. No offense, but your gender has not been pulling its weight."

"None taken," he said. "But please, go on. I'm intrigued."

"The reader risks falling for a type or a trope, rather than a person," she said.

"Not buying it. The same could be said about fairy tales."

"Fairy tales had their moment," Lily said. "Generations of girls hoped their prince would come."

"Hope kills."

"It's a deadly drug."

"Should we work your theories into the podcast?" he asked.

"Maybe," she said. "But first we should come up with a concept, then break down each episode."

"We don't need a concept. All we need is you."

"Are you sure you're not a romance hero? You always say the right thing."

"I'm no hero, Lily. You know it."

"I know you only agreed to the podcast because of me."

Without Ben there would have been no offer. She was no one, as far as Allison Leigh was concerned. Ben, fresh off his MacArthur win, was the draw.

"I'm getting paid to do something I was happy to do for free," he said. "I don't think I made it out so bad." He joined her at the table with water and a bowl of grapes. "Sorry. This is all I have."

"That's fine." Lily reached for a grape. "Next time I go grocery shopping, I'll get us some proper late-night snacks."

"You don't have to do that," he said.

"I want to," she replied. "I like shopping for us."

She wished she hadn't said that. A statement like that would freak out most guys. It made it sound as if she were ready to move in. Ben didn't seem to mind. After a moment, he got up and retrieved the leather box.

"What are you doing?" she asked.

"I saw you looking at it."

Lily stirred uncomfortably in her seat. "You don't have to do that."

"Oh no," he said. "You want insight into my black soul, you're getting it."

It was a classic case of careful what you wish for. Whatever was in the box, it was possible she wasn't meant to see.

He dropped the box onto the table and opened it. She peered inside. It held a collection of leatherbound notebooks, a stack of letters wrapped in ribbon, and a watch.

"Are these his notebooks?"

"His journals," Ben replied. "He spent the last decade jotting down memories. He was working on a memoir. It's all here, all the twists and turns of an incredible life."

"Wow." That was all she managed to say.

"He died alone."

"*Alone* or just . . . alone?"

Although her question didn't make sense, she was confident Ben would tease out the meaning.

"*Alone,*" Ben said. "He had no one."

"He had you."

"No, he didn't. I visited him twice," Ben explained. "The first time, he was asleep, drugged up on morphine. The second time, he was dead."

"Ben, I'm so sorry. No one deserves that."

"He might've," Ben said evenly. He reached into the box for a notebook and thumbed through the yellowed pages. "He married for money and pushed away anyone who truly loved him."

"Including you?" she asked.

"I didn't know him enough to love him, and the little I knew I didn't like."

"I see."

"He was alone in the end," he repeated. "I'm trying to avoid a similar fate."

"You?"

He laughed. "Yes, me!"

Dying alone—corpse consumed by cats—was the scare tactic peddled by the patriarchy to push women into marriage. Why should Ben have to worry about that? He was loved by everyone.

"My track record isn't very good, and you know what they say. The apple doesn't fall far from the tree."

"I don't accept that. You are your own apple."

He drew the stack of letters from the box and dropped it on the table. "See this?" he said. "Letters from women he screwed over, explaining how much of an asshole he was."

"They didn't have Block and Mute buttons back then," Lily said.

"My last girlfriend left me a voice memo listing everything I'd done to push her away."

"You mean Bella?"

He didn't answer.

"What went wrong there?" she asked, guided by naked curiosity.

"We'd agreed from the start to keep it casual. A while later, I stupidly believed that agreement was still in effect."

"This is why I don't do casual," Lily said. "Those agreements are tricky and typically expire after three months."

"Do they? No one told me."

"At which time, the parties must return to the negotiating table and decide either to keep it casual or hash out a new deal."

He offered her a grim smile. "I knew I should've hired a lawyer."

"How long were you seeing her?" Lily asked. It had to have been a while if the whole building knew about it.

"We would've hit the six-month mark in June," he said. "But there's more to it than that. Bella is Rox's best friend's younger sister."

"No!"

"Yes," he said gravely. "And my friend, too, I should add. What do the rules say about that?"

"It's prohibited by statute," Lily said. "Unless, of course, you're damn sure of your feelings."

"I had feelings, but not to the degree that she had."

Lily asked one final question. "Do you still have feelings?"

When they locked eyes this time, she was trapped.

"You know I don't," he said.

"I only know what you tell me, Ben."

"I'll tell you this," he said. "I can't have another relationship blow up in my face."

Most of her relationships had ended without fanfare. She blocked the man's number and deleted any photos. Afterward, she'd order in and open a bottle of wine. Lily wasn't one to key anyone's car or cause a fuss at their place of employment. She wouldn't have taken time out of her busy day to drop off an ex's personal items, either. Anything left behind at her apartment would be donated to charity or disposed of responsibly. Valuable pieces were shipped to the owner with a handwritten note. Her mother had raised a lady.

Ben packed up the box. "That thing Socrates said about the unexamined life? Turns out he was on to something. My father could write lyrically about power dynamics and politics and never once look within. That's what I'm trying to do this summer. Take some time to sort myself out."

"Sounds to me we're on the same quest," Lily said.

"You're going to be fine, Lily," he said. "My life is an electric storm. Pulling someone else into it would be criminal."

"Don't be dramatic."

"It's true. I can't risk it," he said. "Not after the mess with Bella. If I've learned anything, it matters how things end."

Lily heard the warning; nevertheless, she persisted. "We wouldn't have to worry about that. I'm leaving at the end of summer."

Her words were met with silence. He was thinking it over, analyzing every possible outcome. What if it weren't that complicated? In six weeks, she'd be gone. It would hurt, but she'd be back in her city and would get over it.

"In other words, we'd keep it casual," he said finally.

"Yes," she said, keeping her tone as casual as possible. "And we wouldn't have to return to the negotiating table because I'd be gone. It would be just for the summer."

"Where have I heard that before?"

Well, she had more in common with the horny spring breakers of his youth than she'd initially thought.

"You don't do casual," he reminded her.

"You're right." She let out a defeated sigh. There wasn't a casual bone in her thirty-year-old body.

Ben pushed back his chair and left the table to retrieve his backpack. From it, he withdrew a copy of *Around Midnight*. "For you."

He didn't have to buy her books. She could easily download the e-book on her device. In fact, she already had. But what if this was his love language? Who was she to deprive him?

She accepted the gift. "Thank you."

He moved to the couch. "Come. Read to me."

If he'd asked her to kiss him, whip him, strip off her clothes, it wouldn't have been as erotically charged.

She joined him on the couch. He rested his head on her lap. In the soft light of a lamp, her fingers in his hair, she opened the book to the prologue.

Neither of them was dying alone tonight.

Sabato
B.R. Journal Entry, May 19

Born in a remote town in Cuba, sent away to boarding school in Havana, and all but abandoned by his mother, these were the events that marked the early years of Sabato Romero's life. Clever and resourceful, he never went without. Twenty years later, when he landed in Florida, the conditions were ripe for his rise. Tall and handsome, with a weakness for women and cigars. His love was a firefly trapped in a jar: it would not survive the night. By dawn he was gone, searching for another pair of arms that could offer more. He did not confide in anyone, but he bled in blue ink on the page. A lover published one of his poems in a paper. From then on, his influence only grew.

I was born in Miami. Where my mother struggled and often failed, my grandmother and aunts stepped in. Much is written about the tragedy of absentee fathers, but I can't speak to that. I was surrounded by women who kept me warm, safe, and fed. I was loved, my achievements were celebrated, and my every dream encouraged. Even with all that, I knew there were things only he could teach me. Not how to shave or tie a tie— I'd managed on my own. I had bigger questions. How to enter spaces where I clearly did not belong and claim them as my own. How to chart my destiny with only words on a page. How to leave my mark on this world.

The answers may well be buried in the box you left me, filled with your notes and papers. But how can I build on your foundation without destroying my own? Each day, I grow more into you than myself as it is.

Chapter Nineteen

After a day at the beach with Kylie, Lily returned home to wash the sand out of her hair. From the shower, she replied to a text from her brother and left the phone on the ledge in case Patrick had more to say about his efforts to placate their mother. He didn't, but her phone buzzed with a FaceTime request from Ben, who was back from an interview with the local public radio station. She accepted the request from the shower, keeping her phone propped on the ledge, to keep the image rated PG-13.

"Are we still on for tomorrow?" he asked.

"Yes, we are." They were to resume poolside reading in the morning. The goal was to finish *Around Midnight*, post a review, and head out to lunch. Lily wanted to tie up loose ends before they started on the podcast next week. "How did the interview go?"

"Grueling."

She massaged her scalp, working the shampoo to a lather. "Let me guess. They mostly asked about your dad."

"You guessed right." He was at his desk, sifting papers. "Um, Lily . . . *¿Qué haces?*"

"Washing my hair."

"Need a hand?"

"I can manage, thanks."

"I see."

She paused, frowned. "How much can you see?"

"Not enough. Step back from the camera."

"You're adorable."

"Not as much as you." He held up his copy of *Around Midnight*. "How far along are you with this? Did you get to the fun stuff?"

"Not yet. Soon, though," Lily said. They'd read the first chapters together; since then, she hadn't picked it up. She wouldn't admit it to anyone, but now that life was more interesting than fiction, her need to lose herself in books had waned.

"You need to catch up," he said.

"Why? Was it good for you?"

"I don't know." Ben moved from his desk to his bed. He grabbed a pillow and propped it under his head. "I was like . . . he's putting his cock where?"

She let out a shriek, swallowed a mouthful of suds, and spit it up, coughing. "I can hear you from across the hall!" he said, laughing.

"Ben, you're a prude!"

"I'm no prude. It just came out of nowhere."

Lily couldn't respond. She kept hacking like a cat, coughing up suds.

"Are you okay? I'll come over."

"I'm fine," she assured him after a breath. "Also, I told you this one was spicy. You were warned."

"They hardly knew each other. Those moves take trust, and trust takes time."

"The element of danger makes it sexy."

"Not to me."

Lily wondered, but couldn't bring herself to ask, if this difference in approach had set them on the wrong course. That first night in the elevator, she'd thought it sexy and daring to kiss him. He, on the other hand, was just trying to get her name right.

"Anyway," she said, "I'm at the part where the bus breaks down in the middle of nowhere. They check into a bed-and-breakfast for the night."

"Spoiler," he said. "There's just one bed."

In the morning, Ben left a note at her door.

Cloudy, high chance of rain. Let's stay in. Come over for coffee. B.

Smiling to herself, she put the note away and went to knock on his door. He opened it for her, looking warm and soft. His gaze slid down her body, taking in her bathing suit and matching sarong. "Were you really going to sit at the pool in this weather?"

"This is a bright sunny day in Manhattan," she said. But the view from his kitchen window showed menacingly dark clouds.

He drew her in by the knot of the sarong. "The pool will be there tomorrow. We can skip a day and stay indoors."

"Sounds cozy."

It was cozier still when the aroma of coffee filled the small apartment. Ben made them toast and warmed up the pastries Roxanna had brought over from a Cuban bakery as a thank-you for his help. He pulled the blanket off the bed and draped it over her legs. She thanked him and added a proper throw blanket to her running list of purchases.

"We're knocking this out today," Ben said. "I can't stand to hold onto a book for too long."

"That's where we're different," she said. "I like to linger on every page."

She was collecting their differences like her brother collected vintage marbles, each one cracked or flawed in some way.

Under the blanket, Ben curled a hand around her ankle. "Linger on your own time," he said. "Let's get this done."

He got it done in under two hours. At noon, he pressed his lips to her knee and declared, "The End!"

Lily had two chapters to go. She banished him from the couch, curled up, and continued reading, flipping the pages until she, too, had reached the end. Triumphant, she tossed the paperback in the air. "Done!"

Ben was at his desk, sifting through mail. Without looking up, he said, "Rapid fire. What's your rating?"

"Five!"

He met her eyes. "Same."

"Really?" She came to sit at the edge of the sturdy oak desk. "You weren't put off by all the spice?"

"I told you, I'm not a prude," he said. "I've got my kinks. Should we get into it?"

"Get into what . . . exactly?"

"The review. Why? What were you thinking?"

"The review! Obviously." She picked up a brass letter opener from the desktop and slid a finger along the dull blade. "But let's order lunch first."

"Agreed."

When the food arrived, they migrated to her apartment. He brought over beer, and she opened cartons of hummus, falafel, and couscous. It was still drizzling out. They talked and ate. After lunch, Lily got her iPad and opened the Book-Tap app. "Let's do it."

Ben had a notebook with him, but no pen. Lily pointed to her nightstand. "Check the top drawer. There should be one there. I've been journaling in the morning."

"Ah. Healing your inner child?"

"Nope," she answered. "Let's leave that girl alone. She's been through enough."

"If you say so."

Lily watched him rummage through her drawer for a second, then it clicked. Before she could yell for him to stop, Ben had found the ballpoint pen lifted from the resort and every note he'd ever written her, including the one left at her door this morning.

He turned to her, grinning. "Lily! You've kept them."

"It's nothing," she blurted. "I meant to toss them out."

"Should I?" He gestured to the trash can in the kitchen, only steps away.

"No," she said, tapping blindly on the iPad screen. "I'll recycle them at the end of the summer. It's more efficient that way."

"Are you sure? It's no trouble for me to dispose of these."

That grin! If only she could slap it off his face.

"Put them back, Ben."

"As you wish." He dropped the notes into the open drawer and slid it shut. Then he joined her on the couch. "Do you reread them at night?"

"Ben! If you don't stop . . ."

He doubled over with laughter. "You don't know how happy this makes me. You keep my notes. You treasure them."

Lily looked up to the ceiling, which could use some dusting. "Yes, I treasure them," she said through clenched teeth. "Girls don't get notes every day. It's sweet."

"I've said it before. You're a romantic."

He said it like some might say *You're a Gemini* or something equally problematic or disturbing.

"What gave it away?" she asked. "My Jane Austen fan club membership?"

"Jane was a realist, not a romantic. We can get into that another day if you'd like, but you are the real deal."

He had a point about Miss Austen: she knew when to rein it in. A woman with no prospects had to settle for what she could get, and there was no guaranteed happy ending.

"Once I get back home, I'm checking myself in." She had to rid herself of this disease.

"Why?" he asked. "It's not a bad thing."

"It's delusional," she said. "Even my friends who fall in love and get married are, to some degree, more clear-eyed about the venture. I've been to the weddings! The anxiety is palpable. So much can go wrong, and they know it. They're not flinging joyfully into the future."

"You want to *fling* into the future with someone?"

"You know what I mean." She didn't have the flowery language, but he should get her point.

"I know your heart, or I'm trying to," he said. "If you want to fling into your future, no one should stop you. It's your birthright."

"And yours?"

"Me?" he said, brows knit. "No. I don't think so."

Lily sighed. "We're so different, you and I."

"Us?" he said, confused.

"You read fast. I don't."

"Yes, but we're reading the same books. That's what counts."

"I'm impulsive and make stupid mistakes. You don't."

"I don't see that as a problem."

This line of examination was going to lead them straight to trouble. She returned her attention to the iPad on her lap. "This review isn't going to write itself."

"No," he said. "It's not."

"Plus, I really think we should take some time to outline our first podcast episode."

"Outline? Don't suck the joy out of it, Lily. That sounds like work."

"How do you prep your lectures?"

"I don't. A few notes, that's all."

"Oh, I see. This is going to be fun."

"Trust me. It's going to be fine. Now, let's knock this out."

They sat, shoulder to shoulder, like an old married couple, passing the iPad back and forth, finessing the synopsis. Ben first jotted his thoughts on a scrap of paper before typing a final draft into the app. Lily confirmed her five-star rating and added a final note.

BOOKTAP @LegalLyon in collaboration with @Ben_Romero

AROUND MIDNIGHT, by Charlotte Mitchel
Couple: Liz and Austin
Trope: one-night stand/one bed

Synopsis: Solo travelers Liz and Austin meet on a tour of central Italy. Liz, an artist, has recently lost her mother to illness. Austin, a winemaker, is coping with the aftermath of divorce. These hastily planned trips were intended to give each one time to focus inward. Instead, they find each other. On the tour bus, they share snacks and snippets of their lives. When the bus breaks down in the middle of nowhere, the group checks into a B and B for the night. Naturally, there are not enough rooms to accommodate the group. As on the *Titanic*, women and children take priority. Liz and Austin pair up. Their suite is spacious but, no surprise here, there is just one bed. And the things they get up to in that bed have made Ben blush. I would've clutched my late great-aunt's pearls if I had them with me.

Around Midnight is a scorcher from the beginning to end. Add the lush Italian countryside, Aperol and limoncello, espresso poured over a scoop of gelato, a serving of pasta, ripe tomatoes drizzled in olive oil, and what you have is a tale of sexual exploration and emotional liberation under the Tuscan sun.

Lily's Rating: 5 stars

Ben's Rating: 5 stars

P.S. We'd like to take this opportunity to share big news!
Some of you have suggested we start a YouTube channel.
However, we've been offered to host a podcast over the
summer, and that's where you'll find us. Follow Pop Shop
wherever you get your podcasts for our discussions on
modern love and the romance genre. Our next selection is
Boss Babe by Gloria Hernandez, a sapphic romance with
Latine rep. With love, L & B

That night, before bed, Lily found a new hiding place for
Ben's notes. Then, with the lights turned low, she slipped on
headphones to listen to his latest radio interview. She had book-
marked it for a night like this, when she was feeling restless and
needed to hear his voice.

Your local public radio station from Palm Beach to Key West
presents *Sunday Matinee*, a news and culture program, with
host Grayson Mills.

Grayson Mills welcomes acclaimed literary translator, Benito
Romero.

GM: In 2001, your father, Cuban poet Sabato Romero,
delivered the inaugural poem. In his memoir, the president
recounts advocating for a popular country musician. "Anyone
but a poet!" the president writes. It was at the first lady's
insistence that he got the call.

BR: As I understand it, she's a champion of literacy.

GM: The president held out for as long as he could before relenting. Because of this, your father didn't have much time to prepare. Yet he rose to the occasion and cemented his legacy. What will yours be?

BR: I don't think about legacies. Not my father's and certainly not my own. That's a very calculated way to live. I seek meaning in the work at hand. When it's over, I move on to the next thing.

GM: Your literary translations are greeted with much acclaim, which is unusual. What's your methodology?

Surely, such a dry topic of legacies and methodologies shouldn't get Lily so wet, but it did. She reached for one more thing she'd stuffed in the back of her nightstand drawer. The miniature vibrator she never traveled without. Sleek, discreet, it was the size of her palm and generally got the job done. Impatient, she switched it on and slipped it between her legs. Breath shallow, body humming, she heard Ben's voice still pouring out of her headphones, now at the foot of the bed.

"I don't rush it," he said. "I linger on every word. When it's right, I know it's right. And it's the best feeling in the world."

Chapter Twenty

They were bickering when they arrived at the Brickell recording studio and kept on bickering as they showed ID to the security guard.

"We should have worked on a script."

"Why do we need a script to talk to each other?"

"It's not just a casual chat. They'll expect us to spark!"

"We're sparking now!"

They were handed stickers marked *Visitor*. She stuck one to her blouse, and he stuck the other to his T-shirt. The guard placed a call to the show's producer.

"They'll expect banter."

"Who's better at banter than us?"

"The best banter is *scripted*."

"You mean *stilted*."

"Don't tell me what I mean."

"Why are you so worked up? We're going to be fine."

"What if my mind goes blank?"

"When does that ever happen?"

A man's voice cut through the bickering. "Hello. I'm Dave Smith. Welcome to the studio!" Dave Smith looked as easygoing as his name suggested, in a navy polo shirt and khaki pants. "Hope you parked across the street. It's cheaper."

"Thanks for the tip," Ben said.

"Lily, nice meeting you in person," Dave said. "You're funny online."

"Yes, but that's not the same——"

Ben closed a hand around her wrist, instantly soothing her. "She's funny in real life, too."

"Great," Dave said. "That's what we want to hear."

Ben had saved her from drowning in her own insecurity right in front of the producer who was counting on them to deliver, but she didn't have to like it. Lily was frazzled. She hadn't slept well the night before. Ben was his same old self when he'd knocked on her door this morning with coffee in a travel mug. "Ready?" he'd asked with a yawn. Her answer was *no*. On the drive over, she'd wondered how he could be so calm only to realize that a lifetime of creative risks had built his confidence. Lily had no such experience to draw from. She could negotiate a contract or lead a meeting with no problem. She had degrees and certifications to prove her competence. But what qualified her to host a podcast?

"We're on the second floor," Dave said. "Elevator or stairs?"

They took the stairs. On the climb, Lily mulled over Ben's last question. When did her mind ever go blank? Always. Whenever he looked at her intently, brushed her arm with the back of his, or said things like *Read to me*. Or like yesterday evening, when they strolled back to the building after oysters and beer at a nearby bar and he said, "Give me your hand."

Upstairs, Dave went off to retrieve a set of keys. Lily tried one last time to get Ben to understand her state of mind. "When I'm nervous, I tend to ramble," she whispered.

"I love the way you ramble."

Her mind went blank.

The studio was smaller than Lily had anticipated. She and Ben were seated across from each other at a narrow table fitted with microphones. Dave took care of some housekeeping.

"I don't know how familiar you are with what we do here, so I'll give you an overview. Our subscribers appreciate our laid-back vibe. We offer the experience of hanging with friends, talking about the pop culture issues of the day. You don't have to carry the whole show. You're new to this, so we've decided to keep your segments short. Talk about the books you love and be yourselves. No pressure to perform. What you two have done at BookTap will translate well here. Any questions?"

Ben tapped his mic. "How do you turn this on?"

"Good question."

When Dave finally went into the recording room, Ben asked her, "Are you okay?"

"No."

How many times did she have to tell him? She was *not* okay.

"It's fine if you can't handle it," he said. "Leave it to me. I'll do most of the talking."

Lily glared at him. Not only did this man know where her buttons were, he knew the unique pushing sequence to get the exact reaction he wanted. "Don't worry. I can handle it."

He returned her glare with twinkling eyes. "I thought so."

"All right, you two. We're ready to go," Dave said through hidden speakers. "At my prompt, introduce yourselves."

Pop Shop
A Pop Culture Podcast
Category: Arts
Rating: 4.1 stars

June 28: *The Sweetest Lie* **by Teresa Star**
with Lily Lyon and Ben Romero

Lily: Can people change? For as long as I've known Ben, which isn't long at all, we've clashed over this central question. Our opinions on this matter have fluctuated over time, but it's central to Teresa Star's contemporary romance, *The Sweetest Lie*. We've read it, enjoyed it, and posted our reviews on BookTap. Today, we'll discuss how well the second-chance-at-love trope holds up in real life, if at all.

Ben: Lily, I love how you've laid that out. How about a quick and dirty synopsis to get us started?

Lily: I can do quick and dirty. Emma and Max have been dating a couple months when Max gets drunk while on a business trip in Vegas and wakes up married. Emma promptly dumps him. Years later, annulment secured, the couple meet again at a wedding in Malibu. Obviously, she takes him back, and they sail off into the sunset, on a houseboat no less. Was it a mistake, though?

Ben: Waking up married in Vegas is a rite of passage in certain cultures.

Lily: Ben!

Ben: He's truly sorry. He's sober. He's gone to therapy. He's groveled like no man has groveled before. Where's your mercy?

Lily: On the Pacific Ocean floor.

Ben: The guy hit rock bottom, and he's repentant.

Lily: But has he truly changed, like on a microcellular level?

Ben: She'll never know for sure.

Lily: You may have a point about Vegas. Getting hammered and waking up married happens so often in books and films, I get FOMO.

Ben: Sweet Lily ... When was the last time you even woke up hungover?

Lily: That time you took me out for oysters!

Ben: Last weekend? That beer was water.

Lily: You don't know me. I'd get drunk on green tea.

Ben: I *do* know you. One martini is all you can handle, and you probably wouldn't take Max back. If any guy has a chance with you, they better get it right the first time.

Lily: Um ... What were we saying? I forgot.

Ben: We're debating the likelihood of the success of a second-chance romance.

Lily: Right. Where do you stand on that?

Ben: I'll be honest. I'd take the risk, but my instinct would be to protect the ones I love, and I'd advise them against it.

Lily: It's like watching someone walk into a trap. In the book, Emma's girlfriends try to warn her, but she's too far gone.

Ben: What could anyone do in that situation? Asking for a friend.

Lily: You love and support them the best you can. Make sure they know that if or when they hit rock bottom, you'll be there to soften the blow. That's the best you can do.

Ben: What if I'm not big enough of a person to do that?

Lily: I believe you are.

Ben: That's our time.

Lily: Is it? That went by fast.

Ben: Would you like to close us out?

Lily: If anyone wants to read the book that started it all, the details are in the show notes. Our reviews are on BookTap. Join us here on *Pop Shop* through August and don't forget to share this episode with the book lovers in your life.

Ben: What are we discussing next week?

Lily: *Boss Babe*, a sapphic romance by Gloria Hernandez. We'll drop a link below.

Chapter Twenty-One

Kylie offered to host a dinner party to celebrate the launch of their new podcast. Lily saw the offer for what it was: a thinly veiled excuse for the chef to get back into the kitchen. She did not take well to time off, and her forced vacation was wearing her out. Lily accepted her offer just the same, with one caveat. "Dinner *and* book club. We're overdue for an official first meeting."

"Good luck herding those cats," Kylie said.

"Food might help," Lily said. "Thanks, Kylie. This is so nice of you."

"I'm happy to do it," she said. "This is exciting. It feels right to celebrate."

Lily, who hadn't felt excitement in a long time, mistook the sudden rush for an anxiety attack. Late last night, she'd sat up in bed, taking deep breaths until she realized that her unease was actually giddiness.

"You're right," she said. "I'll get the good champagne."

The morning of the party, Lily joined Kylie on her excursion to a farmers market in Coconut Grove.

"I could never host a podcast," Kylie said, as they wandered through the stalls.

"Why not?" Lily asked, her eye drawn to a crate of avocados. "Think of your friend and his cookbook deal and all that. It could work for you, too."

"It's not for me. I'd clam up," she said. "Or I'd rattle on like an idiot. I could never just get to the point, you know?"

"I get it," Lily said. "I was so nervous at the studio. I don't think I could do it alone. Talking with Ben is so easy. It was no different with the microphones. After a while, I forgot they were recording us."

"Uh-huh." Kylie lifted a hefty eggplant from a basket. "What else are you and Professor Romero up to? Anything you'd like to share with the class?"

"I see what you did there, and it's very cute, but I'm sorry to disappoint you. There's nothing to share."

"A shame."

A damn shame, all things considered, but very necessary. Despite their love for words, she and Ben couldn't get on the same page. When she wanted to toss caution to the wind, he reminded her of what was at stake. A great quality in a life part- ner, but they didn't have their whole lives. They only had this summer.

"I'm halfway through the audiobook of *Around Midnight*," Kylie said. "Sorry if I'm falling behind on the book club. I won't be ready for tonight's discussion."

"Never mind that," Lily said. "Ben and I are burning through these books like it's our job, and in a way, it is. You guys take your time. How do you like it so far?"

"It's hot, but there's one thing that gets me."

"What's that?"

"Liz and Austin have the most amazing sex, like right out of the gate. They do and try things they've never done before. It's orgasm after mind-blowing orgasm. I mean . . . what the fuck? Literally!"

Lily laughed. "I got an earful from Ben."

"I've done it. After a few drinks, there's no hotter guy than the one you've never laid eyes on before."

"Or will ever again," Lily added.

"Right? It's fun and a little dangerous, but let's be real. It's never all that good! Half the time, you're playing Twister with a man who doesn't know what you like and can't even ask."

"Would we be having this conversation if we were reading a dragon-slayer novel?" Lily said. "Most likely, we'd be discussing the logic of a magic system. How does that help us in real life?"

"You have a point," Kylie said. "I take back the snarky things I said about romance."

Kylie had a point, too. The story was based on the premise that when you found The One, everything flowed. Good conversation, great sex—no effort required. What was that if not a magical system?

They moved to a stall of heirloom tomatoes. Kylie suggested a caprese salad, a favorite of Austin's, the hero of *Around Midnight.* "Frederico loves it, too, but with a balsamic reduction."

Ah . . . It had been a while since she'd mentioned the Italian architect.

"Most of us are Caribbean," Lily said. "Would it kill you to fry a plantain?"

"Maybe next time," Kylie replied, selecting tomatoes from the crate. "Let's stay on theme tonight."

"Do you miss him?" Lily asked after a while.

Kylie paused and closed her eyes as if she could feel the man she loved in the sunlight. "Every day."

"I've been thinking about the advice I gave you, and I'd like to take it back."

"Oh, really?"

"Yes," she said. "I was very closed-minded three weeks ago." Lily hadn't known Kylie well enough that first night, and her cookie-cutter advice hadn't been helpful. "What if we've been reading this whole thing all wrong? He likes your cooking, maybe he likes you, too. But it's tricky, you know? As your lawyer, I should remind you that the handsome, caprese salad–loving architect is your boss. He may not want to risk getting sued."

"I'd never sue," Kylie said.

"Why?"

"Frederico hasn't done anything wrong. If anything, he might have a case against me."

"Okay, but if he gets out of line, please take him for all he's got."

She shook her head. This morning, her short hair was tucked behind her ears, the edges of which were pink, like prawns in the heat. "It's not worth it," she said. "Word travels fast in my industry. No one would ever hire me."

Lily had heard this argument several times over. If it wasn't the service industry, it was the arts. Either way, she wasn't swayed. "With the right lawyer, you may not need to work again."

"Who knew you were such a shark?" Kylie said. "By the way, did you ever get a chance to speak with Jeremy?"

"Not yet. I ran into him a couple times, but we haven't spoken." Lily averted her eyes, recalling those brief encounters in the hallway at the most inopportune times.

They bought sweet basil for the salad and fresh flowers for a centerpiece.

"I hate to say it, but your advice was spot-on," Kylie admitted when they stopped to sample vegan brownies. "I've got to pull myself together or find a new job. Those are my choices. By the time he gets back, I'll have to sort it out."

"Or you could talk to him," Lily suggested. "Tell him how you feel. You might be pleasantly surprised. Maybe he's waiting for a sign from you. Maybe he's shy."

"That man is not shy," Kylie shot back. "I've seen the way he operates."

"Now I'm intrigued. How does he operate?"

"He's a classic love bomber," Kylie said.

"Really?"

"Oh, yes," Kylie said. "He meets a woman, showers her with attention, takes her out, calls, texts, and buys her gifts. Next thing you know, I'm making their favorite matcha and stocking the fridge for two. A few weeks go by, and he's over it. He gets bored and moves on to the next woman."

The love bomber . . . Lily knew the type. She'd been a victim once or twice and hadn't yet fully recovered. These were dangerous individuals who ought to be on the FBI's radar.

"Knowing all this, why do you want him?" Lily asked.

Kylie deflated. "I don't know."

"Have another brownie. It's on me." Looking to the future, Lily asked, "What's the plan for July Fourth?"

"Usually, we hang out on the roof, get drunk, and watch fireworks."

"Sounds like a good time."

When they were done at the market, they parted ways. Kylie had a few more errands to run. Drained, Lily returned to the building. She crossed the lobby, a dozen white roses wrapped in newspaper tucked under one arm and a tote bag full of fresh citrus on the other. At the elevators, she encountered Jeremy.

For the urban apartment-dweller, bumping into a neighbor, specifically at the elevators, was a peculiar form of agony. She and Jeremy hadn't exchanged more than two words, yet he'd seen her in her pajamas, and she'd seen him stumble home tipsy. She was determined not to make it weird.

"Hey, you!" Lily said, smiling and immediately regretting it. Who even smiles anymore? she wondered.

"Oh, hey," he replied, flat.

The elevator arrived, and Jeremy stepped aside to let her enter first—a gentleman in ripped denim and a Nirvana concert T-shirt. They rode toward their floor in silence, the elevator making a smooth ascent only to stop abruptly somewhere between the third and fourth floors. The lights dimmed in the car, and the hazard lights flashed on.

Lily dropped the bag of citrus. "What's going on?"

"Don't worry," Jeremy said. "This happens all the time."

"All the time?"

"You mean you haven't gotten stuck in the elevator yet?"

"I can't say I have."

He pressed a big red button. A robotic voice assured them that the matter would be resolved shortly. Lily was not at all assured.

"I'm not claustrophobic," she said, "but God, I hate this. Once, I was stuck in an elevator for two hours."

"That's rough," he said.

"If you live in a city long enough, it's bound to happen."

"I grew up in a small town. This is all new to me."

She considered Jeremy more closely. He was much younger than she'd thought. Twenty-two or twenty-three, maybe.

"Where are you from?" she asked.

"New York."

"Oh, come on!"

"Cold Spring, New York," he specified. "Trust me. It's Small Town, USA."

"Well, you seem to be getting along just fine in the big city."

"You're Lily, right? Ben's new girlfriend."

"Yes and no," she said. "I'm Lily, but not Ben's girlfriend. We're neighbors and friends and, well, you get it."

He nodded, knowingly. "Yep."

"And you're an artist," Lily said, steering the conversation away from Ben.

"Yeah, I paint murals and do some digital stuff."

"Kylie mentioned you might need a lawyer to look over a contract."

At the mention of their friend, Jeremy's whole demeanor

changed. He was suddenly brighter and taller. "Kylie . . . She's a real one."

"I'm available to help as much as I can."

Jeremy reached for his phone and, with a few taps, pulled up an email. "It's not a contract," he said. "Just an offer."

Lily skimmed it. From what she could gather, it was a solicitation for original artwork, what he'd described as *digital stuff*. The client was a privately owned art museum. The winning artist would be awarded two thousand dollars. However, the museum reserved the right to use any submitted art in any format, on any platform, in perpetuity.

"What do you think?" he asked. "The deadline is coming up soon."

"Whenever you see the word *perpetuity*, you should back away slowly," Lily replied.

"That means *forever*, right?"

"Forever and ever, amen."

"Gotcha."

"Mostly, this is a clever way to collect original art for free. Maybe you'll win and walk away two grand richer. If you lose, you also lose the rights to your work. Obviously, I can't tell you what to do. We've all got to start somewhere. Going forward, though, it's a good idea to vet your business partners, make sure they're operating in good faith."

"I had a gut feeling," he said, pocketing the phone. "Is this the type of law that you do?"

"In a way," she said. "I'm in corporate law, so I know my way around the four corners of a contract."

"Thanks for the free advice," he said. "It's free, right?"

"Aw, that's so cute!" She tapped him on the arm. "I'll slide my invoice under your door."

Just then, the elevator bounced and continued its ascent. Lily held her breath until the doors slid open on their floor. "Good God," Lily cried. "I'm so relieved."

"Told you," he said. "This happens at least once a month. If you're ever alone, don't stress out. Just press the button, and they'll get it working in ten to fifteen minutes."

"Thanks, but I'll stress out anyway, if that's all right with you."

Jeremy carried her bag to her door. Then he handed her a card with his number. "Here," he said. "In case you're stuck in there, stressing out, just call me, and I'll get the building manager to get off his ass."

"Thanks." He was halfway down the hall when she called out to him. "What are you up to later tonight?"

"Nothing much. What do you got going on?"

"Ben and I are celebrating our new podcast. Kylie is cooking. If anything, you'll get a free dinner."

"Sounds good. What time?"

"Seven, at Noah's apartment."

"I know the place. See you then."

Inside, Lily washed and stored the fruit, set the roses in a jar of water, and sent a quick text to Kylie alerting her that there would be one more for dinner. Then she sat with a cup of tea and her journal to jot down a few lines.

Love Bomber

The landscape of modern love has changed since the nineties, a time when women sat by their phones on Friday nights. The only thing to worry about was whether Mr. Big would commit. Lately, a new crop of genetically engineered men has invaded the dating field. Let's discuss the tactics of the Love Bomber.

This man isn't afraid to give you his number or make weekend plans. He reserves the best table at your favorite restaurant, books flights for weekend getaways. He's into whatever you're into: art shows, the opera, whatever. He'll send you flowers and gifts just because. He acknowledges Valentine's Day as a legitimate holiday and knows which chocolates you prefer. This goes on for weeks, and it doesn't take long before you're hooked. The group chat is buzzing. **I think he's the one and OMG!!!! I love this for you, babe!** You're giddy. You think he might propose. You leave a ring out just in case. Then the missile hits its target. The sky is aglow: for a split second, you believe it's the Fourth of July. By the time you recover from the blast, you're coated in ash and regret. He's fled the scene and narrowly avoids the atrocious aftermath, the sight of you on the ground, your heart bleeding out.

I'm writing from experience. It took a while to recover. I swore I'd never fall victim again, but, of course, I did.

Chapter Twenty-Two

Noah had the largest apartment, a two-bedroom unit on the tenth floor with a slim balcony on which he vaped while scrolling dating apps. Perfect for parties.

Lily showed up alone. Ben had been tapped to help Kylie move her heavy Le Creuset collection, among other things, from her third floor apartment up to Noah's. They'd agreed to meet there, and by the time she arrived with an armful of books, gifts for the guests, she was antsy to see him. They'd been apart the whole day, a rarity now.

Noah greeted her at the door, more handsome than she had ever seen him. His dedication to the sun had caramelized his complexion, and his hair was slicked back and gelled in place.

"Hello, you!" Lily said.

He unburdened her of her load. "What's all this?"

"Our next book club read. *Boss Babe* by Gloria Hernandez. A spicy sapphic. It's a good one."

"Sapphic . . . Cool." Noah dropped the bookstack on the entryway table. "Listen," he said, a bit panicked. "He's here."

"Ben?"

"Nicolas."

"Um . . . Mr. Slow Burn?" she guessed.

Noah looked as if he might explode.

"Hey! What do you want from me?" she asked. "You never told me his name."

"Nicolas Galanis."

"Nice name. Where is he?"

She scanned the living room. Though vast, the living space appeared far more spacious for its lack of conventional furnishing. There was no couch or dining table, only a scatter of ottomans, which lead her to believe they would have to eat Kylie's meal off their laps. Then he came in from the balcony. Average height, average build, wearing a suit from one of those suit warehouse places, but the *swagger*, oh good Lord, the confidence!

"Pas mal, non?" Noah said.

Lily stole another second to admire him. *"Pas mal du tout."*

"Why do you think I keep giving him second and third chances to get me in bed?

To be honest, it doesn't even have to be a bed. The floor is fine. My car works, too. All he wants to do is talk."

She leaned close and whispered, "Do you think something is wrong with him? Like physically?"

"No. I think something is wrong with him mentally."

From the entryway, Lily swept another appraising gaze over Nicolas. He was at the kitchen island, sampling Kylie's food and chatting amiably. Long creases formed at his eyes when he smiled.

What if Ben and Nicolas were the normal, well-adjusted ones, taking their time to get to know Lily and Noah, prioritizing conversation? They were in no hurry to burn through the stops. She and Noah were the horny, impatient ones, dousing themselves in gasoline, willing to set themselves on fire.

Lily gripped Noah's arm and pulled him out into the hall, slamming the apartment door behind him.

"What's wrong?" Noah asked, perplexed.

"We're the ones with the mental issues," she said, jabbing a finger into his chest. "We found great men who want to get to know us, spend time with us, are curious about our lives, share our interests, read with us, and even host a freaking podcast, and all we can do is whine about not getting laid!"

"Not getting laid is not a small thing," Noah said. "Don't dismiss it."

"I'm not. But it's time we act like the mature adults we claim to be."

"I never made that claim."

"You get my point, right?"

Noah mumbled something.

"Great. Let's go inside and act normal," she said. "Is Ben here yet?"

"Present!"

Lily swiveled around, heart beating at an abnormal pace. There was Ben, coming down the hall with all the confidence and swagger her heart could desire. She wanted to run to him but couldn't, not from the high horse from which she'd just delivered her little speech.

"What am I interrupting?" Ben asked. "You two plotting someone's death?"

"Noah needed a time-out," Lily said.

Noah wouldn't play along. "Speak for yourself. I didn't drag myself out here."

Ben was close enough to rest a hand on the small of her back, setting a small fire at the base of her spine.

"See you inside," Noah said, leaving them.

As soon as the door clicked shut, Ben drew her close. "I haven't seen you all day."

"Oh!" she said, as if it hadn't occurred to her. "It was an action-packed day."

"Every minute was agony."

"That's a love bomb."

"Excuse me?"

"Never mind."

"I have something to ask you," he said.

She adjusted the collar of his blue button-up shirt. "Ask away."

"Roxy's wedding is next weekend."

"That's fast."

"She's been planning it a while," Ben said. "She had a bunch of stuff in storage for the first wedding that fell through."

"Oh . . ." Lily's heart could burst. "That's sad."

"Would you like to be my date?"

"Will you walk her down the aisle?"

"I said I would."

"In that case, I'll be your date. Someone should keep an eye on you, make sure you behave. Whatever you do, don't punch the groom at the altar."

"I'll do my best," he said. "The dress code is casual. It's a small wedding, just for a few friends and close family. No need to wear the black dress I love, unless you want to . . . just for me."

"Sorry, can't do it. My mother raised me to dress for the occasion. I won't wear a formal black dress to an informal wedding. It's not in my DNA."

"You're the only person who's going to make this whole thing bearable, so wear whatever you'd like."

How was she to act normal after that?

She took his hand. "Come. We have to meet Noah's guy. His name is Nicolas, and he's something else."

Lily, Ben, and Nicolas had barely exchanged a few words when Kylie summoned Lily into the bathroom.

"Hey, could you come here? I lost a contact. Please help!"

She peeled herself away from Ben, whispering, "I'll be right back." He squeezed her hand before letting go. This was peak couple behavior, and yet, she still didn't know what to make of it.

She joined Kylie in the bathroom. An oil diffuser was puffing in a corner, and the small space smelled of *Baccarat Rouge*. Lily made a mental note to step up her home-fragrance game.

Kylie was seated on the bathtub rim, looking lost. Lily set down her glass of champagne on the vanity top. "Sweetie, don't worry," she said. "We'll find it. Where do you think it might be? Did it fall into the sink or on the floor?"

"I didn't lose a lens," Kylie admitted. "But I think I'm seeing things."

Lily kneeled before her, truly concerned now. "What are you talking about?"

"Is Jeremy hot, or am I hallucinating?"

Lily gathered her friend in her arms. "There's nothing wrong with you. I can confirm that Jeremy is hot. I was stuck in an elevator with him for fifteen minutes today. He's just wonderful, inside and out."

"You're not helping."

"I owe you the truth." Lily straightened up and returned to her glass of champagne. "Now, tell me everything."

Kylie took a few deep breaths before launching into the story. "He came around early and thanked me for looking out for him, which is adorable."

"So adorable."

"He says you two finally had that talk, and you gave him excellent advice."

Lily shrugged. "It's what I do."

"He was telling me all this, and something in my brain rerouted to take in his hotness."

"He looks good in those jeans."

"He's a baby, though. I can't go there."

"Is he, though?"

"He's twenty-four, I'm—"

"I know what you are. Who even cares?"

"Me! I care! I was a mess at twenty-four."

"Sweetie, you're a mess now."

"You're right," Kylie said. "Thanks for reminding me. I needed to hear it."

"On a serious note, how much of a mess can Jeremy be? He's living comfortably, as far as I can tell. How else could he afford his place?"

"The hell if I know. The rent here isn't cheap."

"Maybe he's apartment-sitting for a friend."

"Maybe."

Lily spotted Noah's collection of condoms from a French design house, set out like candy in a jar.

"I may have more in common with Jeremy than anyone my age," Kylie admitted. "Some of my friends are on their second pregnancies. One is on the city council in my hometown in Minnesota. Many own businesses."

"I wouldn't go that far," Lily said. "You may not be on the city council, but you're pursuing a dream, and you're a fantastic cook."

"You haven't tasted my food yet."

"I trust Frederico's taste," she said. "If your cooking is good enough for his discerning ass, Ben and I will eat it up."

"You and Ben . . . You've got something. I can see it."

"Not without your contacts, you can't," Lily shot back. "Now, let's get out of here."

No sooner had Lily rejoined Ben than he was called away to mix Negronis. While Noah was busy troubleshooting the sound system, Lily stole the opportunity to get to know Nicolas. He was nothing like Noah had described—a constant talker or a bore. Nicolas was soft-spoken with elegant manners and inquisitive gray eyes. She could talk to him all day. They passed a small bowl of olives back and forth. She learned that the federal prosecutor had only recently ended a long-term relationship.

"What went wrong, if you don't mind my asking?" she said.

"That's right." He nodded. "You're a love guru."

Lily startled. "I'm a what?"

"Don't you have a podcast on love?" he asked. "Isn't that what we're here to celebrate?"

"Romance, not love," she replied. "There's a difference, and even so that wouldn't make me a guru."

"That's not what Noah says." He laughed. "So maybe you can help me make sense of this. He thought I worked too much."

"Is he right?"

"My therapist thinks so," he replied. "What I don't understand is that he knew what I did for a living when we started dating. He knew I wasn't likely to change. I love what I do."

He explained that, as a senior member of a major crimes unit, he was tasked with thorny cases. At the time of his breakup, he was prosecuting members of an organized crime ring. "It was a difficult time."

Lily searched for something to tell him, some bit of wisdom to impart. "People put a premium on compatibility, favorite movies and books and songs, but that's just surface stuff. You'll find someone who understands how important your work is to you."

"Thanks, love guru."

"You're welcome."

"So . . . you and Ben, right?" he said. "I caught one of his class lectures online. I'm one of those geeks who hopes to write the next great American novel on my lunch break. He's brilliant."

Lily made a mental note to catch one of Ben's online lectures before replying, "He's brilliant, that's for sure. But we're not a couple."

"Sorry. I shouldn't have assumed."

"Don't kick yourself," she said. "It's an easy mistake. I have a hard time keeping it straight sometimes. How about you and Noah?"

He winced at the mention of Noah's name. Lily felt compelled to leap to her friend's defense. "He's a cool guy," she said. "He was the first to welcome me to the building, and he's been my guardian angel this whole time."

"One woman's angel is another man's demon or tormentor," Nicolas said with a little laugh. "He's beautiful and tempting."

"How did you meet?" she asked.

"I hopped on the apps to see what was out there, and somehow matched with him. We don't have too much in common, though. We like wine, so there's that."

The differences between Noah and Nicolas were glaringly obvious, but what of the opposites attract theory or the grumpy/sunshine trope?

"Does anything else matter if you like each other?"

"We're not in the same place," Nicolas said. "I'm ready to settle down. I don't think he'll ever be."

Lily gulped down her champagne. Nicolas's tone was resolute. This didn't bode well for Noah. Ben returned with Negronis, and soon, they were engrossed in a conversation about late midcentury novels, the subject of the lecture Nicolas had caught on YouTube. To the untrained eye, Nicolas had more in common with Ben than with Noah. However, only Noah twisted himself in knots over Nicolas, gave him chance after chance, waited around when he was late, replayed their dates in his mind and for his friends, and combed through every conversation in search of *something*. She wondered if Noah knew Nicolas was grieving a relationship. Had he bothered to ask? Or maybe he'd sensed something was off all along. In that case, he'd been right to be cautious and protect himself. She'd been wrong to keep pushing. This left her wondering why people came to her for advice. *I'm no guru. I suck.*

Noah and Jeremy carried in folding chairs and a table from the spare bedroom. In no time, the table was set with linens, flickering candles, and the roses Lily had picked up at the market earlier that day. They ate family-style. Kylie had prepared fresh pasta to go with the caprese salad: lobster- or mushroom-filled raviolis. Side dishes of broccolini and roasted brussels sprouts rounded out the menu.

Before they sat to eat, Kylie made an announcement. "Guys! Let's thank Lily for gifting us each a copy of the next official book club selection. You'll find one on your seat. Read it, and if you'd like to discuss, come find us at the rooftop bar on a Sunday night. Or not. It's not that serious. Just enjoy yourselves."

"Or find us on BookTap," Lily added. "I get you're busy, and I just want to thank you all for being here, Noah for opening his home to us, Kylie for what looks like a fantastic meal, and Ben for being the best book buddy I could hope for. I love you guys."

Kylie rushed over to hug her, which was so uncharacteristic of her Lily was at a loss for words. She clammed up and took a seat at the table next to Ben. He pulled her chair close to his and pressed his lips to her temple before rising, glass in hand, for a toast. "To my neighbor, my friend, my fellow coffee lover, my reading partner, my confidante, my coconspirator— all things you are to me, Lily. And now you're my cohost. I couldn't be happier. To us. And to another useless podcast the world doesn't need!"

"To another useless podcast the world doesn't need!" the others echoed.

Lily, who had held his gaze throughout, saw in those inscrutable eyes a glimmer of their very first encounter. *Wow. You wait all your life for this feeling to take you, change you, make you new. When it happens, you want to jump off a fucking balcony.*

Ben sat down and asked if she was feeling okay. "You look pale. Is something wrong?"

"Nothing's wrong."

"Did I embarrass you?"

"No, I loved it," she said. "*Loved* it."

He drew her chair even closer, filled her glass with water, fed her lobster ravioli, and even though they were surrounded by people, talked quietly to her as if no one else mattered. They were alone in a world of words, shared thoughts, clashing opinions, inside jokes, shared passions, and joint ventures. She'd never had this with anyone, had never felt like this about anyone.

He leaned in and asked her, "What's going on between Jeremy and Kylie?"

Who cares?! she wanted to scream. *What's going on between us?*

To play along, Lily glanced around the table. Noah and Nicolas were talking, fully engrossed in conversation, and Noah did not look bored. Jeremy and Kylie were swapping stories and laughing, a half-empty bottle between them.

"They're having fun. It's summer."

"I keep telling you, that's no excuse," he said. "This is Miami. It's always summer."

Ben went quiet for a bit before asking, "Remind me when you plan on returning to New York?"

"August 31," she replied and regretted it instantly. His question had heft, loaded to test a boundary. Her answer sounded so definitive, as if she had a plan and a purpose when in fact that was the date her lease was up. She'd gladly move her things across the hall and extend her stay if he asked.

Ben didn't ask. He just nodded curtly and turned away.

Chapter Twenty-Three

By the end of the night, the books doubled as trays and coasters. Noah suggested they head down to their clubhouse, an unfamiliar spot to Lily, Jeremy, and Nicolas. The clubhouse was a pergola by the pool with enough seating for all of them if they paired up. Kylie passed around a container of fresh baked brownies, an after-dessert treat. The night stirred with sounds, the roar of speeding cars, and rowdy music, and the chatter from the streets below reached them on the pool deck two floors above ground. The pool glowed under the city lights.

Ben told the story of the chilly February night he'd stumbled across Kylie and Noah in their so-named clubhouse, drinking and commiserating on Valentine's Day.

Lily listened intently, recording the sound of his voice. There would be a day when Ben and his stories would no longer be accessible to her, and she would have to rely on memory alone. She took in the entire scene, while the others appeared to hang on to his words. His simplest, most mundane stories were peppered with thoughtful observations. Everyone knew how special he was; to be in his company was a gift. Lily could not believe her luck to have found him and these amazing friends in this chaotic new city.

Then things got even more chaotic.

They heard the slam of the door, and the furious tap of heels on the pool deck before they ever saw her. Sierra, in a pink shimmery minidress, showing off long glossy brown legs, emerged from the darkness. She crossed the terrace, heading straight to the edge, gripped the rail, and screamed into the void, "Fuck!"

"Whoa!" everyone cried in unison.

Sierra startled, swiveled around, and screamed. "You scared me!" Her back to the partition, she took them in with wide eyes. "What are you all doing here?"

"The better question is, what are you doing?" Kylie asked.

"What does it look like I'm doing?" she retorted.

"I don't know," Noah said. "Losing your mind?"

"I'm venting. I'm just . . . so frustrated!"

"Talk to us," Kylie said. "We've got brownies."

She came limping toward them in her stiletto heels. Jeremy hopped to his feet, gave her a quick hug, and found her a seat. Kylie handed over the container of brownies. Lily studied Sierra's sullen face, makeup intact despite it all, and her slumped shoulders. Sierra had turned down their dinner invitation for a date, but dating was not for the weak. She should've come to dinner. Kylie's lobster ravioli had been divine.

"It's over," she said.

"With the high value man?" Kylie asked.

"Yep." Sierra bit into a brownie. "And we can stop calling him that. He's worthless."

"What happened?" Noah asked, on the edge of his seat.

She looked him straight in the face. "You won't believe what he asked me."

"Hold on," Ben said. "I need context and a bit of background."

"You want background? How much time do you have?"

"We're in no hurry," Kylie said. "Relax. Take your shoes off. Get comfortable."

Sierra kicked off her Louboutins. "He took me to Mr. Chow."

"Fancy."

"Nice."

"Overrated."

"I've had better at street stalls."

Ben cut through the noise. "This story does not start at Mr. Chow."

"I agree," Lily said. "How did you meet this man of questionable value?"

"We matched on an app," Sierra replied.

Nicolas groaned.

"What's wrong with that?" Noah asked him. "We met on an app."

Nicolas didn't reply, but his pained expression said it all.

"Guys," Ben intervened in his most professorial tone, "you'll get your turn. Sierra, please continue."

"Over the last couple of months, we've been on four or five solid dates. He travels to L.A. a lot, so there have been some gaps. He makes up for it, though. Each time he takes me out, he puts in the effort. Once, he took me to a party at a mansion crawling with A-list celebrities. Another time, we went to dinner and ran into a rapper whose name rhymes with *take*. You get the vibes, right? He ups the ante every time—a better restaurant, a hotter club. He said we'd fly to Jamaica, but that never happened. Last week, though, we were poolside, hanging out with one of the hottest DJs. I'll say this. He's a little dull. I got the feeling he purposely chooses these flashy events to hide the fact that he can't carry a conversation. I tried! God knows I tried. We could never just talk. The connection isn't there. When he asked me to dinner tonight, I was encouraged. It was time we spent a night together without like a whole freaking circus."

She looked to Ben and Lily to confirm that her point was getting across.

"You're good," Lily said.

"Continue," Ben added.

"We get to Mr. Chow. The food is next level. I've never seen prawns so huge, so fresh."

Lily interjected to praise Kylie's cooking. "Kylie made us lobster ravioli. It was perfect."

"It was the best I've had in my life," Jeremy added.

"Aw, thanks, you two!"

"If there's any leftover, I'd love to try it," Sierra said.

"I've got you covered," Kylie said.

"We all love Kylie's cooking," Noah said, impatient. "Now, let Sierra spill this tea."

Sierra grabbed another brownie. "These are delicious, by the way." She took a bite and, with a hand over her mouth while she chewed, went on with her story. "We're halfway through the entrée when he initiates, you know, the talk. I'm thinking, here we go. Things are about to get serious."

"Sorry to interrupt again," Lily said. "What do you mean by *the talk*? Be specific."

"Oh, you know. Where's this going? Blah, blah, blah."

"Gotcha," Lily said. "But where did *you* think it was going?"

"Nowhere fast!" Sierra exclaimed. "I was curious to know his thoughts."

"And we're curious to know how this story ends, so go on," Noah said.

"He says he loves my company and he's having fun. I tell him, 'Same.' He says he hasn't been seeing anybody else. I can't go there because your girl has a roster. It took some time to build, and I'm not going to knock it down just because this one guy took me to a couple of parties."

"Makes sense," Noah said.

"I tell him how special he makes me feel and on and on. And I mean it all! I wasn't catching feelings or anything, but I was always excited to see him again, and that's a start. I tell him I'm eager to see where this goes."

At this point, Lily was eager for this information as well.

Sierra wiped crumbs off her dress, composed herself, and said, "This is when things go south. Ready?"

"Ready!"

"Please! Out with it!"

Sierra cleared her throat. "The man sets down his fork and knife, looks me dead in the eye, and says . . . 'You've seen what I can do. Now tell me what you bring to the table.'"

"What?"

"Holy shit!"

"No way!"

Ben was right, Lily thought. This story doesn't begin at the restaurant. It begins at where this random man found the audacity.

"I would've flipped that dinner table," Kylie said.

"Seriously, doesn't he know who you are?" Noah asked.

"Who is she?" Nicolas whispered, speaking up for the first time in a while.

Noah showed him exactly who Sierra was with only a few taps on his phone. Nicolas nodded, impressed. "Those are good numbers."

"Swim with Sierra is a lifestyle brand," Kylie said.

"It's a whole vibe," Jeremy added.

Lily looked to Kylie and Jeremy. Suddenly, she could see it, the invisible connection—no contact lenses required.

"What does that even mean?" Ben asked, genuinely confused. "What is he asking you exactly?"

Words had meaning. For Ben, the words *what you bring to the table* made no sense. Lily loved him a little more because of it.

"I asked him that same question! He said he was 'going places' and needed someone to support him."

"You're going places!" Lily cried. "Is he prepared to support you, too?"

"I'm going places he's never heard of!" Sierra fired back. "He couldn't find Ibiza on a map!"

Kylie rolled her eyes. "What a jerk."

"What did you tell him?" Noah asked.

"I tell him I'm young, and I'm not looking for a husband. He's young, too. Only twenty-six or something. So like, dude, maybe slow your roll."

"What did he say to that?" Ben asked.

"He tried to play it off and said *I'm* not wifey material. Like what?"

"Heaven help me," Lily whispered, as Ben drew her close and encouraged her to breathe.

"He says what I do for a living is unbecoming," Sierra said.

Unbecoming of what? Lily wondered. First lady? Sierra was young and fun. She shouldn't have to conform to *wifey* standards.

Sierra took another bite of her brownie and went on. "I tell him I'm a content creator, a successful one. He says all I do is pose in bikinis, and how can that last? At this point, I'm seeing red."

Lily couldn't take it. The so-called high value man was questioning Sierra's value. The sickening irony!

"There's nothing wrong with modeling," Jeremy muttered.

"How am I supposed to know how these bathing suits look on real people if someone doesn't post it online?" Kylie asked. "You're doing a public service."

"Thanks!" Sierra said. "He thinks I'm doing it for male attention."

"We don't care what he thinks," Noah said. "He's boring, and we're done with him."

"He's coming for your bag," Nicolas said. "That's never good."

"I'm done with him," Sierra declared. "Done!"

"Sounds like he's getting relationship advice from one of those podcast bros," Nicolas said. "You know the type, right?"

"As the only actual podcast bro here," Ben said. "I think his attitude is chauvinistic, and you can't change that."

"I don't want to," Sierra answered. "I'm *done!*"

"What did he do except take you out to a few parties, anyway?" Noah asked. "*I* can take you to parties."

"He really thought he was doing something," Sierra said. "Like I'd undo years and years of work just to hang out with him. But, guys, don't worry. I'm good. I've got a brand trip coming up to the Maldives! I'm working with a dream brand. I don't have time for this fuckery. Life is good."

Life is good.

They ended the night on those words. After the dinner, and all the camaraderie and closeness it had brought them, everyone went home alone. Kylie took Sierra to her place for the promised leftovers. Nicolas said goodnight and took the elevator to the lobby; he had an early meeting and would not spend the night. Lily, Ben, and Jeremy shared an elevator to their floor. As usual, Ben walked Lily to her door, helped her with her keys, but did not linger.

Lying awake in bed, Lily reviewed the missed opportunities for love and romance: Kylie and Jeremy, Nicolas and Noah, Sierra and Mr. High Value Man, and her and Ben. There wasn't much she could do to help the others. She had high hopes for Noah and Nicolas. Jeremy and Kylie had a shot. Sierra had to get her priorities straight, but she was young, she had time. Honestly, they all had the luxury of time to figure things out—the one thing she and Ben were in short supply of.

They'd wrap the podcast by the end of August, and Ben would have to pivot and prepare for the fall semester. She'd have to pivot, too. She wasn't licensed to practice in Florida, and her best chance at getting a new job was in New York. However, her leaving didn't spell the end. She wasn't one of his spring break girls, the ones who left without a backward glance. She had frequent flyer miles and a gold American Express card. Long-distance relationships sucked, but for Ben, she would finally sign up for TSA PreCheck and fly the friendly skies. Did he doubt it? She had to tell him.

Next thing, Lily was kicking back her sheets, feeling her way to her door in the dark, and marching across the hall. She wondered what time it was. No matter, Ben was likely at his desk, reading or revising some piece of brilliant writing. She raised a hand to knock and froze. *Bad idea. Go back to bed. Tell him in the morning.* Tell him what, though? Announce that she was ready to continue their relationship long distance, a relationship that they hadn't even started? He'd think she was losing her mind. Worse, he'd think she was desperate. Or maybe he'd start to wonder what she brought to the table. *Bad, bad idea.*

Lily backed away from Ben's door, took the elevator to the tenth floor and knocked on Noah's door instead. He opened without first asking who might be stopping by this late. "Lily," he said, "welcome to the after-party."

Noah wasn't alone. Kylie was curled up on an ottoman, stuffing her mouth with the last of the brownies.

"There's an after-party and no one invited me?"

"The real ones know to come by," Noah said.

She moved past him and flopped onto an ottoman next to Kylie. Noah kicked shut the door, splashed the last of the champagne into a glass, and handed it over. "For you."

"What are you guys talking about?" Lily asked.

"The Dow Jones," Kylie said flatly. "What do you think we're talking about?"

"Just asking," Lily said. "Don't get testy. Catch me up to speed."

"First, tell me what you and Nicolas were talking about," Noah said. "It looked intense."

Lily sipped champagne and nestled deeper into the cushion of the ottoman. "It was intense," she said. "Sorry. I can't betray his confidence."

"Oh, don't give us that crap," Kylie cried.

"Your loyalty is to us," Noah said.

"Just kidding, kids," Lily said. "I didn't sign an NDA."

Noah sat on the rug at her feet, eager and ready.

"What I gathered from our short and brief conversation," Lily said, "is that Nicolas is ready to settle down. He prioritizes compatibility above all."

That was enough sharing without getting into the weeds of it.

"I knew it," Noah said. "He's looking for his husband."

"And you're not," Kylie concluded. "Case closed."

"But he's such a great guy!" Lily pleaded.

Noah didn't care. "All the men my age want is to settle down. What's with that?"

"Get yourself a sugar daddy," Kylie suggested. "They have zero interest settling down and give the nicest gifts."

"You should tell him how you feel," Lily said.

"Why should I have to tell him?" Noah asked. "He's a smart man. He should have figured it out by now."

"You're smart, too!" Lily volleyed back. "Use your words."

"No one wants to have fun anymore," Noah mumbled.

"I sure don't," Kylie said. "Fun is overrated. I want what Ben and Lily have."

"But do *they* want what they have?" Noah asked. "That's the question."

The question landed like a dagger in Lily's chest.

"Ben does," Kylie said. "I've seen how he looks at her. But you can't blame the man for being cautious. Remember Belle? Or was it Bella? That was a clusterfuck."

"It's Bella," Lily said, her throat tight.

"Right . . . Anyway, I caught her crying in the elevator one morning like . . . two weeks ago, maybe? So sad."

Lily sunk even deeper into the ottoman, wishing the cushion would swallow her up. She was willing to bet all the money she'd invested in the Dow that Bella had cried in the elevator after catching Lily in her ex's bed, wearing her silk robe.

Noah dismissed this. "Lily is tougher than that. She can handle herself."

Lily wasn't so sure. Whether Ben had wanted to or not, he had pulled her into his electric storm. She'd been quivering with mixed emotions ever since. One minute, she wanted to move into his apartment, and the next, she wanted to run away and shield her heart. At the end of the day, she wanted what Kylie perceived they had, without all the back-and-forth and the red flags she could not bring herself to ignore.

YouTube
Prof. Ben Romero on Endings
850K VIEWS—2 YEARS AGO
[An Excerpt]

Professor Romero writes *Breakfast at Tiffany's* on a whiteboard and drops the marker on the desk.

Prof. Romero: A great American classic. Let's get into it.

A hand shoots up.

Prof. Romero: Yes, Mike?

Mike: Do you moonlight as a bartender? Because a friend of mine said—

Prof. Romero: Not going there, Mike!

Mike: If you do tend bar, let us know. We'll roll through for extra credit.

[Laughter]

Romero rolls up his sleeves and waits for the class to settle down. When quiet settles, he launches into the lecture.

Prof. Romero: Holly Golightly is a comical name: the author chose it carefully. It rings false. A made-up name, but only in part. Lula Mae Barnes married Doc Golightly, which lends some legitimacy to it. *Holly* is the mask Lula Mae wears to forge her way into the city to carve a new life, and it's so fitting. Give me some examples of names of fictional characters that provide some insight of their true nature. There are no wrong answers.

Beverly: Huck Finn! A bighearted country boy, but simple.

Prof. Romero: Good. Anyone else?

Dan: Scarlett O'Hara. She's a firecracker.

Prof. Romero: Agreed. How about you, Mike?

Mike: Cleopatra, a queen. Regal and commanding.

Beverly: Cleopatra is *not* a fictional character.

Prof. Romero: I'd argue that Cleopatra as portrayed in films is absolutely fictional.

Mike: Quick question. Holly Golightly is a hooker. Right?

Beverly: A hooker? Really?

Mike: Yeah . . . For lack of a better term.

Prof. Romero: I promise you there's no lack of better terms. Look into it.

Beverly: She was an escort. There's no shame in it. New York City rent is outrageously high, then *and* now.

Dan: She's a pathological liar. All she does is make up stuff.

Prof. Romero: Holly fled her hometown and escaped a bad marriage. Her creative thinking—what you call *lying*—is a coping mechanism. She makes up her reality as she goes.

Dan: Creative thinking . . . Okay.

Prof. Romero: The novella is a tale of a complicated friendship. A writer becomes infatuated with his eccentric neighbor. The film adaptation gives us a love story. The writer *falls in love* with his eccentric neighbor, and they live happily ever after. Which brings us to today's topic: endings. Let's discuss Hollywood's need to manipulate even the best-crafted stories to tack on a happy ending. Would the film have been less successful without it?

Beverly: If the man is straight, then they have to fall in love, and if they fall in love, it has to work out. I don't make the rules. That's just how it goes.

Prof. Romero: You're right to point out the film's inherent homophobia. They erased the gay character to make the story more palatable to the average moviegoer. The gay writer is clean-cut and straight. In the original story, the friendship doesn't fare well. Holly takes off for Brazil, alone. She even abandons her cat. The writer will spend the rest of his life wondering about her.

Mike: I'm no romantic, but how is that satisfying?

Prof. Romero: That's one take. You've all read the book, and you've watched the movie. Show of hands, who prefers the Hollywood ending? Nearly all of you! Interesting. Let's hear your arguments.

Dan: Are we overthinking this? The movie is a classic for a reason.

Prof. Romero: The novella is no less a classic.

Mike: The book is a bummer. Hollywood was right to tweak it. Everyone knows Capote's best work is *In Cold Blood*.

Beverly: It's hard to begrudge the filmmakers. They gave us Audrey Hepburn in Givenchy gowns and "Moon River" on acoustic guitar.

Prof. Romero: Endings are just as important as beginnings. The movie is more accessible, presents crowd-pleasing tropes, a performance of a lifetime by a legendary actress, and a song that still pulls at our heartstrings today. However, it's worth considering the original ending presented by the author. Capote created a young woman who escaped her small town, only to get chewed up and spit out by the big city. The film is not superior to the book, and the book is not inferior to the film. If you gut the nature of the characters, what is there to compare? As a translator, I prefer a faithful adaptation. Striving for a happy ending at every turn is the best way to get lost. Endings matter just as much as beginnings. And when you write your stories, take a moment to consider all the other possible endings that are not so happy, not so bright, but inherently human.

COMMENTS:

@CBM011000: Bravo!!! Well said! I couldn't agree more!

@AisforAllison: Teaching grad school is no different than teaching grade school. Those questions! LMAO

@Barbara.Myers: If he were my professor, I'd forget my own name.

Chapter Twenty-Four

@Swimwithsierra: Celebrating my independence with Ben & Lily's latest selection: Boss Babe by Gloria Hernandez. Happy 4th! x

As Kylie had predicted, they'd all gathered at the roof to get drunk and watch fireworks. Only Ben was behind the bar and warned he had no problem cutting them off. Sierra joined them this time. With a red, white, and blue popsicle in one hand and a copy of *Boss Babe* in another, and Jeremy acting as cameraman, Sierra captured content before calling it a day.

"Who's actually reading this?" she asked. "Is it any good?"

Ever the champion of literacy, Ben asked, "Why not read it and find out?"

"I'm a busy girl, Ben!"

Ben shook his head and left to serve a group of guys who'd stepped up to the bar. It was a busy evening; people arrived in droves. Their little crew had come early to secure the best seats at the bar and keep Ben company. He'd volunteered to take the shift so that Roxanna could take the baby to a picnic.

"If it's spicy, I'll grab the audiobook for my next flight," Sierra said.

"It won't disappoint," Lily assured her.

"I'm not in it for the spice," Kylie said, sipping on an all-American Jack and Coke. "I'm legit reading these books for relationship tips. Maybe I should date women, because the open and honest communication just blew me away."

"If I dated a woman, all I'd do is raid her closet and use her bath bombs," Sierra said.

"Me, too," Noah admitted. He was drinking champagne, having pledged allegiance to France's tricolor flag.

Sadly, Lily had been boy crazy since the age of thirteen. And yet her most intimate and intense relationships had been with the girls her age. As an adult she found most men, excluding Ben, two-dimensional and boring.

"Do you think it's a woman thing? Or just a sign of a healthy relationship?" Jeremy asked. A true American, he sipped from a longneck.

"What would you know about healthy relationships?" Kylie asked him.

"I know you've got to *talk* to one another," he replied. "I wasn't born yesterday."

"Turn over your driver's license," Kylie said. "I'd like to make sure."

Jeremy hid a smile with another swig of beer.

"I'm decentering men," Sierra declared. "Clearing the roster."

"Don't go crazy," Noah said.

"It's not worth it," Sierra said. "They're a waste of my time."

"It's life," Lily said. The only nod to the holiday was a tiny American flag in her porn star martini. "Nothing is wasted."

"Oh, Lily," Noah said with a hint of pity. "Keep dreaming." He slipped off his sunglasses as the sun had begun to set. The city dripped in gold.

Sierra flagged Ben and had them gather for a group selfie, taking advantage of golden hour. Within seconds, she'd posted the photo to her social media accounts with the caption *Book Club* 🫶.

Lily's heart throbbed with joy, particularly after Ben brought her an order of cheese fries without her even asking. Still, she chastised the group. "Why can't we get together for a proper book club meeting *away* from the bar?"

"No time for that," Noah said. "We've got hearts to break."

"Maybe when I get back from the Maldives," Sierra said. "But that's a big maybe. There's another trip on the horizon."

"We hardly have time to read the books, let alone block out hours to discuss them," Kylie said. "You get what you get. Just be grateful we meet at all."

"But how can we call ourselves a book club if we never meet?" Lily protested.

"Because this is America, and we're free!" Sierra cried.

Everyone laughed, and they ordered more fries and mini hotdogs. Lily watched the sun set. Later she stole time alone with Ben on his break. When the fireworks lit the sky, she closed her eyes. *You get what you get.* She was grateful for this.

Pop Shop
A Pop Culture Podcast
Category: Arts
Rating: 4.1 stars

July 5: *Boss Babe* by Gloria Hernandez
with Lily Lyon and Ben Romero

Miami Beach friends and neighbors Lily and Ben take us on a summer reading spree with romance book recommendations and in-depth discussions on the ways popular tropes play out in the real world.

Lily: Hope everyone had a happy Fourth! This week's selection, *Boss Babe* by Gloria Hernandez, is set in L.A. and features the music industry. It's a love story between a studio executive and a newly signed recording artist. Usually, this sets the stage for a mess of misogyny, but this is a sapphic romance. Pasha, thirty-two, is the young executive, and Monica, a.k.a. Money, twenty-six, is a successful indie artist, new to the label and the object of Pasha's desires. As usual, our full reviews are available on BookTap. Here, we're discussing the tropes. I'd like to begin by saying what a refreshing read! This romance between two smart, ambitious, and business-savvy women is a master class on honest communication. Our book club agreed: men could never!

Ben: Why do you do that?

Lily: Do what?

Ben: Put me in the awkward and unenviable position of defending all men.

Lily: That was not my intention. However, since you've assumed the position, you may as well give it a whirl.

Ben: It's not fair to compare a straight relationship to a queer one. Straight men can't express emotions. It's been studied.

Lily: And where can I find these peer-reviewed studies? *The New England Journal of B.S.?*

Ben: Society raised boys to be stoic, hide signs of weakness, build muscle like armor, and express aggression, not affection. Who raises these boys if not women? Most dads check out and are only ever around for the family photo—you know that.

Lily: [Gasps] Are you saying it's our fault that men are emotionally stunted?

Ben: Our mothers' fault, yours and mine, and every other mother all the way up the family tree to the top branches of the matriarchy.

Lily: *Like father, like son . . . Boys will be boys . . .* Do any of these expressions ring a bell?

Ben: Only in that they're often muttered by women. You've reached for them more than once.

Lily: Just wait until we get out of here! I'll show you who the superior sex is!

Ben: No need. I'll happily fall on my sword and admit that women are superior communicators. They're superior in every way. I'm only kidding. You know I love to wind you up.

Lily: I bet . . . How did we stray so far from the point? And what was the point? I'm drawing a blank.

Ben: *Boss Babe,* a refreshing romance that did not rely on the miscommunication trope. Film critic Roger Ebert spoke of the Idiot Plot. I hate it when the issue between the couple could have been quickly resolved if only they weren't acting like idiots.

Lily: It happens more often than I'm comfortable sharing here. The couple faces an imaginary obstacle, a perceived slight, a miscommunication that breeds mistrust. They act like idiots all the way through, and if they'd only aired their feelings, the whole matter would have been resolved.

Ben: That would be one short novel. Let's talk about what we liked about this book.

Lily: I like very much that the story isn't based on fear.

Ben: Explain.

Lily: The fear of loving again, getting hurt again, the fear of intimacy, the ever-irrational fear of commitment. Those types of fears. In real life, it makes perfect sense. I'm afraid of making yet another mistake. Such a waste of time. In fiction, it's redundant. Do you agree?

Ben: I agree. I'm afraid of hurting someone, inflicting pain.

Lily: That's serious.

Ben: We've talked about this. Don't you remember?

Lily: Yes, but tell me more.

Ben: Not with this mic in my face.

Lily: Go on! Dave can edit it out.

Ben: Dave could never edit it out of his mind. He'd never look at me the same way.

Lily: Fine. We'll keep it moving.

Ben: Thank you.

Lily: Back to our discussion. I don't want our listeners to think that this book is about two women just sitting around talking about feelings. It's fast-paced and spicy. To recap, Monica has just signed with a major label. At the same time, Pasha was recently hired to turn said label around. It's post #MeToo, and the company is seeking to rebrand after a series of misconduct allegations. Pasha and Monica have instant chemistry, but hooking up could cost them both their careers.

Ben: Funny how they relied on a woman exec to clean up the messes of the male execs.

Lily: It's called a glass cliff. Replacing a man with a woman so she can take the fall is classic. Her tenure will be short. It's only a matter of time until she's replaced with yet another man.

Ben: With so much at stake, they should walk away.

Lily: I agree, and in real life, they would've pushed past this to focus on their careers.

Ben: This is not real life, so of course they go at it like rabbits.

Lily: We'll leave it at that because we don't want to spoil it for anyone. Also, our time is up.

Ben: I'd like to take a minute to communicate, clearly and openly, that I love spending this time with you.

Lily: Don't think for a minute that you're out of hot water. You're not. As for the rest of you, the links are in the show notes. Let us know what you think. Join us next week when we discuss *Around Midnight* by Charlotte Mitchel.

Ben: See you then.

COMMENTS:

>**@Bradleyyyy:** Is it me, or are these two hotter than loaded dynamite?

>**@AngelWings:** This podcast is my whole personality now.

>**@user880203948:** Mother is mothering! I don't know what that means, but it's fitting in this case.

Chapter Twenty-Five

It was the second-chance wedding of the summer, and Lily couldn't wait. She wore a pale blue chiffon dress so light and breezy the ruffles caught in the coastal breeze. Picked up at a thrift shop, it was perfect for the occasion. Her mother would have approved.

Ben looked handsome in a cream linen suit selected by Roxanna. After the ceremony, there would be cigars and salsa dancing. For now, though, there were mojitos and mini empanadas for the guests filing into the bayside restaurant. Lily and Ben helped themselves to all that was on offer and stepped onto a wraparound terrace. They staked claim to a bar-height table.

"This is home base," Ben said. "If we lose each other, we'll meet here."

"A man with a plan. Love it."

He gave her a tight smile and stuffed an empanada into his mouth. Lily stirred her drink with a custom *Roxy & Ricky* swizzle stick. Was he nervous? she wondered. Or frustrated? This wedding was happening; there was nothing he could do to stop it.

"Are you all right?" she asked.

He did not have a chance to answer. A rowdy gang rushed up to them. "Cuz!" they shouted.

Lily instinctively positioned herself behind Ben, using him as a human shield. They were four in total, and their ages ranged from the late twenties to the midthirties. They all had Ben's coffee-colored hair and dark good looks. And they were all *lit*.

"Where were you?" one demanded. "You missed the tailgate."

"Oh man," Ben said without an iota of regret. "I fucked up."

"Loser! We poured one out for Tio Alberto and you missed it, so fuck you."

Ben draped a protective arm around Lily's shoulders, and said, "These are my cousins, Anita, Jose, Logan, and Sandra. Everyone, this is my Lily."

Lily waved a shy hello. She'd expected to meet his family and wanted very much to make a good impression, but she hadn't expected to meet them like this. Moreover, or more importantly maybe, she hadn't expected Ben to introduce her as *his* Lily.

Anita stepped forward. "I know who you are. I listen to the podcast, and I love it! Congrats!"

"Thanks," Lily said, loosening up.

"I love it, too," Sandra said. "Only I had to hear about it from a coworker. You could have told us you were hosting a podcast with your girlfriend."

"Or you could have told us you had a girlfriend," Logan added.

"I'll put it in the next newsletter."

Jose laughed good-naturedly. "Good one, bro."

"Benito, I love this for you," Anita said with a pat to his cheek. "You've finally found someone, and she's smart and pretty. I think she's the one! Before you roll your eyes, I predicted Roxanna would get back with the devil, and here we are."

"Why not predict the Powerball, instead?" Logan asked. "Something useful for a change."

"Lily, if you marry this brainiac, you're stuck with us," Sandra warned. "I apologize in advance."

"Also, tailgating at weddings and funerals, or any other event, is tradition," Jose said. "Family gatherings are tricky. Say the wrong thing to the wrong person and all hell breaks loose. We like to arrive early and meet up in the parking lot to share intel. Everybody brings a little something. Ben usually brings the tequila, only this time he left us high and dry."

Ben wasn't moved by any of this. "Dry? I doubt it."

"Sorry to break this up, but you're coming with us," Anita said. "Tia Ada has been asking for you." She turned to Lily. "She can't walk far," she explained, "not even with the cane. No matter what we say, she refuses to go to physical therapy. Maybe Ben can talk sense into her. He's the favorite."

Ben turned to Lily, but she took a step back. There would be time enough for her to meet Tia Ada. For now, Ben should catch up with his family. "Go on," she said. "I'm headed to the ladies' room. We'll meet back here."

"We won't be long," Anita promised.

Ben was led away like a prisoner of war. So these are the cousins, she thought. He didn't have siblings. Last year, his mother had moved out of state with a new husband. The cousins were his safety net. They had their own language and traditions, like tailgating at weddings.

Lily entered the event room and took the opportunity to poke around. The wedding venue was a popular seafood restaurant with a panoramic view so stunning it allowed the owners to get away with watered-down drinks and overpriced entrées. At least that's what she'd picked up, eavesdropping on the guests. Everyone seemed to know everyone. As only immediate family on either side was invited, they chatted liberally. There were couples from every stage in life—old ones with decades of history, and young ones just starting out, with or without kids. No wedding was complete without a contingent of single ladies, trooping in and out of the ladies' room. A string quartet played the standards, from Sinatra to Streisand.

An aisle strewn with rose petals led to an altar. Bride and groom would exchange vows under an archway loaded with orchids. Roxanna had gone to great lengths to plan her wedding, and her mother or Tia Ada must have had a hand as well.

Lily's own mother weighed heavily on her mind. They hadn't spoken for weeks. Her father called repeatedly. She and her brother texted often. He'd also rated their podcast five stars and left the briefest of reviews, which meant their reach had extended far beyond South Florida to Virginia, where Patrick lived with his longtime girlfriend, Coco. From her mother, not a word. When Lily called, she did not pick up. Lily knew, via information from Patrick—and personal experience—that she was on the receiving end of the silent treatment, a tactic reserved for only the worst offenses. To her straitlaced mother, a daughter taking off without a goodbye or a word of explanation was outlandish behavior. She might as well have joined a gang. This time Lily wouldn't fold, as she'd often done in the past. She was no longer her mother's little girl to mold and guide through life. If nothing came of her summer hiatus, she'd finally break the spell of her parents' approval. It was a sad thing to admit at her age, but she'd craved it for far too long. Patrick, older and wiser, had warned her before he head off to college. "Those people will take over your life," he said. "Be your own person." Unfortunately, Lily had not known how to do that at thirteen. Being the baby, the only daughter, her father's favorite, and her mother's crown jewel had fed into her personality early on and aggravated her innate people-pleasing tendencies. She hadn't dared risk their disapproval or their disappointment.

But today she missed her mother. Charlize Lyon loved weddings and would have very much appreciated the personalized touches that Roxanna had added to hers, right down to the cups and swizzle sticks that would fill the recycling bin at the end of the night. Only, if her mother had attended this wedding, she would've spent the evening reminding Lily that she'd missed her chance with Darren. Once Charlize learned of Darren's marriage, Lily would never know peace.

Lily got a fresh drink at the bar and returned to home base. Ben joined her moments later. He looked at her as if searching for signs of damage. "Sorry about that," he said. "I should have warned you about my cousins."

"Did you skip the tailgate because of me?" she asked.

"Oh definitely," he said, without missing a beat.

"Why?" she cried. "You think I'm too delicate to pregame? Is that it?"

"That's it, Lily. Bull's-eye."

She gasped. "What do you take me for?"

"For exactly who you are."

"That's not fair. I can pregame with the best of them."

"I was doing you a favor. My cousins are a lot of things, but discreet is not one of them."

"Then, why let them think I'm your girlfriend?"

"Never complain. Never explain."

"Where have I heard that before?"

"It's more fun this way. They assume I'm dating anyone they spot me with. You could've been my landlord or dental hygienist. It wouldn't have mattered. I like to keep them guessing. If you mind, I'll set them straight."

"No," she said. Nothing wrong with a bit of lighthearted fun. "It's fine. I like your cousins."

"That's good to know, because Anita is planning our wedding right now."

"Lovely! Are you going to propose tonight?"

"Not unless you need my help to secure an inheritance of some kind. A marriage of convenience?"

"You got it," she said. No Regency romance would be complete without one. "Anyway, if you do propose, promise you'll do it in a hot-air balloon. It's my dream."

"You can throw the man overboard if you don't like the ring?" he asked.

"I'll supply the ring. My mother has a collection of family heirlooms. Any one of them will do the trick. I just like the drama."

Lily rattled the ice in her cup. The drinks were criminally watered down, even for a lightweight like herself.

"Have you ever been proposed to?" he asked.

The question startled her. "If I had a proposal story, don't you think you'd have heard it by now? I've shared everything else. There are no great secrets left for you to discover. Oh, and by the way, I'm scared of heights. You'll never catch me drifting past the sun in a basket. Propose to me on solid ground."

He laughed. "Is that the hurdle? Logistics?"

"I wonder if marriage is in the cards for me," Lily said. "I'm devoted to my career. Destined to live a life of solitude. That's just how it goes."

"I'm the artist with a sporadic income no sensible woman would ever marry," he said, playing along.

Good thing she wasn't sensible. "Have you ever come close to proposing to anyone?"

He turned away, squinting at the setting sun, then he slipped on dark glasses. Before her eyes, he transformed into the mysterious man of the night they'd first met. What was he hiding? Suddenly, Lily was desperate to know. Ben had a past, great love affairs and failed ones, but had he ever wanted to devote his life to another person? If the answer was *yes*, it would devastate her. There would be no hiding it. She might take off running to the far end of the terrace, gasping for air. Like Sierra, she might howl in frustration into the void. She wasn't a competitive person, but this time she wanted to be first.

His answer was blunt. "No."

"Oh, thank God!"

"Thank God? What do you mean by that?" he asked, laughing again.

"I'd feel bad for that poor woman, that's all," she said jokingly to better hide the truth. "Marrying a regular guy is hard enough, let alone an artist and certified genius."

"I don't think I'll ever marry," he said.

"Why?"

"I'd take it seriously," he said.

"You'd be the only one ever," she teased. All at once, she recalled the conversation they'd had the night he'd showed her his father's journals. "Does this have anything to do with your father?"

A tic pulled at his jaw. "I swear I've never had to talk about the man as much as I've had to since he died, and I'm sick of it."

"It's a blow you can't ignore," Lily said. "The feelings won't magically go away. If you push them down, their roots will grow deeper. You should talk to someone, and it might as well be me. You've helped me so much this summer, you have no idea. I want to help you, too."

"Lily," he said, lightly tracing the knuckles of her hand, "why are you so easy to be with?"

"Easy?" she choked out. "Wait until I bombard you with free and unsolicited advice. You'll be sick of me soon."

"I don't think I could ever be sick of you. I don't think that's possible," he said. "Which is why I want to protect this."

Her throat tightened. Ben's father was the flaky artist no sensible woman ought to marry. Ben was the hero with the heart of gold.

"Tell me," she said. "Why has your father turned you off marriage?"

Ben went on running a finger along the back of her hand, following the patterns of her veins. "He married three or four times," he began. "It's an approximate guess because one of those wives might've just been a live-in girlfriend. She wasn't quite divorced, at least that's what the research shows. In one of his many obituaries, he's described as a *ladies' man*, feeding into the Latin lover nonsense. What they don't realize is that he married for money. Poets are poor. Unless they're born rich or marry rich, they're poor. There's no way around it. No prize money will keep you living at the Biltmore Hotel, which he did for a time. He seduced aging heiresses, widows, and not-quite-divorced women who funded his lifestyle. He might have loved my mother, but she had nothing to offer. They were never married. He abandoned her for wife number four. The free ride ended when he got old and sick. He died penniless."

"Your father was quite a character."

"He was."

"Are you researching his life for a project? A memoir or biography?"

"Maybe."

"It would make for an interesting project, you know, for the grant. People are fascinated with him and would welcome your perspective."

"Maybe," he repeated.

"Just one thing, though," she said. "The whole Latin lover thing, it's not nonsense."

"You're right," he said. "It's a stereotype."

"Even stereotypes have a kernel of truth."

He smirked. "Oh, yeah? You know this from experience?"

"Let's say I'm researching the topic."

"Tell me more."

"Ben! There you are! I've been looking for you."

The man making his way to their table was the groom, no doubt about it. *The runaway groom.* Looking clean-shaven and well-groomed, wearing a stark-white linen suit with a purple orchid pinned to his lapel, and taking long, nervous strides. He was bald, tan, and of muscular build, the type who frequented the gym, not the cozy local bookstores.

"Rick," Ben said in greeting. "Big day for you. Congratulations."

"Thanks, man. That means a lot."

"This is my date, Lily," Ben said. "Lily, this is Ricardo Perez, Roxanna's husband—shortly."

"Thanks for having me," she replied, "and congratulations."

"Thanks."

"You said you were looking for me?" Ben asked.

"I was hoping we could talk. I have some things to say . . ."

He hesitated. Did he want her gone? Anticipating her reaction, Ben tightly curled his fingers around her wrist, making it clear that *he* wanted her to stay.

"Your approval means a lot to Roxy," Ricardo said. "You think she's making a mistake, and I don't blame you. It's my fault. I need you to know that I'm gonna do right by Roxy and Oscar. That last time, I wasn't ready. I panicked. I thought I had more time to chase some dreams, hit my goals. But none of that matters now. My family needs me, and I want to do the right thing."

"I appreciate you speaking to me," Ben said calmly. "I want nothing more than to welcome you into the family."

Lily credited herself for this measured response. If Ben didn't have such a tight grip on her arm, she would've patted herself on the back.

"Thanks, man!" Ricardo beamed.

"Only, if you ever *panic* again, and your first instinct is to run and abandon Roxy and Oscar, don't."

Ben's tone was almost threatening . . .

Oh damn. Lily averted her eyes and buried her nose in her cup. She slurped down the watery rum, mint, and sugar concoction that passed for a mojito.

Ricardo nodded. "I deserve that," he said. "And don't worry, I won't."

"Good to hear," Ben said. "And again, congrats."

Ricardo turned to Lily. "Roxanna asked me to come back with you, if that's okay."

"Are you sure she asked for me?" Lily asked, confused.

"Yes," he replied. "She said, 'If you see Lily out there, bring her back. I need to speak with her.'"

Well, that was clear enough. What wasn't clear was why the groom was conversing with the bride before the wedding. It was bad luck. Why tempt fate? Things were rocky enough.

Ben released his grip on her wrist and brought her hand to his lips. "I'll be waiting here."

She followed Ricardo through the main room and out a sliding glass door to an area of restricted access, the sacred realm of the bridal suite.

Roxanna sat at a vanity table, adding the finishing touches to her bridal look. She looked lovely in a simple ivory slip dress and her dark hair in a sleek bun.

"Lily!" she said. "Thanks for coming. Don't you look pretty!"

"And you look regal, just gorgeous!" Lily replied. "Very Carolyn Bessette-Kennedy."

"That's what I was going for," she said. "You're the only one who understands. My mother wanted a remake of my *quinceañera* gown, lace, lace, and more lace."

"Your mom can't deny you look lovely."

Roxanna slipped on a pair of white tulle gloves. "Have you met Oscar, my son?"

She pointed to a bassinet in the center of the room. Lily approached it, and her heart swelled. A plump baby with rosy cheeks and a tuft of dark hair was fast asleep, sprawled out on his back, arms flung wide.

"He's adorable," she whispered.

"Oh, don't worry," Roxanna said. "That boy can sleep

through a hurricane. I scheduled the ceremony around his nap time so we could have some peace. He gets so fussy now that he's teething. If he does wake up, we hired a babysitter to feed him."

"Good thinking."

"I asked you here because I need a favor."

"Anything you need."

Roxanna had her hands full: a baby, a wedding, a mother who dreamed of lace. It was a lot.

"My friend Bella is a no-show. First she said she was coming late. Now she says she's not coming at all."

Lily stiffened at the mention of Bella, the image of her crying in the elevator fresh in her mind. Of course she would attend the wedding! Was that the real reason Ben had seemed nervous?

"She designed the wedding program. Her job was to distribute them to the guests. Now they're just sitting in a pile by the entrance. Could you grab them and hand them out? It won't take long. We have fifty-some guests in total. Is that okay?"

Lily blinked and tried to find her words.

Roxanna tore her gaze away from her own reflection in the mirror. "Shit," she said. "You know."

Lily nodded. "She's Ben's ex-girlfriend."

"She's his ex-something," Roxanna said. "Not very classy of me to ask Ben's new girlfriend to do the job of his ex. It's been a crazy day. I can't pin down any of my cousins. They're running wild. Besides, I know you'd do a fantastic job. You're a natural."

Lily had no issues playing hostess. She had other concerns. "Why isn't Bella coming?" she asked.

"Obviously she doesn't want to run into Ben. Somehow word got back to her that he's seeing someone new. I don't know who's smuggling information out of the building. Better not be Noah!"

"Don't blame Noah," Lily said. "Bella . . . ran into us once."

"So you are together?"

"No," Lily said firmly. "I'm not trying to blow up my life right now, and Ben isn't interested in starting something new. He's trying to change."

"*Change?* That's hysterical," Roxanna said dryly. "We don't change. We're stubborn. He's feeling guilty. That's all. It'll pass."

Guilty? Lily swayed uneasily. Despite everything, she'd believed in Ben's innocence. What exactly had gone down between him and Bella? She was done tap dancing around the question. She had to know.

"Listen up." Roxanna reached for her pair of sparkly earrings and clipped them on. "I'm in a rush, so I'll make this brief. *Something* is going on between you two. I clocked it right away. Because of the Bella situation, I tried to intervene. I was wrong. I can admit I was wrong. Ben and Bella, as cute as that sounds, were a car crash waiting to happen. It was painful to watch. The friend group will never be the same and—"

"Honestly, you don't owe me an explanation," Lily interrupted. She wanted to hear it from Ben. "It's your day and—"

"You're right! It's *my* day, and I'm going to speak my mind."

Chastised, Lily sank into the nearest chair. "All right."

"Bella was in love with Ben for years. Instead of just telling him how she felt, she sold him a friends-with-benefits package. When does that ever work? I love the books and all, but life isn't a rom-com. Anyway, Ben was smart enough to know better. Even if he wasn't, I *told* him everything he needed to know. It could only end badly. Did he listen? No. Now here we are." Roxanna let out a long, weary sigh. "Nobody listens."

"I'm listening," Lily said softly.

"Good," she said. "Because you two might be the real deal. You speak the same language. Arguing over books is like catnip to Ben. Why do you think I picked up reading? It was so as kids we could be closer. Honestly, I love to see it. It's high time everyone moved on, and he deserves to be happy. So please, forget what I said that first night. New York is just a plane ride away or a twenty-four-hour drive. You can make it work. I'm marrying Ricky despite everything. I may regret it, but I've got to take a chance. So do you."

"It's not the same. You've got Oscar to think about," Lily said, desperate to erase any parallels between her situation and Roxanna's. "You have his best interests in mind."

Roxanna turned to stare at the sleeping child. "Right," she said, voice shaky. "I only want the best for him."

"All I want is to make it out of Miami in one piece," Lily said. Her voice was shaky, too. "Anyway. I should get out there. Those programs won't distribute themselves!"

Lily never made it back to home base. She seamlessly stepped into Ben's ex-something's role, handing out a booklet of Bella's design. It featured photos of Rick and Roxy over the years, a love poem, and an outline of the evening's main events—the ceremony, cocktail hour, dinner, and dancing. She offered the booklet to uninterested guests, all while mulling over the concept of the leap of faith. Previously, her love life was the only arena in which she'd attempted it. After each leap, she'd landed on her face. But what was the decision to quit her job or to stay in Miami, if not leaps into the unknown? They'd paid off, too. She'd made friends, started a book club, and was now cohosting a podcast.

"What has Roxy roped you into?" Ben approached from nowhere, catching her off guard.

"She needed an extra set of hands. Someone didn't show up, and these booklets were just sitting here, and no one really wants them, and—"

"She asked you to fill in for Bella?"

Lily wasn't going to mention Bella, but since he had . . . "Why didn't you mention she'd be here?"

"She isn't here. Is she?"

"Don't be cute."

"Lily, we don't talk," he said. "But I didn't think she'd skip the wedding. So yeah, I expected she'd be here."

"You should have warned me," Lily retorted. "The last time I saw her, I was wearing *her* robe in *your* bed."

Ben winced, as if the memory still burned.

She handed a booklet to a guest. The older man raised a copy she'd given him moments earlier and declined. Frustrated, she turned back to Ben. "I have questions."

"Do we have to get into it here?" he asked.

"Yes, here." She handed a booklet to a newcomer. "Did you know she was in love with you for years?"

He didn't answer.

"If you knew how she felt and bought into her friends-with-benefits package deal anyway, that kind of makes you an asshole."

Ben joined his hands behind his back. "You've been talking to Roxanna."

"Yes. And?" Lily handed the last of the booklets to the single ladies.

"Okay," Ben said. "And you're done with booklets."

He tried leading her back to home base. She wouldn't let him. According to the program, the ceremony would start soon. He ought to join Roxanna. "Get ready for the main event. We'll talk later."

"We'll talk now," he insisted. "If you think I'm an asshole, we need to clear that up."

She dragged him to a quiet corner. "Talk."

"Bella was one of my closest friends," he said. "I've known her my whole life. We went to school together, hung out, and played video games on weekends. She approved every one of my crushes. To answer your question, I did not know she was in love with me. I should have, but I didn't. I thought she was hung up on her ex. On my end, one thing led to another. We didn't have dates on New Year's Eve and made plans to hang out, like old times. We got drunk and messed around. I knew it was a bad idea, but I shrugged it off. It was the holidays . . . Why not have some fun?"

Lily's heart tanked. Hadn't she done the same? Used "summer" as an excuse to abandon good sense and dive into the deep end?

"Roxanna says I should have known better, and she's right," Ben continued. "This is no excuse, but my father had started messaging me from his death bed around Christmas. I was conflicted. So, what do I do? I act like him, a selfish prick, and hurt someone close." Ben halted, took a breath, and pushed on.

"Bella ended it when she realized I could not love her back, not like she wanted. It just wasn't there. Now she won't speak to me or even risk being in the same room as me. I fucked up and lost a friend."

Clearly, the breakup had devastated all parties involved. There were no villains, no one to point an accusing finger at. Trying to package it in a neat story was misguided and harmful.

Lily straightened his lapel. He shouldn't look so distraught before his big moment. "There," she said. "Better."

Once again, Ricky came around looking for him. "Hey, man," he said. "It's showtime."

"Good luck," Lily whispered.

With a long look, he left her to escort Roxanna down the aisle.

Chapter Twenty-Six

Lily joined the cousins. They introduced her to their spouses and significant others. Only Logan was single because, according to Sandra, he was an unrepentant fuckboy.

The officiant stood waiting at the end of the aisle. In an emerald-green gown that revealed a colorful tattoo sleeve, she was cooler than Lily expected. Then she noted the chestnut hair and creamy complexion and recalled that Bella was Roxanna's best friend's sister. Though Bella wasn't present, she was everywhere. When the woman she supposed was Bella's sister waved from the altar and blew kisses to the cousins, Lily gained a greater understanding at how tightly knit the friend group truly was. For all her love of romance, she valued friendship more. While she could live to the ripe age of one hundred and gladly never see her exes again, losing a friend was a terrible blow.

The time for chitchat ended as the lights dimmed. The string quartet then launched into Wagner's "Bridal Chorus." Lily's heart rate raced when she caught sight of Ben, the bride as regal as a swan at his arm. He'd seemingly brushed his hair and added an orchid to his lapel. He'd never looked more handsome. With a sure stride, he escorted Roxanna down the aisle. It was as if the person he cared for most in the world wasn't about to promise to love, honor, and cherish a man he only had contempt for. No one would ever suspect that he'd opposed the union or entertained any misgivings whatsoever. Roxanna, however, was another story. She glided down the aisle with a smile pasted to her face, gaze fixed on her groom. Why were her eyes, always so vivacious, so dull with worry? Was it garden-variety wedding jitters or something more complicated?

Ben led her to Ricky and joined Tia Ada in the front row. The officiant swept away tears and started things off with a few pre-scripted anecdotes. After a reading or two, it was time for the vows. The couple had written them, and Roxanna would read hers first. She produced a sheet of paper folded down to a square. When she was ready, she cleared her throat. Her eyes skimmed over the handwritten words. "Ricky," she began. Again, that shaky voice. "I have loved you from the start." A pause. "Today, I marry my best friend." A longer pause. "You make me so proud to—Sorry! I can't do this!"

Lily gasped, but no louder than Sandra and Anita or even Jose. They watched Ricardo swoon as though sucker punched. For all his bulk, he couldn't take a blow. Lily was light-headed herself. Earlier, Roxanna had seemed so sure of her decision. What happened to taking a leap of faith and all of that?

"What do you mean you can't do this?" the groom stammered. "What's wrong? Are you feeling all right?"

"There's nothing wrong with me," Roxanna replied. "I've been doing the right thing all along. *You're* in the wrong!"

"Roxy . . . We talked. We worked it out."

"Did we? Everyone thinks we're making a mistake."

"No one thinks that!" Ricardo swept his gaze around the room, trying to rally support.

"Benito does," Roxanna said stubbornly. "He's the smartest person I know!"

From her seat several rows back, Lily watched Ben lower his head and pinch the bridge of his nose.

"I spoke with him earlier," Ricardo said. "He's on board. He welcomed me to the family."

"*I'm* not on board!" Roxanna cried. "Here I am, cosplaying as Carolyn Bessette-Kennedy, looking like a fool! I love you and forgive you, but our baby boy won't be so understanding. I know firsthand how devastating it is when a father neglects their son. If we get married today, so help me God, you better swear that you're ready to be a husband *and* a father."

Following Roxanna's outburst, the fifty or so guests held their breaths, and silence prevailed. Lily's gaze drilled into the back of Ben's head. His neck was rigid and his shoulders straight, despite the weight that had been dropped on him. He was the neglected son. The confident Ben Romero of today had once been a brokenhearted boy, devastated by a narcissist of a father.

Ricky stunned the room by grabbing Roxanna's shoulders and kissing her full on the mouth. "I do!" he said fervently. "I love you, and more than anything, I want us to be a family."

"You swear?"

"With all my heart," he said.

Roxanna brightened. "Okay. That's all I needed to hear."

"Sounds good!" Bella's sister cried. Before they changed their minds, she pronounced Roxanna and Ricardo husband and wife. Everyone hopped to their feet and cheered, giddy with joy but mostly relief. The newlyweds were oblivious to all this. Ricky was as pumped as any gym bro could be on such a momentous occasion. Roxanna beamed: all signs of worry were gone. They were ready to fling into their future.

"What does Carolyn Bessette-Kennedy have to do with any of this?" Logan asked the others.

"Never mind, buddy," Anita said. "Never mind."

"That was intense! How are you feeling?" Lily asked Ben the moment she got him alone. Everyone had migrated to a lower-level dining room for cocktails and dinner. They sat together in the deserted front row. A crew was dismantling the arch.

"I should have tailgated with the others," he said. "They might've warned me a storm was brewing. I wasn't prepared."

"They were just as surprised as anyone, trust me," Lily said. "Jose came close to having a heart attack."

He laughed a weary little laugh. "Was I wrong for inviting you today, knowing what I know about my family?"

She slapped his arm. "Never! I read books for this type of drama, and nothing ever comes close."

"No, seriously," he said. "Are you okay?"

"I'm fine, Ben. It's you I'm worried about. For a minute there, I thought you might jump in and intervene."

He shook his head. "This is Roxanna's fight."

"I think she handled it well," Lily said. "And I think you're amazing."

He dropped a hand on her knee and squeezed. "I'm starving. I could eat anything."

"Your choices are shrimp scampi or slow-roasted pork," she said. "It's in the program, if you'd taken the time to read it."

"Aren't you a fountain of useful information?" He stood and pulled her to her feet. "I'm taking you everywhere I go from this point on."

Ben did not let her stray far after that. He held her hand under the dinner table and only released it to reach for her waist on the dance floor. From Streisand to Celia Cruz, the tempo had picked up quite a lot. Ben was an excellent dancer, and the frilly dress she'd picked for the occasion redeemed itself nicely with each spin. When the DJ paused for a string of shout-outs, he guided her to the bar and ordered two waters.

"I'm cutting you off," he said.

"You can't cut me off!" she protested, laughing sloppily. "This isn't the rooftop bar. You're not the boss here."

He handed her a cup. "Drink your water."

The water was refreshing. Honestly, the endless flow of mojitos plus the champagne at dinner had caught up with her. "Thanks," she said, with a pinch of resentment. "I needed this."

"Oh, I know."

"Want to hear something ridiculous?" she asked.

"Always," he said.

"I lied to you earlier."

He cocked his head. Whatever product had kept his hair slicked back had given up, letting his curls loose. "Why would you lie to me?" he asked. "I don't judge, and there's nothing I haven't heard."

"I was embarrassed," she admitted.

"What about?"

"Earlier, when we were talking proposals . . . I was worried you might have proposed to someone in the past."

He fought back a smile. "That was an unnecessary worry, I can tell you that much."

Somehow, they'd made it out to the terrace. Home base had been taken over by the single ladies, so they moved to the edge. The views were endless, the dark water stitching seamlessly into the night sky. The breeze cleared her head more efficiently than a couple sips of water ever could. They were down to one cup, anyway, and they passed it back and forth.

"It was loud in there," he said. "Now, tell me again how jealous you were. I love to hear it."

"Get over yourself. It's not that serious," Lily said, regaining her communication skills. "I just think a Ben Romero proposal would be extra romantic with poetry and harp music."

"Honestly, I'd just write a note and tape it to her door."

Lily swooned. The woman who came home to that note was the luckiest woman alive.

Exhausted from the dancing, she leaned against his chest.

He wrapped an arm around her shoulder and drew her even closer. "My people put you through a lot today," he mumbled into her hair.

"Your people are great," she muttered.

After a beat, he said, "I find it hard to believe you were never proposed to."

She looked up at him. "Why?"

"I don't know," he said.

"Does it have anything to do with my beauty, wit, and stunning intellect?" she asked.

Ben laughed into the night. "You're the whole package."

"I came close to a proposal," she admitted, quietly. "It fell through. It's my own fault. I was quick and cut him off at the pass."

Ben pulled away and stared at her in disbelief. "The secrets are coming out!" he said. "A little white rum is all it takes."

"It happened so long ago. I was twenty. It's not technically a secret anymore. The statute of limitations has expired."

And yet, Lily thought, the story had been too painful to ever share.

Ben leaned against the rail. "You know the rules. Tell me everything. Start from the beginning. Don't leave out a single detail."

"His name is Darren, and he was my first love," she insisted. "We dated through college. Senior year, it was clear our lives were taking us in different directions. I got accepted into law school in the city. He had a whole life set up in the Midwest. It was my mother's idea for us to get married—a graduation wedding. Can you imagine? She loved Darren. Once a month, he'd come over for Sunday dinner. It's a big deal at my house. My mother makes creole rice and shrimp creole and any other creole dish she can think of. My father plays Caribbean music and drinks dark rum. Essentially, it's nostalgia night."

"Sounds nice," Ben said tightly.

"It *is* nice." Lily took another sip of water. "Darren is as American as it gets. He has his own traditions, yet he very much enjoyed ours. That's rare. You're from the corner of the Caribbean where everything is sultry and exotic. Everyone wants a part of it. Mine is a hard sell even for the most open-minded people. Growing up, I got teased for simply liking my mother's cooking, her rice and beans, her spicy concoctions. I had to vet the kids I brought home."

Ben nodded, encouraging her to go on.

"My mom thought he'd make the ideal son-in-law. Never mind that we were so young, our whole lives ahead of us, and not at all ready to settle down. I didn't want to be anyone's wife. My mother was coming from a wholesome place. Darren was a good guy, but I was sure I'd find another in time. The joke was on me, of course. After we split, I chased one wild rabbit after another. Where did that land me?"

"Here," Ben said, in a soft voice. "With me."

Lily scoffed. "You're the wildest rabbit of them all, Ben."

"In this analogy, I'm the tortoise, not the hare."

"You're a unicorn, compared to some of the guys I've dated."

Ben was somewhat a unicorn: smart, sexy, self-aware, humble, and clever.

"I'm not such a good guy," he said.

"You're good to me," Lily said. "Isn't that all that matters in the end?"

"I'm not so sure," he said. "Let's ask your mother."

"Let's leave Mom out of this."

"Okay," he said. "I think you deserve someone who will make all your dreams come true."

"What do you think I'm dreaming about?"

"A rich husband, a house in the suburbs, a couple of kids, a vice presidency or partnership at a company or firm, and all the iced coffee your heart desires."

"You're not too far off the mark," she conceded. "Except

for the rich husband. I'm comfortable, and I'll probably inherit some money on my mother's side. If you haven't guessed it, my family is well-off."

"Which is why I didn't take you tailgating."

"That's not fair," she shot back. "I'm not a snob. Do I look like a snob to you?"

"You may not be one, but you do look it."

"Ben!"

"Don't you remember that first night at the bar? You and your money clip?"

Lily shuddered at the memory. "Wearing cashmere."

"Was it cashmere?" he said. "I'm not surprised."

"What do you dream about?" she asked. "Since my dreams are so vanilla, let's hear yours."

"I'd like to get out of my rental and buy a place, something similar, maybe even in the building. I like the neighborhood. I can see myself staying there a while. I'd like a residency in Europe at some point, a year or two at a university. I wouldn't stay longer than that. I don't want to miss out on Oscar growing up. I want a kid of my own, no more than one, but I'd have to do it right. If the pressure to do it right is too much, I might not do it at all. I want to publish all my life. It's what I love. When I'm gone, I want students everywhere to curse my name when forced to write critical essays of my work. That will be my gift to the world."

Lily had never heard anyone articulate future ambition and dreams in such a nuanced way. What was the house on a cul-de-sac and a vice presidency compared to a life full of books, study, and travel? Instead of the standard 2.2 kids, one exceptional child who would be loved beyond measure.

"You are a gift to me," she said.

"And you are a precious thing of rare beauty who arrived dressed in cashmere and turned my life upside down."

If this was how he felt, he'd held his cards close to the chest.

Could it be that she'd tormented him as much as he'd tormented her?

"Are you all right?" he asked.

"Yes." She was swooning, that was all.

He removed his jacket and draped it over her shoulders; then, taking hold of the lapel he pulled her close and kissed her. Lily snaked her arms around his neck and sank into him. The first time she'd kissed him, he was a stranger. The second time, he was a riddle she couldn't solve. This time, she knew him inside and out, his past, present, and a glimpse of his future. It was overwhelming. In the circle of his arms, the coil of mixed emotions sprang free. Tears welled in her eyes, even as happiness swirled inside her, and she couldn't suppress a laugh. Ben drew his head back and looked at her through the veil of his lashes. Moonlight lent a sheen to his dark hair. "That laugh," he whispered. "God, I love it." Lily drew his mouth back to hers. His jacket slipped off her shoulders as he tightened his hold on her and lifted her, barely, a half inch off the ground. He'd literally swept her off her feet. No hot-air balloon could ever take her higher.

"Hey! Sorry to break this up, but they're gonna cut the cake." It was Jose, summoning them with snapping fingers, ruining the perfect moment. "Only Roxy would turn her wedding into a marathon event. I've got work in the morning. Let's wrap this up."

Ben turned on his cousin. "Give us a second, will you?"

As soon as Jose was gone, Ben kissed her again. "It's a good thing I let them believe you're my girlfriend, or I'd have some explaining to do," he said.

She caught his lower lip between her teeth and tugged. "Let's go get cake."

"Or we can just skip it," he suggested.

"Not on your life!"

She took hold of his wrist and dragged him inside to join

the others. A moment later, with a mouth full of French vanilla frosting, she kissed him again.

"We can leave now," he whispered in her ear.

They were standing among the others but in their own little world.

"No way," she whispered back. "I have to catch the bouquet."

"If you catch it, they'll try to marry you off to Logan. It's tradition."

"I'll risk it," she said and fed him another bite of cake. "He's kind of cute!"

"You're cute," he said, leaning close to kiss away frosting at the corner of her mouth. "But you're not marrying Logan."

A while later, when her feet started throbbing, they snagged two free chairs in the back of the room and sat together.

"Want to hear something ridiculous?" he asked.

"Always."

"I'm jealous of Darren."

Lily startled. "Darren?"

"Yes. Darren."

"Careful, he's like *Beetlejuice*. Say his name three times and he'll appear," she cautioned him. "Anyway, he's married. I saw his wedding pictures the night I quit."

"You quit your job for the guy?" Ben cried.

"No! Never!" Lily protested. "I got triggered. I just felt so stuck. That banquet had lasted hours, and I couldn't just sit there anymore."

"You omitted this the first time you told me the story."

"Guilty," she said. "I felt so stupid."

Ben raked his eyes over her. "Anything else you'd like to tell me?"

"Only this. There's no reason to be jealous of Darren."

"Not true," he said. "I'm jealous of the space he holds in your heart."

There was no room for Darren in her heart, not while Ben occupied every square inch. If anything, Darren lingered in the back of her mind, triggering curiosity, but no longing or remorse. At times, she wondered *what if?* However, she did not lie awake at night thinking of Darren. She did not randomly type his name into a search engine just to see what might come up. She did not think of him first thing in the morning, her eyes still shut with sleep.

"Maybe you misunderstood," she said. "My mother was infatuated with him. I was ready to walk away."

"By your own admission, he was your first love," he argued.

"Well, then, by that metric, I'm jealous of Bella. Plus, you had that forbidden-love thing going on. She's a close family friend. You would have done better to walk away, yet you were drawn to each other. I can imagine the longing, the pining, the stolen glances, the drama when it ends, and the families left feuding for generations."

Ben took her dessert plate from her. "That's the sugar talking," he said. "Only you could put such a spin on a grim story."

"Sorry. I didn't mean to make light of it," she said. "That's always been my problem, I think. My story with Darren was so flat, so easygoing, and I wanted more."

"I think that's normal at twenty," Ben said. "You do things for the plot."

At the end of the night, Lily did not catch the bouquet. It bounced off her shoulders and was scooped up by one of the single ladies, which was only fair and proper. On the ride home, with a lap full of custom matches and other souvenirs, the ragtop down, and the muggy night air teasing her hair, she admitted to Ben that she'd never had more fun at a wedding in her life.

"Wait till you attend a funeral," he said. "You won't recover."

"So morbid!" Lily scoffed. Then she closed her eyes, hopeful.

Chapter Twenty-Seven

The Icon was lit and lively when they made it back around midnight. They crossed the lobby, rode the elevator, and walked the length of the hallway. The only question was the classic: Your place or mine?

Ben asked for her keys, unlocked her door, and followed her inside. That answered the question.

"Phones go here," he said, stopping at her coffee table. "We're not taking any chances."

To demonstrate, he pulled his out and dropped it there. Lily lowered hers, and all her other stuff, onto the table next to his. Then, slowly, cautiously, she raised her hands to show him that she wasn't armed or dangerous.

"Come here, you," he said, drawing her to him. He removed the silk flower pinned to her hair and brought her curls down around her shoulders. "Tell me how this ends."

What a question! "I don't know. Shouldn't we get started first?"

Lily would not get dragged into a philosophical debate. Not now, anyway.

He looked at her with soft eyes. "Please. I have to know. This can't end in bitterness or resentment or indifference."

"How could it?" she asked. "It's too perfect."

"Anything can go wrong," he said. "You're too smart not to know that."

"This is different."

He weaved his fingers through her hair. "This doesn't feel like a small thing. It feels big. I'd rather do nothing than ruin it, but I have to have you."

"I have to have you, too," she said. "I don't even care if this is a mistake."

"Promise me it won't be."

"Take my clothes off," she demanded.

It took no effort at all. He slid the dress over her arms and tossed it aside. It drifted onto the wood plank floor. She stood before him in her seamless underwear and cinnamon-colored nipple pasties. It was worth the slight pinch of humiliation because his playfulness was back.

He smiled. "We can't have this."

Ben peeled off the silicone patches, freeing her nipples. He then hungrily lowered his mouth over one then the other, sucking them back to life. His hands found their way into her underwear, cupped her ass, and drew her into him, with only his clothes in the way.

"Take this off," she ordered, pushing his jacket off his shoulders. Didn't he know how badly she'd wanted to feel his skin, down to the fine hairs on his arms?

"So impatient," he said.

She demonstrated her impatience by helping him with the buttons of his dress shirt. Once free to discover the map of his body, she traced the outline of the tattoos inked into his golden-brown skin. "How did you pick this floral pattern?" she asked, breathless with admiration. "It suits you."

"We'll get into that later."

He drew her back to him, only this time, her skin met his and the heat from his body scorched hers. Their kisses were deeper, but also looser, messier, just excuses to grab each other. They broke away, panting. Then he was out of his clothes, the pants and everything else just gone. Lily wrapped a hand around his impressive cock and felt it pulsing. "All this for me?"

"Funny girl." He walked her backward toward her bed, his hands low on her hips. "Do you remember that time we went swimming, and your swimsuit came undone, and you lost the bikini top?"

"I'm pretty sure that never happened," Lily replied. Before falling into bed, she swiped aside the bra that did not make the day's final cut, reducing her options to the pair of seamless panties and nipple pasties.

"Must've been in my dreams," he said.

With a hand on the flat of her chest, he eased her onto her back. Her breath labored and slow, she asked, "How often do you dream about me?"

"Often," he muttered into her skin.

Ben was kissing her everywhere. She gripped the sheets and twisted to meet his mouth.

"Bikini wardrobe malfunctions aside," she pressed on, "what are we up to in your dreams? Any chance we're reading a book?"

"Not a chance," he said, laughter rolling in his throat.

"What, then?" she asked.

"We bake cookies from scratch."

"You've got such a sweet tooth!"

"You have no idea." He flipped her onto her stomach and moved to bite into her cheeks before stopping short. "Oh good God!"

Lily squeezed her eyes shut. He'd found her last secret. They were going to have that philosophical discussion, after all.

"What do we have here?"

"A tramp stamp," she said humorlessly. "In my defense, I was in a sorority for a hot minute. The cool thing to do on a holiday weekend was to go into the city and get tatted."

"A tramp stamp is a specific thing," Ben said thoughtfully. "A heart or a butterfly. An infinity sign doesn't fit the bill." He traced the figure with the tip of a finger. "Tell me one of your sorority sisters got one of those."

Lily cackled. "Bethany did!"

"Oh, Bethany," he sighed. "You don't disappoint."

"I'm pretty sure she's had it lasered off by now."

"I like it." He pressed his lips to the base of her spine. "How did you manage to hide it from me?"

"High-waisted bikini bottoms," she confessed. "I won't wear any other kind."

"What else are you hiding?" he asked.

She twisted around to meet his dark eyes swirling with curiosity. "I'm a virgin."

"Not in my dreams, you're not."

"I'll be one again if you don't get inside me."

"Don't rush me. I've been dreaming about this a long time," he said. "I'm going to discover all there is to discover. I don't care how long it takes." He ran his thumb over the spot he'd just kissed. "Look what I might've missed."

Lily sat up and crossed her legs. She would not let this stand. "I've been waiting *far* longer than you. I made the first move, remember? Meanwhile, you took your time, weighing your options. Therefore, I have the superior claim."

He kissed her. "You're going to have to wait, whether you like it or not."

"Why?" she complained.

He kissed her again. "Because the condoms are at my place. Either we head over there, like this, and risk running into Jeremy in the hall, or you wait patiently here for me to get back."

"There's a third option."

He cocked his head. "Let's hear it."

Lily reached around him and yanked open the top drawer of

her nightstand. From it, she produced two packets of condoms in stark black foil. "We're all set."

Ben recognized the monogram of the French design house. "Are you kidding me?"

"They're not mine."

"Whose are they?"

"I stole them from Noah's place," Lily confessed. "He's got a whole collection."

"Sorority girls live such wild lives," he said in a low voice that made her shiver.

"You have no idea."

"I've never used a luxury condom. Is it ribbed for your pleasure by French artisans, or what?"

"Actually," she said, "it tastes like champagne."

"It's time we put that smart mouth to use."

"Let me show you what sorority girls can do."

Lily moved to the edge of the bed and curled her legs around his sturdy ones. Her nails digging into the back of his thighs, she mouthed his beautiful, erect penis, teasing the tip with her tongue, scraping the length with her teeth. Ben's body tightened, and he withdrew from her. Pointing to the condoms, he said, "Hand one over." She did as instructed. He ripped open the foil packet with adept fingers, his growing impatience showing. She spilled onto the bed and watched him work.

Once done, he said, "Give me your foot."

"Excuse me?" Had they unlocked a new kink?

"Now is not the time to be testy."

"Don't you know I'm testy even on my best days?"

"Your foot," he repeated.

She raised a leg and pressed the flat of her foot onto his hard chest. He slid his palms along her shin, down her thigh. "This is what I dream about, touching you, freely, whenever I want."

"Your wildest dreams are about to come true," she teased.

"You have such beautiful skin," he said. "I couldn't stop staring at your legs. I stole every chance I got to touch you."

"Oh, I know . . ." she whispered, smiling.

"Now you know everything."

"I don't know how you feel inside me."

With this man, she had to take her fate in her hands. There was no way around it. She got up, pushed him onto his back, straddled him, pinned him down. "Your dreams are tame, Professor Romero," she whispered.

"Tell me yours."

His eyes were soft, but his grip on her hips was tight. With his taut body between her thighs, she felt beautiful, powerful, and very much in control. "To ride you to the ground."

"I hope you're not waiting for a written invitation."

Lily was done waiting. She couldn't take a drop more of anticipation. But in the blink of an eye, she lost the upper hand. Ben raised her by the hips and buried himself inside her, bringing her vapid dreams to vivid life. She made space for him, breathed him in like air. He murmured something, except the ocean was raging in her ears and she couldn't hear it. She was sure the world had stopped spinning. Then, a bolt of clarity. This was their first time. There would be other times, but never a first. She couldn't afford to zone out and miss it.

Lily caught his face between her hands. "What did you say?"

"Those eyes."

She collapsed into his arms. There was nothing but heat and the sweat of their bodies between them. His teeth grazed her skin. Her nails dug into taut muscles. With her leg locked around his waist and his hand wrapped around the nape of her neck, a frenzied determination took hold. To dive deep into each other. To discover the undiscoverable, the sunken treasure. When they found that rare pearl, held it in their hands, cries of pleasure but also triumph.

Ben Romero was no longer Lily's neighbor from across the hall, her book buddy, fellow coffee lover, or summer crush. From now until the end of time, he was her lover no matter how this story ended.

Pop Shop
A Pop Culture Podcast
Category: Arts
Rating: 4.5 stars

July 19: *Around Midnight* by Charlotte Mitchel
with Lily Lyon and Ben Romero

Lily: Hi, I'm Lily.

Ben: I'm Ben.

Lily: Together we're wasting away our summer, reading books, drinking cocktails, and gossiping about our neighbors. If that sounds like fun to you, stick around. Ben, why don't you introduce our book selection?

Ben: Today we're revisiting a book that we've both rated five stars and I very much enjoyed. *Around Midnight* by a talented debut author, Charlotte Mitchel.

Lily: It's a hot one, almost too hot for Ben to handle, if you can believe it.

Ben: Who's going to believe it? By now, our listeners know me well enough.

Lily: If that's true, please sound off in the comments below.

Ben: This isn't about us. This is about Liz and Austin, our main characters.

Lily: This is our podcast. Everything is about us.

Ben: Even so, we should let the people know what this book is about and why it had us in a choke hold.

Lily: It's a tale of sexual exploration. Liz and Austin are solo travelers who meet while touring the Italian countryside. After a series of contrived incidents, they end up in a quaint B and B with no choice but to share a room with one bed. Instead of the usual negotiations—I'll take the bed, you take the couch, etc.—they go a different route. They decide to make the most of it. After a cool glass of prosecco, things get hot. They abandon the tour and spend the rest of their time in Italy tucked away at Villa Angelina.

Ben: Honestly, that's all you need to know.

Lily: This novel sparked conversation in our book club. One of our friends brought up a good point. It's the question of first-time sex with someone. In this romance, as in most, it goes divinely well. That's not often the case in real life.

Ben: I can't relate, but I'm listening.

Lily: [coughs] I concede that, under exceptional circumstances, first-time sex can go well.

Ben: Divinely well. That's the standard that you've set.

Lily: Do you agree that it generally doesn't shake out like that? It can be awkward, stressful, or even painful when those involved haven't yet established how hard they like it or how fast or any number of parameters that ought to be discussed in advance or intuited over time.

Ben: I'm a quick study. It usually shakes out.

Lily: You're so full of yourself! Has anyone told you that?

Ben: You did, just now.

Lily: I think we've touched on the crux of the matter.

Ben: We've touched upon something. Let's hear it.

Lily: Men have a blind spot. They're unwilling to own up to their inadequacies when it comes to sex.

Ben: Aim higher, Lily. Men are unwilling to own up to inadequacies in any area whatsoever.

Lily: So true! If only they'd stop and ask for directions. The world would be a safer place.

Ben: If only women would articulate what they truly wanted, in and out of the bedroom, clearly and unambiguously, we'd have flying cars by now. There'd be no need for directions.

Lily: What a bunch of crap! Even if we came at you with flare guns, you wouldn't find your way.

Ben: Are you speaking from experience?

Lily: Not recent experience. I'll admit to that.

Ben: Good to know. Let's get back to the tropes.

Lily: Ah, yes! The tropes. Obviously, the one-bed setup gives it away. A little overused, but a crowd pleaser, nonetheless.

Ben: What's your favorite trope?

Lily: Me? Um . . . Friends-to-lovers. It's sweet. How about you?

Ben: The one in which an uptight writer moves into a New York brownstone and falls for his enigmatic upstairs neighbor.

Lily: That's not a trope, that's the plot of *Breakfast at Tiffany's*. Specifically, the movie.

Ben: I'm impressed.

Lily: I watched your lecture on American classics. It's on YouTube.

Ben: No, you didn't.

Lily: I'll drop the link in the show notes for our listeners.

Ben: I think our time is up. Let's wrap.

Lily: I don't know how useful this episode will be to anyone. If you're still listening, just know we appreciate you so, so much. In summary, we believe that sex with a stranger can be divine, but I'm partial to getting to know someone over time.

Ben: Did you always feel that way? Because I remember the night we met—

Lily: Never mind the night we met. I've *always* felt that way. Intimacy is hot.

Ben: Not as hot as the first chapter of *Around Midnight*. Read it and get back to us. We're headed to the pool. [I need to be alone with Lily to find out how hot intimacy can be.]

Lily: [Oh my God! Ben!]

Ben: [Don't worry. Dave will edit it out.]

Lily: [How do you know that?]

"Good stuff, guys!" Dave said over the microphone, enthusiasm cranked high. "Lily, don't worry. I got you. We'll edit that last part out."

Chapter Twenty-Eight

"Want to know what I'm thinking?"

"No."

Lily didn't look up from her paperback. They were in the clubhouse, lounging shoulder to shoulder, finishing up *Crushed Hearts*, the following week's selection by bestselling African American author Kenya Parker. It was the right mix of angst, passion, and drama. She was loving it so far.

"I'll show you, then," Ben said.

He tugged at the high waist of her bikini bottom, edging it down. Lily screeched. "What are you doing?"

"It's time you show me how hot intimacy can be."

"Not here! They'll see us!"

"There's no one here," he pointed out.

It was late in the evening on a Wednesday. After a swim, they'd stretched out in the pergola with their books. The sun had set a while ago, and the pool deck was deserted. Even so, anyone could walk in on them at any time.

"We're totally exposed," Lily said.

"I'll fix that."

Ben rolled up to his feet. With a few tugs on strategically

placed ties, the pergola's heavy burlap drapes tumbled down. They were completely secluded in their cozy little clubhouse.

"It's almost like you've done this before," Lily said, secretly delighted. She switched off her reading light to not cast any shadows.

"No, but I've been plotting it a while," he said. "Now, may I?"

He was tugging at her bikini bottom again. This time, she didn't have the will to refuse him. "Yes, you may."

He dragged the bit of wet fabric down her legs and past her ankles in record speed. "That, too," he said, referring to her bikini top. With a few tugs at the ties, he had it off.

"What about you?" she asked, her breath sharp.

"Give me a minute. I'm busy."

His hands skimmed her body, gliding over her damp skin, still pebbled in places with pool water. Lily propped herself up on her elbows and watched him, coming undone under his gaze. A shiver of worry ran through her. Too much of a good thing was a problem. Ben had put her on a pedestal. There would come a day when she'd have to step down. What then? Walk among the mortals? How could she stand it?

Ben stood and stripped off his wet trunks, bundled them, and looked around for a place to toss them. His golden-brown skin glistened. Could it be that he was unaware of his effect on her? Had she played it a little too cool? His lean, cut, and inked body was the object of her every fantasy and slowly becoming an obsession.

"Ben?" she whispered.

"Yes, beautiful?"

"I touch myself while watching your lectures."

He dropped to his knees between her legs. Eyes shining, he said, "Tell me you're lying."

"That would be a lie."

He lowered his head and pressed his lips to her inner thigh. "Should we discuss Hemingway while we do this?"

"That won't be necessary. I have that lecture cued up for later tonight."

Ben playfully bit her. Laughing, he said, "All right, well . . . Show me what you do."

"I can't! It's private."

"Yes, you can."

"I can't."

"Lily, give me your hand."

"Ben, I would sooner die."

"Look who's prudish now."

She was no prude, not in theory, anyway. Real life was a different matter. With Ben specifically, it was a challenge. Sex wasn't performance art with him. She was vulnerable and open, and that was scary.

"It's not like that," she said. "I have . . . an assistive device."

"There are toys involved?"

"Just the one small vibrator!"

"We'll have to do without it," he said. "Give me your hand."

It was written somewhere, maybe in the stars hidden in the partly cloudy sky, that Lily could not refuse Ben anything. She reached out and touched his face. He kissed her palm then brought her fingertips to her center. "Lie back," he said. "Now, show me."

With those words, he lit a fire in her. The smoke-induced delirium chased away any inhibition she harbored. Lily slid two fingers over her tender nub and drew slow, languid circles, sending tremors down her legs. Eyes closed, she drew her stomach muscles tight and focused on the ever-expanding whirlpool of sensation. Strong waves of pleasure washed over her and retreated, leaving her breathless.

"Look at you, my sweet Lily," he said. "Never hide from me again."

Lily heard Ben's voice in the distance. The waves had taken her far offshore. She was lost to him until he edged her fingers away with his tongue. Lightning struck. Her skin burned hot, the earlier swim only a memory. She gasped when he cupped her bottom and drew her to him. Her legs wrapped around him, undulating to match the strokes of his tongue. Then his fingers were buried inside her. His voice was in her ear, telling her how nothing was private between them, not anymore. "Tell me you feel the same," he said. She could not produce a sound. Her breath was erratic. She bit back every sigh, every cry of anguish that crept up her throat. Soon, her efforts were not enough. Waves of pleasure crashed over her. Ben took her mouth and swallowed her cries. Then he held her shivering body until it was all quiet at sea.

God only knew what time it was when they packed up their things to leave the clubhouse. "How do I look?" she asked.

"Like you've had good sex."

"Ben!"

"It's okay. There's no one out there."

"You never know!"

She peeked through the curtain enclosure. The pool deck was as still and calm as ever. Ben smoothed her hair and kissed her. "Ready?"

"Yes."

"Let's go."

They crossed the deck and called the elevator. Just when it arrived, his phone rang.

"Who's calling me?" he muttered wearily. His messy brows shot up when he read the screen. "Hold on, Lily. I have to take this. It's my agent. She's out in San Francisco. It's still early there."

The elevator came and went. Ben walked off to take the call. Lily sat at the pool's edge and dipped in her feet. When he got off the phone, they'd head up to his place to order dinner, finish the novel, and write a review, as usual. Thereafter, they'd shower, slip into his bed, and make love again well into the night. Every day with Ben was a dream from which she never wanted to wake up. It only got better and better.

Ben paced the length of the pool, the phone pressed to his ear. At times he listened intently. Other times, he burst into laughter. Now he was repeating, "Are you serious?" Finally, he exclaimed, "I fucking love this!" Turning to her, he said, "Lily, Rebecca wants you on this call."

Lily jumped. His *agent* wanted to speak with her? "Why me? What did I do?"

"You'll find out."

He sat next to her at the pool's edge, a hand on the small of her back as if to brace her from sudden impact. He put the call on speaker. "Rebecca, she's here."

A steady voice came over the phone's speaker. "Hello, Lily. This is Rebecca Blackwell with Blackwell and Associates. I've been Ben's agent for a decade now. We handle everything from publishing to media."

Rebecca had handled their podcast deal, but Lily hadn't dealt with her personally. Ben had served as the intermediary. "It's nice to speak with you."

"A New York editor reached out today. She's with one of the Big Five publishing houses."

Lily's heart tanked. There was only one way this conversation could go. Ben had been made an offer, one that was too good to pass up and which would require all his time and attention. Like Lily's father, Rebecca was calling to get Ben to quit reading smut, quit the silly podcast, and get back to work. She wouldn't stand in his way to greatness. But what Rebecca said next made no sense at all.

"He follows you on BookTap and loves your voice."

Lily blinked, confused. Those BookTap posts certainly had a long reach.

"From there he moved on to the podcast, and he's hooked."

"Thanks. I'm flattered."

"He believes you have something there."

"Well, it's a joy to do," Lily said, still confused.

"He thinks you have the makings of a book, and he wants to make you an offer. He assumed I represent you both, but of course I don't. Maybe I ought to? What do you think?"

"A book?" Lily jerked and kicked up water. "I told Ben romance novels are my escape. I don't want to write one."

"We talked about this," Ben said. "There are other options."

"No one is asking you to be the next Nora Roberts," Rebecca said. "What interests the editor are your thoughts on the subject. The way you analyze how common romantic tropes often fizzle in real life."

It was clear that she wouldn't reveal the editor's name, establishing herself as the go-between. Lily respected the strategy, but moving forward she'd need more information.

"Ben could write the foreword, touching upon his experience working with you."

"You'd do that?" Lily asked him.

"I'd do it for you," he said.

That reassured her some, but not enough. What made them think she could write a whole book? A blog, maybe. This would require a lot of reshuffling and delay her return to her legal career. She didn't know how she felt about that. On the other hand, one thing she'd learned this summer was not to turn down opportunities or talk herself out of anything.

"It's settled," Rebecca said. "Ben writes the foreword. Wrap it up in a bow and you've got a bestseller. We'd get you on the morning talk shows, the late-night shows, and dozens of podcasts."

Lily turned to Ben, certain that he'd have a better perspective on this. By the look on his face, his perspective was no different from Rebecca's. He beamed at her with pride.

"I can't believe this," Lily murmured.

"Believe it," Rebecca said. "We've done more with less."

Ben rubbed her back and mouthed *Do it.*

"If you want to entertain the offer or any other that will surely come your way, you should have an agent. If not me, someone else."

Lily had heard Ben say too many good things about his agent to pass on the offer of representation. Besides, Rebecca was the only one with a vision for the project. If she was going to take the leap, she'd need someone competent to guide her.

"Rebecca Blackwell, will you usher me to literary stardom?"

"I'd be honored."

Ben threw his arms around her. His phone came so close to plunging into the water, but he didn't seem to care. "Baby," he whispered into her hair, "I'm so proud of you."

Lily closed her eyes. Each day in his arms got better and better. Each day, an unknown dream came true.

Pop Shop
A Pop Culture Podcast
Category: Arts
Rating: 4.7 stars

August 2: *Crushed Hearts* by Kenya Parker
with Lily Lyon and Ben Romero

Lily: We're back with a great read by one of my favorite authors. This is the third installment of a series set in enigmatic New Orleans with lush depictions of Black life and culture. In *Crushed Hearts*, Madelyn's boyfriend of seven years, Henry, abruptly ends their relationship. Not long after, she meets successful jazz musician Wyatt. Can she learn to love again? Of course she can! Ben and I were more intrigued by Madelyn and Henry, the early years.

Ben: Seven years is a long time to let anything drag on.

Lily: They started dating in high school. This is the classic teenage-sweetheart setup.

Ben: We bring you this episode with apologies to my high school sweetheart, to whom I was a world-class jerk.

Lily: In that case, I'd like to take a moment to extend my sincere apologies to the boy in middle school who passed me a note asking *Will you be my girlfriend?* with answer options *Yes, No,* or *Maybe (Let's meet at the bleachers after class and talk).* A clever, well-crafted note to which I replied *New phone, who dis?*

Ben: No, you didn't!

Lily: Yes, I did. What can I say? He wasn't my type.

Ben: What was your type at thirteen?

Lily: The class president, funnily enough a guy named Wyatt.

Ben: That tracks.

Lily: Anyway, to the boy whose heart I broke, I'll just say you dodged a bullet, my friend. I wish you well.

Ben: Same.

Lily: With that bit of housekeeping out of the way, let's move on.

Ben: I'd like to play devil's advocate.

Lily: Go ahead.

Ben: You already know I have a soft spot for Henry. We've talked about this.

Lily: We have.

Ben: He's portrayed as the evil ex-boyfriend. Only, I can't help but think my guy was in a tough spot. Madelyn was his first, in all respects. She was the first girl he ever asked out on a date. She was the only girl he'd ever kissed, the only lover he'd ever had. When he tells her that he wants to explore and see what's out there, that's not a small request. It's a cry from the heart.

Lily: I reject your argument.

Ben: Of course you do.

Lily: From time immemorial, women have been required to save themselves for that one true love, to keep the so-called body count as close to one—or zero—as possible, should that one true love fail to materialize.

Ben: This book isn't set in biblical times, Lily. It's set in New Orleans circa yesterday.

Lily: Feel bad for Henry all you want but take a minute to consider Madelyn's point of view. Henry was all she knew. He was her world. Imagine pouring all your love, time, and devotion into one man, and for that man to be Henry. What a waste!

Ben: So we agree. The breakup was for the best.

Lily: Absolutely. It was terrible to see Madelyn so crushed over it. I felt her pain at a visceral level. I don't wish that on anyone.

Ben: Imagine going through life without ever knowing that exquisite pain. What kind of monster would you turn out to be?

Lily: Exquisite pain. You *are* a poet. When was the first time you felt that pain?

Ben: My college girlfriend, freshman year. She broke up with me, hopped out of my car at a traffic light, and slammed the door behind her.

Lily: Did she? Good for her.

Ben: How about you? Who was the first to break your heart?

Lily: A guy named Jackson.

Ben: I'm assuming you've changed the name to protect the innocent.

Lily: Of course. His real name is Asher.

Ben: Back to Jackson. What went wrong?

Lily: The classic. It's not you, it's me.

Ben: Ouch.

Lily: Then he just walked away. It was as boring a breakup as you can imagine. I would've preferred the slamming of a door, accusations, and tears, anything but that.

Ben: Tonight, I'll come by to get my books and slam the door on my way out.

Lily: Would you, please?

Ben: Anything for you.

Lily: We should say a few smart things about the book before our time runs out.

Ben: I have a feeling they'll take back my Genius Grant if I don't offer some critical analysis.

Lily: We can't have that. We've been coasting on that award all summer. Go on! Wow us!

Ben: *Crushed Hearts* explores heartache with grace. The takeaway is universal. The heart is resilient.

Lily: Well said! We recommend this heart-wrenching romance. Don't hesitate to share your thoughts in the comment section. We love to hear from you. All the links are below.

COMMENTS:

> **@Rosie_is_reading:** Hey Ben! I'm engaged but say the word and I'll ditch that ring in the Miami River!

> **@Pam909:** Why is my heart crushed just listening to this? I love them so much omg . . . I'm crying.

> **@Books&Wine:** If these two get married, BookTap followers should get an invite. We are DAY 1 Lily & Ben stans!!!!!

Chapter Twenty-Nine

For days, Mother Nature blessed them with torrential down-pours. The rooftop bar was closed and the streets flooded. There was nowhere to go. Where the tourists cursed their dumb luck, taking refuge under awnings, helpless as their beach days dissolved in the waterlogged sand, Lily and Ben were content and cozy in his apartment. They had books, food delivery apps, and each other. They needed little else. When they weren't reading, they wrote. When they weren't reading or writing, they made love. When they weren't making love, they ate in bed and watched movies. If they weren't doing any of those things, they slept in each other's arms, more peacefully than newborn babes.

One afternoon, Lily stirred awake from a nap with one word in mind: *soulmate*. Last night's film was an adaptation of a fantasy romance in which a village girl was married off to a foreign prince. Separated after the wedding night, they were desperate to reunite. They traveled through time, flew dragons, fought wars, and led armies, all just to find each other again. When they were finally reunited, there was no question that the unlikely pair were each other's soulmates.

What was she willing to do to be with Ben? No time travel was required, but she'd have to relocate. Would she leave the city of her dreams? Give up her affordable sublet in the East Village? And what about him? Would he be willing to make room on his dusty shelves for her bright pink books? Add her degrees to his wall? Were they even soulmates? It would have to be ordained from the start, proclaimed in some prophecy, recorded on an ancient scroll or the walls of a cave. That was generally how it worked.

Ben was asleep at her side. Lily propped herself up on an elbow and gazed down at him. He slept on his back, his face turned away from her. Her heart ached as she regarded his features. She'd never experienced anything like this, the rush of love and the fear of loss. What had he called it? *Exquisite pain.*

"What are you thinking about?" he asked, eyes shut.

"Nothing," she replied. "I'm dumbstruck by your animal magnetism. I can't hold a thought in my mind."

He stirred, rolled onto his side to face her. Eyes still closed, he repeated the question. "What were you thinking about? Don't bother lying, Lily. I could hear the gears grinding."

His voice was rough with sleep, which she adored. "I was thinking about you."

His eyebrows shot up. "What about me?"

"You make me happy," she replied.

He reached out blindly and dropped a hand on her waist. "Tell me how."

"I'm more myself with you."

"That's beautiful," he murmured. "What else?"

"I love reading with you."

Finally, he blinked open his eyes. "What else do you love?"

"Your love for stories. Your appetite for details."

"What else?"

"I love your little notes. I'll never throw them away."

He laughed. "Want to know what I love about you?"

"Yes."

"Everything."

It wasn't a stirring declaration of love. Who knew? Maybe he would've made one if she hadn't pounced on him and crushed her mouth to his. They tossed aside the pillows and sunk into each other as rain pounded at the windows and the gray sky turned into night.

Sunday morning brought back the sunshine. But it took a string of text messages to draw Lily out of a deep slumber.

Brunch! Brunch! Brunch! Brunch!

Meet us at 10:30!

Come out of hiding!!

Mimosas aren't going to pour themselves!!!!

Lily read the messages and moaned. She felt torn. Ordinarily, she was a Sunday-brunch devotee, but she did not want to break free from this cocoon. Ben slipped a hand under her T-shirt and rested it on the flat of her belly. The simple contact sent warmth through her body. She moaned again, miserable.

"What's wrong, baby?" he asked.

"We have to go to brunch."

"Says who?"

"Kylie, Sierra, Noah . . . everyone."

Ben yawned. "That can't be right. I don't do brunch, and everyone knows it."

"Check your phone. They must have sent you messages."

"I'm almost certain they haven't, but you can check if you'd like."

His phone was next to hers on the nightstand. The only notification was the weather: seventy-eight degrees and sunny. If anything, the rain had tamped down the summer heat.

She looked down at his sleepy face with longing and regret.

"Don't look so sad," he said. "I'll be here when you get back. Actually, I'll be at my place. Come by when you're done. We'll end the day at the bookstore if you'd like."

"I'd love that," she said. "And don't worry. I'm not usually this clingy. It must have been the rain."

"Cling all you want. I don't have you for long."

Lily showered, brushed through her hair, and slipped on a brunch-appropriate outfit, a white linen matching set and sandals. His words followed her around the apartment. *I don't have you for long.*

Ben kissed her goodbye at the elevator.

"Wait!" she cried, clinging to him yet again. "Where's brunch, anyway? They didn't say."

"Across the street at Lulu's Café," he answered. "Bottomless mimosas and a new DJ every Sunday. It never fails."

On her way over to the brunch spot, Lily's mood brightened. It was a fresh Sunday morning. The recent rain showers made everything new. She was starving and coffee-deprived and missed her crazy friends. In the end, there was nothing as exhilarating as breaking out of any cocoon.

Lulu's Café was exactly as Ben had described. A DJ played house music, and mimosas flowed. The hostess asked if she had a reservation.

"No," Lily answered. "I'm meeting my friends."

Somehow she knew exactly which friends Lily was referring to and led her to a round table near a window. They were all there, all dressed for different events. Sierra had slipped gold barrettes into her afro, elevating an ensemble that looked suspiciously like sleepwear. Kylie and Jeremy were casual in T-shirts and jeans. Noah looked as though he were going yachting later, in a white polo shirt and boat shoes.

"There she is!" they cried when they spotted her.

Sierra moved her purse off a chair and invited her to sit.

A waiter was taking their orders. Kylie gave her two options: waffles or pancakes. "Stick to the basics. Don't get cute," she warned. "Don't even think about the avocado toast. It is way overpriced for what you get."

Jeremy nodded. "She's right."

"Waffles, then," Lily said, taking her seat between Noah and Sierra.

Noah grabbed her face and planted a kiss on her cheek. "You've finally come up for air," he said.

"And you're glowing," Sierra added.

"Well, I've got news!" Lily announced.

The chatter came to a halt. Four pairs of eyes were pinned on her face.

"Don't make us wait for it," Kylie said.

"I have a book deal!" Lily had sat on the news at first, waiting until she'd officially signed with Rebecca Blackwell. Then rainy season had dampened the news, somehow making it less real. But the sun was out, and she was feeling optimistic. "Or . . . I may have a book deal. It's in the works."

"Great," Kylie said.

"Yes, congrats," Jeremy added.

"It's the logical next step," Sierra said. "Your book reviews are slamming. The podcast is a hit. It was just a matter of time. Have you considered starting an online course?"

"No, I haven't," Lily replied. "Thanks for the idea."

"Will you quit practicing law?" Jeremy asked.

"No," Lily said. "It's in my DNA. Besides, law is like a tool kit. You can build any career you want."

Jeremy nodded and wiped the thick curtain of bangs from his eyes. "Cool."

An awkward silence settled at the table. This was not the reaction Lily had expected. Her friends appeared slightly underwhelmed by her big news. A book deal, whether it materialized or not, was big. She was going to be a published author. It had taken a while for it to sink in. Rebecca had followed up with a call on which she and Lily worked through the outlines of a potential publishing contract. Afterward, Lily had not slept well. Could she do this? The question kept her up, staring at the ceiling. An opportunity fell at your feet, you couldn't kick it away. How crazy that her silly idea to read romance books by the pool had gained such speed and momentum, drawing people from everywhere through the reviews, the podcast, and maybe now a book.

That next morning, the storms had rolled in. Ben had skipped his run and was sleeping pleasantly beside her. He'd been publishing for years: a book deal didn't scare him. She had reached for her journal and flipped through the first notes she'd drafted for the podcast. *Romance tropes versus reality. Apply popular romance tropes to real life.* She sat there, weeping. It was all there, the DNA of a book.

"Are you sure that's all you have to tell us?" Kylie asked.

"Isn't that enough?" Lily protested. "This is a big deal, guys!"

Lily demanded their enthusiasm. She would not let them shrug off her news.

"We're happy for you!" Sierra exclaimed.

"We thought you were going to finally tell us about Ben," Noah said, fulfilling his role as the group's straight shooter.

"If you don't want to talk about it, you don't have to," Sierra said. "But FYI, the whole building knows what's going on."

"You *have* to talk about it," Noah said. "I've had a crush on Ben for years, and I'm living vicariously through you."

Kylie fixed her a mimosa from the bottles of orange juice and prosecco on the table. "Maybe you need loosening up," she said. "Drink this."

Lily sipped her mimosa, all while squirming in her chair. *Wow,* she thought. *You wait your whole life to have a friend group to dish with over brunch. When it happens, you don't like it. It makes you uncomfortable, and you'd rather run home and crawl back into bed.*

"Is he any good in bed?" Kylie asked.

The question caught her off guard, and Lily coughed up the truth. "Yes."

"We knew it!" Sierra screamed in her ear.

Lily covered her face with her hands while the others cheered, and the waitress dropped off a fresh bottle of prosecco at the table.

Jeremy excused himself to go to the restroom. As soon as he disappeared through the barn doors at the back of the restaurant, Kylie shared some news of her own with giddy delight. "Lily may not want to share details, but I will," she said. "Jeremy is exceptionally well-endowed. He's hung like you wouldn't believe."

"I believe it," Sierra said. "He's got that energy. Quiet confidence."

"You and Jeremy hooked up?" Lily asked, fully aware of the double standard she was peddling. She wanted every scrap of information regarding her friends' affairs, while keeping her own under lock and key.

"No!" Kylie exclaimed. "We've been hanging out a lot, though. The weather's been shit lately, so we headed to Hotel Blake to use the indoor pool. He came out of the water, and his tiny little suit left nothing to the imagination. It made me start paying serious attention."

"You really should," Sierra said. "The poor guy follows you around everywhere like a puppy."

"I'm not fool enough to think it would actually work," Kylie insisted. "I wasn't born yesterday."

"We know!" Noah said, exasperated. "You were born exactly three decades ago. We don't want to hear about it anymore."

"I'm done playing around," Kylie said. "I'm looking for

something long-term, someone I can bring home to Minnesota."

"I've known you a while," Sierra said. "I've never once heard you talk of Minnesota. You're just looking for excuses."

"Minnesota is my home. I'd like to raise my kids there, someday. Besides, I miss snow."

Lily wasn't buying any of this. Kylie hadn't applied the Minnesota standard to the Italian architect. Why limit it to Jeremy? Besides, it was easy to miss snow in seventy-eight-degree weather.

"I'm never moving back to Tallahassee," Sierra said. "Anyway, I don't think I can. They'd chase me out. I've burned too many bridges."

"I never thought I'd leave New York or the tristate area," Lily said. "But I've always lived a short train ride away from my parents, and I'm kind of sick of it."

Jeremy returned. The waffles and pancakes arrived, along with bacon, hash browns, toast, and sausage.

"I may be moving back to France."

Noah made the announcement so quietly they might have missed it. It was instantly drowned out by the music, chatter, and the orchestra of their forks and knives.

"What did you say?" Lily asked.

He set down his utensils and fixed them with his clear blue eyes. "I may be moving to France in the fall."

"What?" Kylie cried. "You can't do that!"

"But *you* can move back to Minnesota?" Noah fired back.

Jeremy swiveled in his chair and confronted Kylie. "You're moving to Minnesota?"

"No," she replied honestly. "It was just a thought. Anyway, this isn't about me."

"My sales figures have been solid lately," Noah said. "Last week, we had a visit from headquarters. They took me to lunch and made me an offer. It's too good to pass up."

So much had happened during the rainy season, Lily's head was spinning. "What about Nicolas?"

He gave her a look that said it all.

"Is this why you insisted on brunch?" Kylie asked. "For you to drop this news on us?"

Chastised, Noah nodded, eyes cast down. This blew Lily's mind. She'd never seen her bold friend so low.

"Am I the only one who sees this as a good thing?" Sierra asked. "He's going to Paris! That's the dream!"

"Saint-Tropez," Noah corrected her. "I can't live far from the water."

"That's an even better dream!" Sierra cried. "Make sure you have a guest room or a pullout couch."

"I'm going to cry," Kylie said.

"I'm going to cry, too," Lily said. "You were my first Miami friend. I'll miss you."

Noah scoffed. "Lily, what do you have to be sad about? You're leaving soon."

"How soon?" Kylie asked.

"At the end of the month," Noah tossed out casually, as if this weren't loaded information.

"Before you all go, we should have a night out," Sierra said. "We haven't hit the clubs all summer."

"Since when do we ever hit the clubs?" Noah asked.

"Fine. I'll meet you in the middle. How about a pool party?" Sierra suggested. "Nothing but day drinking and dancing. I'll organize it."

And while they all talked about day drinking, Lily sat with the realization that she was leaving at the end of the month. Not at the end of summer or at the end of her lease, as she liked to vaguely think about it, but in a few short weeks.

I don't have you for long.

"How are the waffles?" Kylie asked. "Do you like the Chantilly cream?"

"Love it."

In truth, Lily could hardly taste a thing. Ben had made her promise things would end smoothly between them, which meant that he'd accepted that things would end eventually. She did not want it to end at all.

After brunch, she and Kylie indulged in window-shopping before heading back to the building. Most of the boutiques were tourist traps, offering bikinis, cover-ups, and T-shirts with catchy Miami slogans.

"What am I going to do about Jeremy?" Kylie asked when they reached the end of the block and were ready to circle back.

"You're going to invite him to your place, pour him some wine, slip into something more comfortable, and seduce the boy, Mrs. Robinson."

"Very funny."

"Did you talk to him? If he knows where you're coming from, maybe he'll understand."

"What if it's all in my head and there's nothing to talk about?"

"Then it's in my head, too. He's clearly into you, Kylie. If nothing else, he's taken your mind off the architect. That's a bonus."

"Nothing is ever going to happen between Frederico and me," Kylie said. "I'm not his type. He likes the glam girls. My fingertips always smell like garlic."

"Then he's an idiot," Lily said.

A group of local boys whizzed by on skateboards. Their beach towels were tied at their necks, flapping behind them like superhero capes. That would have been Ben at twelve or thirteen, Lily thought fondly.

As though reading her mind, Kylie asked, "How are things really between you and Ben?"

"Perfect, which sucks because it's over soon. Why can't I have nice things?"

"I hate when that happens," Kylie said. "Life dangles a good thing in front of your eyes and takes it away."

"I've been in denial," Lily admitted. "I've pushed it out of my mind, and now it's all I can think about. I'm leaving soon."

Kylie rummaged in her purse for lip balm. "What does Ben say?"

"I think he's been counting down the days, preparing himself."

"That's smart," Kylie said. "Maybe it's time you do the same."

When Lily got back, Ben was in the shower, his gym clothes tossed carelessly into the hamper in the corner of his bedroom.

She knocked on the bathroom door and heard the shower curtain draw back.

"Lily? Come in!"

She took that invitation at face value, stepped out of the proper linen matching set, and joined him in the shower. "I thought you might need a hand."

Ben was lathering shampoo in his hair and grinning at her. "Did you have fun without me?"

"Not as much fun as I'm going to have with you."

She kissed him hungrily under the hot stream jet, shampoo suds making their bodies slick. He squeezed her breast under his wet palm, making her gasp.

"Remember that time when you took my video call in the shower just to torture me?" he asked, kissing her neck. "That wasn't a dream, right?"

"No, but this is."

Ben laughed a throaty laugh that died abruptly. "Wrap your legs around me."

Even though she'd started this, Lily couldn't bend so easily. "Under one condition."

"What's that?" he asked.

"Call me Liliana and I'll do whatever you want me to."

His dark eyes flashed. "Liliana, do what I tell you."

He did not have to ask twice. She was determined to make the most of what little time they had left with no reservations.

Lily's Notebook

Archetypes

The Italian architect is the catch. So is the French baker or the American lumberjack, the British rock star, the Canadian hockey player, the biker, the cowboy, the race car driver, the self-made millionaire, the heir to the company who might as well be the heir to the throne. Who am I missing? What do they have in common, aside from their height and their sun-kissed skin? They are unattainable, inscrutable. They may not even exist. Writers create them from scratch, down to the dimple in their cheeks and the twinkle in their eyes. Even so, these are the types we pine for, men who won't spare us a second glance. We're not tall, pretty, rich, connected, or famous enough to hold their attention. Given a chance to get to know them better, we may learn they don't live up to the hype. However, we will never get that chance. The rejection stings. Only when we hit the bottom of a bottomless-mimosa brunch can we admit to our friends that the pain is real. The truth is they are not worthy of us. A real man defies archetypes. He's everything you need him to be, and nothing less.

Pop Shop
A Pop Culture Podcast
Category: Arts
Rating: 4.9 stars
RATED #1 Podcast in Arts & Culture

August 16: *Just Friends* by Angelica Key
with Lily Lyon and Ben Romero

Ben: Let's talk about instant chemistry.

Lily: Or more importantly, the lack thereof.

Ben: Is it real? Imagined? Let's try to define it.

Lily: Women define chemistry as that flutter of butterflies in the stomach. You either feel it or you don't. When you do, it's the most extraordinary feeling. You'll chase it no matter where it takes you.

Ben: You'd chase a butterfly?

Lily: Not literally.

Ben: Butterflies don't live that long. Some are lucky to last a week.

Lily: The same can be said for most relationships.

Ben: Basically, we're talking about attraction. Sometimes it's there from the start. Other times you have to scratch the surface to find it.

Lily: We agree you shouldn't have to dig a tunnel with a spoon to get at it, right?

Ben: Agreed. Want to introduce our book?

Lily: This week we're discussing *Just Friends* by Angelica Key, a friends-to-lovers romance based on the principle of opposites attract. Jack is in tech, and Bobbi is an artist. However, as hard as we tried, we couldn't pinpoint the area of attraction.

Ben: We gave up.

Lily: It's a shame, too! These are my top tropes.

Ben: What do you like most? The friendship graduating to a relationship part?

Lily: Yes! That part! I love it!

Ben: If you mess up the relationship, which isn't hard to do, you also lose a friend. How do you recover from that?

Lily: I can't imagine, and I'm glad you brought that up. This is another fine example of how tropes can trip you up in real life.

Ben: Keep your friends close and your lovers closer. Just don't mix the two.

Lily: Give me a second. I need to write that down.

Ben: Write this down, too. Opposites attract is bullshit. You're either compatible or you're not.

Lily: Too compatible and you fall in a rut. There should be some tension.

Ben: We're compatible. Where does that leave us?

Lily: Just friends?

Ben: [Laughs] Okay. Maybe.

Lily: Bobbi should've left Jack in the friend zone. Sometimes it's for the best. Have you ever been friend-zoned, Ben?

Ben: Absolutely. Several times.

Lily: I'm shocked. Who would put you on the bench?

Ben: You might find this hard to believe, but I was once a bookish nerdy kid with acne and unruly hair.

Lily: Did you ever ride a skateboard?

Ben: Yes. Why?

Lily: No reason. I want a complete mental image.

Ben: Add this to your image. I had no date for my junior high prom. I was either the third wheel or the designated driver through high school until things picked up sophomore year.

Lily: In other words, you had a normal teenage experience.

Ben: Still hurts!

Lily: Oh God!

Ben: How about you? Did you serve any time in the friend-zone supermax prison?

Lily: As a matter of fact, I have. I'll show you the mug shot later.

Ben: Tell me all about it.

Lily: He was a Wall Street type.

Ben: You and those finance bros ...

Lily: For a while, they were my weakness!

Ben: Tell me what he did.

Lily: It's more what he *didn't* do. He never kissed me, never tried. When I asked, finally, what was up, he came clean. I wasn't his type. He wanted to be friends.

Ben: He should die a slow and painful death. You're everybody's type. If he can't appreciate that, he's a useless human being, taking up oxygen for no good reason.

Lily: Wow!

Ben: I don't mess around when it comes to you.

Lily: Thanks, buddy!

Ben: [Laughs] You'll pay for that later. But we're lost in the woods now. The topic is chemistry. What do you do when it's not there?

Lily: One of our book club members had a similar problem. What started out as a slow burn sort of fizzled out. I was rooting for them and hoping for that spark that would set them on fire.

Ben: My uncle took my cousins and me camping once. He couldn't light a campfire to save his life. We gathered sticks, and he doused them with lighter fluid. The s'mores we made later that night were toxic. I'm sure of it.

Lily: I don't see where you're going with this. Is there a moral to the story?

Ben: There's only so much lighter fluid you can pour on any situation before it's hazardous to your mental health.

Lily: Moving on from our mutual friend, we don't like to tear books apart on the podcast. What are some of the things we loved about this novel?

Ben: It was one of the funniest we've read.

Lily: That mini golf scene is hilarious. I cried!

Ben: I know you did. Adorable.

Lily: We were all over the place today! Maybe it's because you've made us the number one podcast for arts and culture? What an honor!

Ben: It went to our heads. We'll do better next time.

Lily: Which is next week, for a bonus episode!

Ben: Fun stuff.

Lily: That's all we have for now. My buddy Ben and I are off to play a round of mini golf. Thanks for joining us. Bye!

COMMENTS:

> **@KharmaQueen:** Screaming!!! The way that man went feral!

> **@ReadingAustenInBoston:** I DON'T MESS AROUND WHEN IT COMES TO YOU!!!

> **@User8495uyt7t950404:** The speculation is over. They've pretty much confirmed they're dating!

Chapter Thirty

Ben had her back against a wall. There was no nice way to put it, no chic and tasteful turn of phrase to convey what he was doing to her. He was fucking her brains out. Lily, breathless, scratched his back and cried out his name. "Ben! Oh my God, Ben!"

"Am I your buddy? Is that what I am to you?"

Shocked, she went still. "Is that what this is all about?"

The pettiness! He'd played the long game, and she loved it. How long had it been since they'd recorded that podcast? He'd been ruminating on it like the vengeful Virgo he was.

"Well played, *friend*!"

Those were the last words she managed to utter. He bent her over the couch and had her crying out to God. When the knock came on their door a while later, Lily didn't know if it was their dinner delivery or a disgruntled neighbor coming round to complain about the noise.

It was Noah.

"If you're going to talk about me on your podcast, you should at least buy me dinner," he said.

Lily and Ben stared at their friend, standing in the hallway with a pinched expression on his face.

"Don't even bother denying it," he continued. "I'm that guy in your book club who's digging a tunnel with a spoon or whatever. I know it."

Lily turned to Ben, who simply shrugged and said, "Defend yourself, Counselor."

Karma had come for her tonight. She was going to pay for everything she'd said on that episode.

Lily drew Noah inside and had him take a seat at the kitchen island. "I apologize," she said. "I should have asked you first. It wasn't premeditated. We don't rehearse these things, as much as I would like to. It felt so natural to bring up examples of real relationships. Sometimes, I forget they're recording. Sometimes it feels like Ben and I are chatting about books by the pool."

"You could've mentioned me by name. No one at work believes I'm the guy in the podcast."

"Your coworkers listen to us?" Lily asked, surprised. She couldn't imagine his sophisticated sales associates listening to her and Ben rattle on about tropes and stuff.

"A few of them," he replied. "They read the books, too. Everyone loves you guys, but you still owe me dinner."

Ben opened a bottle of wine. "We ordered Peruvian. Want to stay for that?"

"Sure."

Noah got comfortable and rolled up his sleeves, flashing a new watch. "I see you staring," he said to Ben. "It's a vintage *Santos de Cartier*. Trendy now, but it's a timeless piece."

"I have a vintage watch that I'm looking to sell," Ben said. "Could you help me with that?"

"Sorry," Noah said. "I don't handle Timex or Casio."

"Hey, Casio is cool," Lily protested.

Ben took the insult in stride. "I'll grab it," he said. "Take a look and give me your honest opinion. Fair enough?"

"Cool."

Ben set aside the bottle to let the wine breathe. He went

over to the bookcase and returned with the leather box. He set it on the kitchen island. After some rummaging, he pulled out the watch that Lily had glimpsed that time he'd showed her his father's notebooks and letters.

Noah let out a low whistle. "*Mec* . . . That's a Patek Philippe 2499 in rose gold. It could be worth something."

"I'm not sure it even works," Ben said.

"It likely needs to be serviced, that's all." Noah's voice was soft with admiration for the timepiece. "Why would you want to get rid of it?"

"It's not mine," Ben replied. "It belonged to my father."

"He left it for you," Lily said. "He must've wanted you to have it."

Ben came around the island and kissed her hair. "Don't get sentimental, Lily. It was probably a gift from one of his wives."

Lily caught him by the waist and held him close. "Don't you want to keep it?"

"I'm never going to wear it," he said. "Do I look like a rose-gold Patek Philippe guy to you?"

"No," she said with secret delight. *And thank God.*

"You'd have to get it insured and keep it safe," Noah recommended. "You can't leave it in an old box on a bookshelf. Anyone could get at it. Either buy a safe or leave it at the bank. Every year, get it serviced."

"That's a lot of upkeep for something you won't wear," Lily admitted.

"This watch is a loaner," Noah said, pointing to his Santos. "I belong to a watch club. That takes the trouble out of it."

"Would you like to buy it?" Ben asked Noah.

"Even with my promotion, I can't afford it," Noah said sadly. "If I were you, I'd sell it and pocket the money."

"That's the plan," Ben said.

"If you want me to help you out, we'd have to act fast. I won't be around for long."

"Oh no . . ." Lily said, knowing what that likely meant.

"I accepted the job offer," Noah said. "It's much more generous than I thought. Relocation expenses are included, a lease on an apartment, too. I'll have a year to sort myself out and find a place of my own."

"That's a good deal," Ben said.

"It's a great deal," Noah said. "When I moved to Miami, I lived in a hostel for a month. My clothes kept getting stolen."

"Get ready for houseguests," Lily said. "I caught Sierra searching flights."

Noah narrowed his eyes on her. "How about you, Lily? What are your plans?"

"I'm not sure when I'll visit, but it's on my bucket list."

"I meant when will you start looking for a new job?"

"Soon," Lily stammered. The last person she'd expected to get a lecture from was Noah.

"Let her enjoy her last couple weeks," Ben intervened.

He rubbed her lower back, tracing wide circles, coaxing her to relax. It only made Lily tense up more. *Last couple weeks.* He made it sound so definite. As if they had no other option except to separate. In her mind, there were no hard limits. Couldn't they work out an alternate ending? Was there no possible future for them? Would they ever talk about it? Or was the plan set in stone? Once he dropped her off at Miami International in his beloved BMW, would that be the end of it? Hadn't he said he loved her? No, he hadn't. He'd said he *loved everything about her,* which wasn't the same. Lily closed her eyes. She was better than an ostrich at burying her head in the sand. She intended to enjoy these final few days, regardless of the outcome. She hadn't done all this work just to fall apart over some guy. Once she left this building for good, she might never know true happiness again. Noah was off to a bright, sparkling future, a dream job in a dream location. Lily had found those things here. There was no use looking for it anywhere else. In a city known for its artificiality, she'd found her authentic self. Too bad she'd have to leave that girl behind.

Pop Shop
A Pop Culture Podcast
Category: Arts
Rating: 4.95 stars
RATED #1 Podcast in Arts & Culture

August 23: *Arm Candy* by Vikki Ong
with Lily Lyon and Ben Romero

Lily: At last, we have a classic romantic comedy! Our book of the week is *Arm Candy* by Vikki Ong. Beyond obsessed!

Ben: I was not as obsessed as you, but I enjoyed it.

Lily: Don't you miss the simple rom-coms of the nineties? And the usual cast of characters? Julia Roberts, Nia Long, Meg Ryan, Angela Bassett, Drew Barrymore, Julia Roberts—

Ben: I miss Robert De Niro, Joe Pesci, Sharon Stone, Ray Liotta, Lorraine Bracco, and once again, De Niro.

Lily: Our nineties nostalgia could not be more different. That's a subject for another podcast. Let's focus on this super fun, fast-paced romance set in beautiful Singapore. Ben, could you give us a brief synopsis?

Ben: Jon Tan is a notorious womanizer and major fuckup. Desperate to prove to his dying grandfather that he deserves to inherit the family business, his plan is to hire a so-called nice girl to accompany him to a reunion. He's willing to shell out a quarter of a million dollars.

Lily: I'm nice enough. Should I lend out my services? In this economy, it's all about multiple streams of income.

Ben: I'd love to swim in that stream.

Lily: Put your money where your mouth is, honey.

Ben: That's essentially what Candace Song says to Jon. They're in the same boat, rowing upstream, desperate to run family businesses.

Lily: She's watching, helpless, as Candy's Sweet Shop, the confectionery business that's been in her family for decades, is losing ground. They're no longer competitive. No banks will lend to them. She needs an infusion of cash. Before you say anything, Candy's Sweet Shop is on the nose. It's meant to be cute, but it ain't.

Ben: It's a form of virtue signaling. Why not say she *wants* the money? Instead, she *needs* it to save a candy shop, of all things. If it wasn't a cute shop, it would be a dog shelter or a charming B and B, anything to tug at our heartstrings.

Lily: I agree. Let's be the greedy capitalists that we are! Who in their right mind would walk away from a quarter-million dollars? Not me.

Ben: Me, neither.

Lily: That kind of money could change your life. It could put you through school, help you start a business ... In some cities, it could buy a house.

Ben: Not in this city. Let's get into the tropes.

Lily: Fake dating, obviously. How did we get this far without running into it? It's one of the most popular tropes around.

Ben: Maybe because it's the least realistic. Not having a date for a wedding or whatever is no reason to rope someone else into your misery.

Lily: Ben Romero, I specifically remember you roping me in on more than one occasion. *I* was your arm candy.

Ben: Those dates were not fake. You know it.

Lily: I'm so glad this is a podcast. No one can see me turn into a ripe tomato.

Ben: More like bright red cherry hard candy, if we're staying on theme.

Lily: Speaking of themes, this story centers around family, which I like.

Ben: A daddy's girl through and through.

Lily: Who? Me?

Ben: Yes, you!

Lily: I won't deny it. I'm working on it.

Ben: Candy's job was to look pretty, but she successfully brokers a peace treaty between three generations of the Tan dynasty. It's remarkable.

Lily: She missed her vocation. Candy is a natural-born diplomat. She should close shop and head to Singapore's version of the State Department.

Ben: I was on the grandfather's side. His son ran the family business to the ground. It took decades to rebuild. Now his no-good grandson wants to take the helm. I don't know about that.

Lily: Jon Tan is the consummate party boy. He barely made it through the elite British private school he was sent to. He wrecked the sports car he was gifted at sixteen. He's been spending the family fortune in London, which is where the couple meets.

Ben: He's pulled himself together, but it's a case of too little, too late.

Lily: I resent that it's a woman's job to get him over a line.

Ben: She was compensated fairly.

Lily: He offers Candy an insane amount of money to accompany him on an all-expense-paid trip to Singapore. Most people would just take the trip! No further compensation required. This makes me think his grandfather is right. Jon is not a good businessman. Like his father before him, he will ruin the family business.

Ben: What does this business involve?

Lily: It's not important. Two charming people fall in love in a breathtaking setting. There's food and culture and family drama. Those are the main points.

Ben: This is a book about men. Interesting how the women do all the emotional heavy lifting.

Lily: The men would crumble without the support of these women.

Ben: I'd crumble without you.

Lily: Somehow, I doubt it.

Ben: I'm crushed. We'll sort this out later. What else do you like about this book?

Lily: Am I the only one who liked it?

Ben: You're not alone. The food descriptions made my mouth water. The banter was great.

Lily: You know how much I love banter.

Ben: The bantering we do over good banter is insane.

Lily: What exactly didn't you like?

Ben: The willful ignorance of the characters. They were clearly falling in love. Candy is so observant, and yet she couldn't pick up on this? It was beyond clueless.

Lily: Nice nineties reference! Except, it might've seemed too good to be true. Remember, they have very different backgrounds. She didn't belong in his world. She was only pretending.

Ben: You know who wasn't fooled? Jon's grandmother. She knew the deal from the start. I loved her.

Lily: She was sharp! I loved her, too!

Ben: Let's wrap this up with a cute bow for our listeners.

Lily: Jon and Candy think they're pulling something on Grandpa Tan, but the joke's on them. In this bighearted rom-com, three generations come together to bring these hopeless lovers together.

Ben: Well said, Lily. Now I like it a little more.

Lily: Then, I've done my job.

Ben: That's it for us.

Lily: See you next week. Until then, give love a chance.

COMMENTS:

    @fr33spirit: Who's going to tell them? This is love. Duh!

    @Dylan22: Don't crush his heart, Lily! 🏠

Chapter Thirty-One

I would crumble without you.

Somehow, I doubt it.

I'm crushed. We'll sort this out later.

WHEN WILL WE SORT THIS OUT? AT THE DEPAR-TURE GATE?

"Baby, wake up."

Lily turned to Ben's voice and buried her nose in his throat. She breathed him in until her heart rate steadied.

He stroked her back. "You were talking in your sleep. Were you having a bad dream?"

"Yes."

He gathered her close and whispered. "It's okay. You're here with me."

For how long?

The summer was nearing its end. She would have to start planning her return trip soon. Though it killed her, she would not raise this question with Ben. In so many ways, she'd inserted herself in his life. If he wanted her to stay, he would have to ask.

"Hungry?" he asked. "I'll make us breakfast."

She nodded and reluctantly let him go. Then for the first time in weeks, she sat up and reached for her phone instead of her journal. Old habits were creeping back. She tried focusing on the day ahead. Ben was making coffee in the buff. That was promising.

Whenever they spent the night at her place, he brought over his coffeepot and made sure she was fully stocked on his favorite brand of espresso. Slowly, her studio was taking on the qualities of his place. Books were stacked everywhere. Her kitchen drawers were stuffed with individually wrapped plastic utensils and packets of sugar, ketchup, and soy sauce. He'd even left a leatherbound notebook at her bedside to jot down his thoughts late at night. If this wasn't the ideal setup, what was? Possibly a one-bedroom apartment to hold all their stuff. A kitchen with more natural light and a better view from the window. Cookware and proper utensils for when they eventually eased up on food delivery. There would be room for a large desk or two desks side by side, one with his laptop, the other with her high-resolution monitor. A custom-designed bookcase to hold her books and his impressive collection. Plants, plants, and more plants. Maybe they'd adopt a pet, a little dog to take for long walks on the beach.

All these things were simple enough. Lily wasn't asking for the world on a platter, or the moon or stars that might fall out of reach. She wanted what they had with a stamp of permanence. She wanted the aroma of his coffee to fill her home. For that, she would give up her bodega order in a second. Simply, she wanted a life that glowed with his love. Walking away from this was the nightmare she could not wake up from.

Her phone buzzed with a FaceTime request from her brother. Lily did not feel the urge to run across the hall as she did whenever the people from the real world intruded in this new one she and Ben had created. For one thing, there was no place to run to: they were already in her apartment. Besides, it was only Patrick.

"Heads up!" she called out to Ben. "I'm hopping on a video call with my brother."

"Should I throw on clothes?" he asked.

"Nope! I like you just the way you are. Just stay out of frame."

Ben winked and slipped on headphones. Each morning, he listened to a literary podcast hosted by the *New York Times.* Knowing this about him made her love him even more.

She adjusted her pajama top and accepted the call. "Hello, Dr. P!"

Patrick favored their father. He was handsome in a nerdy way and practically lived in a white coat and tie. It was odd to see him dressed casually in a faded T-shirt, seemingly lounging at home, even on a Saturday morning.

"Wow!" he exclaimed. "You look great. That Miami glow up is unreal."

"Four out of five doctors recommend it."

"Good to know. I may try that someday . . . Hold on just a sec. I'll get our parents on the call."

"Why would you do that?" she cried.

He gave her a quizzical look. "Didn't you get my text?"

"What text?"

"Last night. I sent you a heads-up."

"Heads-up for what?" she asked.

If this was an intervention, there was no need. Her Miami sojourn was ending soon.

"Lily, take a breath," Patrick said. "You're freaking out for no good reason. This is not about you. It's just a family call."

Without any further warning, he added their parents. There they were, sharing a square box on the lower corner of her phone's screen. Her father's widow's peak more obvious than ever. Her mother's face arranged in a scowl.

"There she is!" her mother exclaimed. "I thought my daughter was dead or kidnapped. But no, she's alive and well in Miami. She knows how to use a phone, too. She just chooses not to. Now that I've seen your face, and I know that you're well, I will not say another word."

Lily darted a glance Patrick's way. *Tell me again how this isn't about me!*

"She's on vacation," Patrick intervened. "You're familiar with the idea, right? They're not just for the top one percent. Common people like us take time off every day."

Lily nodded approvingly. The least her brother could do was defend her.

"We have nothing against vacations," her father said. "Your mother and I are planning a cruise next month. But Lily is no longer in college, she's a professional. There's no summer break."

Her mother broke her vow of silence. "What your sister has done is relocate to another state without a word to anyone."

"It's only temporary, Mom!" Lily scoffed. "And I called you many times. You never answered."

"You called twice," her mother said icily.

"And you quit your job!" her father exclaimed. "Your name is no longer on the company website."

Lily didn't bother denying it. Deep inside, she was thrilled to no longer be associated with such a life-drainer. Her days were far more exciting now.

"Always another story!" her mother lamented. "We don't know who you are anymore."

"Who I am is an adult," Lily asserted. "If I want to unplug in Miami for a while, that's my prerogative. I'm not hurting anyone. I can afford it. It's not on your dime."

"This is not about money," her father insisted.

"And this is not about Lily, either," Patrick cut in coldly. "I called this meeting, remember? If you can believe it, I've got stuff going on that I'd like to discuss."

They all fell silent.

"I'm moving back to the city," he announced. "I've been offered a position at New York-Presbyterian."

That wonderful bit of news had the bonus of getting Lily's parents off her back. She cheered with exceeding enthusiasm. "Yay, Patrick!"

"Congratulations, son!"

"That is a fine hospital!"

This was the sort of career move that made sense to their parents. They could tell their circle that their son, the doctor, was now at Presbyterian. Their friends would nod appreciatively and recount the surgeries and procedures they'd all had done there.

"It will be so nice to have you and Coco close," Mom said. "Sunday dinners have been so lonely lately."

"Coco is not relocating with me," Patrick said evenly.

"What does that mean?" Mom asked.

"It means I'm heading back to New York, and Coco is staying here in Virginia."

Lily came close to dropping her phone. Patrick and Coco had been together for ages. "Are you breaking up?" she asked.

"Yes, we are," he replied in a detached, clinical voice that Lily didn't care for.

Was this the voice he used to break bad news to the parents of the children in his care? Or was he hurting and masking his hurt with indifference? Had Patrick always been like this? Unable to acknowledge his failures and weaknesses? He'd only gather their family to announce impressive news, a new job or promotion. Or was this just how men were, taking breakups in stride?

Their parents hadn't noticed the change in Patrick. Her father focused on the job, sharing that the hospital was ranked number one in the state. Her mother casually mentioned that she approved of the breakup. "What grown woman goes by the name Coco?" she asked. "She's not an actress. She's a pharmacist!"

"Please, Mom," Lily said, while texting Patrick privately.

LL: Stay on the call. Let's talk after this.

PL: Sure thing. I'll wrap this up. I have something to ask you, anyway.

Once the meeting was adjourned and their parents were off the call, Patrick got straight to it. "I wondered if I could crash at your place, since you're not there. That would go a long way to make the move easier."

Playing musical chairs with apartments to facilitate big life moves was the theme of the week.

"I'll be home soon," Lily forced herself to say. "But you can always crash with me. We'll make it work."

"Are you sure?" he asked. "I don't want to cramp your style. Are you seeing anyone?"

"That won't be a problem," she said hurriedly. "What's really going on with you and Coco? You've been together, like, six years, right?"

"Seven," he said. "It's over now. She moved out a couple months ago."

"Months ago!" she exclaimed. "Why didn't you say anything?"

"When do I ever say anything?" Patrick replied. "That's not how I roll."

"Consider rolling in a new direction, please. You can't keep everything bottled up."

"You're my kid sister," he said. "I'm not coming to you with grown-folks' problems."

"I'm not ten anymore, and you're not that much older than me."

When she was ten, and Patrick fifteen, the difference in age was staggering. There was nothing they could agree on, no new toy they could share or movie they could happily watch together. She was a bratty kid then, and he was a brainy teen. Now they were adults. There was no reason they couldn't talk.

Patrick sighed. "There's not much to say. Something was off. I couldn't put my finger on it. One day, she packed up and moved out. I think someone else was in the picture, but let's not go there. All I want is to put this whole thing behind me."

Lily wasn't too surprised. She'd always found Coco to be rather cold. "Okay," she said. "Look out, New York! Pat is single and ready to mingle!"

"Shut up."

"On a serious note, is that why you're moving back? To put distance between you and your ex? I assure you, there's enough room in the state of Virginia for the both of you."

"It's a good move, careerwise," he said. "Besides, I miss the city. I'll get to reconnect with my friends, and I'll be closer to the family hub, Sunday dinners, and all that. You've shouldered the burden a while. What I'm saying is take your time. You deserve a break."

Lily swallowed past the lump in her throat. "You're just saying that because you want my apartment."

Patrick chuckled. "That's true."

Lily did not dare look up from the phone screen. She was aware that Ben was stealing glances at her. She could feel his gaze sweep over her then move away. What had he made of her family drama? Though she'd told him all about her parents, their overprotectiveness and limited worldview, this would be the first time he'd witnessed them in action. Today, they'd been in rare form.

Before saying goodbye to Patrick, she encouraged him to use their mother's spare key to move his stuff into her apartment whenever he liked.

"Thanks, sis," he said.

"Sure thing. See you soon."

Chapter Thirty-Two

Sierra had reserved a poolside cabana at the famed Fontainebleau. A flat-screen TV was on to the sports channel. A complimentary bottle of champagne sat in an ice bucket.

"Does this work for y'all boomers?" she asked, after showing them their digs for the day. She was obviously pleased with herself.

"I approve," Noah said.

Lily approved as well. She was in a party mood. Rebecca was actively negotiating a publishing deal. Evenings, she worked on her essays. Lily Lyon, essayist. That had a nice ring to it. She wouldn't abandon her legal career, but the book advance could buy her some time, give her an opportunity to revamp her career to her liking. She only needed time to figure it out. For now, though, she'd enjoy the last days of summer, prepare for the one remaining podcast, and pretend her love life wasn't on the edge of a cliff.

There was nothing wilder, more carefree, than a summer pool party at a Miami resort. Everyone was having fun. Even Ben appeared to be enjoying himself. With the brim of his baseball cap low over his eyes and a beer in hand, he swapped stories with the others. Roxanna had joined them. Lily knew he'd been looking forward to spending time with little Oscar. When a DJ started her set, Roxanna protected his delicate ears with noise-canceling headphones. Jeremy, Nicolas, and Sierra's date, a guy named Ted, rounded out their group. "He's in real estate," Sierra said, referring to Ted. "Which means he's making bank or broke. There's nothing in between. He's cute, though."

Lily agreed. "Yes, he is."

Ted had a handsome face, a sandy-brown complexion, and the tricky smile of a master salesman. No way he was broke.

"He's been stalking my social media for weeks. I decided to give him a try."

Lily admired the younger woman's can-do spirit. At her age, she'd have been sobbing over her last relationship for weeks.

Ben and Roxanna left with Oscar for the kiddy pool, just when Kylie came rushing back from her swim. "You won't believe this."

Lily, stretched out on a sunbed, looked up from her e-reader. "What is it?"

"Frederico is back!"

"From Italy?"

"Yes! He cut his trip short."

Kylie showed her the text message she'd received seconds earlier. No pressure, but if you want to come back to work early that would be amazing. I'm home today.

"Hold on. When were you scheduled to return?" Lily asked.

"In two weeks."

"Ha!" Lily settled back down. "Tell him *Nice try. See you in two weeks.*"

"I can't do that."

"Oh yes, you can," Lily said. "What are you doing?"

Kylie scrambled around the cabana stuffing her personal items into her beach tote. "Leaving. I've got to stock his refrigerator."

"Are you serious?" Lily asked, dumbfounded. "Look at where we are! We're celebrating."

Kylie tucked her damp locks behind her ears. "I don't have anything to celebrate. This job is all I have."

This wasn't true, not by a long shot. However, she knew better than to argue with someone in that state of mind. Lily recalled how lost she'd felt the night she quit her job, crying into a eucalyptus-scented towel in the sauna. She'd relied on her position to shape her identity for far too long. Her ideas and creativity stretched beyond the corporate cadre. Yet she'd allowed them to move her around like a pawn. The night she walked out, she was ready to walk away for good. Then again, she wasn't in love with her CEO, which had made walking away that much easier.

"Kylie, don't do this. You're settling for crumbs."

"I don't have time for your food analogies!"

Lily tried a different approach. "Don't you see? He's the black cat, and you're the golden retriever."

Kylie shoved a bottle of sunscreen into her tote. "I don't understand you."

"I think you do," Lily said, flatly.

"I can't get into this now, Lily!"

"What's the rush? Can't this wait until Monday?"

"He won't be home then. If I want to see him—" Kylie caught herself saying the quiet part out loud. She could return to work anytime, but Frederico was home now. This was her chance to see his golden face again.

"All right," Lily said. The kind thing to do was to let it go.

"Could you do me a favor?" Kylie asked. "Tell the others I had a work emergency or something."

Lily made a face. "Jeremy, too?"

"Yes, Jeremy, too," she said. "It's work. He'll understand."

Without meeting her eyes, Kylie waved goodbye. She hoisted

the beach tote onto her shoulder and stomped away on soggy flip-flops.

Lily watched her go with a heavy heart. She wasn't looking forward to breaking the news to Jeremy, just as she wasn't looking forward to day drinking without Kylie. But she was a big girl, getting used to life's minor disappointments. She put away her e-reader, adjusted the ties of her bikini, and went off to find Ben and Roxanna.

Watching Ben splash around the kid's pool with his baby cousin lifted her mood for a while. However, when they returned to the cabana to find Jeremy sitting alone, her mood tanked.

"Have you seen Kylie?" he asked.

"Kylie had an emergency."

He ripped off his sunglasses. "What kind of emergency? Is she okay?"

"I'm fine!"

That was Kylie, red-faced, making her way back to the cabana on her soggy flip-flops. "I just had to make a call. It's sorted." She dropped her tote and peeled off her bathing suit cover-up. "Want to head out to the beach?"

"Yeah," he said. "Give me a sec to grab a water. Want one?"

"Very much. Thanks."

Jeremy jogged off. Lily didn't budge, waiting for an explanation. Kylie approached, looking sheepish. "I don't have to stock his refrigerator."

"No, you don't."

"And I'm no golden retriever."

"*You're* the black cat," Lily said, nodding.

"I got as far as the lobby when it hit me," she said. "This is bullshit. What did I think was going to happen? I'd fill the fridge with organic vegetables, and he'd fall in love with me? I've worked for this man for two years, and we've never had a serious conversation. I'm just another high-tech accessory in his smart home."

Lily went over to her. "Why not stock my fridge, instead? Ben and I would so appreciate it."

Kylie showed her the message she'd sent Frederico before turning back. **Nice try. See you in two weeks.** He acknowledged it with a thumbs-up emoji.

"I'm proud of you, sweetie."

"Thanks, Mom."

Jeremy came jogging back, his long hair flopping behind him, and off he and Kylie went.

Ben showed up next to her. "What did I miss?"

"Shh . . . I'll tell you tonight."

"I'll hold you to it," he said. "What can I get you from the bar?"

"Aperol spritz."

He dropped a kiss on her shoulder. "Coming up."

Finally, Roxanna came to say goodbye. "I'm heading out. Oscar's had enough. It's too hot out here for him, he won't wear the hat, and he hates sunblock."

The baby squirmed in her arms, making angry little sounds. Any minute, he'd blow.

"I'm just glad you came," Lily said.

"I wouldn't miss it. Ben says you're leaving next week."

Lily kept an even smile on her lips, neither confirming nor denying the statement.

"That's too bad," Roxanna said. "I would've liked to get to know you better, but with the baby, it's tough."

"What else did Ben say?" Lily asked.

Roxanna had her back to her, inventorying her mommy paraphernalia. "Nothing much."

Ben returned with her spritz, but Lily's celebratory mood had fallen flat. He took Oscar from Roxanna and offered to carry him to her car. With his cheek pressed against Ben's chest, the baby instantly relaxed. Roxanna wasn't swayed by this. She gave Lily a brief hug. "I better go before he screams his head off. This better not be our goodbye!"

"It won't be," Lily said.

"Anyway, you've got to come back to visit us. Maybe next summer?"

"Sure," Lily said. Though, she knew full well that if she left Miami with her heart in her hands, she'd never return.

Chapter Thirty-Three

"There's a book event this afternoon. Want to go?"

They were at their favorite coffee shop on Española Way, at their usual table on the patio, in the shade of a yellow tab tree. They came for the ambience as well as the food. It had the best iced lattes, the espresso drinks that Ben preferred, fresh baked pastries, the friendliest barista, good music, and a quirky cat that rubbed up against Ben's ankles whenever he placed their orders.

They were regulars at this point, stopping for lunch once or twice a week. They'd worked on their review of *Crushed Hearts* at this table. After lunch, they often returned to the building for a quick swim then spent the afternoon reading. Ben had committed to stay on at the bar through the end of summer. If he had a shift, Lily would join him there. He'd make her a martini. She'd take her usual seat at the corner and finish her reading for the week, as Ben would've already made quick work of their book selection. When he had a chance, he'd come over and discuss a plot twist or share a laugh over a particularly funny scene. They had a running game going, rating the love scenes in tequila shots. A five-shot rating was scorching hot, and only *Around Midnight* had earned that mark. When their friends came around, they'd order a shot and add their ratings to the list.

If Ben wasn't working, they'd order in or head out for dinner. Sometimes, Kylie and Noah would join them. Once, Jeremy had tagged along. All five of them had ended up at a dive bar, playing pool until three in the morning.

Lily tallied these experiences: the lunch dates, the evenings at the bar, the dinners, either at Ben's place or a local restaurant, hanging out with mutual friends, reading the same books, and when tired of reading, watching movies projected onto the blank wall across from his bed. Add to all this their morning-coffee ritual and evening tea followed by a long walk, and what did you get? It was obvious to her. What were they doing, if not cosplaying as a comfortably married couple?

Although the questions ate at her, she said nothing. Instead, she adopted her mother's pinched tone. "A book event sounds nice. Where at?"

"The Betsy," he replied.

"Really?"

"Yes. The hotel is known for its engagement in the arts."

Lily brought a hand to her chest. "The Betsy is where it all went down!"

"What happened there? Was there a crime?"

"It's where we stayed for our corporate retreat," she said. "Where I walked out of the banquet, fell apart in the sauna, packed up in a hurry, and quit my job on the fly."

"Forget it," he said. "I don't want you triggered."

"We have to go."

"We don't have to do anything."

"We have to do this," she insisted. "I walked out of that hotel in shambles. I want to go back as I am today. Better. Happier. More secure than ever."

Ben reached for his espresso cup. "Let's just skip it."

"I'm going, with or without you," she said.

"Doubt it," he said. "It's by invitation only. The author is a Nobel laureate, and some important people will be there."

"We're going. I'll wear my revenge dress."

"Listen, Lady Di," he said, amused. "Have you considered that the people you're enacting revenge on are no longer there? Unless it was an unusually long retreat, they ought to be gone by now."

"The walls will remember," she said solemnly.

"You're out of your mind," he said. "But I like that line."

He opened his notebook and wrote it down.

The South African prisoners'-rights advocate, Greyson Aubrey, had been awarded the Nobel Peace Prize some years back. His recent publication, an antiwar book, had earned him credible death threats. For that reason, security was tight at the evening's cocktail party. If you made it past the chaos of the checkpoint, the hotel's courtyard offered a serene oasis. Despite this, Lily was agitated. Once she'd stepped through the hotel's portico, she'd been teleported back in time. Her revenge dress was the same black one she'd worn the night she'd quit. Coming here was a risk. She could easily slip back into this persona, get reabsorbed into corporate America.

Those dark thoughts dissipated as soon as Ben stepped close and whispered in her ear, "Are you okay?"

"I will be, in a minute."

"I'll give your former employers one thing," he said. "They picked a cool venue for their retreat from hell."

It was a storied hotel, built in the 1940s and named after Betsy Ross. To keep things respectable, the event coordinator had picked this venue over others which were better known for their nightclubs than their historic architecture.

They spotted the elderly Greyson Aubrey seated in a corner with a view of the courtyard. His walking cane rested beside him. He was swarmed by admirers. Lily and Ben thought it best to stay away for now.

They split up. He went to the bar and returned with champagne. She hunted down a cocktail waiter and loaded up on small bites. They set up camp at a cocktail-height table. This was their MO, for all events from here on out.

"First this," Ben said, referring to their spread of goodies. "Next we buy the book and get it signed. We circle back for a second round, and then we're out of here. Does that sound like a plan?"

Lily raised her flute. "We'll be in bed by ten."

He grinned lustfully. "I like the sound of that."

And so did she, very much.

Their mouths were stuffed with puff pastry when Allison Leigh sailed up to their table, her silver bob glistening in the afternoon light. "Look at you! My rising stars!"

Ben wiped his mouth with a cocktail napkin before greeting her. "Hello, Allison."

"Good evening," Lily said.

"Hello, Lily, my genius!"

"Me?" Lily said, confused.

"Oh, don't do that," Allison admonished her. "Don't dim your light for anyone."

"I wouldn't," Lily assured her. "Ben is the certified genius in our duo."

"That goes without saying, but *you* are the revelation of the summer," Allison declared. "Ben is your perfect complement. I had a feeling about you two. I pat myself on the back every day."

"Cheers to you," Ben said, teasing.

"You listen to me, Ben Romero," Allison said. "The next time I reach out to you for any project, I want you to remember this day. I'm great at what I do. I have a nose for talent. I knew you two would be a hit, and I was right."

"Are you done?" Ben asked, laughing.

"No, I'm not," she said. "It's not official yet, but I hear they want you back for a second season."

"What?"

"I suspect you heard me just fine," Allison said. "Why are you surprised? You have the top-rated podcast in the region. There's no reason to pull the plug. A Summer Love Book Club Series—it's an evergreen idea. Lily brings the expertise, and you, Ben, bring the gravitas."

"Lily is leaving next week," Ben said bluntly.

"Leaving for where? Mars?" Allison deadpanned. "If not, she'll likely make it back in time. Besides, this is the twenty-first century. There's no need to record in studio. With the right software, you can record the podcast from your bedroom closet. Think about it. Although, this is what they call a no-brainer."

"Can you believe this?" Ben asked, as Allison walked away.

What Lily couldn't believe was his reaction. *Lily is leaving next week.* Ben had fully accepted her imminent departure. The discussion she was holding out for would never happen. There was no alternate ending. They were done.

I'm leaving next week, she acknowledged to herself.

It was time she behaved accordingly.

Chapter Thirty-Four

"I don't know about another season," Lily said. "This summer was perfect. I don't want to ruin it."

"You're right," he said. "The sequel hardly ever lives up to the original."

Lily stuffed a pastry in her mouth. For once, she didn't enjoy being right.

"Mr. Romero?"

Ben turned to a young woman who'd tentatively approached them. The lanyard around her neck identified her as a student volunteer.

"Yes," he said.

"Mr. Aubrey would like to speak with you."

"How does he know who I am?" Ben asked her.

The student was more than willing to volunteer this information. "He's a fan," she said. "So am I, by the way. I'm registering for your class in the fall."

"Thanks. See you in the fall." He turned to Lily. "Will you come with me?"

"No. Go ahead," she said. "I'll get the books and join you soon. It's more efficient this way."

Lily needed a few minutes alone to calm down. Ben

squeezed her hand and went off for his private audience. At the bookstand, Lily chatted absently with the seller, waiting for her heartbeat to stabilize. The man handed her a receipt and asked if she could use a drink of water.

"I'm fine," she said, though sweating profusely. "Thanks for asking."

She wasn't fine. She had that sick feeling that she was making a mistake. Or was it this hotel? Returning had brought her face-to-face with a former version of herself, one who questioned her every decision.

When she joined Ben, the Nobel laureate was praising his father's work. "He wrote about power better than anyone."

"That's what they say," Ben said, already turning to Lily, taking the books off her hands, drawing her close.

"Is this your wife?" Greyson asked.

"No," Ben replied. "This is my . . . Lily."

"Ah, my mistake," Greyson said with a laugh. "In my time, we were herded into the institution, two by two, like cattle. Your generation does not have that problem. I envy your freedom. It's a pleasure to meet you, Lily."

"The pleasure is mine," Lily said, calmer now that Ben had his hand at her waist.

Greyson resumed his line of questions. "Would you say your father was satisfied with his body of work overall?"

"I couldn't say for sure," Ben said. "We never discussed it."

Greyson studied him for a while. "Father-son relationships are complicated, aren't they?"

"We did not have much of a relationship."

"I see."

"What are you working on, presently?" Greyson inquired. "If you don't mind my asking."

"I've started a few projects. All have stalled."

"You might be working on the wrong thing. If there's something you need to get off your chest, it will stop you from moving forward, as cliché as it sounds. I did not win the Nobel for literature. I won it for peace." He laughed again, pleased with his attempt at self-deprecating humor.

Cliché or not, Lily understood exactly what he meant. If Ben didn't deal with the box on his shelf in one way or the other, he'd be forever stuck.

"If Lily has no objection and if you can survive far from the sway of palm trees, you may want to consider the University of Amsterdam," Greyson said. "I know they're looking for someone, and I'd put in a good word."

"Thank you," Ben said. "I'm honored."

Lily, though, swayed like a palm tree in a hurricane. Ben kept her steady with a tight grip on her waist all while promising to keep in touch with the author. She hadn't recovered when he steered her away. His words returned to her. *I'd like a residency in Europe at some point, a year or two at a university.* This was his dream. He asked so little from the world, he deserved this.

On the drive home Ben was quiet and withdrawn. Lily, deflated, melted into the passenger seat. It was settled. She was returning home next week, and Ben would leave for Amsterdam. She would give up her passenger princess status, and he'd trade his car for a bicycle. If Allison had her way, they'd record a second season of the podcast from deep within their respective closets. They'd never read in bed again.

"Are you okay?" Ben asked.

"Me? I'm fine," she stammered. "You?"

"I'm still thinking about what Greyson said."

"What is there to think about?" she asked. A Nobel laureate offers you a job, you take it. *If Lily has no objection . . .* Cute, but irrelevant. She'd never stand in Ben's way.

"He thinks I should write about my father."

Lily reached out and stroked his thigh. "Would that be so bad?"

"Yes."

"It might do you good," she said. "Your feelings are locked up in that box."

"That fucking box," he muttered. "I know I should do something with it, but all I want to do is set it on fire."

She couldn't blame him. He'd worked hard to distinguish himself from the not-so-great Sabato.

Ben took her hand and brought it to his lips. "You didn't look happy tonight."

Lily searched for an excuse. "It's this dress, and that hotel."

"I told you revenge is futile."

They drove the rest of the way in silence. When they got back to his place, they let the books spill to the floor. Ben turned the dead bolt and drew her to him, pinning her back to his chest. "Let me love you, while I still have time."

Lily spun around and kissed him unreservedly. This love was never meant to outlast the summer. What did that matter when they had each other tonight?

Ben's Journal
June 10, Lily

It's only been days, and I'm fond of you. I know the rhythm of your footsteps, even the sound of your dishes when they crash into your sink. I wait for you to knock on my door. I wait because knocking first would take things too far, cross the line that I've drawn between our doorsteps. I wait because my heart needs to be sure. I've wasted my time and the time of others. I've used people and I've been used. I've been careless. I've loved and quickly erased the mark of love on my heart. Some have called me heartless, but that is not true. I've felt everything, and then I shed that skin to start anew. But with you, my firefly, my gentle breeze in the cruelest spring, I want to move gently.

July 19, Lily
Lily, bring your impulses to my door. Come over in the dead of night. Ask for anything. Lay your soul bare. Show me your body. Press your lips to mine. Laugh into my mouth. Scrape me under your nails. Take me inside of you. Don't hide a thing. There's nothing that torments you that doesn't torment me. There's no shame so deep inside you that I wouldn't dive in to find and discard. It's only been a few weeks, and I know you won't stay long. When you fly away, my firefly, it won't be because I hurt you or disappointed you or let you down or harmed you in any way. It will only be because I cared too much to trap you in a jar.

August 12, Love
We don't have a say in when or where we fall in love. I suppose we'd all appreciate if it showed up in the most convenient way and the most conventional package. It won't. We want a love that won't require too much of us, won't force us to grow or move or make a single compromise. If it were as easy as ordering from a menu, I would not choose you here and now. Not with you still in doubt about your future and me still battling demons I thought long-defeated. Not with your stubborn streak and my pride blocking the way forward. Not with the fear I see in your eyes and feel in my gut. Maybe in a month or a year or

even ten, but certainly not now. Lily . . . falling in love was as easy as tripping blindly into the void. Now comes the hard work: climbing out of that ditch.

August 24, Lily
If you can't say goodbye, say nothing at all. I'll do the work and let you go. I owe you this. You give so freely of yourself. All my greedy heart ever does is take.

Chapter Thirty-Five

From then on out, every experience was the last. The last lunch at their café, a last stop at the bookstore, the last podcast episode, and possibly, the last ride to the building if they decided to stay in this evening and the next. Frankly, Lily's heart couldn't take it.

Late one evening, while Ben was at a faculty meeting, she went down to read by the pool. It didn't take too long before she put the book away, stripped down to her bikini, and dove in for a swim. Normally, she'd never expose her color-treated hair to chlorine without extra protection, but she did not feel like her normal self. She floated with her arms spread wide and gazed at the cloud-streaked sky. She felt trapped in silence, her inability to speak openly with Ben was part of a bigger problem, a lifelong habit of bottling complicated emotions. Growing up, she never confronted her father like Patrick routinely did. The day she broke up with Darren, she'd asked him over for a talk but never actually said anything. He'd guessed by the look on her face that it was over. More recently, she hadn't exactly confronted her boss before quitting the job. She simply sent him a curt email, expecting him to read between those few lines. This was something she would have to unpack with a therapist, but there wasn't time for that now. It was too late, anyway. If she'd spoken up before they'd met Greyson, before the offer for him to join the faculty at the University of Amsterdam, maybe they could've worked something out. Like the clouds dissipating before her eyes, the time had passed. Lily had started crying well before she realized it. Sobbing, she swallowed chlorine water then made her way to the edge of the pool where she sat, head between her knees, coughing and crying.

A half hour later, Ben sent a message.

Dinner?

Yup!

Lily wiped her tears, pulled herself up, and headed upstairs.

Pop Shop
A Pop Culture Podcast
Category: Arts
Rating: 5 stars
RATED #1 Podcast in Arts & Culture

August 30: *The Thought of You* by Julia Carr
with Lily Lyon and Ben Romero

Lily: I'd like to discuss story structure.

Ben: That would be a first for us.

Lily: I have thoughts, Benito.

Ben: *Dime, mami.*

Lily: This romance has no third-act breakup. A rarity.

Ben: I like it. The third-act breakup is too expected.

Lily: But does the story lack structure because of it? Like it skipped a beat?

Ben: I'm okay with it.

Lily: Me, too. I guess we don't find fault in this story, except for the way the couple falls in love. It's the phenomenon of Insta Love, more commonly known as love at first sight. Do we believe in it? Are we skeptical? How do we feel?

Ben: Clearly, you're skeptical.

Lily: And you're not?

Ben: Sometimes you just know.

Lily: That's what our main character, Blake, said.

Ben: It's cliché, but lately I'm more forgiving.

Lily: To fall madly, deeply in love with someone you've never met in your life? I don't know about that. Love implies trust, and trusting a stranger, well . . . that's the sort of thing that can get you killed.

Ben: So cynical!

Lily: Where's the lie, though?

Ben: Have you ever met someone and felt an instant connection?

Lily: I don't recall.

Ben: Is that right? Should we refresh your memory?

Lily: I plead the Fifth.

Ben: Let's try this. What was your first impression of me?

Lily: That's easy. *How can I get this bartender to take my order?*

Ben: It was a busy night!

Lily: I waited a long time.

Ben: Want to know what I was thinking when I first laid eyes on you?

Lily: Yes, please.

Ben: Bummer. Our time is up. Join us next week when we discuss polyamory. Get into it.

Lily: Don't tease them. This is the last episode of the summer.

Ben: Sadly, it is.

Lily: The idea of hosting this podcast was so daunting, we nearly turned it down. I can't believe it went by so fast.

Ben: We had fun.

Lily: Yes, we did. And from all the comments, we're confident our listeners had fun, too. Thanks from the bottom of our hearts for joining our summer love book club. I know I will never forget it.

Ben: I want to thank you, Lily, for making this possible. I'll never forget this experience.

Lily: [Pauses] That's very sweet.

Ben: Our time is up, for real this time.

Lily: Bye, everyone. Remember to give love a chance.

Chapter Thirty-Six

From the recording studio, they drove straight to the building. Ben parked at his reserved spot in the garage and cut the engine. "I have to see Noah about the watch," he said. "The appraisal is in."

Lily could not face Noah right now. He'd take one look at her and just know. "I'm going for a walk," she said. "I'll meet you later for a last swim?"

"Why last?" he asked with a tight smile. "The pool isn't going anywhere."

"Who knows? What if it rains tomorrow?"

"It's not like you to be so pessimistic."

She took one look at his face and knew what he would say next. *Do you want to talk?* The answer was *no*. There was nothing to talk about. Her flight was booked. Dr. Jake had scheduled a walk-through. The time for talking was over.

"Say hi to Noah for me, please."

Lily climbed out of the car and walked away briskly. She exited the garage through a side door, stepping out onto a busy corner. Midafternoons in Manhattan were chaotic, but Miami Beach had its moments. Tourists raced past on foot, on Vespas, or in sexy little sports cars. The city drew people from all over the world looking for fun. When they returned to their lives, they'd annoy their friends with accounts of their time in the sun. *I spent a week in Miami . . . Unreal!* they'd say. As if the city were a fictional place and the locals, paid actors. Ben, Kylie, Noah, Roxanna, Sierra, Nicolas, and Jeremy were as real as anyone, and so was her love for them.

Lily hadn't made it around the block when she got a call. She stopped abruptly on the sidewalk, phone in hand, staring in disbelief at the caller ID.

Slowly and with caution, she brought the phone to her ear. "Mom?"

"You know, Liliane," her mother said in a breezy tone, as if picking up a conversation they'd started over a glass of wine, "I lived in Miami once."

"I . . . didn't know that."

"It was the summer I turned sixteen. We hadn't been in the US long. We stayed with relatives. Your grandfather couldn't find a job and decided to move us north."

"You never mentioned it."

"It was such a brief time, but I loved it," Mom said. "So warm. So sunny. I could see myself staying there forever. You know how much I struggle in winter. But there was no work for your grandfather at the time. There wasn't much work for him up north, either, to be honest. So he started the business. You know the rest of the story."

Lily had heard this story millions of times, minus their short stay in Florida. Her grandfather, a civil engineer in his native country, had moved the family to New Jersey. Frustrated with menial jobs, he'd started a thriving construction business, firmly landing the struggling family at the tippy-top of the middle class within a decade.

"I appreciate how hard my grandfather worked and how much he sacrificed. If you're trying to guilt me for taking time off—"

"Either you quit your job or you were fired, but you're not taking time off. Be serious, Liliane."

"Fine!" she cried. "I quit my job. I don't think there is any shame in that."

"I'm not trying to shame you," Mom said. "I want the truth. That's all. Is this why you never called me?"

"I called you twice!"

"Early on Sundays when you knew I'd be at church," Mom retorted. "That's an old trick, Liliane. Don't think I wasn't on to you."

"Fine. Can you blame me, really?"

"Yes, I can," Mom replied. "There's no excuse. Were you afraid I'd belittle you?"

Lily stepped under a shop awning to get out of the sun and out of the way of foot traffic. "Or shame. Or manipulate. Or any combination of the three."

"Is that what you think of me?"

"You gave me the silent treatment!"

"You went away for a weekend and never came home! Your father had to track you down."

"Okay. Maybe you have a point."

"I'm not here to score points."

"It won't happen again. I'll be home soon."

"I'm not asking you to come back."

"Don't you want me to?" Lily asked, miffed. Was her mother willing to cut her off after two short months of absence?

"I had never seen you looking as beautiful, as rested, as on our call last weekend. You were glowing, and I thought maybe Lily has finally found happiness."

"Mom, I saw you on that call. No way you were thinking that."

"Well, it's true. Patrick would never let anyone talk him out of his choices. You were always holding out for your father's approval."

"Yours, too! Don't worm your way out of this."

"In that case, you have it," Mom said. "If you're happy in Florida, stay there. Enjoy the weather, the beaches. Our people are meant to live in the sun. I'll visit often, sit with you, and flip through magazines while you read your books."

Hmm . . . How often would she visit? Lily wondered, even as she tried not to burst into tears on the sidewalk. She'd been labeled a daddy's girl since childhood. As it turned out, all she ever needed was her mother's blessing.

"Would you take care of Monster?" Lily asked.

"I picked her up weeks ago," Mom said. "She's flourishing in the den."

Long after the call ended, Lily stood under the shop's awning, taking all this in, until a sales associate came out and handed her a catalog. "In case you're interested, we're running a sale."

It was a polite way of saying *Come in and shop or quit loitering*. The shop was a high-end boutique, and the catalog was thick and glossy. On its cover, Jeremy—*their Jeremy*—was posing on a rowboat like a young Paul Newman. Jeremy, who only ever wore faded T-shirts and ripped jeans, was sporting a polo shirt and pleated shorts. Lily, who'd been weeping a moment earlier, started laughing. The mystery was solved! Jeremy wasn't a starving or struggling artist, he was an honest-to-goodness *model/artist* of the kind every New York waiter claimed to be. He was probably doing better than all of them combined. Did Kylie know this? She couldn't wait to find out!

Chapter Thirty-Seven

Lily's dash to the building's elevators came to a halt when she ran into Sierra, rolling her stainless-steel suitcases across the lobby. She wore her hair in long braids that curled at the ends. Her dark sunglasses slid down the bridge of her nose.

"Hey, lady, where are you off to?" Lily asked.

"The Maldives, babe! The Maldives!"

"When will you be back?"

"Two weeks."

"Oh no! I'll be gone by then."

Just because her mother was fine with her staying, didn't mean Lily was fine with it. What would be the point if Ben was leaving for Europe, anyway?

Sierra dropped her travel bag and pulled Lily into a hug. "We'll keep in touch on social, right?"

"Of course." She showed Sierra the catalog with Jeremy on the cover. "Did you know about this?"

"Oops! The cat's out of the bag." Sierra laughed. "Jeremy is a model. He's done *Swim Week* and everything. I don't know why he keeps it low-key. If I had his bone structure, watch out!"

Lily was laughing, too, until Sierra asked, "What's the plan with you and Ben? Are you doing the long-distance thing? It sucks, but you gotta do what you gotta do."

Put like that, it seemed so simple. The long-distance thing . . . The sad truth was, she and Ben did not have any sort of plan.

Lily tried to pivot. She grabbed the handle of a suitcase. "Let me help with that."

Sierra wasn't deterred, though. Once outside, with all the pieces of luggage accounted for, she resumed her line of questions.

"Seriously, though," she said. "What's going on with Ben? I'm obsessed with you guys. Please say you have a plan."

"It's not that easy."

Sierra groaned. "If it doesn't work for you two, what hope is there for the rest of us? And what about book club? I gained five thousand followers on book content alone."

"Posting about books is great, but you should read them, too. Download something for the plane."

"Sure, but that's not the point." Sierra took out her phone and checked an app. "My ride will be here any minute," she said. "Listen up. You and Ben are perfect for each other. There's a lot of fake shit out there. You two are the real deal. Work it out!"

Lily stared down at her feet, ashamed for taking relationship advice from a buoyant twenty-two-year-old with designer luggage and sparkly lip gloss. Yet here she was.

"I'm telling you," Lily mumbled, "it's not that easy."

"Don't be idiots!" Sierra cried. "What was it you were always saying? Give love a chance?"

That was the awful truth. She and Ben were idiots, their love story patterned on the Idiot Plot and hinged on a miscommunication trope. What had she done these last few weeks except wait on Ben to read her mind, pick up on her cues, and apply his genius to save their relationship? Waiting for a man to figure things out was the definition of idiocy.

A black car pulled up to the curb. "Well, that's me," Sierra said with a sad little smile. "I'm so glad I met you, Lily. You're one cool bitch."

That was high praise from the coolest bitch Lily had ever met. She pulled her copy of *The Thought of You* from her tote bag. "Take this," she said. "And go kill them in the Maldives. I'll be watching on social."

The driver tossed the luggage into the trunk, and Sierra climbed into the back seat. Lily stood waving goodbye until the car slipped into the flow of traffic.

Chapter Thirty-Eight

Her talk with Sierra left her buoyant. Lily floated across the lobby, high on self-confidence and girl power. She *was* that bitch. It was time to reclaim her power. She would decide her future irrespective of a man's opinion on the issue. Yes, she'd done the dumb thing and fallen for her neighbor, but that shouldn't condemn her to a life in exile. If she wasn't ready to leave, she shouldn't have to. What was the rush anyway? So little of her former life remained. Her brother was moving into her apartment. Her mother had custody of her plant baby. Most crucially, she did not have a job. New York was not a city for navel-gazing. If this building wasn't big enough for her and Ben both, she'd move out. The thought alone pierced her heart. She loved it here. She loved the marble floors, fluted columns, gold leaf accents, faulty sconces, and every crystal chandelier—authentic to the period or not.

"Hey, Miss Lily," the doorman called after her. "You've got a package."

His name was Al, and she loved him, too. Lily reversed course and followed him to the mail room where she signed for a huge box.

"What's in that thing, anyway? An oven?" he asked.

Al was from New York, Bronx specifically. They'd long bonded over this.

"A suitcase," Lily said grimly. The day after Greyson's book signing, she realized her dainty carry-on would not hold the bulk of items that she'd accumulated over the summer and ordered the oversize suitcase online.

"If you want, I'll break it out of the box. It would be easier to wheel it into the elevator."

"Smart man," Lily said.

Al broke out an industrial box cutter. With a few quick moves, he freed the suitcase from its packaging. "Here you go."

"Thanks."

"Of course, if it doesn't work out and you wanna return it, you don't have the box anymore."

"You might've pointed that out before you took it apart," Lily said.

"We'll figure something out," he said good-naturedly. "Have a safe trip!"

Lily held back from telling Al she would not be traveling after all. She thanked him and wheeled her shiny new suitcase to the elevator. She'd stash it away then find Kylie.

The old building was blessed with great Wi-Fi and a strong cellular signal throughout, even in the elevator. She gave Kylie a call. Her friend answered cheerily. "Hey! We're all on the roof. Join us."

Lily loved the roof.

"What are you all doing up there?" she asked. It was almost three o'clock. Happy hour didn't start until sundown.

"Jeremy and I were hanging out," Kylie said. "Ben and Noah showed up. Now they're huddled in a corner. I don't know what that's about."

The appraisal. There was a good chance Ben's father's watch was worth a lot. That was money he could use for the future—a future she would have no part of. A future he refused to discuss with her. It was as if nothing existed beyond her departure date, as if she'd board the plane and disappear into thin air.

"Guess what?" Lily asked. "I've solved the Jeremy mystery."

"Which one? There are so many."

"I know how he can afford his apartment."

"Spill!"

"Is he around? I can't tell you if he's standing right there."

Kylie's voice dipped to a whisper. "Come on. He never tells me anything."

Jeremy's distinct voice cut through the background noise. "What are you whispering about?"

"Nothing," Kylie chirped. "Could you be an angel and get me another beer? This one is warm."

"Sure thing."

Kylie waited a beat then whispered, "He's gone."

"I'm not so sure I should tell you."

"Are you kidding?"

It no longer felt right to snitch on Jeremy. The self-effacing young man from Small Town, USA, was probably too embarrassed to boast about a modeling career. Besides, he enjoyed a kind of attorney–client privilege she couldn't ignore. "You two have a relationship. If he wanted you to know, he'd tell you."

"What relationship? We're just friends."

"Who's just friends?"

It was Jeremy again.

"Jesus!" Kylie cried. "Why are you back?"

"I forgot my wallet. Why are you so jumpy?"

"I'm not jumpy," Kylie said. "I'm just yapping with Lily. Now, go."

"Are you telling Lily that we're just friends? Is that what you're doing?"

"That's what we are," Kylie replied firmly.

Kylie didn't have a nuanced take on life. Things were black or white. They weren't friends-to-lovers or friends-with-benefits, they were just friends. But seriously, how many friends did a girl need?

"That's not what I think," he said.

"What *do* you think, Jeremy?" Kylie demanded.

"I think you're smart, sexy, and so much fun," Jeremy replied. "Your cooking is so good it makes me want to cry. I've been trying to paint the exact color of your hair for weeks. I think we're good together. But if you want to be friends, we'll be friends."

Kylie must have dropped the phone, because the next sound was a loud thump.

Lily let out a silent scream. Kylie and Jeremy had a true connection. It was worth exploring. From the muffled sounds coming through her phone, she imagined they were exploring that connection right now.

Lily was in such a state she hadn't realized that the elevator was still and likely had been for a while. Panic seared through her. She pounded on the big red button and screamed into her phone. "Kylie! Pick up!"

A moment later, Kylie was giggling into the phone. "Shoot, I forgot about you."

"I'm stuck in the elevator!" Lily cried. "Between the third and fourth floors. Tell Jeremy! He knows what to do!"

"Does he, though?"

"Yes!"

Kylie relayed the message then resumed their conversation. "Jeremy is calling the building manager. Now you've got to tell me what's up with him. If it's something illegal, I need to know. Girl code."

"You can't invoke girl code in an emergency."

"What's the emergency? Everyone gets stuck in the elevator. It's an inconvenience. That's all."

"Kylie, I'm trapped in a suspended box. Any second, I may plummet to my death!"

"Ugh! Drama queen."

"I'm afraid of heights, and I have a touch of claustrophobia," Lily explained between deep, rolling breaths. "We all have our issues."

"Noah," Kylie called out. "Come talk your friend off the ledge. She's stuck in the elevator."

Next thing Lily was speaking with Noah. "Relax," he said. "I'll order you a drink. It'll be ready when you get here."

Lily gripped the handrail. God bless Jeremy for taking action. If she stayed in this building, she planned on writing a strongly worded letter to management, or maybe she'd start a petition to get the elevators repaired. What was the point of a law degree if you didn't terrorize your community?

"I've got news," Noah said.

"Yeah?"

"I turned down the promotion."

That bit of news flipped her upside down. "Are you insane? How can you say no to Saint-Tropez?"

"France isn't going anywhere," he said in his blasé way. "I moved here for a reason. I want to be young and messy in Miami. I'm not ready to give up that dream."

"I get it," Lily said, nodding. "If you're not ready, you're not ready. No one should pressure you."

"That's the good news," he said.

She slumped onto the elevator floor. "Is there bad news?"

"It's over between Nicolas and me."

"Oh no," she moaned. "But why? You're not moving anymore."

"That doesn't matter. We want different things."

She repeated the last bit of advice, as it applied here, too. "If you're not ready, no one should pressure you."

"It's for the best."

"How are you feeling? Are you okay?"

"I'm French," he replied. "I think it's cool we figured it out. No hard feelings."

"We should all be French," Lily muttered.

Noah laughed. "I'll miss you, silly Lily."

Like with Al, Lily refrained from telling Noah the truth. She'd break the news to Ben before telling the others. She'd draw on her inner French girl to do it, cool and contained. *I'm staying, Benedicto. Do with that information what you will.*

"So, um, where's Ben?" she asked, her voice clipped. "Is he still up there with you guys?"

"He took off the second he heard you were stuck in the elevator," Noah said with a chuckle. "He's probably on his way to rescue you."

It was hard to be mad at a man who had dashed off to save your life. That was when it hit her: it was hard to be mad at Ben, period. He was perfect, neither alpha male nor cinnamon roll. He was simply an amazing human being. He wrote her notes. He brewed her coffee in the morning and mixed perfect martinis at night. He bought her books. He listened with the patience of a saint to everything she had to say. Handsome and smart, with a touch of social anxiety to keep him humble, Ben was perfect. How could she blame him for the sticky situation they were in? How could she resent him in any way? But she *did* resent him. How could he just . . . let her go?

When the elevator finally kicked into motion, Lily was relieved but not relaxed. She hopped to her feet, ready for a fight. Her fingertips tingled with rage. Sure enough, when the doors opened to their floor, Ben was there, standing stock-still, arms folded across his broad chest, eyes level. She'd never seen him so self-contained, and frankly, it unsettled her.

"You were trapped in there and asked for *Jeremy* to help instead of me?" he asked.

His tone unsettled her, too.

"Jeremy and I have an understanding," she said. "Get used to it."

He strode into the elevator, slammed a button on the panel, and before the doors joined behind him, his hand was in her hair and his mouth was crushing hers. He kissed her with sweet possessiveness. Lily clung to him, her fingers digging into his shoulders. She was disoriented. Were they on their way up or down? How long had she really been trapped in this elevator? What had happened to her tingling rage?

Ben abruptly broke the kiss, leaving her panting. "It's back to you and me and a suitcase in an elevator, isn't it?"

She'd forgotten the suitcase. Lily reached for it as it rolled away. "I'm not leaving," she announced, chin high.

"Sure looks like it."

"Never mind what it looks like," she said. "I won't leave Miami until I'm good and ready."

"But you will leave eventually."

"Frankly, that's up to you."

He studied her a while then said, "Let's talk."

The doors slid open to the pool. Ben strode out of the elevator. Unless she was willing to risk getting trapped alone again, she had no choice but to follow him.

The pool deck was as serene as the morning of their first meet up. They marched over to their usual pair of lounge chairs, which hadn't been moved since they'd placed them side by side. Lily dropped onto one and waited for him to sit across from her.

Finally settled, Ben stared at the flat blue surface of the pool. "When were you going to ask me?" he said quietly.

"Ask you what?"

"To follow you to New York?"

"Never!" Lily cried. "I would *never* ask you to follow me. That's insane."

"Why insane?" he said.

"You should never follow anyone to New York," Lily said. "I know how this works. It's a demanding city. When it gets nasty and the winters harsh, you'll resent the person who dragged you there. You'll find the people rude, and all you'll see is trash. The subway, the bodegas, the museums and shops, Wall Street, and every play on Broadway will lose their appeal."

"If you don't want me there, just say so."

"That's not it."

"You made it clear to your brother, when he asked about your place, that you weren't in a relationship and there was no one to worry about."

"Because!" she cried, unsure of what to add.

"I would do it," he said. "I would follow you anywhere."

That was sweet, but Lily had to quash this idea. "Forget New York," she said. "Why haven't *you* asked *me* to stay?"

"I can't do that," he said. "Your apartment, your family, and your career are in New York. So is your Monstera."

"That plant is flourishing without me—I've seen the pics. I'm the one who's wilting, waiting for you to tell me how you feel."

"Lily, you know I love you!"

"No, I don't!" she cried. "You said you loved 'everything about me,' which is technically not the same."

He stood and stared down at her, those velvet dark eyes taking her in. "If I love *everything* about you, isn't it reasonable to conclude that I love all of you?"

"I'm more than the sum of my parts!" she declared.

"Are you going to argue with me like this for the rest of our lives?"

"Yes! This is me. I'll never change."

"Change is overrated," he said. "We are who we are."

Lily rose to her feet and took his face between her hands. "Please don't use my family or career or apartment as an excuse.

Patrick can have my place. My mother will visit. I wouldn't be the first New York lawyer to take on Miami. I'm sure there's a secret society of us somewhere. All I'm saying is that we have options. We don't know what kind of life we'd have up north, but we know what we have here. And FYI, if you don't ask me to stay, I'll stay anyway and go on living across the hall from you, but I'll *never* speak to you again."

"I won't be across the hall for long."

Lily's heart faltered, but her spine remained rigid. "Right. You'll be in Amsterdam."

His long, thick brows crumpled with confusion. "Amsterdam?"

"For the position at the university," she explained. "It's your dream."

"No, it's not."

"But you said—"

"I don't remember saying anything about moving to Amsterdam."

"It's your goal to live and work in Europe for a while. You said so."

"I'm taking a break from chasing goals. I met a woman this summer who taught me that it's okay to stop and take a break."

"Is that right?" Lily said. "Have I met her?"

"Funny girl," he said, smiling down at her.

"What will you do during this break?" she asked. As much as she would have loved to, they couldn't read by the pool forever. They had to earn a living.

"Take the box down from the shelf, riffle through it, take notes, and write the damn book," he said. "I've got to come to terms with my father or I won't move on. Greyson said a lot of things the night we met him, but that's what stuck with me. Not some invitation to Amsterdam."

Now that was true growth. "I'm so proud of you."

"Thanks, beautiful," he said.

"Why would you have to move out of your apartment?" she asked.

"To buy a new one. I'm in the market."

"Since when?"

"Since meeting with Noah this afternoon," he said. "I'm interested in a two-bedroom on a higher floor. A couple are sitting vacant. I'll get a hold of Dr. Jake and work something out."

Lily put aside her pain and suffering to better absorb this bit of information. "How many apartments does Dr. Jake own?"

"Quite a few. Once I sell the watch, I can afford to take one off his hands."

"Wow! How much is it worth?"

"We'll get into that later."

"All right, well . . ." Lily said with a sigh. "In case you've lost track, this is the moment you make a big, romantic declaration and sweep me off my feet. Bring your A game."

A family of four arrived with a wagon full of inflatable toys. They got settled nearby and switched on a portable radio.

Ben took her hand. "The setting matters," he said. "Come with me."

They were back in the elevator with the suitcase, kissing madly all the way up to the roof. It was early. The bar was sparsely attended. Kylie, Jeremy, and Noah were chatting at a table. She couldn't wait to join them and share the big news. Book club at the bar would continue through fall! However, Ben avoided their table and made a beeline to the very edge of the terrace.

From the top of The Icon, Lily imagined they were close enough to touch the sky, but she felt no fear. The city unfolded below like an origami piece. The ocean whispered beneath the constant hum of traffic. Ben tucked a finger beneath her chin.

"Do you want to know what I thought the first time I looked into your beautiful eyes?"

"Yes, please."

"I thought you were stardust," he said. "I saw everything in your hazel eyes, the whole world, the universe. I thought, *She's magic.* There was nothing you could do to change my mind. You could lie to my face, you could steal from me, and I wouldn't care."

Lily whispered, "The first time your eyes met mine, I thought, *Damn, he's hot.*"

Ben tossed his head back and laughed. "I get that a lot."

"Now I think you're the love of my life, my soulmate," Lily said. "If not you, then I don't want one. I'll happily go without a great love for the rest of my life."

"In that case, you better cancel your flight home."

"Give me a sec," she said, patting her pockets for her phone. "I'll do it now."

"It can wait."

The salt breeze picked up. Ben brushed her hair away from her face. "I love you," he said. "And I've known it from the start."

"Liar."

"It's true. It was love at first sight. The moment you handed me your voucher for complimentary rosé, I was done for."

"Shut up."

"You looked so lost, I wanted to take you home, care for you. But I was afraid. After Bella, I didn't want to make another mistake."

Lily put a finger to his lips. "I know."

"I sent you a myriad of mixed signals," he said.

"A flurry of red flags!" she cried.

"Forgive me?"

"Depends. Do you love me?"

"So much."

Her eager golden retriever heart lurched forward. She threw her arms around him and buried her face in his neck. Breathing in his familiar scent, she whispered, "I love you, too."

Ben pulled her closer. "I love your heart, your laugh, your wit, your wild imagination, your body, your hair, your scent in the morning . . . everything."

Lily closed her eyes. The colorful city vanished from her view, but her future lay clear ahead.

Pop Shop
A Pop Culture Podcast
Category: Arts
Rating: 5 stars

July 1: *Call Me Sentimental* by Lorelei Scott
Season 2 of our popular Summer Love Book Club with authors
with Lily Lyon and Ben Romero

Lily: Hello, everyone! Welcome back to the Summer Love Book Club. The same rules apply. Ben and I will be lounging by the pool, sipping cocktails with our friends, and reading romance books all summer. Ben is as grumpy as ever, and I'm still a little ray of sunshine. Together, we'll comb through the tropes and see how they fare in real life. As always, our reviews are on BookTap. Ben, say hi!

Ben: Hey, everyone! I've missed this. Before we start, we should congratulate Lily. She passed the Florida Bar exam and will soon appear in a courtroom near you.

Lily: That's not the kind of law I practice, but thanks! Could you please introduce our first read of the summer?

Ben: To launch our second season, we chose *Call Me Sentimental* by Lorelei Scott, a historical romance set in Ireland. Let's get into it.

Lily: I don't know how we've gone so long without reading anything set in Ireland. It's a travesty! And this is our first historical! So we're starting out strong.

Ben: It's a marriage-of-convenience story. A penniless British royal marries the daughter of a wealthy Irish merchant. Despite her riches, Mary can't find a match because her daddy's money is dirty and sweaty and new.

Lily: At the age of one and twenty, she's just wasting away! I'm sad to say this story depends on the miscommunication trope for drama. Baron McCarthy loved Mary since the night of the great ball. If he'd only said so, this story would be over by page fifty. It's what you once called the Idiot Plot, remember?

Ben: I've had a change of heart since then.

Lily: Have you?

Ben: I was too harsh. It's tough expressing overwhelming emotions. And it's not a failure of communication if you don't have the words to articulate your inner turmoil. We should extend some grace to these fictional characters who are obviously struggling.

Lily: Is that right?

Ben: Call me sentimental, but that's how I feel now.

Lily: I might've had a change of heart, too.

Ben: Really?

Lily: My heart belongs to you now, and it's forever changed.

COMMENTS:

@yaya21: Dead.

@SMITH: They're baaccckkkk!!!!!

@DesignedbyBella: Good luck, you two!

@Beckyandherbooks: It's going to be a great summer.

* * * * *

Acknowledgments

This novel is a shared dream. I could not have done it alone.

My editor, Errin Toma, had the vision. Thank you for trusting me to bring this story to life. You are the best, and I hope we have a long collaborative future!

Thank you to my agent, Jessica Alvarez, for your hard work, diligence, and guidance. I so appreciate you!

All my love to Ariel Gonzalez, husband and creative partner. So many of my dreams would wither without you.

Big hugs to my siblings: Dominique, Hermine, Murielle, and Martine. Special thanks to Martine for coming along on this wild ride.

Finally, I wish to thank any reader who finds this book and shares the joys with others.

Remember to give love a chance.

Nadine